THE COURIER WORE SHORTS

SHEILA
KINDELLAN-SHEEHAN

THE

COURIER

WORE

SHORTS

Véhicule Press

Published with the assistance of the Canada Council for the Arts, the
Canada Book Fund of the Department of Canadian Heritage, and the
Société de développement des entreprises culturelles du Québec (SODEC).

Cover design: David Drummond
Typeset in Minion by Simon Garamond
Printed by Marquis Printing Inc.

Published by Véhicule Press, Montréal, Québec, Canada
www.vehiculepress.com

Distribution in Canada by LitDistCo
www.litdistco.ca

Distributed in the U.S. by Independent Publishers Group
www.ipgbook.com

Printed in Canada on FSC certified paper

for
Gina, Cynthia & Denis

and

Bob Dillon
A friend lost suddenly on
July 28, 2013

Characters

MADISON HOLMES: diligent, successful literary agent, about to sign a second big-name author; consolidates her one-woman agency

THOMAS HOLMES: Madison's father, physician and fallible

Rejected Authors

CLAUDE BEAUCHEMIN: arrogant, frustrated, semi-retired lawyer who thought publishing a book would be easy for a man of his talents

STEPHEN GALT: detective, known as 'Prose' to his fellow cops, a cowboy who's been passed over; a publisher was his ticket to the big time

JEAN PAUZÉ: McGill post-grad, desperate for a teaching post opening up at McGill University; needed a big house to publish his dissertation

YVETTE RANGER: 74-year-old, the first French female pilot in Quebec, a decent writer, life amuses her; delighted to be considered a suspect

Major Crimes: The Team

TONI DAMIANO: 42, lieutenant-detective, lead on the Holmes file; tough, confident, complicated and beautiful

PIERRE MATTE: Detective Damiano's partner, fact and detail expert; goes by the book, a good partner with foresight

RICHARD DONAT: chief, 'the boss,' demanding, difficult, abrupt, chooses the right lead on the high-profile case

TROY TURNER: officer SPVM, (Service de police de la Ville de Montréal) young, ambitious, opportunistic

TOM GRAHAM: American agent who has lost his mega author to Madison Holmes

TRACEY DOYLE: young mega-star author with a $20-million contract represented by Madison Holmes

ANGELA MARINO: Doyle's mother, high-end successful lawyer, brutal and stunning

MATHIEU ROY: young witness; a little truant who decides he wants to be a cop like Damiano

JEFF SHEA: Damiano's estranged husband

LUKE SHEA: 15, Damiano's son

Chapter One

THE FOUR EMAILS were sent on Monday morning just after nine. They were identical and written with sincerity, clarity and finality. Endings were difficult for literary agent Madison Holmes. Endings meant failure, cutting away from authors and their work and her belief that she would find homes for their books. She chose her words judiciously:

> Mid-October marks almost two years that we have worked together. We were, I fear, caught in the market turmoil. As I have often said, the competition in the literary market is fierce, and we have been unfortunate in our timing. It appears now that we should move in different directions.
>
> I hope you have wild success – I trust that my editorial work has been of some help. I truly wanted this to work and am saddened by this turn of events. You have been a delight to work with and I wish you only the best. Madison Holmes

She thought briefly about the emails' impact because most authors didn't have her tough skin. It would be more difficult still because of the sudden viral marketing success of her principal author, Tracey Doyle. The breakthrough story with Doyle's photo and hers beside it had run in all the major media – print, Facebook, YouTube, blogs, Twitter and iPhone feeds. It was a featured story on CNN News. *First-time Author Hits the 10,000,000 Mark!* Doyle's fourteen-year-old heroine had drawn new blood from the vampire craze. In a burst of appreciation, Doyle had said *I owe this success to my agent, Madison Holmes. She's tireless, reassuring and unafraid of the big publishers.* Agents are never famous, no matter whom they represent. A more seasoned author might not have shared her success. The young author, Tracey Doyle, had pulled Madison Holmes into the spotlight with her and changed the agent's life. English-speaking Montrealers were quick to celebrate both women.

Madison knew that the authors she let go would feel short-changed. Undoubtedly, they had hoped to jump on the bandwagon. Ironically, Doyle's work was actually inferior to the four authors she let go. Narrative skill didn't much matter. *Wow* and simplicity were *in*. Asia *was* today's market. North America now averaged only 14% of the pie. Social-networking teens had created Doyle's overnight success and the techies were still punching out new numbers. The young author had Stieg Larsson's numbers without his style. Doyle, a twenty-four-year-old Canadian, had just signed a five-book deal with a major New York house with a $20-million contract.

For Madison, great news just kept coming. In late October at the Waterfront Festival in Toronto, Martin Connor, an enterprise unto himself, had approached *her* with his personal card and asked her to call him that night. Madison left the rowdy gathering at a downtown bar on King Street early and hurried back to her hotel room. She'd permitted herself one glass of white wine. Clearing her throat, speaking aloud to test her voice, pacing before she stopped, Madison stood with rubbery legs and tapped in the number. 'Hello, Martin, this is…'

'I know. I appreciate punctuality. It's a rare bird in this business. First off, congratulations with Doyle!'

'Thanks. It's still hard to believe.' Harder to compute that Martin Connor was on the other end of the line. Her own voice rang in her ears as it did when she was nervous.

'Shouldn't be. I'm familiar with the work behind the scenes. For the past year or so, I've been scouting for a new agent. Tom Graham and I have worked together from the beginning of my career, but he has been struggling with his prostate. We've come to an impasse. I have seven or eight books in me. The literary scene has changed. Agents multi-task today. They have power. I come with baggage, a marketing manager and the gang that goes with that. As my agent, I'll want you to brainstorm with my manager so that he can tap into the magic you've discovered, to sell rights and to ensure that the marketing is done properly. You'll work behind the scenes, but you'll have a marked influence on the process. I made my success book by book, but that's a thing of the past as Doyle and a few others like her have shown. Texting, tweets and chats mean sales. I'm woefully behind these viral times. I'm sticking with my publisher, but I want you to tackle my contract. It's a renewal year; there's room to manoeuvre. You obviously have great PR skill sets – I want into this new scene. It's that simple.'

'Doyle is my first mega star,' Madison said with honest but hesitant pride. Her shoulders shook involuntarily and she steadied herself. The conversation seemed an out-of-body experience. *Does he know who he's talking to?*

'You've had a taste – that's what I want, someone young and hungry.'

'I'm 34.'

'I'm 57, you're young.' Connor gave Madison a few seconds before he continued. 'The Salon du Livre begins on November 17th. I'll be in Montreal for that. How about lunch at the Ritz on the 16th, say one o'clock at the Café de Paris? The food's great and it's a good place to talk. In the meantime, give this some thought.'

'I will.' The two words shot out before Madison could hide her eagerness.

'If anything comes up between now and then, you have my private number.'

'I'll be there, Martin.'

Madison stood very still for a few minutes after the call, stunned. Then she was jumping like a kid. Her heart kept skipping long after she had stopped. She took a good look at herself in her full-length mirror. *Young?* She pinched a little fat on her hips. An early morning run till all her muscles screamed would take care of that. The hint of crow's feet was punishment for the tan she still had. Filler she could now afford would camouflage that. Clothes! Definitely. People had said she was strikingly attractive. All in all, at 5' 7", with long legs, she was a pretty decent package. Most dates focused first on her dark and wistful eyes. For the next two days she worked in a fury of activity, with only two weeks to get herself and her work in shape. Most days she was proud to be in the 47% who didn't see marriage as a good fit. Other days, she wasn't. Writers seemed to fill her life, and she had now hit a bull's eye. For the time being, Madison didn't want to share the red circle.

Madison had gone out on her own, and not by choice. Last in, first out had brought about her independence. Spence Agency, where she had worked for six years, was about to discover an Othello loss if Connor worked out. They were already gritting their teeth about Doyle. If Connor signed with her, she'd be working with two of the most successful authors in the industry. Spence Agency would forever regret that they hadn't had the foresight to keep her on.

Madison owned the second unit of a triplex on rue de Saint-Vallier only because a gay couple who were good friends with her ended a seventeen-year relationship. When neither one could afford the rent alone, Madison used her mother's inheritance that she hadn't wanted to touch and bought the place. Cancer had left so little of her mother at the end that Madison wanted to leave the inheritance intact for a while because it was her mother's final gift. Her mother would have wanted her to remain in Montreal West, but Madison enjoyed a French-speaking environment. The Plateau was now *the* place to live. Rue de St-Vallier was on the edge of it, and Madison was fine with edges. Her friends Mireille and Nicole had completely renovated their unit, and Madison felt guilty enjoying the comfort they had lost. She had six rooms in all and converted two of them into offices. In one she stored the files and manuscripts that had begun to creep up the left side of the wall near the door. The sunnier room, with the wooden balcony overlooking a charming old lane, she used as her working office.

She was still excited about Connor's call two days later. She got to her knees in the file room, grabbed a number of manuscripts, some still boxed, and stacked them on the recycling pile at the back door. *Haven't read them by now, never will.* Even though Madison received manuscripts by email, she still preferred printed manuscripts. She had also taken charge of her career and, for once, was not at the mercy of a publisher. Waiting on a call could last for weeks on end. She remembered too well how her nerves tightened another inch with each passing day. Well, that was the past. Madison now intended to get with the times and stop accepting boxed scripts. Since money wasn't a problem, she'd go the electronic route and print emailed manuscripts herself. Paging through her mail, she noticed that three of the released authors had already written. Claude Beauchemin was no doubt composing a lengthy missive. Negative vibes really hosed her. *Flogged their books for two years! I need to run.*

She left her iPhone behind and let it all go. She slipped on skin-tight navy shorts and a matching jacket and laced her Nikes in double knots. With a water bottle, she scooted out the front door and down the 52 stairs from her landing. On the last step, her right foot flew out in front of her and her body followed, except for her hand that clutched the railing to prevent the fall. Anchored to it, her body flew around the railing like a curve ball. Her forehead smashed into the cement planter with a heavy thud. A neighbor darted across the street to her aid. Madison sat on her bum holding her forehead. *What the…?* Madison checked her hand. There was no blood.

'Est-ce-que je peux vous aider?' the neighbor asked.

'Non merci, ça va.' Madison got to her feet, bent over and examined the stair. When she spotted the bottle of shampoo leaking its contents she swore and kicked it into the street. She refused to allow a bad start to ruin her day. Off she ran, leaving the neighbor shaking his head. By the time Madison got to the Fairmount bagel shop, her head was throbbing. A bruise had already begun to show at her hairline. She wolfed down two hot bagels, blamed the fall for her lapse, and cabbed it home.

Chapter Two

THREE DAYS EARLIER...
Claude Beauchemin printed out the rejection letter and stared at his monitor, reading it for the eighth time. He studied each word. Words, individual and clustered, mattered to him. As a retired lawyer, he'd worked with them all his life. He folded the copy and tore it apart, dumping the pieces into the recycle bin. Printing another copy, he memorized every word as the air around him splintered.

Five filing cabinets took up the side of one wall in his office. He pulled the first drawer open and examined the 63 color-coded rejection letters, now 64. Four years ago, he'd felt that each rejection was a learning experience. *The characters were not well drawn, the story line was 'done,' implausible action sequences, amateur prose, an arrogant narrator, huge editing work required, not for us...* Claude had worked on them all, ALL. In his youth, he'd represented Canada in badminton, and he had tennis trophies. Nudging sixty, he'd cycled to Ottawa with two younger men and kept up with them. A bankruptcy lawyer, he'd acquired the upper duplex on Westmount's Lansdowne Avenue in payment from a bankrupt client. Beauchemin had learned something of life. When he was just out of law school he felt that firms would heartily welcome him. That didn't happen, so he knocked on doors until he found work. Most other lawyers didn't make millions either, he discovered. Unexpectedly, he'd weathered his forced retirement when the firm downsized and still worked at the law off and on from his home with three loyal clients. He was certain publishing a book couldn't be harder than passing the bar. For him, it was. Holmes's letter didn't deserve a file. He slammed the cabinet shut.

Some rejections had come from his connections, top agencies and large houses. Back then he was thrilled they had taken the time to write, and he wrote back with effusive thanks until he realized they were standard letters. Still, he had been pleased his work hadn't lain in a slush pile, waiting for the recycling bin. He noticed his dog-eared *2011 Guide to Literary Agents* at the back of the cabinet. The leaden weight of all those query letters that he had written with the hope of a novice unsteadied Beauchemin. The single words he had fought over with his writing group at the Westmount Library mocked him now with their impotence. He was back where he had begun four years ago, but worse, because the leads were used up. The antique mirror above his desk reflected failure. Beauchemin didn't see the physical man, a short, balding, stubby man with sloping shoulders and small eyes.

The second cabinet housed the query letters accompanied by the agents' requests, some for twenty pages of the manuscript, some for three chapters, a few the whole manuscript, "ms," all dead ends, chipping away at his ego and effort. Yet he had endured because he couldn't let go.

Beauchemin had done research. He had gone to writers' conferences, studied at libraries, followed Ken Follett's lectures on thrillers and read Erskine Childers' *The Riddle of the Sands*, the first thriller. No one was better prepared for his first novel. No one deserved it more. A muffled laugh released some of his tension when he remembered that Childers was an executed Irish republican. *At least the poor bugger published a book!*

The last cabinet contained all 41 copies of the manuscript that he had printed to send out, to rework, and to perfect. Front and center in this file was the translation of his book from English to French. It cost him four grand and two different translators for work that ate up almost a year of his life. His book had lost some of its buzz, but Beauchemin had attacked it again because Holmes had taken him on. *It works for me in French and I have connections in France. I'm excited, Claude.*

Now that she had Doyle, Holmes had given him the kiss-off. He'd bragged to all his friends, he had shown them posters he had designed, and almost promised a publishing date. He'd have to dodge all of them. What a trusting fool he had been! He punched the desk with a closed fist and yelped in pain. There was one positive. His research skills were vastly improved. He could find anyone. Her photo was on the web. He realized he could pass Holmes on the street and she wouldn't recognize him.

The phone rang. It was his wife Louise, who had begun to check up on him. She worried about his growing obsession with his book. *Growing obsession*, her very words! Louise didn't understand. Claude didn't pick up. She often came home later than usual to avoid talk of the infernal book. Well, he'd take care of himself and he'd steer clear of the writing group at the library. *Damn!* He'd bought and read Doyle's book. A waste of good trees! Other people's success made him anxious because he felt left out. He had talent. He couldn't allow news of the rejection letter to reach his friends. No way! The air felt very close in the house, and Beauchemin went out to the back porch. Three leaves still clung to a branch. He took the broom from a side wall and struck the branch. The first two fell easily. The third was stubborn. He clobbered the branch until the leaf came down in pieces. *The season's over – you should know that.*

Chapter Three

MADISON FROWNED when the phone rang because she was still prepping for Martin Connor. It was already November 6th. They were to meet in ten days. When she saw it was Doyle, she lowered the volume on a Wynton Marsalis solo. 'Hi Tracey, what's up?' Madison padded her enthusiasm whenever she spoke to Doyle. Good business.

With her mother listening in, Tracey wasted no time getting to the point. She was the star after all. 'It's our contract.'

Madison's back stiffened. 'Okay…'

'You're my agent and my publicist for the next five years.' Doyle spat out her words, and they struck Holmes like an indictment.

'Uh huh.' Doyle's sudden turn from their usual conversation hurt Madison, giving her a fright, but she attempted to reason calmly with her young author. 'We agreed to both hats when you and I signed the contract, and you know that I've been doing PR all along, Tracey. You know pretty much how many hours I put in for you.'

'I know, I mean I guess, but that's adding an additional 5% to the 15% you're already taking as my agent. My mom's a lawyer. She said it's a lot of money. I'm *writing* the books and I'm losing 20% of my royalties to you.'

Ungrateful little sod! In saner times, I would never have taken you on. Timing is all you have. Your work… There was no point finishing the sentence. A prominent vein in Madison's neck began to pulse convulsively. 'Tracey, I've always been up front with you. Most publicists work for a fee – an hourly rate – and would even cost you more! I'm charging you only 5%. Breaking a contract is a costly prospect. Litigation would hurt our reputations. I can't believe you're even thinking of such a thing.' Madison paced furiously back and forth to avoid an explosion. She could not lose this author!

'My plans for you are long-term. I'll have you everywhere. You won't be a two-year 'trash-celeb' as so many authors have been. No one will see your book in bookstore remainder bins or as massive quantities waiting in a warehouse to be pulped. You'll enjoy a long, successful career. That's always been my goal. Our contract is more than fair. And acting as your publicist, I've already set up our schedule for the next three months: TV talk shows, reviews and interviews, book club dates, multiple signings in prestigious places, we're in schools with the kids who buy your books, we're in new bookstores, museum shops, university bookstores, visitor centers, libraries. I've even worked on blog seeding. All you have to do is get the next book out. And I'll be glad to edit the work as usual.'

Tracey wasn't swayed. She liked her power. 'I know you work hard, but 20% is still a lot of money.'

'Good publicists have a long list of clients. If you go elsewhere, you'll be one of many. It will take time for them to get to know you. We already have a relationship. You'll pay top dollar to establish one with another publicist. I've let some of my authors go to give you more attention. Aside from this discussion, something very exciting has happened. An American icon wants to sign with me. He's been "big" for years. We're meeting very soon. He wants in on the new scene. I plan to cross-pollinate you two and gain mass publicity. You're a smart young woman who can teach him about today's world – he can teach you the track to longevity. He's one of the greats. The three of us will come out winners. No other authors will have better numbers. With me you have someone who knows you and cares about you long term.'

'Still…'

'Everything you dreamed of, I managed to get for you. What first-time author ever snags a five-book deal?'

'I know, but…'

'Tracey, think hard about this. If you sign with a new publicist, I can't hand over the three-month agenda I've prepared. If this prospective author signs with me, he'll draw more business my way. I'm doing very well on my own. Still, I firmly believe I'm the best person for you right now.'

'I didn't mean to say you're…' Tracey's argument flagged.

'Get back to me with your decision.' Madison's heart was leaping. 'In the meantime, I'll stop working on any promo plans. I have other pressing business.'

'Madison, don't…'

'Sorry, I have another call, Tracey. Remember, together we broke into a very tough market and we wiped out other contenders. We're a winning team, a good fit from the very beginning. Don't forget that. Once trust is broken, it comes back in pieces.' Madison cut the connection. Her cheeks were splotched with deep red and she stood open-mouthed. Madison put her head in her hands and groaned. She muscled up her nerve to check her email. If Connor hadn't responded, then… She exhaled. He had written to confirm their meeting. She rocked back and forth before she rose and picked up Doyle's file. She felt like burning the damn thing. Instead, she dropped it onto a pile of *might get around to it*. A bolt of nerves caught Madison off-guard. How much did Doyle's presence play in Connor's decision to meet with her? If Doyle walked, would Connor reconsider? *I have to find some way to keep Doyle.*

Madison opened her desk drawer and flipped on her Sony digital recorder. She recorded important conversations. If the conversation proved not to be important, she'd erase it. This call was high priority. For a good minute, Madison fell back against her chair, stared at the ceiling and took deep breaths.

Angela Marino had steered her daughter into the call. 'Tracey, don't let Holmes scare you into staying. I have connections. You can do better.'

'Mom! I like Madison, we…'

'Best interests at heart, ha! Who but a mother has that?'

'You don't understand. This is *my* book!' The more Tracey wavered, the stronger Angela's resolve. 'This isn't about you, Mom,' Tracey whispered in a thready voice.

'What? Never mind, I heard you. Darling, let's not pretend you're another Dickens,' Angela said with deliberate offence. 'You *need* the best out there. And I intend…'

'How can I do better than a five-book deal with a $20-million dollar contract?'

'I think I can. It's the future I want for you. Now doesn't last. Don't you see that Holmes made her name on you? I want the best.'

'Mom, please.' Tracey knew she'd been a disappointment to her attractive, successful mother. A single photo of her father who'd left when she was an infant, was evidence that she had managed to inherit the worst genes from both parents. Deferring to her mother had gone on so long that it had become second nature. Yet she was startled by the vehemence of her mother's selfish interference. Unsteady, Tracey struck back for the first time ever. 'Are you jealous of me, is that it, Mom?' The words came out in a hoarse whisper.

'What would I have to be jealous of?' Angela sneered. 'Talent? Have you actually read your book? I'm a law partner. Money? Anyone can make money.'

Tracey's face drained of color, but she held steady. 'Don't ruin this for me, Mom.'

'Are you threatening *me* now?'

Something like mad panic had crept into Tracy's words. 'Please stay out of my life. This belongs to me. Leave it alone, Mom.' Tears welled up in her eyes. 'Sometimes, I wish you had had another child.' Tracey ran past her mother.

'That makes two of us.' Angela's nostrils flared in disgust. 'I haven't finished yet. Don't you dare walk out on me!'

Chapter Four

MADISON COULDN'T SLEEP the night after her hang-up with Doyle. 'If you can eat, eliminate and sleep, you're ahead of the curve.' Her grandfather had recited this credo when she was seven. Twenty-seven years later, she understood the old man. An entire bottle of Jacob's Creek cabernet hadn't knocked her out. She paced, swore, kicked her blankets off the bed and punched her pillow flat – nothing broke the bar of nerves. Masochism might help so she sat, half drunk, half sleepy, half scared, at her computer reading the authors' emails. She chose Detective Stephen Galt's first, known as "Prose" at the Crémazie Division. *Well, this is a cop-out.* Despite her rigid fear, Madison laughed so loud, she burped up some of the wine and it dripped down her chin. 'Great pun!' *I'd booked my flight to Hollywood. Figured the big boys might want me as a professional consultant. I have another book. I hope you will read it. What's strange, Ms Holmes, is that few people ever turn their back on a badge. Prose.* A cold chill ran across her shoulders.

Yvette Ranger's email, her seventy-four-year-old author, the first female pilot in Quebec, was elegant in its disappointment and clear as a blue sky in its rebuke of her. *I didn't expect you to be swayed by such a silly book as Doyle's. I thought better of you and readers.* Madison felt the cut and saw its truth. The last email she read was Jean Pauzé's, a McGill University post-graduate history student whose manuscript traced the origins of McGill's historic stone Roddick Gates. Pauzé protested that Holmes had wasted his valuable time and had exhibited a glaring lack of foresight in rejecting Montreal history that well deserved its day on bookshelves and eBooks. His *oeuvre*, actually his dissertation, had been highly praised, he reminded her. He decried the mediocrity of present day writing, including hers. Verbal abuse didn't score a TKO for Madison either. *Not one of them thanked me for my effort. Ingrates!* She bare-footed it back to bed, rolled herself into a ball shivering until the first light slipped between her vertical blinds and drew sharp white lines across her navy sheets.

Her throat was dry from the wine, and she knew that her breath was foul. Turning on to her back, Madison rubbed the sleep from her eyes and got up. She tossed the white quilt to the floor, and ripped off the sheets. 'If I'm going down, I'm going in style.' With that, she picked up her sheets, walked briskly down the long hall and dropped them in a wicker basket. From her linen closet beside the bathroom, she reached in for her new Anne de Solene sheets that promised a marriage of elegance and purity.

The pale blue sheets had set her back $700. When the bed was made, she stripped, except for her white slippers, took her long night shirt with her and headed for the tub. A bath would wash off yesterday and the near panic inside her ribcage. She wanted to be clean, to regain her strength and confidence. The blow drier provided a good hair day. That was a start.

The next boost was food. While her Iranian flatbread was toasting, she ate a bowl of cut cantaloupe, strawberries, raspberries and a banana. Madison grabbed the hot toast with her fingertips. Wincing she dropped the pieces quickly on a plate. Smearing them too generously with blueberry jam, she added thin slices of aged Gruyère cheese. She drank her coffee hot and black. The food dulled the growing panic. Madison looked around the kitchen, the main reason she'd bought the place. The walls of the rectangular room were a cosy caramel, the counters and stools a light gray. A selection of teas and small coffee tins beside an espresso machine were carefully arranged against the only wall free of major appliances. The wood floor was light and warm. The whole room was awash with summer sunshine that streamed through the back door and the window. The yellow bars installed on the windows and doors in the condo added the comfort of safety. She would have loved to eat out on her balcony that overlooked the 100-year-old lane, but November put an end to that pleasure. Despite the food and the bars, Madison jerked forward on her stool, elbows on her knees, hands in fists in front of her when the phone rang. Doyle? *Funny, I never thought of an assault coming from a phone.* It was just before six.

Alarmed, she reached over and took the receiver without checking the caller ID. 'Madison Holmes.'

'How's my favourite daughter?'

Exhaling, she answered, 'You only have one, Dad, unless you're calling to confess a past. It's early! You scared me a little.'

'Bad night, it happens. Nothing unusual. But something's up with my girl. I hear it in your voice.'

'I can handle it.'

'Sure you can, but you might want a second opinion. I'm in that business.'

'No speeches, no talk of eggs and baskets.'

'First, do no harm.'

'Good enough.' Madison gave her father the facts about Tracey and the four authors she'd let go.

'A head butt definitely, but it doesn't have to be a bare-knuckle affair.'

'What?'

'A boxing term – but you get the meaning, right?'

'I do.'

'Your plan?'

'Connor's presentation is redone. I'm ready for him.'

'With Doyle, I mean.'

'I don't know – do I call, do I wait for her?'

'Give it a day, and then I'd call. You're her agent, you have a contract. The longer you wait, the more time they have for hunting. The mother's your main problem. She can drain you legally, and all she loses is her time.'

'But Doyle's an adult, Dad.'

'Parents inveigle themselves into their adult children's lives. It's a new phenomenon. Keep up your ties with Doyle – get her back on your side. You know her too. You're the miracle worker. Today, read manuscripts, add a few authors. Forget the others. You gave them plenty of time. You'll do just fine.'

'Wish I had your confidence.'

'It's a well-founded belief in a fine agent.' Thomas Holmes tried to project authority and confidence in his daughter. 'Now, I do have to get back. Dinner?'

'I'll call you later on that. And – thanks.'

He heard the strain in her voice. They'd talk things out at dinner. He had his own problems that he hadn't shared with his daughter.

What could she say to Doyle that she hadn't already said? What soft spot would turn the girl around? She had no time to lose. Her best thinking occurred in her office, so she headed there. It was November 8th. In eight days, she'd meet Connor. Madison began another review of her presentation. She heard the footsteps on the stairs, carpeted or not. She supposed it was a courier. The regular mail came later. She hadn't accepted any new manuscripts, but first-time authors sometimes thought they could bypass *no unsolicited manuscripts* by sending theirs by courier, which might impress the agent enough to accept them. *It can't be legal papers from Doyle already. It's only been a day!* When the bell rang, she peeked through the blinds and was instantly relieved to spy a courier with a familiar cardboard box. A manuscript. Normality restored. This author might just get lucky.

A low gray November sky meant it was cold outside. Madison pulled the foyer door behind her as she unlocked the front door. She looked quizzically at the courier when she saw the shorts and gloves, scarf and cap. The mix was odd. Madison might have hesitated, but the situation with Doyle distracted her.

It was cold so she invited the courier in so she could sign for the package. There should have been something to warn Madison, an inner signal, a sudden chill, a threatening sky, a hesitancy, something, but there was nothing.

Before the courier closed the front door, a gust of wind blew the foyer door open. Madison reached around to close it properly. As she was turning back, the courier levelled the first blow, catching Madison at the corner of her left eye, knocking her violently off balance into the side wall. Blinded by spurting blood, immobilized with shock, she couldn't raise a hand to defend herself. Involuntarily, she bounced forward into a haymaker that drove her sideways through the glass window of the foyer door. She fell hard against the jagged shards at the base of the frame. A low moan betrayed the pain at her collapsing lung, but she hadn't screamed. Most of the broken glass fell on the carpet runner. Bent in two, pinioned by the shards, Madison still managed a coherent thought. *I'm watching my own murder.*

The courier breathing heavily never said a word. Madison felt the door being pushed open, dragging her with it. She felt the courier staring down at her, could hear the heavy breathing. The next blows struck the side of her head. Madison couldn't feel pain. She couldn't count the blows either. The thought came back. *I'm watching my own…*

The courier stood silent once more, waiting, before kicking Madison's legs. There was no response. Removing his blood-smeared shorts and gloves, the courier reached for pants stowed in the messenger's bag, put them on, stuffed the shorts, gloves and manuscript into the bag with the gloves and cap and reversed the jacket. The extra shoes weren't in the bag. The shoes!

Without warning, there were footsteps. The courier stopped breathing. The vertical blinds on the front door were closed, but the door wasn't locked. If the caller tried the door… Was it possible to see anything from the side of the blinds? If it were another courier, he'd snoop, not wanting to have a come-back. The caller stopped at Holmes's door and rang, then rang again. The courier heard a few steps off to the left. The caller was looking in at the office. Was there a view of the hall from that window? Another ring, then the phone rang four times before voicemail picked up. Whoever it was hadn't left but stood not three feet from the courier, who pressed himself against the wall. There was no movement from Holmes. A thump at the front door startled the courier. Finally, the sound of footsteps growing faint.

For the next two minutes, the courier stood stock still, listening. Reaching into the messenger bag a second time, the courier grabbed the shorts and used them to smear the bloody footprints. But there was nothing to do with prints that might be left on the balcony and stairs. The courier was forced to wear the blood-smeared shoes. The courier opened and closed the front door quietly, using the jacket to avoid fingerprints. Stepping over two manuscripts that lay against the door, the courier rushed down the stairs, careful not to use the railing. On the sidewalk, this unremarkable individual turned right and disappeared down rue Beaubien. Madison's front door remained unlocked.

No one on rue Beaubien noticed the bloody shoes until the courier reached a lane and stopped.

Chapter Five

AT SEVEN THAT MORNING, emergency nurse Michelle Aubin had survived a double shift at the Hôpital St-Luc on rue St-Denis. Two years from retirement, such shifts needled every bone in her body and the hemorrhoids that had developed from long periods of standing. She ought to have taken the Berri métro, but she needed something in her stomach to take the edge off the long night. In the students' quarter, near the University of Quebec, UQAM, it wasn't hard to find a greasy spoon. Eggs, sausages, bacon, hash browns, white bread toast, and black coffee did a number on her functioning arteries, but she didn't care. On the métro, her head lolled back and forth, as she fought sleep. She got off on rue Beaubien and stepped into a mini-gale of driving rain. The wind was kicking up dirt and discarded fragments of paper from the gutters. Montreal in November.

She regretted buying the condo on the top floor. The stairs had grown tougher. She'd bought her place 27 years ago when the selling point was having no one above her. A few mumbled groans escaped as she began her climb. She spotted the wet manuscripts as she passed Madison's condo and was tempted to ignore them, but grumbling up the final flight to her door, she grabbed the key to Madison's condo and lumbered back down. Owners looked out for one another. Furthermore, she liked the Anglo.

Michelle put the key in the lock, but it wouldn't turn. *Merde!* Examining the key, she saw the "M" taped to it. It was Madison's alright. Michelle tried it a second time without success. The three condo owners had come to hate their special keys: *serrure a pêne dormant* and *serrure á mortaise*. Custom-made by the now defunct Meubles de Québec, it took one key to lock the antique pine door from the inside and another to open it from the outside. If lost, the owners had to send the codes to the Paris manufacturer, so they had all purchased extra, expensive keys, to their chagrin. Reaching down, she picked up the packages, and on a hunch, tried the door. It opened.

An instant dread leached the frustration and fatigue from her body. Smeared blood on the foyer floor was the first thing she noticed. Blood was her job. Then she saw Madison lying on the floor with her legs crossed. She dropped the manuscripts. '*Mon Dieu!*' Michelle could feel a deadness in her legs when she took in the mangled body of her friend. She let out a low breath. Heedless that an assailant might still be inside, she stepped carefully into the condo, inching her way past the foyer door so as not to further injure Madison. Blood had pooled on both sides of the door and she had to kneel in some of it to reach Madison. Michelle felt a familiar hollowness whenever she saw the victims of horrid crimes. A home invasion sprang to mind. With the remarkable calm of her profession, Michelle placed two fingers on the side of Madison's throat. Surveying the damage and Madison's horrible predicament, she felt inside her bag till she found her cell phone and called 9-1-1, and then the Montreal General Hospital which had a trauma center. Both numbers were familiar to her.

Michelle related the situation with precision and detail and gave her profession. The responder then knew the information was accurate. 'The pulse is thready... The fire department would need an electrical saw... The victim cannot be lifted off the glass because of the possible additional damage to vital organs. For the moment, the glass is serving as a block against additional blood loss. What you need is a human stretcher, two paramedics supporting the victim's back on both sides of the frame and two others: one for the hips and legs, the other for the shoulders and head. In transport, the victim should continue to be hand-held. I suggest you bring a metal splint for support. She may not survive the hour. It looks like she lost more than three pints of blood...' Once all the information had been relayed, Michelle rushed to the bathroom for towels. Gently, she lifted the bloody head less than an inch, resting it on her knee under the towel. With her fingers, she pried Madison's mouth open very slowly but expertly for another airway. She brushed bloody hair off Madison's face and used the other towel to wipe blood from her nostrils. Next she worked around the eye. The principal livid gash appeared to be at the corner of the eye. The first sign of hope. Michelle's face was flushed; her face wet from tears. Her voice was a hoarse whisper. 'Madison, it's Michelle, I am here...' She stroked the hair not soaked in blood and reached for Madison's hand and held it. She looked cautiously behind her, but the rest of the condo was quiet. 'I am here – help is coming.'

Two of Madison's fingers closed loosely around Michelle's.

Chapter Six

THE SCREAM OF SIRENS converged into an ear-splitting chorus as fire trucks, ambulances, squad cars and the Crime tech white van came to screeching stops on rue de Saint-Vallier. Paramedics flew up the steep classic Montreal outside stairs to Madison's second-floor condo carrying their equipment as though they were bags of air, followed by Crime techs. Officers immediately closed the street from Beaubien to Bellechasse. Two squad cars parked in a "V" at either end of Saint-Vallier did that job while other officers orange-taped the stairs and blocked off the sidewalk to foot traffic before moving up to the second floor. The officers were forced to wait outside because there was no room for them.

The paramedics and the Crime techs worked in perfect unison. The paramedics bagged Madison with oxygen and blood as soon as they'd typed her. The firefighter, saw in hand, waited. Another stood ready in the hallway. The print tech, suited up, hatted, gloved and slippered, knowing the victim might end up in a freezer bed, took his whorls and composites from every angle he could get to. The scene was badly contaminated, so he worked quickly. He stepped outside and snapped photos of the door, inside and out, the balcony and stairs. Other techs marked off footprints and fingerprints, mostly partial, taped and measured them. Officers stood on the balcony during this work.

A metal splint was set up on either side of the door. Madison was covered and supported carefully by kneeling paramedics. Michelle had stepped aside, letting go of Madison's hand because a tech needed to bag both hands in case she had managed to fight back. Michelle did not realize her face was swollen and slightly disfigured from crying.

When the saw began, she didn't turn away. The foyer door was old and thin. The saw first cut through its left side, a foot above Madison, then the right. A firefighter held the door as his mate cut, then he took the piece and placed it against a wall in the hall. The four paramedics braced themselves, holding Madison firmly and still as the firefighter cut away the bottom of the door only inches below Madison. Lastly, he cut away the sides. The plastic protective sheet was lifted off. The next movements seemed surreal.

Without a wasted second, the paramedics lifted Madison, the splint and what remained of the frame and carried their special burden down the steep stairs, slowly, like the casket of a slain soldier. No one spoke, not even the neighbors who had congregated on the other side of the street. When the paramedics reached the sidewalk, one could sense a collective sigh of relief that no one had fallen, not the victim who floated precariously up and down with each descending step, nor any of the paramedics who strained visibly under the weight of their charge. Madison disappeared into an ambulance, the doors closed. The two squad cars blocking Bellechasse burst into life and sped up the street and positioned themselves behind the ambulance. The two at Beaubien backed up to escort the ambulance. The screeching of the sirens began anew as the entourage sped to the Montreal General Hospital.

Two officers stayed with Michelle, waiting for detectives. Her hands were bloody. The help she had given to the victim contaminated the crime scene. The leads on the case would want to interview her. They waited inside the foyer for detectives to arrive. The attempted murder charge might well be upgraded to murder if the victim did not survive. One of the officers began to take notes. 'Madame Aubin, please recount the events leading up to you finding Ms Holmes.'

Before Michelle could answer, detectives mounted the stairs, one male and one female, and both immediately frowned at the crime scene. They had left their cards on the dashboard and their radio on the rear-view mirror to avoid the ticket quotas. Even the police were not immune to the City of Montreal's money grab. 'Madame, Detective Toni Damiano and Detective Pierre Matte.' Damiano looked at the officer with the notepad.

'Je n'avais pas le temps de poser tous mes questions.' Nevertheless, he filled them in with what little he had and handed over his general notes.

The detectives, wearing gloves, walked carefully around the scene, at times crouching to observe details. Detective Damiano used a pen to touch some of the marked areas and regretted that the crime scene was contaminated. She'd have to live with that. She reread the notes. 'Weapon?'

'We haven't located one. Officers are combing the area outside.'

Detective Damiano looked at the boxed manuscripts.

'Madame Aubin found them outside.'

When Detective Damiano's face expressed irritation, the mask of age that would one day descend on this forty-two-year-old woman was visible. She sat back on her heels and shrugged her shoulders. This situation didn't rock her world view, but it did stall her usual fast pace. A mother of a teenage boy, Detective Damiano had a strong heart and a set of hard rules that she employed on the job and at home. As tall as her partner at 5' 10", everything about this detective suggested intensity and power. Detective Matte had taken her on a few times in their last nine years together and had learned that Damiano fought till she wore him down and won. He was no match for her Italian temper. That was fine by him some of the time although he never admitted that to the other shields.

Michelle's ankles hurt. She wanted to go home. Because of what had happened, the scene seemed to slip out of focus. She craved a bath and her own bed. Being detained after she had explained everything twice to one of the officers provoked her. The female detective asked if the techs had taken photos of her clothes, and her person. Michelle nodded. She felt a jab as sharp as a paper cut when told she'd have to surrender her clothes and be fingerprinted. She was a suspect, after all she had done?

Detective Damiano was the obvious lead detective. She looked at the tape and pointed to the kitchen as a better place for the interview. 'Madame Aubin, s'il vous plait?'

Michelle walked sluggishly behind her, very much aware of her own haggard appearance. Detective Damiano was impeccably dressed in a dark blue pant suit over a pale yellow shirt and a subtle gold rope chain. Michelle glimpsed the sleek, shiny navy sneakers. This woman cared to dress well and it was obvious. Detective Matte, with his close-cropped brown curly hair and long legs, followed, tagging and labelling the blood smears Michelle's shoes were leaving behind. Michelle looked back at him, thinking he reminded her of an insect at work. Once they were both seated on stools, Detective Matte took out a notebook and handed it to his partner. Detective Damiano read what he had gathered before she handed it back to him. Michelle suggested that they speak in English. It was obvious that the detective's French was a second language.

'Fine. Please understand, Madame Aubin, you are the primary and therefore most important witness. We are dealing with a very serious crime. Madison Holmes has a high profile with the media so there will be close scrutiny of this case. There was no evidence of a break-in, the security system was disengaged, and Ms Holmes's Rolex and wallet were left on her dresser. Nothing appears to have been taken. This suggests that Ms Holmes opened the door to her assailant who left by the front door. From the notes, I see that this door cannot be locked without a key. You've told an officer that door was open when you tried to give the manuscripts to Ms Holmes. Is that accurate?'

'Yes. I tried to open the door with the spare key I have when Madison didn't answer. It was by chance that I tried the door. I was about to leave.'

'Since the attack was brutal, perhaps fatal, would you please account for your whereabouts before you discovered the victim? I know you own the condo above this one.'

Michelle let out a deep sigh and began to recount the events, but deliberately abbreviated them. Her day was becoming more miserable, and her annoyance was evident in tone and posture. Enough was quite enough.

If Madison lived, she had saved her life!

'Would you know the name of the restaurant where you ate?'

'No, I wouldn't. I have a mental block with names, any names. But they know me and I could get it for you after work tonight.'

'Thank you.'

'I am in no way responsible…'

'This is a necessary elimination procedure.' Detective Damiano spoke in a matter-of-fact tone, yet Michelle saw that the woman never took her eyes off her.

'Now, the door. You are certain it was unlocked?'

Michelle gave the long version for this answer and repeated the story of the keys. 'We never leave our doors unlocked, especially not with the number of home invasions that we read about.'

'Does the owner on the first level also have a spare key to this condo?'

'Yes. Detective Damiano, I find your questions insulting. I'm exhausted and I need some sleep. If your next question is *were we friends,* yes, we were. We all worked hard and had different hours and might go days without seeing one another, but there was no animosity. Madison was a welcome addition to our *quartier.* She improved our English, we her French. Séparatistes can get along with Fédéralistes. We thoroughly enjoyed heated political debates. Serge Lavoie is the other owner. He works for Radio-Canada and leaves for work very early.'

Detective Damiano gave Michelle the once-over and her eyes narrowed. 'Do all three of you live alone?'

That question incised itself on Michelle's memory. Her answer was clipped, 'For now, yes.'

'Would you know if Ms Holmes was seeing anyone?'

'News like that we'd share and celebrate. Madison was preoccupied with her work. I don't think she was seeing anyone, but her father would know for sure.'

'Do you know a contact number for her family?'

'Madison has only her father. His number must be on her phone.'

'Detective Matte will accompany you to your condo and wait for your clothes and take your prints.'

Michelle was summarily dismissed. Every tired edge of her felt sharp. She whirled around. 'Excuse me, Detective, we're both civil servants here. I would have appreciated a nod of thanks.'

'Certainly you do, but you also have to appreciate that contamination of the crime scene has made my work more difficult.'

Michelle sucked in air as the detective turned away, the kind that can loosen a filling. 'We do differ then. Your work is crime – mine is saving lives,' she said to the detective's back. Back in her condo, Michelle quickly removed her clothes and threw on her blue robe. At the door, she handed the blood-stained clothes and shoes to Detective Matte and watched him place them in plastic bags already labelled. And then he took her prints.

When she was finally alone she washed the black ink from her fingers, Trembling with anger and an encompasisng fear, Michelle poured a gener-ous double scotch and took it to bed. Madison might stop breathing and die. Michelle examined her hands and observed how her work had roughened them, how caring for others had gnawed away at her. *There was a time when I could attract women like Damiano...* She drained the glass. The warm liquor slipped down her throat and into her stomach. She let some of it rest on her tongue for a moment. What had she to show for any of those years of swinging between women and getting it wrong? It all seemed so long ago. If she could have one day back, she'd spend it with Francine and be kind. Michelle knew she wasn't a finisher, she liked the chase. That time had passed and now she was alone with her scotch, and was as vulnerable as Madison. Not quite alone, for a ponderous old tabby, Racine, waited until Michelle quieted down before he climbed the footstool he needed to get onto the bed and curled up against Michelle's thigh. He had heard the list of old lovers and he wasn't in the mood to hear the litany again.

Detective Damiano reached her first conclusion. *The attack was per-sonal.* She wanted to see the victim for herself. Victims personalized atrocities for her, but she knew the clues to this crime were in the condo, particularly in the office. Matte was fully engaged in the work she had as-signed, but the set of his shoulders told her that he didn't appreciate being treated as a tech. 'Detective!'

He came to her wearing a scowl. He hated that his skill worked against him, keeping him a step away from managing a case. Damiano had cracks, but he'd covered for her, more than once. 'I want my first lead to be a quick solve. You are the best detail cop I know, Pierre. While I'm at the hospital, I want you to comb through the victim's files. You're almost a hacker, you're that good – find what I need. I won't be long and I guarantee you will inter-view with me. For the time being, this office is our focus. The victim was a literary agent; makes for many unhappy people. Find me the names. We can't miss any of them. Your notes are top-grade. I have trouble reading my own.'

Detective Matte said only one word, '*Compris.*'

'I want this fucker. The attack was brutal.'

'We're on the same page,' Detective Matte agreed.

Chapter Seven

DETECTIVE DAMIANO found the phone number for the victim's father. 'Mr Thomas Holmes?'

'Speaking.'

'This is Detective Damiano. Is Madison Holmes your daughter?'

'Yes…' Holmes's voice was suddenly strained.

'Sometime this morning, Ms Holmes was the victim of a home invasion.'

'Is Madison alright?'

'She was rushed to the trauma unit at the Montreal General Hospital. I'm still at her condo, but I'm leaving for the hospital and will meet you there.'

'Is she alive?' His voice was thin and full of panic.

'She's critical. Do you know if your daughter had been threatened recently?'

The line went dead. Peeling off her gloves and shoving them into her pocket, she stalked out of the condo and took the stairs almost too quickly. At the edge of the tape, officers were holding back reporters leaning over the yellow tape with notebooks and recorders. One TV crew had arrived. Mustering a calm she didn't feel, Detective Damiano approached the nearest and gave a terse statement. 'When I have further information, I will issue a report,' she said sternly.

'Was Madison Holmes involved, Detective?'

'That's her condo, right?'

'Give us something.'

'Should the neighbors worry?'

Detective Damiano ignored the media and motioned over two of the uniformed officers and led them back to the bottom of the stairs. She took out her digital camera and ran through some of the photos. Making very certain she was out of earshot, she said to the officers, 'The head's a bleeder, so the assailant had a lot of blood on him or her. Begin the house-to-house. Someone must have seen something. Squeeze whatever you can from her neighbors. Report directly to Detective Matte upstairs,' she pointed to the condo. 'Understood? If you discover anything, have Matte contact me immediately.'

Detective Damiano sped with her siren whining and blue lights flashing from the sun visors as she leap-frogged through the inevitable traffic gridlock on rue Saint-Denis. Taking a right on Pine, she picked up speed and parked on Cedar Avenue. Tossing her Major Crimes ID card on the dashboard, she rushed past pathetic die-hard smokers at the Cedar entrance, past hospital staff and patients, past the beeps and boops from equipment and elevator chimes to the trauma unit. She hated the smell of urine, antiseptics, cleansers, body waste and fear that hung in the heavy air. Gurneys, loaded with dirty sheets, clogged the halls. The floors were shiny with grime that mops had passed over and machines had polished. The walls were covered with hand washing notices. Under them hung soap dispensers and some had leaked their blue suds down the walls. Patients hooked up to saline IVs moved like gray ghosts, dragging their bags and poles with them. Detective Damiano heard the *tick tock* of her own life beating down. She hated hospitals. Lowering her eyes, she tried to ignore everything around her by hiding in her head.

At least the slow process of house-to-house interviews and collecting statements was underway. She was about to call the chief Crime tech when she spotted a man talking and listening to two physicians. Her call would have to wait. When she heard the name Holmes she knew she had the right person. Madison's father listened intently to one of the physicians. The other physician turned and saw Detective Damiano take out her badge, yet he didn't say a word when she drew closer. He did edge to one side making some room for her.

'Tom, so far we've been fortunate. If Madison hadn't received the medical assistance from her neighbor, we wouldn't be having this conversation.'

Detective Damiano bit into her lower lip. *I didn't intend to be that rude, but this is my first case! She may have saved her life, but she also messed up the crime scene.*

'I've told you that she fell through the glass door. We have that from the paramedics. Her body must have knocked most of the glass from the frame because she didn't suffer a total collapse of the pneumothorax. The lung should heal on its own. With oxygen, it's slowly coming back. Scans also indicate the other shards have not compromised any of the major organs. There was also no evidence of sexual assault.'

Holmes suddenly appeared even taller than his six-foot frame, and straighter with the strength of relief. 'Then Madison's not in critical condition.' The relief didn't last. As a physician, he knew to probe further.

'Tom, that's the good news. Madison has also suffered an acute subdural hematoma. She was repeatedly struck just above her eye on the left side of her head. The eye, though severely swollen, is not in jeopardy.'

Whatever air was supporting Holmes left his body in a pitiful slump. The corridor itself seemed suddenly airless. He covered his eyes with his hand. His head nodded from side to side and his shoulders sagged. 'Is she in surgery?'

'Yes. They've removed a section of the left side of the skull to drain the hematoma, lessen the intracranial pressure and control the bleeding. We're doing our best to prevent further damage to delicate brain tissue. Additionally, we've induced a coma.'

A worried moment hung in the air. Detective Damiano allowed it to linger before she made her presence known.

'Excuse me, Mr. Holmes. I'm Detective Damiano.'

Holmes turned in a daze. 'What?'

'Detective Damiano. I called you about your daughter.'

Ignoring her, he turned back to the physicians. 'Madison's condition is grim, then. I've said those same words myself to patients. Never understood until now the full threat behind that four-letter word. My daughter is facing possible paralysis, loss of vision, or permanent disability, *if* she survives…'

'Tom, that's the worst of it. I'm not speaking as a physician now, but Madison seems to be on some lucky tear. Her luck might hold. If she makes it through the surgery, we'll maintain the coma to reduce further swelling.'

'May I see Madison? I don't want my daughter to die before I see her.' He spoke the last sentence in a thin whisper. Sweat had already made rivulets under his nose, and they began to run down the sides of his mouth.

'Stay here.'

'Where would I go, Stephen?'

'I'll do my best, Tom. Now let me do my job.' Both physicians left. An awkward silence ensued.

Detective Damiano didn't have the time to wait, but had listened intently to the exchange. *Odd*, she thought, *Holmes is expecting the worst even though the attending physician is offering hope.* Damiano tossed the thought to the back of her mind. 'Mr. Holmes, this is a very difficult time for you, but I do need to ask you just a few questions. I want the person who attacked your daughter.'

For the first time, Holmes seemed aware of her presence. 'You called me? I'm all over the map.'

'Yes.' She saw how thin Holmes was, like a gangly teenager. On a man of fifty-eight the look seemed frail. You could make out his shoulder bones through his gray suit jacket. His face was kind, but broken and drained of color. She extended her hand and it met a firm grip. He held her hand for a few seconds, reluctant to let it go.

'If I knew who hurt my daughter, I'd kill him. I wouldn't need the police.' His face hardened as he released her hand. He spoke with such venom that Detective Damiano didn't doubt him. She'd feel the same way if someone hurt her son Luke.

'You're under a great stress, but you can't utter death threats to a police officer. When did you last speak to your daughter?' She felt Holmes was watching her closely as she spoke, measuring her.

'Last night. We'd planned dinner together tonight.'

'Was your daughter worried about something?'

His answer was a moan.

'Sir?'

'Madison was upset. I told her to be strong and plug ahead.' The consequences of his words struck like a bolt and Holmes winced. 'What did I do? I sensed she hadn't slept, but I thought she'd be... I didn't help – she needed me...' Holmes turned away and hid his face. His body shook.

'Sir,' she gave Holmes a few seconds before she spoke again. 'Tell me what was bothering her.'

Holmes shook his head, visibly upset, before he hazarded eye contact. 'My daughter's most important author, Tracy Doyle, was threatening to leave. She'd just released four others who responded with angry emails. I told her to forget them and go after Doyle. I tried to keep things light. My daughter is very independent, but I see now that Madison would never have broached the topic if she weren't concerned. I felt her fear, but she's so capable, I thought...' He smiled ruefully. 'I might have...' His face blotched with tears.

Detective Damiano's cellphone rang, against hospital regulations. 'I have leads and info,' Detective Matte reported.

'I'm on my way. Collect what the uniforms have from their door-to-door as well.'

'Done.'

'Excuse me, Mr. Holmes, I must get back. Before I go, was your daughter seeing anyone?'

'What?' Holmes didn't seem to be aware Damiano was still there. He didn't correct her on his title either.

'Was your daughter seeing anyone?' Damiano spoke loudly to get his attention.

'No, not for quite some time. She was engrossed in her work. Find the sub-human who attacked my daughter and keep me informed, please.'

'Well...'

'About killing this bastard, I spoke in anger and stress.'

'I know that, Sir.' But she didn't. At that moment he looked capable of murder. 'I will contact you, Sir.'

'Thank you, Detective...'

'Damiano.'

'Madison would want you on her case.'

'Ms Holmes will have 24-hour police surveillance.' Damiano felt Holmes's father was scrutinizing her.

Chapter Eight

FROM HER CRUISER Detective Damiano arranged round-the-clock security for Holmes. The next call was to her estranged husband. 'Jeff?'

'Guilty, Detective.'

'Cute. I've caught my first high profile and from the looks of things, I'll be putting in a lot of hours. Plus there's top brass pressure to close the case.'

'What's the problem? I have Luke this week.'

'I'm thinking ahead.'

'No change there. I have a life, Toni.'

'I covered you this summer.'

'I'll hold your I.O.U.'

'This is work, Jeff.'

'Always was. Do you eat? Are you ever free for lunch?'

'You know where that leads. Thanks for Luke. Tell him I love him.'

'What about me?'

'A slight movement on my Richter scale.' Jeff was a talker. Four months had done little to convince him they were separated. The family should be together, he said. Damiano rolled her shoulders, and closed her ears. The travails of her alpha male. She waited for a chance to cut him off. 'Jeff, gotta go.' She didn't have a talent for marriage. It felt like a heavy tarp thrown over her. Compromise and hooks that held her down. Damn her limitations! She had no time for analysis.

Last year there were 49 murders in Montreal, most of them 'stupid' crimes, solved in a day or two. Holmes wasn't dead, but her attempted murder was the buzz of the office and soon a media virus. She stared through the window and her brow furrowed. Jeff had taken cheap shots at her 'career.' *Why is that badge everything to you? What about me and Luke? What do you want?* Want? She wanted time to box this case. She intended to eat and sleep the Holmes assault. It was her lead.

Her next call en route was to her friend who headed up Crime. 'Hi Marie! Damiano.'

'Knew you wouldn't wait for the full report.' Marie Dumont had a strong nose, a Quebec chin, long and pointed, a full, warm smile and wide hips. She tore into her work like a tank on a mission. Damiano and Dumont were women in a rush and worked well together.

'The media's out with the story, or what they have of it.'

'Figured as much. We worked it fast because the victim was still alive and being rushed to Trauma at the General. We've taken blood samples from the hands. The head wound bled profusely. On site, I'd say the samples belong to the victim, but the lab will verify the results. No defensive wounds on the hands, no broken fingernails, no scratches and no push-away bruising. The victim was struck on the left side of the head. It appears, I say with caution, that the assailant was a south-paw, but that idea might be misleading. The foyer is small. We figure the victim turned away from the assailant, perhaps to get the phone, or simply to close the door behind her. She was struck as she turned back. There was no room for the assailant to strike from the right because of the wall, not if he or she wanted the element of surprise.' There was a pause Damiano recognized. 'Having supper? Not poutine, Marie?'

'I'll have you know it's a New York delicacy now. No complaints from my Denis. To continue, we have no weapon. Have you any ideas on that?'

'I'm still thinking about your arteries. Fries with cheese curds and brown gravy – a doctor eating that mess?'

'Come on, Toni! The weapon had a point or a sharp edge. By process of elimination, it wasn't a blunt object, wood, glass, hammer or crowbar. We found no trace evidence on the floor or around the wound area. We didn't have enough time with the head, but we did with the floor of the foyer.'

Detective Damiano jerked on her brakes, double-parking on Pine Avenue, flashed her emergency lights. 'Our weapon might still be there. Dammit! Gotta go! I'm already getting the horn and middle fingers from drivers. And the idiots know I'm a cop. Keep me posted, Marie.'

'Goes without saying.'

Caught in a mess of honking drivers, Detective Damiano revved her car and burned rubber until she zigzagged her way out. Deliberately aggressive, she was soon screeching up rue Saint-Denis where she pulled a right on Bellechasse and left on rue de Saint-Vallier. It was almost two o'clock on Friday. She forged her way past the tape. 'Don't these gore freaks have something better to do?' She spoke to no one, but acknowledged the uniforms who were keeping people well behind the tape. She found Detective Matte hard at work. Matte texted faster than a teenage girl. He continued for a few seconds, copying Holmes's files to his iPhone before he printed what he had been working on.

'Let's hear it,' she said, charging ahead with the grace of a pit bull.

'Holmes dumped four of her authors. I have copies of the letter she sent to them and their replies, all angry. The wordy author *didn't* respond, unlike him from a quick look at their correspondence over the past two years. This Claude Beauchemin is a good start. Detective Stephen Galt, of the Crémazie division, is one of her discards. He emailed, *few people ever turn their backs on a badge.* Not a wise move. Prose, that's his nickname, may have been pissed, but he sent the email. Finally, I have the tape of the call between Holmes and Tracey Doyle, the gazillion best seller, who was threatening to find another agent. The conversation was heated for obvious reasons, but there was an existing contract. Apparently, Doyle's mother is a lawyer and she appears to be behind this sudden move. Holmes recorded her suspicion about the mother following their conversation. Holmes may have been incorrect, but I assume she knew her author. It's a lead no matter how you look at it. I have all these files and the tape.'

'Excellent, Pierre. Not good for us or Detective Galt – a cop perhaps involved in our investigation. Collect the copies and we'll begin the interviews. I spoke with Holmes's father and to Marie at the lab. Marie said the weapon might have been some sort of book, not a phone book, a heavy, hardcover book. We're on slippery ground. It would have to have been one hell of a heavy book with a sharp, strong edge. We thought of a bible, but much larger than a regular bible. For the moment, the weapon remains a question mark, sorry.'

Damiano walked slowly around both offices in the condo examining the books and the piles of manuscripts. Most of them were piles of paper. However, some were boxed. She reached into the middle of the pile and tugged at a box until she got it free. The heft of the box set off her alarms. Damiano trusted those bells, signals, not intuition. She raised the box above her head and swung it down hard. It struck the manuscripts with a heavy thud and cut through several sheets. 'Pierre!'

He poked his head around the corner of the office.

'I think I have it!' Her words crackled with excitement.

'What?'

'The weapon! A boxed manuscript. It's heavy and the sides of the box are strong and sharp enough for that kind of damage. Look." She brought the box crashing down a second time on the pile of manuscripts. "See that gouge?'

'By God! You may just have it, Toni.'

They shared the moment of elation in silence before Matte spoke.

'There were two on the balcony – we should have caught that! We did look at them and, although they were wet from the rain, we found no trace evidence of blood or any indentation suggesting they were used as a weapon. Are you thinking of another one altogether?'

'That's exactly what I'm thinking. Damn! That's what it was! How perfectly ironic! Holmes is an agent and has her head bashed in with the symbol of her work. No chance for misdirect here. What else would be sent to her condo but manuscripts and mail? I'll lay odds that the assailant was smart enough to take it back with him. He'd also be covered in blood, back splatter at least. Must have brought a change of clothes. This assault was ugly,' Damiano said, more aware of the emerging facts. 'At least we have our weapon! We have to work these suspects, but we can't narrow the field to these four either. Throw our nets wide. Apparently Holmes was not seeing anyone, so that avenue is cleared. Did you find other numbers?'

'She worked at Spence Agency before she went out on her own. I have the number. I'll get her phone records. She had meetings coming up. I have those numbers too.'

'Check them out. I want all the fish in the net.'

'Alright.'

'Their prints are most likely not on file. Galt might be the only exception. Because of all the blood, the contamination and the daily traffic in and out of this condo, my guess is that none of the prints Crime took will be a clear enough match for our computerized records. I was wondering if Holmes ever had authors to her condo. If not, that's good for us. Whatever partials we get will help us with these four authors, or even her superstar. The unidentified prints can be used against theirs,' Matte enthused.

'The victim's father would know the answer to that, or perhaps Aubin upstairs.'

'Detective?'

'Yes.'

'I appreciate this is *your* first lead, but I'm not just an endorsement of your work.' He took a step back.

'What's your problem?' Insulted, Detective Damiano turned and glared sharply at Matte. 'I don't *use* my partners, Detective. We're a team and that's how our results will appear, but I am the lead here.' Her message was clear – he was her subordinate. She didn't say if he was unhappy, he could apply for reassignment. That fact was implied.

'I didn't intend…'

'But you did, Detective. We've worked together for nine years. You should know by now that I'm fair. You have skills that I have to use. You're my partner for God's sake.'

'Sorry Detective. In school, geeks were shoved into urinals. Now we're in demand. In my first case, before you and I hooked up, the lead claimed my work as his. This is a high profile case for me too. My career is important to me.'

From the beginning, she had preferred that Matte was gay. It worked well for both of them – freed them up from potentially messy situations and set them up as strong individuals working together. Today, Matte's spiky hair began to irritate her, but she spoke calmly as she leaned forward. 'Pierre, grow up. I'm not running a daycare. Get to work and I'll forget this conversation.' For the next few hours they prepared for the interviews. 'What about the neighbors, Pierre? What have the uniforms reported?'

Detective Matte leafed through the notes he had been given. 'No eyewitness or I would have reported that right off. One neighbor saw couriers, but she sees them regularly. One thing she did say is that one from UPS was wearing shorts. She saw the brown shorts.'

'Today?'

'Yes.'

'Male or female?'

'That's the thing. She focused on the shorts because of the weather. That's all she recalls. I checked the two manuscripts that *were* delivered. Both were FedEx.'

They rose in unison and began to look for a delivery from UPS, a large envelope, a box, anything with Friday's receipt date, but found nothing. Matte looked at his notes again. 'Another thing she said was that the trucks usually double-park in front of the condo blocking traffic, but she saw no UPS truck. That's how she saw the shorts.'

'She doesn't remember anything else about this courier?'

'Said she was vacuuming and didn't really pay much attention.'

'How old is this woman?'

'Late sixties, I guess.'

'Doesn't recall if the courier was carrying anything?'

'The uniform said he repeated his questions and got nothing more. All she homed in on was the shorts.'

'The attack was well executed. The only flaw is Holmes surviving. We start with this Beauchemin. Get his facts together. I have a call to make.' Detective Damiano wanted to call Thomas Holmes, but getting through to him would take time. She had another idea, glanced through her notes and called.

The call was about to go to voicemail when a gravelly, sleepy, angry voice answered. '*Oui?*'

'Detective Damiano, Mme Aubin. Sorry to wake you.' More grumbling. 'The surgeon at the General credits you for saving Ms Holmes's life.' The grumbling didn't stop. 'I have one question. Do you know if Ms Holmes invited authors to her condo?'

'*Jamais, sauf Tracey Doyle.*' Michelle had had enough.

'But she might have without you knowing.'

'*Possible.*'

Detective Damiano let the hang-up go. If they found even partial prints of any of the four authors, they had their first break. She was about to rejoin Matte when her cell rang.

'It's Marie. Quick question. Is Detective Stephen Galt working the case with you?'

Detective Damiano let the significance sink in. 'No.'

'Well, his partials were found on the front door. You there?'

'Don't share this information with anyone.'

'Oh-oh.'

'Pull up whatever you can, we'll get the other elimination prints and send them to you.'

'Not good for Detective Galt.'

'No one, Marie. Get me other prints.' Detective Damiano hung up the phone and joined Matte.

'We have our first suspect.'

Chapter Nine

DETECTIVE MATTE DROVE to the Crémazie precinct in Montreal East. Leads didn't drive unless they wanted to take the wheel. During the short drive along the Metropolitan service road, the detectives were silent. Damiano mentally prepared her interview with Galt. Matte knew when to be quiet. The interview room was on the first floor. Dragging Galt down to Place Versailles, the central division, would seem a deliberate affront. She'd take heat on that. Galt worked the Crémazie Division. The interview room, away from the detectives' offices on the second floor, would be best.

When they entered the penitentiary-gray building, she called Place Versailles from the corridor. She wanted to avoid a viral gabfest on Galt, but she needed his schedule.

'Galt's working nights. Here's his private cell number. Anything I can help you with?'

'Thanks, I'll get back to you if I need help, Detective Pouliot, is it?'

'That's me.'

'Alright.' *Damn! Galt was off this morning. I can't eliminate him as a suspect.* Instructing Matte to get up to the interview room ahead of her, she called Galt. 'Detective Damiano. I'm sorry to call you on your down time, Detective.'

'Not to worry, Detective Damiano. I heard the news through the grapevine an hour ago. You've landed a big one. We've never met personally, but I've seen you at meetings. Everybody has,' he added with a smirk. 'Whatever help you need, Detective. I'd like to be involved. Holmes was my literary agent, so I can jump right in. Partnered up yet?'

Detective Damiano gave him an 'A' for his art of misdirect, yet she detected a guarded expectancy behind his words. 'Is it possible for you to get to Crémazie, say in an hour?'

'I'm a cop – no prob there.'

'I'll be in the interview room.'

'Why?'

'Space.'

'Your call.' Galt's tone had changed. 'See you at four.' An instant anger had winched his voice a little higher.

'Good.' She hurried up the steep stairs to the detective offices. For the next hour she worked on questions for Galt while Matte worked up the next suspect. At 3:45 pm Matte watched Damiano until she gave him the signal to accompany her. The rectangular interview room was a poor relation to a boardroom. Except for the table and wooden chairs, the room was bare, and purely functional with no distractions for suspects. Damiano and Matte sat on the same side of the table with a spare chair between them. Matte had the legal pad he used ready with pens and his recorder. Damiano had one question sheet.

At 4:05 pm, Detective Galt walked into the room like a recalcitrant student with one of the best slow swaggers Damiano had seen. Almost six feet, he reminded her of an aging high school football hero. He took off his charcoal suit jacket and tossed it on the table. The sleeves of his white shirt were already rolled. Damiano noticed he bit his nails. His ginger hair was gelled like Matte's, but definitely thinning. Galt went to the head of the table, pulled the chair out and sat spreading his legs to their limit. Damiano allowed Galt to jockey and assume the pseudo control he needed to establish.

She moved her sheet and turned her pen in her hand, but didn't say a word.

Galt picked up on her power silence and arranged his features into a guarded mask. 'So, shoot.'

'Thank you for coming down. Detective Matte, please hand Detective Galt the letter.'

Galt reached over and grabbed it from Matte, took a quick look and smiled. 'I was pissed and pulled a bit of rank. Holmes had my book for two years, lots of promises and all the bunk. Poor taste and bad timing as it turned out. Happens to the best of us. You're not going to make something of this are you, Detective Damiano?'

'Have you ever met Holmes?'

'Wait a minute, Damiano, I asked you a question.'

'Simple procedure, you know that, Detective. Now, answer mine.'

'No, I haven't.'

'No?'

'No! What are you doing here? Am I a suspect?' His voice rose in sudden alarm. 'I'm a detective, Damiano. I'm on your team.' Galt switched gears and tried to be conciliatory. 'Look, this is a high priority file, but don't make me a target of your investigation. Use your head. Don't trash my whole career, my pension and my family. Jesus! Are you reaching, Damiano?' Galt saw he'd gone too far. 'I never met Holmes. Is that clear enough for you?'

Damiano hated being rimmed by one of her own. Her armpits were sticky and she backed her chair up ever so slightly as though Galt's presence offended her. He had the charm of a wasp. 'Do you know where she lives?'

'She never gave me that information.' Galt pushed his chair closer to the table to make his point.

'Did you find it yourself?'

Galt knew what Damiano could find with a trace. 'Once Doyle hit the big time, Holmes's face was everywhere. I'm sure I'm not the only author who went looking for her.' Galt brought his knees closer together. The left twitched noticeably.

Damiano wiped imaginary dust from the table. 'Have you been to her condo?'

Galt steepled his fingers and held them in front of his nose. Damiano wouldn't be asking the question unless she had something.

All three detectives knew it was a 'gotcha' moment.

'I went to her place last night.'

'You said you were working.'

'Took a ride.'

'You got away with that?'

'Nineteen years on the job gives me some leeway.'

'You said you never met Holmes.'

'I didn't. I knocked and rang. I could see light inside the condo, but no one answered. Thought if we met, she might reconsider. I brought my second book with me, hoping for a read.'

Detective Damiano glanced at Matte to see if he'd picked up the import of Galt's answer. He had written "manuscript" and underlined it twice.

'What?'

Ignoring the question, Damiano asked, 'Where were you this morning between nine and eleven?' She dropped his title.

'In bed. Working nights, remember? Maureen got the kids off to school before she went to work.'

'You were alone then.'

'Don't mess with me. I'll see you with my rep next time.' Galt sat up straight and then rose in a last-stand gesture.

'Before you go, hear me out. This interview is not easy for me or Detective Matte. We're all cops. You can make this investigation very public with your rep and all, or you can cooperate and we can do the search, with perhaps only your wife knowing. I need a sample of your DNA, a search of your premises, the manuscript and your shoes. If you're cleared, you're off our radar.'

He sat back down. 'How did you know I was there?'

'You left your prints on the door.'

'Ah. A cop who intended to assault Holmes would know to wear gloves.'

MOM: motive, opportunity and means, thought Damiano. *The first visit might have been a ruse to set up an alibi. Galt said he was pissed.* The tension she saw in his hands suggested an explosive anger. He'd never be a good poker player.

With a quick nod from Detective Damiano, Matte produced the swab kit, and Galt stood up and opened his mouth. Matte dropped the swab into a plastic tube, sealed it and labelled it while Galt drummed meaty fingers on his forearm.

'Give me a time for the search. I've seen the after-mess.'

'I'll have Crime there tonight. We can't wait for your family to be out of the house. Perhaps you might see to that yourself. Crime won't be there till seven.'

'You know I'm on the job tonight, Detective. Consider what this will do to your reputation with the shields. You won't find rat shit there, but you already know that.'

'I can't run this investigation according to your schedule, Detective. I want to eliminate you from the file asap.' She could almost see the pores on his face grow larger and darker.

'Sure you do.'

'I'm following procedure.'

'Wiseass bitch!' Galt muttered loud enough for them both to hear. He rose, knocked his chair into the table and shouldered his way through the door without a word.

Galt's aggression made Damiano feel he was lying. He was thinking of his own reputation, not hers. If Galt was good for this crime, her solve might turn out to be a downhill ride. Nailing one of your own never went down well. 'All this over a book! A vanity project.' She looked over at Matte.

'It's a different world. Ego, insecurity, vulnerability.'

'You've written?' she snorted with what Matte heard as disdain.

'So?' he answered defensively.

'In one way, I'm not surprised. You're smart. Where did you publish?'

'That's the thing – four years and still trying.'

'Ah,' Damiano said, 'another rejected wannabe, but you're not attacking anyone.'

'Believe me…'

Damiano had no interest in having her face in front of cameras or featured in the press and didn't want to understand those who did. Closing books was her thing. 'Who's our next interview? We can't afford to lose any time.'

Chapter Ten

THOMAS HOLMES LEANED heavily against the hospital wall, shaken and rattled. Perspiration ran down his ribs, back and front. He didn't want to bend, but he saw that he had. He wanted to think the patient was somebody else, but it wasn't. Distressed by the memory of his wife Becky's illness and death, he had no intention of going there in his thoughts, but surging doubts dragged him back. An overwhelming sense of failure weighed him down. In Becky's battle, he'd been as useless as City Hall. He'd contacted the best physicians, secured a private room at the Royal Victoria Hospital – the large room reserved for VIPs – read all the reports, but he kept working with his own patients. He hadn't sat with her or touched her or listened because he couldn't accept losing her. Madison was alone with Becky the afternoon she died. Thomas was seeing patients. After blowing two lights, he'd made it to her bedside eleven minutes too late. Becky had been conscious to her last breath. 'Tell your father I forgive him.' Her lips were warm when he kissed her. Her forgiveness drained him.

Thomas pushed away from the wall. If this tragedy was a chance at redemption, he couldn't fail a second time. He squared his shoulders for the fight. Barging into the ICU he looked around to find Madison among the other patients. It took only seconds before he saw her head heavily bandaged, stained by a seam of blood and yellow mucus. His body bucked from the impact. Then he saw her hand and recognized Becky's wedding ring on her index finger. He walked hesitantly to the bed as though his presence might cut the delicate thread of her life. His face collapsed in pieces as he watched the rise and fall of the respirator. Even with the heavy bandaging, he saw that the left side of her head had swollen like a football. Her nose was broken, flattened and looked like wet putty. Tears leaked from his eyes when he reached for her hand. 'Hang on, Maddy. I won't leave you alone. Hang on for me.'

He heard the slap of shoes and turned.

'Sir, you have to leave.' The nurse's face was kind, but adamant.

'I'm a physician,' he whispered.

'Here you're just a father and you have to leave. You can have two minutes an hour from now. I gave you five minutes and I broke my own rules, so, please…'

Thomas kissed Madison's hand. It seemed so fragile and small and yet, to him Madison was tough and he wanted to be close to that. During the bleakest of times, Madison had Becky laughing while he stood outside the room, fighting for his sanity. The physician who couldn't face mortality in his own home.

'Please, Sir!' Her voice was as solid as granite.

The nurse heard Thomas give a low moan as he left the room. He had no intention of holding up another wall and went in search of a washroom. Inside a stall, he called his office with his decision.

'But you can't possibly think Doctor Helle can take over your practice as well as his own for six months! He's cutting back as you know. Doctor Holmes, I don't know where to begin. Do you have any idea of the number of patients I'll have to place? More important, you need to work.'

Holmes stiffened when he heard the last sentence. 'Follow my instructions, Irene. I have to be with Madison now.'

'But Doctor, Thomas, you know about the GP shortage in the province, please don't… what about that other issue, issues really?'

'Irene, I haven't the energy to deal with any of this.'

Irene heard something breathing and frightening in his voice. 'I'll do my best. Take care of…'

He'd hung up. Next, he went looking for a chair that he carried back to his post outside the ICU. He took out the iPhone 4S that Madison had taught him to use and accessed her email. He had her password as she had his. He cut, pasted and sent what he found to his computer. He had the authors' names and he memorized them. Thomas meant to settle with the monster who had attacked his daughter. His head hadn't been clear since the attack, but he wasn't going to wait for the police. He couldn't bear to see patients because he had nothing for anyone but his own flesh and blood. Scrolling through Madison's emails to get a sense of the rejected authors, he got up and paced like a man possessed.

It seemed obvious who the police might want to interview first, but Thomas knew from his profession that answers often came from the less apparent. An older woman, Yvette Ranger, was an interest, but he went with the student. He read the emails from Jean Pauzé, the McGill postgrad. His words were manufactured and edgy and smelled of youth who sneer at life without having lived it. *Hmm! We all thought we were Atlas,* Holmes smiled ruefully. It took him no time at all to track down his address in the McGill student ghetto. Thomas had a starting point.

The sudden appearance of Madison's principal physician startled Thomas. 'Thomas, the most recent tests reveal no developing clots or fever spikes, good signs. Unfortunately, there's a media circus out on Pine Avenue but police are corralling them behind a roped-off barricade. I called Detective Damiano who ordered me to say nothing but that the patient's condition is critical. She demanded there be no leaks from anyone or she'd follow up with charges of obstructing an investigation. I took care of that. There are also officers in the halls blocking reporters from entering the hospital. When you were in the ICU did you notice the orderly close by your daughter?'

'Couldn't see anything but Madison.'

'Undercover in whites and there are two more in this hall. Have to give it to Damiano. This attacker is still out there and she wants to make *damn sure*, her words, your daughter is safe. Good head on that one. . .'

'I agree. The white coat?'

'Here. The fact that you're a physician might lessen Denise's ire, the iron matron of the ICU. Go to your daughter. I'll take the brunt of it.'

'Thanks, Stephen.'

'Get some sleep at home, doctor's orders. You can't live here and I can't fight Denise off for 24 hours. I need her.'

Thomas tipped a salute. Both men walked into the ICU.

Chapter Eleven

'PIERRE, GRAB SOME FOOD and take the search at Galt's home tonight. He won't be as abrasive with you. Look for . . .'

'Freshly done laundry, shoes, garbage, nail clipper, nail clippings, manuscripts and boxes. I know what we want.'

'That's why you're going.'

'I'll call Claude Beauchemin. From your facts, he's arrogant and no doubt stepping through the interview before I even get there. He'll think he can get the better of me. That's where I want him. Sorry, Pierre.'

'You'll be interviewing him again,' he said confidently. 'I want in on the second.'

'If that's the case, I'll need you.' With that, Damiano walked briskly to her locker up on the second floor, reached in for a crisp white shirt and a cosmetic bag and headed to the washroom. She grabbed a Red Bull from her purse and drained it. Five minutes later, she looked as fresh as if she'd just showered. Matte could take care of himself. Once she was on Sherbrooke Street, she kept her eyes peeled for the Westmount Library and took a left on Lansdowne until she spotted the address of the duplex.

It was definitely Lower Westmount, vintage but solid. Plumbing was probably the only renovation these homes had seen in eighty years. She parked out front and left her ID on the dash with a blue light flashing inside the car. The steps were cement and the small porch weathered red brick with stone. Beauchemin himself opened the door.

'Claude Beauchemin, Detective.' He led her up a steep staircase that had seen better days. Worn shoes were parked on various steps. No sneakers and no lights, except for the one on the top floor. He swept across the room and stopped by his pride, a baby grand piano. He directed her to a chair with a sweep of his hand. It struck her as condescension rather than anything effeminate. She chose another and immediately sank into it, impaled on the surviving coil. Beauchemin wore a blue shirt rolled to the forearms, khakis creased at the thighs and crotch, and tassel loafers. One of the tassels was hanging by a thread. He was balding and his eyes were small and deep-set. The living room was decorated in SPARSE. Damiano found the oak floor appealing. Her eye caught sight of the office because it appeared packed and very functional. One side of the room was lined with colored cabinets, the other, bookcases. A large old desk against the far wall had the usual computer and printer close by. She spotted a scanner, a digital recorder and a laptop on a small table beside the desk near stacks of new computer paper. Everything looked unused. Damiano smirked. What a pretentious phony!

'Do you know why I'm here, Sir?' Damiano turned back to Beauchemin who appeared to be waiting for a compliment.

'My wife called from the hospital. After the police, hospitals are news centers. What a tragedy!' He bowed his head and managed an approximation of emotion. When he looked up, it was gone.

'Your wife called from the hospital? What hospital?'

'Yes, the General. Louise works in Admin. Holmes is there, under serious, private supervision.'

Damiano met his gaze but gave nothing away about her surprise at his wife being at the hospital. He had an especially unattractive face. There was something waxy and cold about the man.

When she reached for her notes, he began talking. 'I'm not certain what hat I should wear for this occasion.'

'Excuse me?'

'If you've done your work, you know I'm a lawyer and an author.'

'You've published elsewhere then?' Damiano made a mental note to watch herself. Every case had a screw-up – he wasn't going to be hers. It didn't stop her from wanting to blitz him, but she waited for his reaction and kept her hands relaxed.

His demeanour changed in a flash. 'I'm halfway through my second book. And I was very close. I also have other…'

'Then the rejection letter from Ms Holmes must have hit you pretty hard.' The battle was engaged.

He blew out a derisive breath. Beauchemin felt a pinch behind his left eye. 'Most certainly disappointed.' Anger winched the sides of his mouth.

'Mr Beauchemin, I dislike additional paperwork. Let's make this interview as short as possible. I want to eliminate you from the suspect pool.'

'Suspect? Why?' he asked indignantly, pulling himself up from the best chair of the lot.

'Let's just go through the necessary protocol. Have you ever met Madison Holmes?'

He bit his lower lip.

'Sir?'

'No, I never have.'

'You did hesitate, may I ask why?'   .

He cleared his throat. 'I went to Blue Metropolis book fair last year and she was there. I saw her but I didn't introduce myself.'

'From afar then?'

'You could say that.' He knuckled his eye, blocking her out.

'Can you account for your whereabouts this morning?'

'This is insulting!'

'I haven't eaten since breakfast – remember I said I hate paperwork. Honesty works best for me.'

'I drove to Wal-Mart for USB sticks they had on sale.'

'You bought a few?'

'Already sold out. Then I drove to the Lakeshore. I do my best thinking beside Stewart Hall, by the banks of Lake St. Louis.'

'Did you talk to anyone?'

'I go for peace and quiet, Detective.'

'Do you know where Ms Holmes lives?'

He made a restless movement. 'Figuratively?'

"Don't go symbolic on me. I'm not a publisher.'

'I've Google-Earthed her address.'

'Have you ever been to her home? Before you answer the question, I have a search warrant for your home and an order for your prints and DNA in the works. I hope you will volunteer to help with this investigation. The rejection letter and your many emails to Ms Holmes are grounds for probable cause. As a lawyer, you should know this.' Damiano assumed a friendlier mode. 'However, if you've never been there, and our techs will find nothing on you, then I'll cancel the warrants. Crime techs aren't TV heroes, but we couldn't do our work without them. They need more than forty TV minutes, that's all.'

'It was a release letter,' he corrected her. His cheeks suffused with color.

'Off the record, what is it with you authors? You're a lawyer. Why do you need the stress and rejection? The odds are heavily against you. I don't get it. What's the attraction?'

'It's a losing battle between reason and compulsion. You'd have to be in it to understand.'

She thought he was about to pull a U-turn and rant about life as an aspiring author, but he sat up aggressively instead. 'Well?' Damiano persisted. She turned when she heard freezing rain spitting against the side window and ricocheting off the panes. 'Sir?'

He hated going bald. He looked over on his left shoulder where he spied two hairs. He might have lost another at Holmes's condo. 'Yes.' He dropped his head and his cheeks fell into developing jowls.

'You were at Holmes's residence.' Avoiding the question mark, she kept her voice calm, almost soothing.

He nodded, conceding.

'When?' she whispered as a friend might.

'Yesterday morning around eight. I deserved a face-to-face. No one answered the door, I swear.' Beauchemin felt his life drain into Damiano's notes.

'Ms Holmes was attacked this morning.'

He shook his head violently. 'I wasn't there today.' Then he ran for a bathroom outside the kitchen. 'I don't feel well.'

Damiano meant to stand outside the door, but she spied the cashews near his seat, hurried over and shoved a handful into her mouth and chewed like crazy, whipped out a Red Bull and gulped that, trying not to choke. She sucked cashew bits from the front of her teeth and swore off the Red Bulls. Beauchemin was angry enough to assault Holmes. He was an arrogant little man, but Damiano knew enough not to trust intuition. It got her stupid.

When he reappeared, grimacing, Beauchemin tried to swallow the lump in his throat by parsing his predicament in his head. Panic jumped him again at the humiliation of an arrest. His family, his friends! He squared his shoulders and stretched to his full height, but Damiano was still taller. Had she told him he looked pathetic, he would have believed her. Beauchemin made no attempt to talk block her, cop jargon for lying. He had no alibi. He couldn't cut through the glue on that one. Louise should have come home to run interference for him, instead of going to her mother's. 'I'll contact a lawyer.'

'I'll wait for the Crime crew.'

Chapter Twelve

BEAUCHEMIN DIDN'T LOOK like a runner, so Damiano stepped outside but stayed under the porch, protected from the ice pellets. She felt a strong urge to slam Galt and Beauchemin into interrogation rooms and sweat them, but a niggling thought kept her steady. *This raft of wannabes might all look good for the assault.* She punched in another number. 'Go,' she said to Matte.

'We'll find nothing here,' Detective Matte said. 'Galt booked off. He's stomping around behind the techs after he herded the family into the car, and they're just sitting out there in the rain. Attitude! He called his buds at Crémazie, so we can expect a backlash tomorrow at our division. I booked the other two interviews, one tomorrow late morning so we can meet first, one tonight, the seventy-four-year-old. Says arthritis has made her a night owl – I'll take it if that's okay by you? Hope I didn't overstep, but I know you want to move on this high profile. Beauchemin?'

Irritated but starving, she hadn't the belly to backhand his efforts. 'I'm impressed. Tomorrow, we'll figure out how best to handle the gazillion book author and her lawyer mother. It's good to schedule these interviews. Saves us time and lets our suspects stew. The usual route of surprise would have taken us longer.'

Matte hid his relief. 'Beauchemin?'

'You nailed that.' She relayed what she had. 'Tonight, see if the old wannabe has grandsons who might do whatever for the inheritance.'

'You want in?'

'I'm staying put. Beauchemin has no alibi and I doubt he finished in the top third of his law class. He could have been at Holmes's place this morning. His writing room's a shrine. Reminds me of a friend who owns the best clubs, bag and golf rags but can't sink a putt two feet from the hole. This prick might have felt we'd never suspect him, and that's the reason I don't want him alone before Crime gets here. How about seven tomorrow morning at Place Versailles, we'll use Coupal's office? He's off for the week.'

'I'll be there and call if anything good comes from tonight.'

'Before you go – Beauchemin's wife works at the General. I'll alert the uniforms we have there. I don't want her hanging around like a troublesome gnat!' Scanning her list she found the number for the uniform outside the ICU. 'No one but hospital staff you recognize is to get closer than five feet to Holmes.' She told him about Louise Morin. 'Keep her out. Advise Holmes's physician.'

'But she's Admin.'

'I don't give a rat's ass what she is – I don't want her there!'

'Her father's been in the room for the last three hours.'

'Any change in Holmes's condition?'

'No medical alerts – all quiet here.'

'Find Holmes's principal physician – have him call me asap. He's Stephen something. Don't mix him up with Detective Galt. Got two Stephens in the mix. I have another call.' Arching her back, she saw Beauchemin through the window, sitting woodenly in his chair. 'Yes, Chief.' Richard Donat was always referred to as the 'big boss.'

'Where are we on this?' He gave Damiano four minutes. 'You're pulling out all the stops and, as we like to say, we're looking into all possibilities, because that's what I've been telling the media, right?'

Grimacing, Damiano said, 'I know we have to push the PR buttons.'

'It's not what you know. It's what you get done. See me after you brainstorm with Matte tomorrow morning. Set up an airtight plan for this author Doyle and her mother – they have clout. Angela Marino, the mother, has connections on both sides of the law. We can't afford bad press if we fuck this up. Understood? With all the goddamn hacking and media ambushes, we're exposed. Every screw-up will be tweeted, texted and the rest of that bullshit. I gave you this file for a reason, Damiano.'

'I appreciate your confidence.'

'Means nothing. Results mean something. You wanted high priority. Well you have it – get the job done. Catch this freak on your own hook. I can spare two guys. Grab ass on this one!'

Damiano knew that the short wiry Chief Donat felt his strongly accented foul language added two inches to his height and used it to control his division. She didn't discount the fact that he could just be another short bully, but she spoke to him mostly in English and addressed him as *Chief*. 'Doing all that, Chief. Haven't eaten since...'

'So?'

'Matte and I are okay for now.' The chief rang off. Damiano turned to see Beauchemin with a cigar and a small fire in an ashtray. She ran back to the door, but an Abloy had locked her out. Damiano banged on the door.

Beauchemin took his time getting to it. Blocking her way, he asked casually, 'What's the problem?'

Pushing him aside she ran for the ashtray and found a pile of black ashes. 'What did you just burn, sir?' She had the ashtray in her hand and felt like hitting him with it.

'The cellophane from the cigar.'

'There's too much ash for cellophane.'

'Maybe there was a Post-it. I didn't see anything else. It's a large ash-tray.'

'Don't play me, Monsieur Beauchemin.'

'I can assure you...'

'Sit down and put out the cigar while I package the ashtray and the cigar for Crime.'

A smirk crept across his face when Damiano turned her back on him.

Chapter Thirteen

JEAN PAUZÉ HAD EXPECTED THE call, but it stole his breath when it came. The cops soon discovered that Holmes had summarily dumped him and his manuscript. They'd also have his email. His interview, scheduled for eleven the next day, buzzed through his thoughts like the fruit fly he couldn't kill in his studio apartment. At the moment, in student jargon, Jean was acting like a total 'tool,' in his dirty wool hiking socks, frayed jeans and stained work shirt. He was shoving empty forties of beer, McDonald's wrappers, pizza boxes, half a sandwich from Schwartz's deli, crushed Coke cans, weed, pipes, butts, one shrunken black banana – all the detritus that had piled up – into cardboard boxes he'd found in the basement of the Barcelona apartment.

Although he wore expensive gold-rimmed glasses, he wasn't part of the corduroy university crowd. For one thing, he was twenty-seven, and somewhat of an isolate in the McGill Ghetto. McGill students lived in this mix of row-houses and low to mid-rise apartments. The students were beginning to move out as the Plateau gentrified and became too expensive. Jean should have had his doctorate and moved on too, but with no options, he stayed put, waiting to make his dissertation defence. He had planned on Holmes giving his name a real boost with a big-name publisher. His advisor had told Jean that there was a one-semester Canadian History course opening up at McGill and that he was great friends with the dean. The position might lead to further work. If his dissertation went to a large trade publisher he'd be a shoo-in. A university press didn't carry weight, not the kind that could land such a post. Often, his advisor had confided, university presses were pressured into publishing works by someone they wanted to hire. He knew they wouldn't want him now. Jean's dream had exploded in his face.

By nine that night he was standing in a shower, trying to wash away the stench of fear. Shivering as he stepped out and towelled off, he put his arms through a blue cotton work shirt and pulled it over his head. It was the only clean one in the place. He stepped back into his jeans and went barefoot, looking for socks. He threw a pile of clothes into the center of the room, got coins and soap from the kitchen a few feet away and hurried down to the basement where he threw the mess into a machine. He figured the cops would acquire a search warrant. While he waited for the 28-minute wash, he studied his reflection in an old tarnished mirror.

A few years back, with his longish black hair, glasses and skinny student body, he reminded himself of a young Beatle. He had a full-length dark wool winter coat that he wore three seasons of the year. Now his scrutiny went to his temples where he knew his hair was receding and to the beer paunch that looked odd against his gaunt frame. He looked like a Beatle who had aged ten years on his way to a concert.

When the phone rang around eleven, he coughed up his beer and it sprayed down his shirt. He wiped his mouth with the back of his hand and reached for the phone. His hand shook. 'Oui?'

'Un étudiant dans votre immeuble a gagné une pizza gratuite, mais je ne peux pas le rejoindre. La voulez-vous?'

'Euh…'

'Pas de problème. Je vais la manger. J'ai encore cinq livraisons à faire ce soir.'

'Minute, je vais la prendre.'

'Impossible de stationner. Déscendez la chercher.'

'J'arrive.'

'Je suis à la gauche de l'immeuble, dans la deuxième alcôve. Y mouille ce soir.'

Some pizza place wanted to give him a free pizza because they couldn't reach the guy in his building who'd ordered it. All he had to do was run out to the front of his apartment and take it! Jean hopped into his yellow work boots, grabbed his coat and took the stairs running. He was starving. Hunger was part of the reason for his spiking nerves. Rushing out the front door, he had a fleeting thought. *Why didn't the guy stand under the front awning? He was probably closer to his car and didn't want a ticket for delivering a free pizza.* The second alcove was also at the front of the building. It was dark but he could see the corner of the pizza box. Jean's Adam's apple bobbed up and down once before he fell to his knees screaming. His assailant struck him four times. Then he leaned down and grabbed Jean's Bose ear buds and searched his pockets for cash before he left.

Soon there was a small crowd running around him like chickens with their heads cut off. Jean was lying face down on the cement still screaming. Finally, somebody called 9-1-1. No one heard a car take off. No one saw anything.

Chapter Fourteen

Earlier that night, Detective Matte peeled out of the City of Laval using flashers, now attached to the sun visors, and the odd blast of siren because of serious traffic on Highway 13 and the Trans-Canada Highway. The search at Galt's place had been a waste of time unless Crime came up with something. Matte sped down boulevard St-Jean, but let up when he turned left on St-Louis. The thirty-five-minute drive had taken Matte nineteen. John Rennie High school was to his left, Pointe Claire City Hall to his right. Kids hung around empty buildings like Krazy Glue. The last thing he needed was to take one of them out. On Maywood Avenue, he looked for the Maywood apartment building which wasn't far from the swimming arena that had trained Olympic champions. It was well after 10 o'clock. The red-brick building was new and well lit. In the darkness, he could make out the clump of trees behind it. Matte hurried up to the front entrance and almost lost his footing because black ice was forming. He buzzed 218. The door clicked and he walked briskly to the elevator on his right, got off at the second floor and saw a woman waving him down the hall.

Yvette Ranger had one hand on the doorknob and the other on a handle of her walker. She wore a camel skirt and matching cashmere sweater with a red pashmina fastened with a gold pin. She had an expansive smile and flair, even pushing the walker. 'Do come in. I'm rather excited to be interrogated by a detective.' She motioned him toward a chair.

In better light he saw a definite twinkle in Ranger's eyes and then a library that took up one wall, and art. The other walls were covered with photos of her youth, planes, horses and children.

'Mme Ranger, I just have a few questions for you.'

'Too bad,' she sighed. 'I was quite ready for my defence, as they say. The attack on Madison Holmes is dreadful in our city, dreadful anywhere.'

'May I ask where you were today?'

'I wish that I had somewhere dashing to tell you about. Unfortunately, I was here. I did go out back, quite against regulations, to feed a stray cat that seems to have adopted me. That was the extent of my escape. Will you charge me for that misdemeanor?'

The twinkle and the remark brought a smile to Matte despite his fatigue.

At that moment, a heavy tawny cat jumped up on Matte's knee; he jerked, scaring it off.

'You don't like animals, Detective?'

'It's my best suit,' he said abruptly, picking off cat hairs from his pants. He rubbed his nose and realized that cat hair floated through the air. 'Were you disappointed with the rejection letter from Ms Holmes?'

'That's not a terribly astute question – you must know the answer. Ms Holmes called me early on when she accepted the manuscript. She was a serious, conscientious young woman. I respected that and I must say I envied her youth. I was far more disillusioned by her capitulation to the drivel of this Tracey Doyle than I was at the letter I received. I didn't know if I was up to the editing that I've learned has brought many a good writer to her knees.'

'Do you have children, Mme Ranger?'

'Three. Two sons and a daughter.'

'Are they in the city?'

'One works for the U.S. government. He's in Bangkok. The other is on the West Coast. My daughter is close by, but my grandson is away in the military. So you see, I did not send anyone to commit this outrageous crime. You were going there with your question, I assume. Violence is both vulgar and crass and beneath me.'

'It's part of my job,' he said proudly.

'Pity for you, young man, that you spend your life in such ugliness.'

Matte smiled weakly and zoned in on Mme Ranger's thick and bulky ankles.

'These legs were my wings and both have been sadly altered and grounded. I was the first French female pilot in Quebec, but that was long ago,' she said sadly.

Matte smiled with admiration and looked over at the photos of the planes.

'I flew those!' she sighed as Matte rose. 'Detective, I had hoped to prove more interesting.'

'You have been – thank you. Good night.'

'Let me walk you to the door.'

Matte walked slowly back to his car and stood thinking for a moment. He suddenly saw himself with his details and notes, scurrying around like a wireless mouse. To change his thoughts, he got into the car and called Damiano. 'How's it going?'

'I just got out of Beauchemin's. My breath is foul; I've been buried in bullshit. The boss called. I have to meet with him after our interviews tomorrow. He wants the file closed. He warned me about Angela Marino's varied connections, Mafia included. We have to tread lightly there – he should hear what the bitch put her daughter up to. On tape, you can feel her mother coaching her.

'Beauchemin sat in one chair, staring blankly at his piano and stuffing his face with nuts. He stonewalled us from the outset. I told Crime to scour his office without their usual "B-" care. That got him up.

'He began barking out orders to Crime like a cutthroat lawyer – too much of a weasel to bark at me. The guys ignored him, and I held him from getting one foot inside the room with the threat of obstruction. I'm sure Beauchemin didn't leave any trace for us if he committed the attack on Holmes. He's meticulous. I enjoyed the mess I made in his office. At one point when his folders were all askew on the floor, I thought he was close to tears, or murder.

'Beauchemin's a planner. Crime said he'd reformatted his computer with a write-over. The attack on Holmes was cold, efficient and researched. I figure his place will probably be a dry hole for us. This guy knows how to clean up. That won't stop me. He was at the crime scene and he's an angry man quite capable of great harm. What about Yvette Ranger?'

'Charming and insightful but a dead end.'

'Narrows it down – good. Can we meet at six, not seven? We have to commit to 24-7. I don't want add-ons from the boss – we can make this case.'

'I'll be there.'

Damiano headed straight for her condo on Hutchison Avenue just above the very chic Laurier Avenue. Before she got out of her car, she called Pizzaiolle across the street and ordered her usual black olive pizza. The minute she was inside her place, she peeled off her clothes, started the shower and kept moving because she was freezing from lack of food and the damp cold. She turned up the heat and hurried to her small, well-equipped kitchen, and poured herself half a glass of pink vodka and then found the Ambien above the stove. She had two left, gave them two full seconds and popped both, using the vodka as a chaser. Now the race was on.

The hot shower came first, the towelling and the hairdryer second and then she ran to her closet and laid out her clothes for Friday. She took out her best tailored navy blue suit and reached in for a new blue-and-white-striped Lauren cloth shirt that she'd leave open at the neck. A hint of last summer's tan lingered. With her gold Swiss mint piece, she'd look good. The shiny new blue designer Nikes with matching silk socks were her final touch. She laid her leather police shoulder bag and her .45 beside the clothes. The duty weapon was neatly concealed behind the bag and at full aim at 1.1 seconds. As yet, all she'd done was practice the move.

The nuts and the sugar had left ridges on either side of her tongue. The pills and the booze were kicking in, but she was so hyped that she wasn't getting their full effect. Damiano swore off Bulls and pills. She wanted this case. She needed to be sober and clear-headed. Now that a soft buzz was invading her body, oaths were easy and always made when sleep came with a chemical guarantee. She wanted 'down' before she ate. When she heard the phone, she threw on her terrycloth robe and buzzed the waiter up. The five-buck tip, her usual, was handed over as she took the pizza. She always appreciated the time he took to run across the street for her. She put the box on the dining room table, opened it and grabbed a slice that was devoured in five bites. Licking her fingers, she went for the index cards she used for cases and began to print them with the facts they had. The photos, the facts, their notes, and the call slips would be neatly arranged on Damiano's corkboard at work.

When the phone rang again, it startled her. It was almost eleven and it was her son Luke who should be in bed. He had an early hockey practice. The last thing she wanted was to lose the quiet buzz that would help her catch four hours of sleep. 'What's up and why aren't you in bed?'

There was no response for a few seconds.

Damn! 'Luke?'

'You missed parents' night.'

'Ah Jesus! Didn't your father tell you about the case?'

'What's the difference – you're always busy. Dad was there.'

'The good parent.'

That drew an easy extroverted laugh from Luke, and she loved him for that. 'What did I miss?'

'My math teacher!' The mood was back.

'I don't have time to guess. What about him or her?'

'Whatever.'

'I am who I am, Luke. Stop being a hardass and tell me.'

'Did you ever even want me, a kid I mean?'

Luke's sullen mood was evaporating her buzz. 'I was 23 hours and 37 seconds in labor with you. Around hour 23, no I didn't want you. Then you came and the doctor put you on my chest. Your head rested against my chin and I knew I was stuck 'cause it was the best day of my life.'

'89%!'

'What?'

'In math.'

'Wow!'

'Yeah, that's why I wanted you there, Mom.'

'I did miss something.'

'Not if I make a 90% next term.'

'I'll be there.'

'Whatever. Get back to work.'

'Goodnight, genius.'

'As long as you know.'

'I do now.' It was almost past midnight before Damiano got to bed. She had to be back up at four-thirty. She padded into the kitchen and reached behind the soda crackers for her special stash of Ambien, reached for the vodka and fixed herself another cocktail then fell into bed.

Chapter Fifteen

THOMAS HOLMES LAY on the bed with his arm stretched across Becky's side. In the semi-darkness, he could make out a few crystals hanging from the chandelier she had chosen for the room. He heard the ticking of the grandfather clock in the hall. Where had he lost his life – where was he, the man he'd been when he began to lose control of his own practice? The weight of Becky's death struck him full force with each beat of the clock's pendulum. Medicine had erased the faint line of faith he had taken with him into adulthood. Madison was alone in a coma. She couldn't forgive him – she might never speak again. But he didn't want forgiveness. He wanted to strike out. He wanted to earn her forgiveness. There were times when he didn't understand what Becky had meant when she said she forgave him. At the time, he'd heard only condemnation in those words. They still played with his head. Thomas was unaware that he was moaning and weeping. Not that this hadn't happened before. Soon his body rocked in uncontrollable spasms. His screams, keening through the late night, were not unlike those of Jean Pauzé. And then Thomas stopped all sound. *Tell your father I forgive him?* Becky's forgiveness didn't matter as he lay shivering. He would never forgive himself. He was a doctor and he had missed both calls for help from the two people he loved most. At this late hour, he saw himself for what he was, a coward who hid behind the misery of others to avoid his own.

Groping for the switch, he turned on the lamp beside his bed. He pushed himself out of bed and into the shower. He couldn't sleep while Madison was alone in the hospital. He had to keep the family together, merit the forgiveness. As soon as he could, Thomas, edgy and jittery without sleep, left his home in darkness on Westminster in Montreal West and drove back to the General. He should be at work. Patients were growing frustrated and business debt was mounting.

In the east end of Montreal, at Hôtel Dieu Hospital on rue Saint-Urbain, Jean Pauzé was still in surgery. The police had tried their best to extract information from Pauzé at the scene, but the kid's distress and low pain threshold had negated anything useful coming out of his mouth. His screams had risen well above any questions he was asked, as his saliva had sprayed the air. 'Knock me out, for Christ's sake, man! I can't stand the pain!' The younger cop had caught something about pizza. He'd looked around but had seen no pizza – hadn't smelled it either. Despite the cold,

Pauzé was sweating from the pain. Disappointed, the cops had hustled back to their car and followed the ambulance to the hospital.

The fractures in both knees required more work than simple settings. The kid would require an aluminum joint in one of them. By the time he was taken to recovery, his parents had been notified and waited for him in a ward. Pauzé had been fortunate. Though he'd been found with no ID, another student tenant heard the commotion as he approached his apartment. He'd gone to investigate and identified Pauzé for the police. With that information, they called his parents. The uniforms waited outside the door to the ward. They had to get something on the apparent mugging. The older cop poked his head around the corner and looked in at the ward with cool curiosity.

The older officer took his partner aside. 'Broken kneecaps could mean a settling of accounts.'

'The guy's not crisp.'

'What the hell is that supposed to mean, college boy?'

'It's a street word for a pusher or a mule. Does he look like either?'

'Drugs on campus – what was I thinking?'

'I graduated from McGill. Pushers and mules – they have a presence. Kids know who they are. I didn't use, but I knew who they were. Pauzé, he might have been selling papers – he looks that part. There's good money in that too.'

Unwilling to concede the point, he ended the talk. 'Could be we're reaching – coulda been a random mugging.'

They waited for well over an hour before a physician appeared and spoke with the parents. The cops inched into the ward and listened.

'He should be awake any minute now,' his physician told the Pauzés.

The cops blocked the physician's exit. 'When can we question the victim?'

'Give the parents a few minutes. Then you can question him. Keep the questions short. Pauzé's still under the influence of the anesthetic.'

The uniforms walked in behind the parents, had a few words with them and waited. Pauzé's mother had gone to fetch ice chips and a water jug. Pauzé came to while she was down the hall. The older cop held up four fingers and began timing and then stepped forward. 'Monsieur Pauzé, Officers Fortier and Houle. What happened tonight?' Officer Fortier wanted answers.

Pauzé grabbed the water glass from his mother as soon as she returned and drank greedily, and then vomited within seconds, spraying anyone within range. Fortier got hit. He fought with his temper and won, but this kid was going to answer his questions. He took a facecloth from Mme Pauzé and wiped himself off. 'What happened?' The question was brusque.

Pauzé stared mournfully at the huge plaster casts on both legs that went well above his knees. The legs were suspended in some kind of traction.

'Monsieur Pauzé?'

Pauzé tried to focus. He would have preferred to cry. 'How am I going to get around?' he moaned.

Officer Fortier had had enough waiting. 'Jean, we need some help here.'

He turned his gaze to the cop. 'As I'm reaching for the pizza, the sonofabitch takes me down with a bat and keeps hitting me!'

'What? A pizza guy attacked you?'

Pauzé rubbed the side of his head. 'I am so drugged and sick. Can you come back a little later? I have to sleep.'

Officer Houle pulled his training officer aside. 'Shouldn't we hand off? This is a felony, we don't belong…'

'As soon as I get some answers – I gotta get something out of this. Grab your chance. That's my philosophy.'

'Yeah, but…'

'A few questions, that's all.'

Pauzé tried to intervene for his son, but Officer Fortier would have none of it.

'Look, we want whoever did this to you. This perp didn't want to kill you. Start at the beginning.'

Officer Houle stepped out and called the Crémazie Major Crimes division. Detective Galt had gone back on the job to get away from his wife. Before the call came in, he was spitting mad. 'Damiano's a freakin' pit bull!' Both fists were balled.

'What? Damiano's a great piece of…' The voice came from two desks away.

'I've seen fine-looking pit bulls that could tear your face off. The bitch is at my face.'

'Has she collared you, Galt?'

'No and I'll make damn sure she doesn't.' He grabbed the call. 'I'm there.'

'What?'

'Broken legs. A mugging.'

'You want that?' the detective called over.

'Beats the shit out of growing old on a chair,' Galt shot back as he got up to leave the room.

'Take it. Calm down.'

'Don't you freakin' start, Deschamps!'

At the hospital, Officer Houle walked back into the ward. 'I called it in. Detective Galt's taking this.' There was an edge to his voice.

Chapter Sixteen

DETECTIVE GALT USED HIS badge to force his way into hospital parking. He had no trouble locating the victim, but was turned away by a physician and the parents. The victim needed to sleep for a few hours. Galt went looking for vending machines, bought coffee, sat down alone in a hallway, spread his legs and tried unsuccessfully to catch some shut-eye. He got to his feet and took a tour. He remembered studying about this oldest hospital in Montreal founded by... *right, Jeanne Mance.* Stopped and read some of its history and how it had been moved to its present site in 1961. The hospital had its own museum with its name translated into English in the last photo he checked out, the 'hostel of God.' Now it was part of CHUM, Centre Hospitalier de l'Université de Montréal. Galt checked the time. One hour was all he wanted to waste.

When Galt reached the room, the victim was awake and moaning. From the extent of the injury, Galt knew this was no crash and grab. He told the parents to leave the room, and they did so reluctantly. Pauzé focused on the plainclothes cop. 'Detective Galt, Major Crimes Division, Monsieur Pauzé. Forget what you told the other officers and tell me what happened from the beginning.'

Galt listened and took notes. 'Did you get a good look at the man?'

'No, I saw the edge of the box and reached out. Next thing I knew I was on the ground and he was smashing the bat against my legs.'

'You must have seen him then?' he asked sharply.

'He wore a dark knit cap down to his eyes, the collar of his jacket was pulled up, and so I didn't see much of his face. It was raining, cold and dark. It happened really fast. I heard my bones popping. Shit! I heard my own screams. I thought he was going to kill me! He did me in a few seconds! So goddamn fast. Had no chance to defend myself.'

'Was it a kid?'

'Nah, the guy was older.'

'Tall, short, heavy, what?'

'Tall, size? I don't know – he was wearing a heavy jacket.'

'This is a weak ID – are you holding back?'

'No! It was fucking dark – it happened fast like I just said – he busted my legs and I may never walk again. You think I wouldn't help you find this bastard?'

'How did he get your number?'

'How should I know? He was trying to give the pizza to someone else – didn't seem to care if I came down to get it or not.'

'That's how he got you to come down?'

'It wasn't just a mugger then?'

'What did he take?'

'My ear buds. Didn't have my wallet with me. The pizza was a free-bee.'

'Not worth all this hurt. This could be personal, Jean.'

'What?'

'Too much damage for ear buds.'

'Shit!'

'Who do you owe?'

'The government.'

'Do you push?'

'No.'

'Use?'

'Maybe weed.'

'Why would someone target you?'

Pauzé fell silent.

'What? Term papers and essays?'

'A few.'

'So, a kid got caught with a bad paper. Thought kids went online for that stuff.'

'Too easy to trace. I actually research the papers I write.'

'So, how was he caught?'

'I recycle.'

'What does that mean?'

'I use one more than once sometimes with a few alterations.'

'I'll need a list.'

'This could ruin me.' Pauzé teared up again. 'Ah man! There are only four students. They would have called me first, demanded their money back. Detective, if it's not one of them, can you keep this quiet? This has been a bad time. Oh, God! All those years of work and I'm about to defend my Ph.D. I can't compute any of this.'

'What?' Detective Galt leaned forward on his chair.

'I'm supposed to be at Place Versailles this morning. The police want to interview me. I have to call them and tell them I can't make it. Ah man!'

'Stop with the *Ah man!* What's that about?'

'My whole fucking life is falling apart. I don't get any of it.' Pauzé's heart began to beat like a first-time shoplifter. 'Ah man!'

'Jean, pull yourself together. What about Place Versailles?' Galt's face tightened.

'Madison Holmes. You must know about that.'

'Go on.'

'She was my agent.'

'Was?'

'She dumped me, after two freakin' years! I told my professors I'd have my dissertation placed with a real trade house. That was the key to my future, to a temporary job opening that might lead somewhere. Two years of my life shot down. And now this,' he wailed, looking at his legs. 'All because some chick writes about a vampire babe and idiots love blood. I gave Holmes history and she dumped me.' He lost all sense of humiliation and wept. He looked lonely, younger than his twenty-seven years and as scared as a kid, raw and open. 'Please write up the attack as random. I can't lose my education and my life. I won't press charges.'

'The case has been opened.'

'Let me at least check with the four students first. If they didn't do this – it's random. Detective, please don't report me for the papers. I'm beggin' you, man.'

'I want the names. If nothing comes out of it, I suggest you stick to your own work for the future.'

'You have my word. I can't press charges. I have to save myself. You can see that, right? Would you call Detective Matte to say why I can't be there?'

'I'll do that, but they will no doubt come here to interview you on the Holmes case.' Galt got to his feet and tossed his coffee cup into the waste basket beside the bed. 'For the last time, did you see who did this to you?'

Pauzé tried to back away. 'No, I swear.'

Galt left the room pumped, even secure. He had Pauzé in a knot. He'd come back on Damiano like a migraine.

Chapter Seventeen

THE TWO DETECTIVES rode up in the elevator together at Place Versailles in east-end Montreal, the principal headquarters of Major Crimes. Since they'd be using Detective Coupal's office, they secured their guns in their lockers but took their lunches with them.

'I have photos of Jean Pauzé and Yvette Ranger. I put them together with my notes last night.'

'Well,' Damiano smiled, 'I have Galt, Beauchemin and Angela Marino. Galt was easy. Caught Beauchemin on my camera phone, Marino from LinkedIn. Photos keep me focused.' They didn't speak again until they reached the corner office that offered them a modicum of cover. The glass walls made privacy difficult. Damiano put up three large corkboards and they both began to head each with the photos. Damiano's comic book printing looked like a template, the letters were so uniform. Matte had his own notes, and they worked till all the notes were up on the boards.

'I didn't bother with Tracey Doyle,' Matte said. 'From the taped conversation, I figure she wanted to stay with Holmes. I read a few chapters of her book online. The impression I have is that Doyle swims in the shallow end of the gene pool. Her mother is another story. She was the force behind the call.'

The small office smelled fresh, part muted cologne and gel and expensive perfume. They wouldn't leave the room except for coffee refills. 'Well,' Damiano said, 'let's go back to the beginning and clear up the loose ends.' Damiano was chewing gum and licking her lips.

'Detective, whatever you used last night has to stop.' He held her gaze.

'Family stuff, the stress of my first lead – I had to sleep. I'll be fine. Just take care of your end.' Her neck had blotched red, but she said nothing more. Her tongue felt like sand. 'I want to meet again with the nurse, Michelle Aubin. We can't forget she found Holmes. I need to be assured that Madison didn't blow off Aubin sexually. That might have caused Aubin to attack Holmes and cover up by saving her life. Rejection is a bitch, we all know that. I thought of that late last night. I want you to interview the witness who saw the courier. Grill her, Matte. Maybe there is more to be had from her. We'll put Ranger aside for now.

'Look at the attack. It was cold, calculated, brutal, intended to murder, well executed. Took a planner, and almost smells like a professional hit, but I don't think it is. A pro is dispassionate. This attack was personal. On my way to work, I called Holmes's physician. She's critical but stable.

He will have her moved to a private end of the ICU. This attacker has to be shitting bullets. If Holmes regains consciousness and remembers, we know what happens then. We have to keep her safe, or we're busted back to sidewalk duty. That can't happen. I'm concerned about her father, there's no telling what he'd do if she's hurt a second time.'

'Let's begin with Beauchemin. He's a strong candidate for this attack. Claims he was at her condo the day before the attack, but my gut tells me he was there the day of. His alibi has no credence, no witness and no verification,' she snorted with disgust. 'He takes me for a promotion climber and a plodder. He'll learn.' She told Matte about the ashtray incident. 'He was baiting me.'

'We have to move quietly with these rejects and Doyle. I'm not discounting her yet, and we tread very carefully with her mother. We can't look for logic. We have a cop, two lawyers, a post-grad and a successful commercial author. Egos and anger – that's what we have. To kill some agent over a book! These are educated people, and one of them planned a brutal murder. Holmes should be in a fridge at the morgue – she lucked out.'

'Holmes worked for each author and never asked for any money up front,' Detective Matte added. 'She played by the professional code.' .

'That's what's remarkable. Neither Galt nor Beauchemin felt any kind of emotion for Holmes. The sense of entitlement is nauseating. Not a moral to split between them.' Damiano reached for her brown bag and stuffed her mouth with a peanut butter and jam sandwich. 'I'm starved – can't help it.'

Matte smiled.

Licking jam from her fingers, Damiano continued, 'We're not dealing with dummies. Whoever did this was careful not to leave any trace behind. The perp wore a hat. I'm sure of that. So, we take their photos and put hats on each of them. We use uniforms to head to the métro, to rue Beaubien and rue de Saint-Vallier, and the nearest taxi stand. Somebody saw this assailant – he didn't just dissolve.'

'I can take care of that.'

'What part?'

'Altering the photos.'

'Really?'

'Uh-huh.'

'You surprise me, Pierre.'

He smiled again, a record for Matte. 'I'll call the Spence Agency as well.'

The room began to fill with detectives arriving on the job. A few made it a point to walk by Coupal's office talking loudly. 'Galt got to them,' Matte said.

'Not all of them. That's the blue wall. I have breasts, so I know the walls.'

Matte didn't point out he was also a target. A gay cop – not an easy life on the force. Montreal was known for its tolerance, but male bastions still fought to maintain their macho image. Matte watched his every move in the division. He had no choice.

It was just before nine when they were both startled by a loud knock at the door. Detective Galt had filed his report at the Crémazie division, signed out, had breakfast and then driven to Place Versailles. Damiano got to the door, just as he was about to open it. She'd seen Galt. Matte stood quickly and hid Galt's photo.

Opening the door, she stepped outside the office. 'Detective Galt, I didn't call…'

He cut her off. The detectives at their desks had seen Galt barred from the room. Women like Damiano were the armpit of the force, he thought. *Castrators!* His square chin hardened and he spoke through his teeth for the audience. 'Caught an interesting assault early this morning.'

'And?'

The bitch is rushing me! 'You'll need notes,' he said, gesturing inside Coupal's office and making a move towards it.

'How about we sit at that empty desk? I'll get my pad.' Damiano was gone and back before he got another word out. 'Thank you for coming, Detective. I appreciate the assistance.'

What the fuck can I do with that? Galt yanked out the chair. His colleagues were watching. He threw his notes on the desk and sat back.

'Well?'

'Sometime after eleven last night, Jean Pauzé was attacked outside his apartment on Hutchison. Had both his legs broken, suffered multiple fractures. He wanted me to tell you that he can't make his interview with you. He's out of surgery but he's stuck in a shitload of plaster and traction at the Hôtel Dieu.'

Damiano didn't look up from her notes. Galt wasn't about to share his. 'Leads?'

Galt relayed the pizza story. 'It was a take-down, not an attempted murder.'

'Was Pauzé into something?'

'He was pissed about a rejection letter from his agent, Madison Holmes.' He smirked. 'Didn't recognize the assailant. Too dark, he says.' He gave Damiano the rest.

'That's not what I asked you.'

Galt wasn't going to risk his career for Pauzé. 'He wrote papers for students and sold them - had four clients. He recycles.'

'Not always healthy.'

Galt couldn't choke the whole laugh. It sounded harsh, laced with fluid hatred. 'I'll get to the cheats tonight. No double-time for muggings.' Galt got to his feet and left before she could dismiss him.

Damiano's mind floated possible reasons for the mugging. Students, perhaps. Galt? Made for a great detour. He could have hacked into the police files. Beauchemin was a snoop. He might have found the names. Did he have the time? Pauzé could have set the attack up to drive suspicion away from himself. The last conjecture struck her with sadness. Holmes! Had he just destroyed himself? She hoped he'd been at the hospital, but her gut was tight. That didn't bode well for Holmes. Matte looked up when Damiano came back into the office.

'We can be back for eleven. Get your notes. We're on our way to the Hôtel Dieu.'

'What?'

'Matte, do the Spence Agency later. Pauzé was mugged last night.'

Chapter Eighteen

Before they left Coupal's office, Damiano called security and had the office locked. As they were walking out, Matte was shoulder-bumped by another detective. Damiano side-stepped her intended bump. Matte turned, about to react, but Damiano pulled him forward. 'No time for pushback.'

Pauzé's parents were out in the hall, asleep from the long night. Pauzé lay in bed gnawing his thumb. His pulse pounded. This wasn't supposed to happen! He held a receiver to an ear. 'So you're okay? Good, I'll give you three other numbers. Don't hand the paper in and tell the guys not to hand them in either. Call them for me. I'm not going down alone. You guys came looking for me.' He gave out the information. 'Got it? Get back to me.' How would he know they weren't lying to him? *Merde!* He began to grind his teeth. A train of coke would jump him into clarity. He could do some reconnaissance with a good head. The adrenaline spurting into his bloodstream was jamming his thoughts together.

Damiano walked into the ward first, drew the green curtain around Pauzé's bed and squared herself up to him. Her eyes picked at him before she said a word. He wiped his hands on the sides of the mattress. 'Monsiur Pauzé, Detective Damiano and Detective Matte. We can conduct our interview here if you're up to answering questions?'

He had nothing to push through the roadblocks. 'The drugs aren't helping that much. I'm in a lot of pain.' His face was strained with discomfort.

'We'll try to get through this as quickly as we can then.'

'I don't know about anything.'

'Well, let's see if perhaps you can be of some help. Detective Galt filled me in on your attack, so I'll come back to that later. Where were you yesterday morning between eight and eleven?'

'Home studying for my defence.'

'Of?' she asked.

'My dissertation.'

'The manuscript Madison Holmes had?' Matte asked.

Pauzé's cheeks flushed. 'Yes.'

'Was anyone with you yesterday?' Damiano continued.

'No, I have a small bachelor apartment.'

'No classes then?'

'I'm finished with that,' Pauzé said with pride.

'Do you own a bike?'

'Yeah.'

'Would you give me permission to take a photo of it? Is it in the apartment?'

'Wait, wait!' He ran his hands through his hair and it took a beating.

'I can have a warrant this afternoon, but your cooperation would be appreciated. Detective Matte will take your fingerprints and a saliva sample for DNA to eliminate you as a suspect.'

Had he left anything? He began cracking his fingers. The other cop was already writing something out. 'You're talking a search too?' His voice was shrill.

'Afraid so.'

His parents suddenly appeared, but Matte walked them back out.

'I am in so much pain!' He rocked back and forth like a child.

'The sooner you help us, the sooner we leave you in peace. Well?'

Matte offered Pauzé a pen and the sheet. Pauzé signed and drew his breath back between his teeth while depressing his call button. 'I need to kill this pain!'

An aide appeared and told Pauzé he wasn't due for pain medication for another hour. He answered with a four-letter word, and she ignored him and left. Pauzé began to cry, taking both detectives by surprise. 'Holmes ruined my career, and I've pretty much ruined what was left. I worked for seven years, every summer, just to crash. I don't get it.' His body throbbed as he wept. 'Are you calling the dean?'

'Not my case. Detective Galt caught the case.'

'Just so you know, Holmes actually wasted three years of my life! It took me almost a year to reach her and have her take me on. Then she trashed the next two years.'

'Madison Holmes is an agent, Monsieur Pauzé, not a publisher.'

Pauzé wasn't listening. 'Unless you're a writer, you'll never understand. To sit and wait, check the email every day, keep believing, and end up with a freakin' rejection letter. It's hell!'

'But...'

'She made me a promise she'd find me a publisher!'

'Don't know about authors, but she didn't cause the recession. That's what did you in.'

'She knew it was happening – she should have returned my book. Give me a chance to look elsewhere. I thought I'd be working by now. I only began writing those papers to stay in my shithole. Can't you see what she did to me?'

'Did you see anything helpful about the individual who attacked you last night?'

'I told the other cop it was too dark.'

'Nothing?'

'Fuck! My eyes were sore, so I didn't bother with my glasses. I could see the pizza box. The guy's a blur. He was beating me with a bat! I felt it was happening to someone else. Look at me! I may never walk again! Ah man!'

'Madison Holmes is fighting for her life.' Damiano spoke very slowly.

'I don't give a shit about her! What about me?'

Damiano looked at Matte who cautioned her to cool it. She had downed a Red Bull – he was sure of that. He guided her out of the room.

Once they were out of hearing range, Damiano let loose. 'I wanted to take a bat to his writing hand! All three, Galt, Beauchemin and now Pauzé look good for the attack. '

Damiano was buzzed.

Matte fumed because he knew why.

Chapter Nineteen

MATTE WAITED UNTIL they were inside their unmarked cruiser. 'You have to stop the cocktails. Your mouth and lips are dry and you're hyper. I noticed; the chief will too. He worked vice. When he does pick up on it, we're both screwed. Worse, one of the suspects might well figure you out. Have you thought of any of that? Do you want to crash your first lead?'

Matte had never taken Damiano on. For a few seconds she sat on the edge of her fury. It was too easy to beat up on Matte, or it used to be. What came out was hissed. 'I hate people who can sleep under stress. You're probably one of them, aren't you?'

Matte ignored her. 'We can't foul out on this one. That's all I'm saying.'

'A baseball metaphor from you!' She didn't want to but she laughed. 'I'm not taking narcotics. It's one Ambien for God's sake.' The whole truth wasn't going to work here.

'And the Red Bulls and the night chaser, right? Chalk it up to nine years of working with you.'

'You and your goddamn details! Kids drink Bulls – quick energy.'

'You don't need them.'

'Says you – moderate little you.'

'If you need a sleep-aid, take one Ambien. Forget the rest. This case is as important to me as it is to you. I'd never turn you in, Toni, you know that.'

She did. 'The case races around in my head at night.'

'It's the Bulls. Damn, you know that. Kids take them to study all night.'

'Enough therapy. Did you get the Spence Agency number? We're almost at the office.'

The conversation withered. They took the stairs in silence. Once they were inside, Damiano walked toward her locker. 'Water,' she called back, 'only water.'

Matte got on the phone and punched in the number he had found in Madison's friend's condo.

'Spence Agency, Ashley Kimpton.'

'Detective Pierre Matte.'

'Oh God, is this about Madison?'

'I'm investigating the assault on Ms Holmes.'

Damiano had walked into the office and nodded approvingly at Matte.

'It's just horrible. I still can't believe it. I spoke to Madison a few days before she was attacked. We're friends. She was on top of the world. Martin Connor was going to sign with her. How could this have happened?' Kimpton seemed near hysteria.

'Martin Connor?'

'The American mystery writer. He's an enterprise unto himself. Madison and I had a great talk. She even suggested that I might come to work with her if he signed. Why do such things happen? Madison was peaking. This is just so terrible that I can't really believe it's happened.'

Kimpton was close to tears.

'Since you were friends, you would know if there were any hard feelings at the agency because of Ms Holmes's success? I have to ask these questions.' *Tread lightly.*

'Detective Matte, we're professional people, but we're human. Who wouldn't feel a little envy? We felt pride too. Madison was one of ours. No one but me knew about Connor. He hadn't signed yet. Madison swore me to secrecy until he did. I've kept my word. I can tell you one person who wouldn't have been happy was Connor's agent. Have you contacted him? Madison met Martin Connor and his agent at the Waterfront Festival. I'm not suggesting anything. I know how I'd feel if I lost a client of that stature.'

'Did Ms Holmes mention the name of the agent?'

'No, but Martin Connor could give that to you. Madison must have kept Connor's number on her phone. You should be able to find it. If not, he's well known. He'd be easy to locate. Can you tell me how Madison is doing? I couldn't get anything from the hospital.'

'I can't give out specific information, Ms Kimpton, but Ms Holmes is hanging in.'

'I'll keep her in my prayers. Do you need anything else?'

'I know where to reach you if I do Ms Kimpton.' Matte gave Damiano the rundown. 'I have an American number that I did not have time to check out. Try that.' He knew Damiano wanted to make the call. They both sat together for a minute. The feel of the case took a slow, steadier spin. The lead in Damiano's head had worn off, the buzz stopped vibrating. The adrenalin rush was sudden and real, not synthetic. The wedge in the case was solid.

'Think of what this agent would lose when Connor walked – status, income. What he'd feel – professional humiliation, and worst, the deep sense of betrayal. If this isn't the right number, we can still locate him.' Damiano had given each of the four nouns weight.

'Had another thought.'

'You would.'

'If the split was amicable, then…'

'Already had it. Let's hope.' Damiano punched in the number.

'Yes?' Connor was puzzled. Not many people had his unlisted number. The ID of the caller was unlisted as well.

'Mr Connor?'

'Speaking.'

'Detective Damiano, Montreal, Major Crimes.'

'Detective, this call must be concerning Madison Holmes. I have been trying to get some information on her condition. I was directed to you and was about to call you today. Apart from what the press came out with, there has been no additional information about her progress.'

'Police orders for Ms Holmes's protection and for the file.'

'I'm a New York author. I was to meet with Madison on the 16th of this month.'

'Ah! I'm glad we've connected, but I still can't disclose any information about Ms Holmes.'

'I know police protocol. Actually, I'm calling with news for her. We were about to broker a business deal. I had a nasty fall from my bike. It looks like I'm facing rotator cuff surgery, so I wanted to tell her, if she is recovering, that I'm still interested. We'll both need recovery time. I hope my continuing interest might cheer her.'

'I will give Ms Holmes this message – just can't give you a time.'

'I see you've found my private number. I would appreciate any update you can shoot my way.'

'Actually, Mr Connor, I have a specific reason for this call. I do need the name and contact number of your agent.'

Connor was big in the mystery genre, big with a capital "B." It didn't take long for him to see where Damiano was going. He couldn't respond immediately. He felt sick. 'My God.'

Damiano waited patiently.

'If I'm in any way responsible…'

'The break wasn't mutual then?'

'Partings never are. I gave Tom, Tom Graham, a generous settlement. Our parting wasn't sudden. I wanted changes in my career for the past couple of years, but Tom was stubborn and set in his ways. He's also been diagnosed with early-stage prostate cancer. I had in my mind he might welcome the time to concentrate on his health. I was dead wrong. The break was brutal. I lost his friendship and earned his bitterness. But I can't believe Tom would… I can't tell you how badly I feel. Tom is a good man who would never…'

'Did he know Madison's name and whereabouts?'

'He was with me at the Waterfront Festival. He didn't fly there with me, said he wanted to drive and think. We met up in Toronto. I hoped that I might connect him with new writers because he was adamant about working. He met Madison. He guessed the rest that afternoon and walked off.'

'So you don't know when he got back to New York?'

'I gave him the space I thought he needed, for his illness and for our situation. I've left it to him to get back to me. He hasn't.'

'Do you think he knew about the attack on Ms Holmes?'

'He would have. The media covered it, but he didn't call me.'

'Would you give me his private number, please? I have to direct you not to contact him, Mr. Connor.'

'I understand. I can't recall a time when I've felt so low. I hope you have other suspects. Tom's a devout Catholic, a family man and a great friend for many years. I cannot believe he'd… Doesn't compute.' Connor gave Damiano the information she needed. 'May I ask you for any feedback you can give me?'

'What I can.' Damiano turned to Matte who had heard the conversation on speakerphone.

He saw that Connor's sadness had affected her.

Damiano spoke to herself mostly when she said, 'It still amazes and saddens me to see the spreading effects of a single crime.'

Chapter Twenty

DAMIANO PUT THE phone back down. Matte was already on his iPhone. 'Pierre!'

'Here's a photo of Tom Graham and Martin Connor,' he said, handing her the phone. 'They could be brothers, or could be you're with someone long enough, you end up looking alike.'

Damiano took the phone. 'Older frat boys! Good American hair and teeth and the proverbial blue shirt and tan slacks. Before we see the chief, we should talk to Graham to see if he was in Canada the day of the attack. If he was back in New York and can prove it, we're out of luck, but we will verify his location with evidence. Agreed?'

'Call him.' Matte sat beside the speakerphone.

Damiano cleared her throat and made the call. Having the private number was a real help. The phone rang three times before it was picked up.

'Yep?'

'Tom Graham?'

'You got me.'

'Detective Toni Damiano, Montreal, Major Crimes.'

'Then I hope you don't got me!' The levity seemed forced. 'I suppose I know what this call is about. You've probably been speaking with Martin, so you are aware that my life is rocky at the moment. Before you go ahead with your questions, let me say that I am still shaken up about the loss of this contract and the suddenness of our split. However, I begin cancer therapy in three weeks. Although Martin might like to think he's foremost in my thoughts, I can assure you, cancer has knocked him and his new agent off my podium.'

Two jarring blows coming from different directions had left Graham bitter and angry. Damiano felt pain. She couldn't always stay aloof.

'I represent a crime writer so I'll cut to the quick. I suppose you want to know if I was in Montreal or thereabouts the day of the attack. I even know the dates. Just a sec, I'll get the clippings I saved. Well, yep, I was in Montreal, actually I was down at the Old Port.'

'May I ask what you were doing in Montreal?'

'Escaping the realities of my life. Back home my wife is devastated on both fronts. We still have two sons at Princeton. The boys are wondering about money. Mara knows me too well. There were changes I flatly refused to make for Martin, so I can read blame in my wife's every glance. It's all too heavy. This is the first private holiday I've taken. I just needed space for me and my grief to come to terms. I didn't want to share any of it or feel the heat of condemnation from her. I fell in love with Montreal a long time ago. I was born in Outremont; my mother was French-speaking. We spoke French at home. She died tragically when I was thirteen. Your city allowed me to hide for a while in a place where I felt safe. Does that make any sense to you, Detective?'

'It does.' *Madison Holmes thought she was in a safe place. She didn't think she had to hide.*

'I hope you do.'

'Now I suppose you want to ask me if I bludgeoned this Madison Holmes. In instances of betrayal, I always felt the woman should go after her husband. If I wanted to kill anyone, I would have gone after Martin. We grew up together in this market – we had a bond. However, my attention was divided. I'm looking at six weeks of laser prostate therapy three times a week, more if I can handle it, followed by nausea, headaches, the works. After that, I'll take up Kegel exercises for incontinence. That should be lots of fun.'

'You're angry.'

'To the core.'

'I appreciate your honesty.'

'Martin had the absolute gall to introduce me to her. I mean what kind of a friend does that?'

'I do sympathize.'

'Clears me out with a severance package and goes to a woman who struck the jackpot with timing and luck! Jesus! Martin never thought of how humiliated I might feel. Then the fucker introduces her to me! Thinks I won't figure out the obvious? What a moron, never saw his cracks, but he has them. I guess we all do,' Graham conceded and commented astutely. 'You're a good listener, Detective. That's a skill. You waited till I worked myself up into a good lather. That's what you wanted, right?'

'I think you knew where you were going, Mr. Graham.'

'So, what's next?'

'The usual, prints, DNA, a lineup.'

'You really believe all this is necessary?'

'I do.'

'Any chance you can come to Manhattan for the prints and DNA? I'm trying to conserve my energy. The lineup would have to be set up before my therapy begins.'

'I'll check with my chief and get back to you.'

'You have no worries on one front. I'm not going anywhere.'

'You'll hear from me within the hour.'

'Good by me.'

Damiano looked at Matte. 'What's your take?'

'Looks as good as the others. Americans are generally friendly people. They're not the easy reads they might first appear to be.'

'Let's check in with Donat.'

Chief Donat was remarkably calm, attentive and brief. 'Matte can hold things together here. You'll drive down. With all the recent budget cuts, I don't want to spend money on a flight. Can you leave today and be back tomorrow? I don't want any time lost on the file.'

'I can.'

'Have you done your homework?'

'Upper West Side, Precinct 24, and the number for the Detective Squad is 212 678…' She added Graham's address as well and handed Donat a copy.

'I'll contact our Liaison Officer for cross-border interviews – I might even call through to the precinct myself and save time. Expect a call from your American counterpart. You realize you might not be alone on the interview.'

'Won't be a bother.'

As soon as they left, Donat popped a med for his acid reflux. Damiano would be driving there all night and back in the afternoon. He knew what he was asking of her. She impressed him, often did. He didn't feel well enough to bark anyway, though it was a habit he enjoyed. *Good cops like Damiano could take it.*

Damiano gave Graham a quick call. With the thrill of a root canal he said he'd await her arrival. Damiano liked him; liked a man with a sense of humor. Wasting no time getting back home, she packed what she needed. Once she was on the road, she turned on her digital recorder and sped to the Champlain/Lacolle border crossing. Damiano left the hardware at home and identified herself as a cop at the border, to save time. She stopped once for gas and a bathroom break. Before ten that night, she was on the outskirts of the city and stopped at the first Comfort Inn she spotted. She ordered a Boston pizza and orange juice, threw her clothes on the bed and dropped down beside them. Her phone rang. She reached over to the night table and picked it up. 'Detective Damiano.'

'Detective Rutgers, Precinct 24. I hear you have an interview tomorrow with a Tom Graham in my jurisdiction. Chief Donat tells me Graham is compliant.'

'He's expecting me.'

'We're talking preliminary, right?'

'Correct.'

'Think you might need help? I can park outside the place if you like.'

'I believe I have this covered, Detective, but you're welcome to come along.' Damiano hoped he wouldn't. She passed on Graham's address and time of the interview as a courtesy even though Rutgers appeared to have the information from Chief Donat.

'If you smell an arrest, I have to be there.' He gave Damiano his number because it was confidential, as was hers. 'If it closes with the prelim, you don't need me. Does that work for you?'

'It does, and thanks.'

'Take care out there. This is New York after all.'

The Ambien had come with her and she broke one in half. *One and a half should do it for the night. Can't be heavy-lidded tomorrow, especially if Rutgers ends up coming.* When the pizza arrived, she was too tired to attack it and picked at it instead. She set the alarm for 6:30 a.m., went out to the car and verified the directions from her GPS, stripped, guzzled most of the OJ, got into bed and fell off the planet till the shrill of the alarm woke her. Beside the clock, she spied the forgotten Ambien. *Wow!* Alert, clear-eyed, energized, she showered and dressed, gnawed at the cold pizza, finished the OJ, brushed her teeth and left. A power surged in her head, airing her brain. *Wow!* She felt good.

Just before 8:30, she rang #4, an elegant townhouse on 49 West 87th Street, between Central Park and Columbus Avenue. She noticed that there were ten units in the rustic limestone building. *Quiet money.* Rutgers was nowhere around.

Graham answered the door, in a black V-necked cashmere sweater and casual pants and loafers. 'Come on in to the office. It's at the back. Mara's out running.'

Damiano felt that yesterday's easy exchange had evaporated.

'I called our attorney. Maury said he couldn't block what you want. A court order would just put off the inevitable. Have a seat.'

The room was artfully appointed with subtle recessed lighting, pale eggshell walls, a page-cut walnut desk and book shelves. It could have been a film set.

She opened a small black case. 'I'll take the swab first, then the prints.'

Graham didn't resist. 'Any other questions?'

Did you do it? 'The situation in Montreal is not ordinary. I will call a lineup. You did say you'd present yourself. It'll take place before your therapy. Why put yourself out for that?'

'Truth?'

'I hope.'

'Much-needed distraction. It's brutal here. Mara's probably right that I screwed myself with Connor and destroyed my livelihood. I knew he'd already made up his mind, but I didn't push him. I couldn't crawl. Should have in retrospect. Guilt works at times. Cancer crushes your body and your spirit. Maybe a lineup will cheer me up,' he snorted. 'You never know. At the very least it'll get me out of here.'

'Can anyone alibi you for the morning of the attack?'

'You don't invite others in when you're hiding.'

'Ordering a drink, whatever?'

'Sounds like you're on my side.'

'I'm trying to get at the truth.'

'Good luck with that chase – I never have.'

'You do have motive, and you were in town.'

'Enough, I can recite the rest of it for you. I've hit the trifecta: summarily dumped, diagnosed with cancer and a suspect in an assault. Beat that!'

'Did you check out her place?'

'I think you've hit a wall, Detective. I'll see you out.' Graham turned on Damiano in a heartbeat. He extended his hand at the door. 'I appreciate you making the trip.' His hand was wet with sweat. 'I don't know if this,' looking down at his hand, 'is the cancer or fear. You'll do your best to nail that down, won't you, Detective? You like the job, I can feel it.'

His eyes narrowed. The anger was there. Damiano felt its sudden threat and was glad to leave. The uneasiness never left Damiano on the long drive back. His anger was well-founded, not arrogance.

Chapter Twenty-one

DETECTIVE GALT wasted no time getting back to the hospital. Jean Pauzé jumped, startled by his return appearance. No time wasted with small talk. 'Monsieur Pauzé, were the four papers you sold for the same course?'

Pauzé appeared worn and strained, much older than his twenty-seven years. 'Detective,' he whined, 'you said if nothing comes of...'

'I already told you that the case has been opened. Your assault may be linked to the attack on Madison Holmes and what happened to you is a felony. Something came of it.'

'I'm not pressing charges! What part of that don't you understand? I won't help you destroy my life!'

'Answer the question.'

'Yes, but I told the students to use my papers as a guide for their own – not to hand mine in.'

'I'm meeting with them in an hour. I'll sort all that out. The professor's name and the course number?'

Pauzé mulled over his situation and saw no hope of dodging. 'Dr. Harold Nagel, Canadian History 301, but you don't have to talk to him because none of the papers have been handed in. They're only due Monday.'

'You've been busy.'

'Excuse me?'

'Continue your recovery Monsieur Pauzé.' Detective Galt left for his interview with the students. In the Crémazie parking garage he made a fast call to McGill Faculty of Arts, asking for Nagel and getting lucky. Nagel was in his office. Galt asked his questions.

'Just a second, Detective, I'll run their names through my class lists. I certainly don't know my students by name. My TA might. Well, yes, yes, yes, and yes. They're all mine. May I ask what these questions are about?'

'Not on an open case, Professor. Have you received papers from any of these students?'

'I have the sense, Detective, that it's been a long time since we were both in school. I'll be lucky to get them late Monday. Would you like to speak to my TA? She's young and a real stickler for details.'

'Thank you, yes.' When Galt had what he needed, he headed into the Crémazie building. The students were huddled together, slouching against a corner wall. Galt herded them down to the main interview room, left three outside and ushered the tallest one into the room. Galt was accustomed to suspects lying to him, but this arrogant, head-high, dare-you approach surprised him. No one in their group had attacked Pauzé, this was their first 'tutorial,' they were working together on their own papers last night, using Pauzé's as a guide only, and no one had had any intention of cheating. Galt had tried once to corner a squirrel and didn't win. He'd learned from that experience.

Galt admired Pauzé's sick-bed organizational skills – he'd gotten to each of these kids. His only pushback was forcing the students to wait while he spoke to Nagel's TA. She'd only seen one paper, and their grades were unremarkable. The thought did occur to Galt that one of these kids handed his paper in and got nabbed by the TA, but a parent paid her off or donated handsomely to the university, guaranteeing a hush-up. Either way, how could he prove that? Galt was back to square one.

While Detective Galt was facing an impasse, Detective Damiano was carrying her notes to the boss's office. Chief Richard Donat had not asked to see Matte. Damiano stood outside his office, mentally preparing.

The Chief saw her approach and wasted no time. 'What are you waiting on?'

'After the long drive to New York and back, I'm not up to your games, Chief.' She did find the strength to give him her report on Graham as though she were a drill captain. He tried to hide a crooked smile.

'You've got four possibles with Graham?'

'That's good addition. They all have motive. Graham the strongest. He will present himself for the lineup and his DNA and prints have been sent to Marie. No point guessing. It's goddamn confusing is what it is. The hook is there, but I can't sink it yet.'

'Ah Jesus, four!' Donat had permanent dark circles under his eyes. He looked hollow because he had one of those thin faces that never looked good to begin with. Prominent blue veins marked his temples. He was never called a hunk behind his back. Racoon was his tag. Damiano liked the racoon.

Damiano went through their list of the other three.

The boss drummed his fingers on the wooden desk while he listened, and brought his fist down when Galt's name came up.

'Prose, *our* prick?'

Damiano nodded.

'Shiiiit! The idiot went to Holmes's place and he wonders why he's never made lieutenant? What a cluster fuck-up for my department if he whacked Holmes! The uniforms and their guns are doing a number on the whole department as it is – we don't need this! What's your gut on Galt?'

Damiano frowned.

The papers on his desk jumped as the boss slammed both fists on the desk. A sheet fell to the floor.

'Leave it. Explain this other attack.'

She gave her limited report. 'Galt will fill you in on the rest. He caught it.'

'Fine. Damiano, give Galt nothing on Holmes! I can't risk the smell of collusion. I lose my job and by God, I'll bring you down with me. Clear? I gotta work on some spin for the media call-up or heads will roll before we have a straight lead.'

They were both startled by the hum of her smart phone. 'Galt.'

'Take it.'

'Are you pursuing the file?' Damiano listened as Galt reported on what he had learned. 'Uh huh. Thank you, Detective.'

'Shoot!' Donat ordered.

Damiano reported the conversation. 'I think the attack is somehow related to my case.'

'How?' he asked.

'One thought is that the attack is a blind, set up by Beauchemin, Galt or Pauzé himself.'

'The second?'

'Thomas Holmes. He's very angry, carrying loads of guilt and he made threats. I hope I can clear him.'

'A blue chip cluster fuck-up! What about Angela Marino?' The boss was tense.

'Is there any chance of getting a wiretap on her phones? She's connected. We've traced her case files.'

'No cause. Besides, Marino's too smart for taps or text mop-ups. She'll horsewhip and stomp you. Start with the "wonder kid" author – see what you can get on Marino.'

'Fine,' Damiano said too crisply.

'Now, get out there and close the book on Holmes. I'll feed the swarming press. Galt gets nothing from you! That's not a warning – it's an order.'

Donat walked out of his office after Damiano had left, right into the frown of his long-time secretary. 'Why do you come down so hard on Damiano? She's one of your best badges.'

'You must have heard Damiano. The good ones give it right back to me. You hear everything, even with the door closed.'

Chapter Twenty-Two

DAMIANO'S MOOD WAS as gray and cold as the weather. The fear of an unsolved file almost choked her. The confident smile she worked died as she walked past colleagues to Coupal's office. That didn't much matter because the male detectives zoned in on her hips that asserted themselves with every step. Matte was ready to say something, but she dove into her purse and yanked out another peanut butter and jam sandwich, tore it and inhaled it. She threw some crusts into the wastepaper basket and wiped her hands on discarded paper.

'You could choke, eating like that.'

'But I won't, so lay off my eating habits. I ate a Christmas decoration when I was two – had only a few cuts.' She brought Matte up to date on Graham.

Matte opened his lunch, two diamond-cut tuna sandwiches without crusts.

'Figures.'

'I tried to set up an appointment with Tracey Doyle. Thought I'd leave her mother to you.'

'What time?'

'There's a glitch.'

'What?' she asked, clearly irritated.

'She's staying incognito at the Ritz-Carlton and, can we go there?'

'The boss's nostrils are blowing smoke. We'll go anywhere. Stuff your mouth while I clean up a bit.'

Matte took all his notes with him, Damiano only what she needed. 'Doyle sounded like she'd been crying.'

'Good – better for us. Give it some gas, Pierre,' Damiano said as they drove.

When they arrived at the storied hotel on Sherbrooke Street, Damiano jumped out of the unmarked car. They had no time to waste.

'Mais, vous… Mademoiselle,' the doorman began to protest. Only at the Ritz would the doorman have the nerve to discourage cops from parking in front of the hotel.

She pushed a card into his hand. 'Police! Cas urgent.' Matte hurried after her. 'Run back and give him a twenty.'

'My own?'

'Tough. I'm lead after all.'

They were ushered up to the Royal Suite. 'Some bolt-hole!' Damiano said, knocking loudly, waving off the bellhop.

'Why can't you just say hideout like the rest of us?' Matte asked Damiano.

'I keep up with the buzz talk. You should too.'

Matte shook his head.

Tracey Doyle opened the door wearing a luxurious white terry cloth robe, tied loosely, with the hotel's blue insignia on the breast pocket, over a powder blue turtleneck and pajama bottoms. The robe was stained with pink splotches and what looked like pizza sauce that had somehow dribbled on the blue socks. The white belt dragged along the floor. She waved two fingers behind her back, ushering them inside like help.

The largest suite of the Ritz was sumptuous. They followed Doyle into a double-sized living room where a fire blazed in the marble fireplace at the side of the room. Damiano figured the dining room could easily seat eight and she saw a study and more rooms down the hall. She sat beside a sky-blue marble lamp. Matte sat on the other side of the room. Every article in the room was posh and old and classy.

Doyle grabbed her bottle of pink vodka that had left rings on a lovely marble table, took a long swig and circled them. Her face was bloated and blotched from crying. Damiano would have called her a Plain Jane years ago, and crying had dropped Doyle down another level. Damiano tried to find one attractive feature in the author's face and couldn't. Her hair was long and stringy, her face Canadian pie, her eyes swollen from tears, her teeth heavily braced. Doyle, thought Damiano, looked like she was carrying all her shit around in her loopy socks.

'Ms Doyle, I'm Detective Damiano and that's Detective Matte and we have a few questions. Would you please sit down? That will make things easier all around.'

'Please don't think I had anything to do with hurting Madison!' A fresh wave of tears, a voice shrill with hysteria. 'She was the only person in my whole rotten life who believed in me. I can't sit – I just can't. I wish I could see Madison. I want to tell her I didn't mean anything I said. My mother doesn't know where I am, you know. I just walked out. Wait till she sees what I'm paying for this place! It's my money. It's my life and I can do what I want with it.'

'May I call you Tracey?'

'Like we're friends or something?' Doyle stopped circling and bent sideways awkwardly, glaring at Damiano through her owl lenses.

'No,' Damiano admitted, 'like I'm someone who thinks you might fall and injure yourself, like someone who thinks you should put the bottle down. Tracey, I don't think you attacked Madison Holmes, but I need your help with some questions.'

Doyle put the bottle down and dropped into the nearest chair, drawing her robe closed. 'I wish I could take back what I said to her ...'

'We all have that wish at one time or another.'

Matte looked admiringly at Damiano. It had taken her just a few words to win Doyle over.

'We heard what you said because Ms Holmes records important conversations as do we. Would you mind if Detective Matte tapes this conversation?'

Matte turned on the recorder when Doyle didn't state an objection.

'My mother forced me to call and told me what to say.'

Damiano and Matte nodded and thought the same thing. Holmes had been right in her assumption. Their silence kept Doyle talking.

'I told her I had a contract, and she laughed in my face. She said she had all sorts of connections and to leave everything to her. My mother never cared about me my whole life. Everything is about her. She's everything I'm not: beautiful, intelligent and powerful. Then when I made it, by some freakin' miracle, she wants in!'

'Maybe she was a little envious, Tracey.'

'Of what? She said I had no talent, and that anyone could make money, but she could set me up for life!'

'How could she break your contract without incurring huge losses?'

Doyle laughed a short, sad, knowing laugh. 'Hmph!' Her eyes teared again. 'She can do anything,' she whispered. Doyle sat up feeling that words were falling loose, that the balance in the room had changed.

'I feel you still love her.'

'My therapist said that's the tragedy of wounded children. You know what's funny?'

Damiano waited quietly.

'No matter what my mother did, I could never get out of my contract. You should see the thousands of FB messages, YouTube podcasts, texts and tweets I've been getting telling me to be loyal just like my vampire character. I couldn't leave Madison if I wanted to. I never wanted to in the first place.'

'Maybe your mother was exaggerating when she said she could pull strings, whatever, to get you out of the contract. Maybe she was just trying to control you.'

It turned out that Doyle was not a fool. She caught the tone and the direction of the questioning. She also caught sight of the recorder.

'You're recording this?'

'We told you at the outset we were, Tracey. We can stop if you wish.'

Damiano signalled to Matte and he turned the recorder off.

'My mother's not stupid. You should leave. I'll never testify against her.'

'I won't put your name on the information you gave us, Tracey.'

'You wanted me to junk my mother. You're not my friend. Just leave!'

And, Damiano thought, the kid was right – about everything.

Chapter Twenty-Three

The detectives hurried back to their car and they drove off.

'Angela Marino's office is on McGill College Avenue. We're close by. I'd like to catch her unprepared. There is a professional smell to the assault, but I think her daughter might be right. Marino is just not that stupid. She might even be able to have a body buried in some hole and tied to a bag of lye, but would she? She seems much too selfish to harm herself.'

Matte sat inert beside Damiano. It was her call.

The adrenalin rush that went with risk-taking had earned Damiano lieutenant, but she didn't want to end her day presenting herself at an antiseptically brutal meeting with the boss. At times, she grated on her superiors but her deft political savvy and good looks had kept her in the top department. 'Make the appointment. We'll do this by the book.'

'Good decision.'

'Where are you with the photos?'

'The uniforms have them. I've sent Graham's as well. We have to be patient. A small break is all we need.'

'Patience! We have to get an edge on this thing. What time is it?'

'Almost two.'

'Good. We can scrape the bottom of the barrel. Nurse Aubin must still be home. She works nights. I'll tackle her and you go at that witness. Needle her with your detail shit!'

'Detective!'

'Alright, skills. We need forty-eight hours in a day. I hate these gray days – they feel like handcuffs.'

They double-parked and used their flashers. Damiano ran up the flights of stairs and was breathing easily when the door to the condo opened. For a moment, she didn't recognize Aubin.

A look of satisfaction crossed Aubin's face before it turned to a scowl. '*Oui?*'

'I have a few more questions, Madame Aubin.'

'I'm meeting someone,' she spoke harshly.

'Call her and tell her you'll be late. May I come in?'

Aubin's facial features tightened, trapped as she was. She stomped back inside her condo and Damiano followed her. A question arced around Damiano's head like electric bolts. She knew what it was. Racine the cat knew too and ambled out of their way. Aubin sat in a chair nearest the front door, waiting for the question she knew was coming. *Had she ever…* Let this cop ask. Aubin wasn't going to help her.

The room was decorated with style and a subtle feel for color. *Flair,* Damiano thought.

'It's my job to look closely at the person who finds the victim, the first person at the crime scene.'

'And saves her life,' Aubin added.

'Yes, there's that. Holmes is an attractive woman. I've seen her photos before the assault.'

'And?'

'You know where I'm going.'

'She's single, and straight.'

'Straights don't always walk on the lines. Did you make any advances towards her? I have to be direct. You saved her life, but you found her, had lots of her blood on you and you contaminated the crime scene. I can't let this angle go without all questions asked and answered. *You're gay, you see a good looking woman, you cruise her.* She didn't like reducing herself to a stereotype, but she had no choice. She had to ask.

Aubin felt her secret slipping loose. She wiped some imaginary lint from her cream-colored slacks and rubbed the pads of her thumbs together.

'Well?'

'I was interested.' Aubin looked at the floor when she answered.

'Don't make this harder on yourself – get it out.'

'I was disappointed, and hurt, but that occurred when Madison first moved here. We later settled as friends.'

'No lingering animosity?'

'Madison was full of life. It took too much effort to feel animosity towards her. Quite frankly, after work, I didn't have the energy.'

Well, thought Damiano, she hadn't picked up any dregs scraping the bottom. She rose. 'Holmes is lucky to have a friend like you.'

Aubin got up as well. 'It's always worked both ways.' They walked out together.

Matte was back in the car, so that didn't bode well. 'Well, this was a bust. How about the witness?'

'Nothing. I checked her window. It does have its limitations. The woman made a valid point. Couriers running up and down Holmes's stairs are a daily event. That's the main reason she didn't take special notice. Brown shorts, that's it.'

Damiano's phone rang as Matte was pulling out. 'Go slowly – I want to hear every word.'

The tech who had mopped Holmes's computer presented his finds to

Damiano. 'There were two recent viral attacks on her computer.'

'Explain.' Damiano sat forward listening and put the phone on speaker so Matte could hear too.

'What crooks are doing today is infecting PCs with a virus that sits on the PC (though it can be detectable) and then the trojan will send personal data to an outside location of the crook's choice. We found two trojans. If the crooks only want limited information, then they're usually successful before the owner detects the virus.'

'I'm back to my rejects; Graham fits right in with the lot. If I understand this correctly, that means that two individuals might have stolen access to Holmes's PC and to the names of the other rejects.'

'Correct,' the tech said proudly.

'Can you track the source?'

'If the intruders IP spoofed the trojans to confuse us, our job will be more difficult, not impossible. The majority of PC owners do not encrypt their files. That's why their contents are really unprotected.'

'Work through dinner on this!'

'I brown bag, but I can eat and work.'

Damiano gave Matte her first smile. 'The attack on Pauzé *is* connected. I'm sure of that now. Two of these fuckers knew the names of the other rejects. We have an edge. I have to interrogate Thomas Holmes. I hope for his sake he had nothing to do with the attack on Pauzé. I have a bad feeling.'

'Feeling? You?'

'Gut.'

'Better.'

'Get back to the office.'

Chapter Twenty-Four

A FEW HOURS EARLIER, Jean Pauzé's condition worsened. His left leg had swollen badly. His surgeon had placed Pauzé on standby for further exploratory surgery. The pain meds were increased. He moaned quietly in a druggy daze and wasn't at first aware that there was someone beside his bed. His eyes, already red-rimmed, grew wild when he saw who it was. He lay there like a cornered animal. His fear upgraded to terror and he pushed himself deeper into his pillows. 'I said I won't press charges. I haven't said anything. Look, I know I got myself into this. My leg's fucked up and I need more surgery. Please, leave me alone.'

His visitor studied Jean's face and left. There was still time.

Jean had gripped the sides of his bed. His knuckles were white. He was completely alone. He'd never bring his parents into the mess. He knew for the first time what it meant to be afraid, not like a kid, like a man who knew he might die.

It was the next afternoon when Madison's physician tapped Thomas on the shoulder. He appeared to have fallen asleep on his feet. He signalled for Thomas to follow him out of the ICU. 'Come down to my office, Thomas.'

'I'd rather stay close. I had to take a break last night.'

'Well, the news is good. There was no apparent oxygen deprivation. That was my initial fear. The recent scans also show a decrease in the swelling. We brought Madison into surgery last night to reattach the skull piece. The procedure itself was unremarkable. Her progress *is* remarkable. I'm not often surprised, but your daughter's ahead of the normal schedule for this type of injury. I was glad to find that you had gone home for much needed rest. What's wrong, man? You look as though you're ready to pass out.'

Thomas covered his eyes and rubbed his forehead. He rebooted. 'I'm fine – it's just that I was expecting the worst.'

'Thomas, when we finish talking, go down to the cafeteria and get some food and coffee into you. If you don't go, I'll block you from the ICU. Take stock, Thomas. Later today, we intend to bring Madison out of the coma. Then we wait and that might take a few days. I'm looking for encouraging signs. Once she's conscious, we'll see if she recognizes you. If she does, you'll ask her a few simple questions to see if she understands. I'll check to see if she can follow directions. I believe that she'll be able to breathe on her own. She's a strong young woman and I think she's lucky, so I can't have you collapsing. Have I made myself quite clear? Madison is safe. There's good police protection. Get to the cafeteria.' He watched as Thomas walked away reluctantly.

He fished into the breast pocket of his white coat and found the number he wanted. 'Detective Damiano?'

'Dr. Orr?'

'Yes. I have news.'

Damiano's face lit up. Progress! 'Very good news, Doctor. Is her father with her?'

'I sent him down for food. He's taken a beating and struggling.'

'He's heard the encouraging news?'

'Yes, but he's despondent. That concerns me.'

Damiano tried to understand. 'He'll be back to the ICU then?'

'I'd give him ten minutes. I can't keep him away.'

'The privacy issue is even more important, Dr. Orr. Please alert your staff again. No one in Admin is to get wind of this.'

'Understood.'

'I'm heading down soon to speak with my men.' Damiano looked over at Matte. 'Pierre, pay a visit to the techs – get them moving. You probably know as much as they do. I can handle Holmes. Don't get that sour look on your face. You might end up with a better lead. We have to move – can't do everything together.' Damiano walked out of the room before Matte could whine.

Driving through the road construction chaos on the way to the hospital did not have a calming effect on Damiano's nerves. *Complete insanity!* Flashers didn't help much. Nothing could. She spent almost twenty minutes negotiating one block, watching seven lights change. Once she was finally at the Montreal General, she blocked out everything but the ICU. First, she spoke with the uniform at the door. 'Were you on last night?'

'Shoulda been in bed, but I filled in for a friend I owe.'

'You're keeping a log of the ins and outs?'

'Yes, Lieutenant,' he answered, pulling out his spiral pad.

'I don't want the whole list. What time did Thomas Holmes leave the ICU last night?'

'Well,' he ran his finger down the first page, 'at four-fourteen, he left to take a leak. He was back in six minutes.'

'No! No! When did he leave for the night?'

He turned to the third page. 'Let's see. Eight-twenty-three.'

'You're sure he didn't come back?'

'Woulda had to get by me – he didn't. He looked bad, Lieutenant.'

'Is he in there now?' she asked pointing to the ICU.

'Oh yeah. He's back. Came out once to talk to Dr. Orr.' He went back to his notes.

'Forget the time. Get him out here, please.'

For the first time as lead, Damiano wanted to be wrong.

Holmes made it very clear he wanted to be with his daughter. 'Dr. Orr is bringing Madison out of her coma. Why am I out here?'

'Dr. Holmes, I've just learned of your proper title. I'm very pleased for the promising news, but I need you to come with me for a few minutes.'

He blew out a derisive breath. 'I can give you exactly two minutes. Whatever energy I have I will spend on Madison. Hope restored is as difficult to deal with as hope lost. My place and full attention is with her, not wasting time with you, Detective.'

'This won't take long. There's a small office not far – we'll go there. I'll ask my questions as quickly as possible.'

Damiano had seen the cubicle with a desk and three chairs and had decided on taking it for the interview. She closed the door once Holmes was inside. The walls were hospital gray-white and peeling in the corners.

'What is this about?'

'Late last night, one of the rejected authors was attacked. He's in the hospital – he also underwent surgery.'

'Good! What does that have to do with me?'

It was clear to her that Holmes was pissed. He was haggard, but full of fight. 'Where were you last night between nine and midnight? Before you answer, I know you weren't here.'

A sudden tension began to pull at the corners of his mouth.

'You knew all the names of the rejected authors Dr. Holmes, and you threatened to do them harm.'

His face was drained of color so his sudden smile seemed sinister and ghastly. 'I wish I had, but I drove out to the cemetery to sit with my wife Becky. There was a lot I needed to say to her. I find peace when I'm there with her. Now I'm going back to be with Madison.'

'Do you own a baseball bat?'

'About 43 years ago.' He turned away.

'Dr. Holmes, would you consent to a house and vehicle search?'

'Secure a court order. Aren't you the detective on my daughter's case?' He braced his shoulders and banged a fist against his leg. 'Do your job – find the monster who tried to kill *her*! Nothing else matters to me.' With that, Holmes got up and left to be alone in his personal hell.

He might have done Pauzé. Was that the reason for his despondency? *Huh!* Her nerves frayed, her heart beat so hard that her shoulders began to shake. *This is worse than playing Fortress on Mahjong Titans! It looks so simple but the game's a bugger. I need more than an edge. I need a crack!*

Chapter Twenty-Five

DAMIANO WALKED BACK to the ICU and waited. There was a steady flow of medical staff in and out of the unit. She assumed most of the action was for Holmes. 'You watching all this?'

The uniform was checking and madly scribbling notes. 'Yeah, yeah. Two new white coats.' He began texting.

'What are you doing, Officer Turner, is it?'

'Yes, Lieutenant. Making double sure that Officer Bourque tracks them. He's at Holmes's bedside. Just a sec. He should get right back to me.'

'Well?'

'He's slower than I am and wordy. Gotta practice texting speed. It's a game really.'

Damiano paced up and down the hallway with her natural hip-swinging stride. The case was beginning to eat her up. So many suspects without a real bite. The damp November wind seemed to have invaded the hallways and she pulled her faux cashmere jacket tightly around her. She was tired and hungry.

'All the doctors are with Holmes. Dr. Orr says they have to be patient. I guess nothing's happening, Lieutenant.'

Damiano's phone began to vibrate. 'Text me as soon as anything happens and pass that on to your replacement. Holmes is still at risk and you are responsible. Get your head out of your notes for now, Officer Turner. Address me as Detective. It's less formal.' Damiano hurried back to the small office down the hall she had used for the Holmes interview and read the text she'd just received. 'Call me.' She got right back to Matte. Had he found an opening in the case? 'Pierre?'

'We have the first intruder.'

'Drop the suspense – spit it out.'

'Galt. Actually, his sixteen-year-old son. The kid sent the virus from his friend's house.'

'What was the garbage about the trojan coming from a remote area?' The room was claustrophobic, and she could smell her vanilla-laden perfume as she shook her head. 'He put this on his kid? I'll nail this body-conscious prick to the wall!'

'Hold on, Damiano. There's still the other trojan. Remote just means the crook is not using his own computer.'

'Don't ever tell me what to do, Detective Matte. I hear you. I just didn't want to bust up a cop's life and have the blue flack fly back in our faces.

Where's the fucker now?'

'He caught the Pauzé file. He must be on that.'

'How long does the tech figure it'll take to track the second trojan?'

'No one can give you a time on that.'

'We need better techs.'

'What happened with Thomas Holmes?'

'He's morphed into the Iron Man, but meaner. Thinks we've lost our direction with his daughter's case. He's a doctor, for God's sake, and he could have beaten Pauzé without a shred of conscience. He knew all the names. He gave them to me, and he doesn't have an alibi for the time of the beating. I've never dealt with people like this conniving group. I have an odd feeling about him.'

'It's his only child.'

'All the same.'

'What do we do about Galt?'

'Ah damn, wait for the second intruder.'

'Any news from the hospital?'

'They're bringing her out of the coma and like every other bleeping procedure – it takes time.' Damiano poked her head out and saw Dr. Orr at the door. 'Gotta run. Bring some food back to the office for us tonight.'

'You paying?'

'I'll cover you.'

'Sounds good.'

She ran back to catch the physician. He saw her and waited.

'Any news?'

'She is breathing on her own with a tracheotomy for now and she's in and out of consciousness.'

'When do you feel she'll be fully conscious?'

'We wait and see, but I'd hazard a few hours. She's a lucky woman so far. From the beginning I said that to her father, but I was really trying to console him. I may have been right.'

'What about her memory?'

'As long as she still has the "trach," she can't talk. Even without it, coherent conversation might take some time. I can't rush Ms Holmes. Patience isn't your forte, Detective.'

'Can't afford it in high profile cases.'

'Pressure cooker?'

'On high burner.'

'Well, I can't accelerate this process, Detective.' He went back inside.

Damiano would have to suck up the delay and she began to pace and plot out what she had. Something had pumped Holmes. A talk with his dead wife? Bullshit! A beat down on Pauzé would do it, make him feel that he'd done something to avenge his daughter's assault. A fifty-eight-year-old could swing a bat. Then there was Galt. He used his own kid. He knew they had him in their crosshairs, so he might bust up Pauzé to deflect attention from himself. Galt was angry and aggressive. That was a fit too. As for Beauchemin, she figured he didn't have the time for Pauzé. On the other side of things, Pauzé could have been hit by one of his student clients, but kids were into chest and head stomping. If they could crack Pauzé's attack, they might be able to move forward on the Holmes assault! She still felt strongly that they were connected. Tom Graham's trifecta, as he called it, might well have created his raging demon. He had reason to hate Holmes and Connor. Damiano didn't expect luck. She'd never had a smooth landing, not even on a plane. Orr reappeared.

'Detective! She's conscious! You may come in with me for a few minutes, but you're to stay in the background. Absolutely no questions – you could send Ms Holmes into shock.'

Damiano nodded reluctantly.

Chapter Twenty-Six

In the ICU, Detective Damiano focused first on the IV drip, the monitoring equipment and the drains before she looked at the victim. She was a homicide cop after all. The previous victims she had seen at Parthenais, the Montreal city morgue, were dead, past fatal damage, past breath, past caring. Madison Holmes's head, though heavily bandaged, still revealed massive swelling and the enormity of the assault. Damiano gently put her hand to Madison's head. Thomas Holmes noticed and glared at her.

Conscious? How could anyone tell? Damiano wanted to scream at the injustice of this assault, at the long road back that Holmes faced in recovery, if she recovered. And then she saw it. The right eye opened, not fully, but clear and focused. Damiano stood stock still. She watched the eye as it scanned those closest to her. Then it settled on her father. 'Maddy, I'm here, honey. I'm right here. Stay with me now.' He had been holding her hand.

Damiano watched, transfixed, waiting, like everyone else around the bed that stood at the far end of the ICU in its own cocoon. The eye didn't leave Thomas Holmes's face where tears fell sloppily, dripping from his chin. Holmes lifted his daughter's hand and Damiano saw it. Madison was holding his hand as well!

'Do you see?' he whispered to Dr. Orr.

'She's tough, damn tough, Thomas. Stay with her and talk to her. She needs you.'

Holmes nodded, wiping tears from his chin. Damiano understood now why Holmes might have attacked Pauzé. If that were Luke lying on the bed, she would have gone at Pauzé's head, never mind his knees. Dr. Orr guided her out of the ICU.

She left the hospital determined and pumped. The case was complicated and she was tired without her boost from the Red Bulls, but she couldn't risk the caffeine shakes that Matte would catch. This case would not become political. No heads would roll because she'd close the file. Madison Holmes's face followed Damiano down the elevator. What was it about the eye? It took seconds for Damiano to figure what it was – it was strength, raw strength. As soon as she passed the die-hard smokers clustered at the front doors of the hospital's Pine Street entrance, a knifing wind cut into her rib cage. She dug her clenched fists into her pockets, tucked her head down and ran for her car. *Global warming, ha!* Everything seemed more depressing in November. She hated what awaited Quebecers: freezing rain, ice pellets and snow. Snow lovers were the worst. They encouraged the stuff.

A sudden sheet of freezing rain lashed the front window of the car. Damiano was struck by the meanness of nature and the misery she dealt with every day that spread like that rain. The wipers began their work but the right blade was already slipping over fast-forming ice. 'I really needed this now!' Pulling to the side of the road, she turned on her flashers. Damiano got out of the car, reached over and grabbed the wiper. She peeled off the ice with her fingertips, hopped back into the car and slammed the door behind her.

If Galt had anything, he would have called her, if just to ease himself out of her sights. Had Matte figured out that he was a paper detective and would more than likely never be a street detective with a lead? He was a good badge, a solver, but a second man. Galt was made for the street but he'd never be a lieutenant. Maybe there was some justice after all. As soon as she could see through the front windshield, she took off. She hated to contact Galt, but she had to know if he had made any progress with Pauzé's assault.

Galt didn't take her call because a few minutes earlier he had walked the campus quad and found the TA. Galt wasted no time with her. Her shirt was worn at the cuffs, and the brown sweater was balling. The young woman didn't appear to have come into money recently, but he figured he'd throw a scare into her. 'Ms?'

'Faigan.'

'You did say that you hadn't marked any papers from these four students, but…'

'I didn't. That hasn't changed,' she said defensively.

'This is a felony case, Ms Faigan.'

She sat up, leaning towards Galt.

'With a court order we could track your bank accounts and search your place in case you took cash, thinking you could hide that.'

'Go ahead! You'd be wasting your time.'

Galt drummed his fingers on her desk before he left. Once he was outside, he flipped open his phone and called Damiano.

'What is it, Detective Galt?'

'Pauzé. Got nowhere with the students. The TA didn't blink. Doesn't mean there wasn't a payoff.' He pressed the phone into his ear. 'You think it's connected to Holmes?' Galt deserved a 'B' for effort. He was persistent, but Damiano could see his act for what it was, an attempt to steer attention away from himself.

'I can't discuss the file with you.'

'Right, you want me for this, don't you Damiano?'

'Don't flatter yourself. My job, like yours, is finding bad guys. If you're one of them…'

That bitch will not cut me a break! 'Watch your back, Damiano.' Galt hung up and stalked off. He'd given her panties a good twist she wouldn't forget.

Damiano pulled the car over again and slammed on the brakes. Ice flew off the windshield and the car slid to a halt. *The jackass just threatened me!* She thought about reporting Galt and changed her mind. *You used your own kid! Now I really want you.*

Chapter Twenty-Seven

THE ROOM WAS STIFLING and dark. The courier gripped a black marker so hard that it split in two, and the broken plastic cut into his hands – blood trickled across his palms. *She didn't move when I kicked her. I checked her neck – she had no pulse. Damiano's playing me.*

His injured hands dropped to his sides. One rubbed against his pant leg and left a stain. The rest of the courier seemed stuck in place. A thought wrapped itself around his skull, compressing it like a vise. *If she recovers – and remembers my face....*

Had Detective Damiano been close by, she would have seen the panic etched on the courier's face.

Chapter Twenty-Eight

LOUISE MORIN, BEAUCHEMIN's wife, felt tension in the office soon after Madison Holmes arrived at the hospital's trauma center, but that was normal when a celebrity case ended up at the General. She asked how Holmes was doing, without noticing that the bulk of the tension was directed at *her*.

The head of Admin had hovered, waiting to pounce the second she asked that question. She pulled Louise from the room and whispered a little too loudly. 'The police have ordered me not to give you any information regarding Madison Holmes.'

'Are you serious, Gina?'

'I am sorry, Louise. Please don't go asking anyone else either. It'll be my neck,' Gina warned. 'I had to inform the others about this situation.' She seemed elated to be 'on the job.'

Colleagues – friends Louise had once thought – whispered in corners, a few glancing over at her. Louise wanted to shout, 'I had nothing to do with this terrible assault. Holmes was Claude's agent, but he'd never do something so inhuman! To even think that he...' The faces of her colleagues were titillated that suspicion had touched one of their own. Protesting the ridiculousness of such suspicion would only serve to widen the web of doubt, so she worked quietly. When the work day ended, she left alone.

The day of Claude's police interview, Louise couldn't bear to go straight home and deal with her husband so she went instead to her mother's. Bathing her mother, towelling her off and dressing her, preparing dinner for them both while attempting to coax a smile from her mother released some tension, but nowhere near all of it. Her mother's life was difficult and lonely. Sometimes Louise looked closely at the woman who had borne her, trying to find the mother she'd known. The onset of Alzheimer's had kicked the broken pieces of her past aside. That day though, her mother called her by name, and Louise had held her mother close. When the sitter arrived at nine, Louise left for home. *Mom still knows me.*

She paused a minute at her front door before turning the key. The only light was coming from Claude's sanctuary. The odor of wine struck her first.

Claude weaved his way out of the room, holding the wall with one hand. 'I could have used your help tonight! I needed you! Why didn't you head straight home? At least come see what the cops did to my room.'

Louise didn't move.

Claude didn't notice because he had already turned his back. 'Do you know how many times I called you today? Hey, are you coming?'

'Fourteen,' Louise called after him.

Claude stumbled back out to square off with Louise. 'That's all you have to say? Do you have any idea what I've been through today, the indignity of it all! This Detective Damiano went after me as if I were a nobody! Furthermore, she didn't believe a word I said. Don't ask me how I know that, I'm a lawyer – I know. Are you just going to stand there?'

'Claude, I'm tired, I've had a full day. I need a shower.'

'Well, I need to talk.'

'Can't it wait for twenty minutes?' Louise walked past him to the stairs and flipped a switch. 'I need a few minutes of quiet time.'

'You never even looked at the study.'

'It'll still be there when I get back.'

'I'll be here too – I'm not going anywhere either. I need another drink. By the way, I'm sorry about the Pinot Noir. I needed something good in my life today.'

When Louise was halfway up the stairs, he shouted after her, 'Why didn't you take at least one call?'

'Because I couldn't.'

'You knew I wanted to know about Holmes.'

Louise looked squarely down at Claude. 'The police ordered all Admin to watch me and make certain I know nothing about Holmes. They're treating *me* like a suspect. Do you understand now?'

'What?'

'You'll have to wait, Claude. I need to regain my sanity.'

Claude didn't say another word. He dropped into the nearest chair, and his head fell back against it. He was snoring like a drunk when she reappeared. Louise had an urge to leave him there, but she didn't. Instead she made strong coffee and woke him. 'Claude, we have to talk.'

'I have a splitting headache. And what's the point? You weren't here. You used to support me, Louise, and now you don't. What more is there to say?'

'That's why we have to talk. I'm thirteen years your junior – I'm not your mother. For the most part, you're still a little boy and everything revolves around you. Until Mom became ill, I didn't mind. You can be a charmer when it suits you. But Claude, I will not be part of tabloid tripe!'

'What's up with you? I'm the one who needs help.'

Louise quickly explained how she was made to feel at work.

'You can't blame me for that.'

'For God's sake, Claude, grow up!' Louise trembled with emotion. 'Before you began writing, we were a reasonably contented couple, better than most. You have anger issues, but dammit, Claude, who doesn't? You lost your father young, your mother made you feel you didn't measure up and then the firm turfed you. Why in heaven's name did you take up writing? You've done the research – you know how few writers get to see their work in print. How many of your friends are ten years into a book that will never be published – it's become a joke to them and a hobby. You were different. You were positive with the rejections. You accepted them and learned from them. Then this thing took hold of you and now obsesses you so that's all you think about. What was so different with Madison Holmes? She's just an agent. Why did her dismissal break you? You've had rejections before.'

Claude sat with his elbows on his knees holding his head. He was crying when he looked over at Louise. 'She believed in me. I had begun to believe in myself. Then she dumped me.'

'I've always believed in you.'

'Not the same.'

Louise held back her tears. 'Fine, Claude, I'll stand by you but spare me a soul-wrenching confession, if there is one. To do that I need to have some respect for you. If I ever learn that you assaulted Holmes, I'll leave you. Now, I'm going to bed.'

If Claude had felt Louise might be a willing accomplice, feeding him information, he saw he was sadly mistaken.

Chapter Twenty-Nine

MARA GRAHAM, SHAKEN as well by the recent events, had cut her run short and was back in time to see Damiano leaving. The woman was attractive, sure of herself. She hadn't bothered to check the street before driving away. Mara hadn't missed the Quebec plate. A sudden queasiness gripped her body. Perspiration from her run dried up. Tom had stayed on in Canada, Montreal he'd told her. Mara couldn't move. She couldn't deal with the drastic changes that had assailed their lives. When they were young, they had marathon fights, long and lingering make-ups, but trust throughout their marriage had been a grace appreciated like health until you lose it. They loved one another and adored their boys. Their team was strong.

When her legs lost their stiffness, she ran the short distance into the townhouse and found Tom in the solarium smoking a Cuban cigar. His father had given him a box that Tom hadn't touched because his father had lost his battle with the same cancer he was about to fight. Mara could recall his father, a tall, proud man puffing away saying, 'Don't let anyone think that dying has infringed on the simple pleasures of my life. The only thing missing is my Porsche. And my cigar arm out the window!'

Tom turned when he heard Mara.

'I was just thinking that your father was quite a character. Do you have an extra cigar?'

Tom reached into the box and handed her one, first lighting it for her. 'Sit yourself down.'

They puffed away in silence for a few minutes. 'Who was the woman?'

'Lieutenant Detective Toni Damiano.'

'From Quebec?'

'Yep.'

'For the Holmes assault?' Mara's hand trembled and she almost dropped the cigar. She inhaled deeply. She wanted Tom to talk to her. Hysteria never worked.

'Pretty woman. Montreal has pretty women. It's a fact you know. They have flair. Mom had flair – Dad told me more than once.'

'You must have passed the litmus test; you're still here.'

'Thanks for skipping the sermons. Why didn't I fly and come back with Martin? Why stay on in Montreal?'

'Would it have mattered?'

'Not then – not now. I could never have flown with Martin. I saw the betrayal coming, but I just couldn't get my head around it. Martin and

I were like brothers. We were doing well. The numbers were good. Why didn't he just have a mid-life affair? Instead, he chose to fuck me up the wazoo. My colleagues will know, my golf buddies, our mutual friends. Losing face is not for sissies. Money will be a problem after the year is up. The authors I have now might want to jump ship. I have no paddle and I might lose the canoe with it. You know what really sticks in my craw? Martin knew I had cancer. After you, he was my best friend and I confided in him. The shithead knew and he went ahead anyway and dumped me.'

'Tom, let's tackle one thing at a time.'

'The bullshit is simultaneous, Mara! You can't separate it. I can't put the goddamn cancer aside. This Detective Damiano took my prints and DNA and wants me to appear in a lineup. How does that hit you?'

'Why didn't you have David with you?'

'I called. David said he couldn't help me with that. We could delay, wait for a court order. Damn, delay? I have the first treatment in a few weeks.'

'Why you?'

'I was in Montreal when Holmes was attacked.'

Mara took a puff and blew the smoke out slowly. *Why didn't you just come home?* She wanted to scream.

'You heard me, right?'

'I can smoke and listen.'

'A lineup means they have a witness and, if Holmes recovers and remembers, they have a star witness. The cop didn't give up anything on her condition. The case has drawn a lot of scrutiny. There's pressure on the cops to nail someone for the attack.'

'Have a little faith, Tom. One month ago we were fine. We will be again.' She doubted her words.

'Mara, I was scared when Dad died, scared for me, I mean. I'd finally let that go, and look what happens.'

Mara put out her cigar. 'You shouldn't be smoking with cancer.'

'A lot of things shouldn't be but they are.'

'Do I have to worry, Tom?'

'On all fronts. That's my guess.'

Chapter Thirty

DETECTIVE GALT WAITED at home for his wife before he went on duty. When he heard the garage door opening, his throat worked, but it took a full minute for him to formulate what he wanted to say. Maureen was an investment advisor with a large company and made near double his salary. If the home search and herding the family into her car that night had brought her to the tipping point, what could he say? When he saw her, he figured she must have been crying in the car because her eyes were swollen and the whites shot through with red. 'I thought you might want to talk.'

'Why?' She lugged her briefcase and purse into the house past him. 'The kids are at soccer practice but they should be home any minute.'

'I had no warning about the other night. That bitch Damiano has it...'

'In for you? My God, Stephen, stop! Stop blaming everyone else. You're not a lieutenant because of some whatever – it's never your fault.'

'I haven't the time for your litany tonight.'

'I'm a cop's wife, so I learned more than I wanted to know about the police and their politics. Damiano couldn't have gotten a warrant just because you were one of Holmes's authors. So you did something, right?'

'You don't get it. She's...'

'Talk to me! What did you do? Let me guess. You went to Holmes's house to what, tell her off? Is that it? That sounds like you.'

'Will you be happy if she takes me down for the assault? You'll have a solid reason to leave me, won't you?'

'You need help, Stephen. It's never bothered me that you haven't made lieutenant. It's eaten away at *you* and us by extension.'

'The only goddamn help I need is Damiano off my back. She got warrants so easily for the Holmes file, and I couldn't get a single warrant for my assault on Pauzé. The boss told me I had no cause. He wouldn't order them. It's amazing what long legs and a good rack can do for you on the force!'

'Stephen.' Maureen's voice was soft, pleading.

Galt's anger cracked. 'Min, I might have screwed myself and Corey.'

'Corey? What does our son have to do with this?'

'When I got the blow-off from Holmes, Cory was home. I swore and kicked my chair over. I said I'd like to know if I was the only reject. You know our kid's a computer whiz, so...'

'Tell me you didn't ask Corey to hack into Holmes's PC.' Maureen's forehead creased and she began tapping her teeth with the side of her thumb. She whipped around and caught Galt with a wicked slap across his face that knocked him backwards. For a second, they were both shocked. 'You and your bloody books! No goddamn wonder Damiano has her sights on you. But Corey?' She raised her hand again, but Galt caught it.

'I didn't ask him, alright? He did it anyway.'

'He wanted you to notice him, you jackass! For the past three years, the books have swallowed you. Sex is the only good thing we have, and it's become confrontational and that's a disappointment too. I want you, no, I demand you call Damiano and tell her you're behind the hacking. Get Corey out of this.'

'Alright, alright!'

'Corey will not have a record – do you hear me, Stephen? I'm taking the kids to my parents while you sort this out.'

'Fuck, Maureen!'

'What? Call me tonight about Corey. It's not a threat – don't make it one.'

'I gotta get to work. I'm nowhere in my case and I can't see that I'll be able to close the damn thing either. It's all gone to hell!' Galt left the house quickly before his wife had a chance to say anything else. He thought of going back to the hospital to see Pauzé, but he was certain that whatever the kid knew was locked behind a deadbolt of fear. Yet that fear didn't translate to the four cheats or the TA or Professor Nagel. No one was about to implicate himself, and, without warrants, where could he go? He drove to Crémazie, spoke to no one and began to fill out the official report on the dates, time and details with a summary of the suspects involved and his interviews. He worked for an hour, checking his spelling. If he couldn't close the file – he wanted, at the least, to hand in a legible report. He checked his memos as well and glanced at other paperwork. He flipped open his phone and called Damiano. He had to make the call.

'Yes, Detective Galt.' Damiano made no mention of the threat.

'I've gotta come clean about something.'

'I know about the hacking – you knew the names of the rejected authors.'

'I blew up when I got Holmes's letter.'

'So…'

'My son was there, and he… I didn't know… put this on me… leave the kid out of it… he's fifteen. It's my shitload.'

Damiano thought of Luke and what he might do for her. Damiano hated do-gooders, didn't trust them. 'It's on you then. I'll straighten things out with Crime.' This shift bothered her.

'I owe you.'

'You're in this knee-deep, Detective.'

'The hacking is nothing. You have no proof.'

Damiano laughed. The *cojones!* 'Accumulation, Detective.'

Chapter Thirty-One

DAMIANO WAS TRYING to stomach the fact that she had just tampered with evidence as she sat, hands clenched on the wheel, trapped in a mess of traffic that wasn't moving. Matte's call broke some of that tension.

'We have the second trojan! You won't believe who it is.'

'Spare me the guessing.'

'Our seventy-four-year-old Yvette Ranger, not her, actually, her son Michel. He lives in L.A. and does freelance work for the Gates Corporation. I drove back to Pointe-Claire, verified that Michel has not been in Montreal for the past five months. He was in a business meeting the day of the attack. Three colleagues verified that, but I had it out with Ranger. Know what she said?'

'Facts!'

Matte read from his notes. 'Detective, the only crime I plead guilty to is curiosity. Michel wouldn't disclose the names of the authors, but knowing I wasn't being cast aside because I'm an old biddy made me feel better. There are no age limits on pride.'

'Or stupidity, I suppose. You make the call, Pierre.'

'We move on.'

'Agreed. I'm driving back to the office.'

'See you there.'

Damiano had driven half a block in three minutes. Sherbrooke Street was no better than St. Catherine. She didn't see she'd fare any better on de Maisonneuve Boulevard, so she fumed and concentrated on her favorite swear words. Then she did her best to understand authors. *They write with hope and desperation, selling themselves. If my case goes bad, I can blame the system, the witnesses or Matte, whatever. Writers expose themselves, and publishers can turn their work aside with a simple form letter – not a good fit for us – you're not good enough! Anything can happen, I suppose. People have shot one another over a parking space. Graham's rejection was brutal.*

Damiano suddenly thought of Luke's teacher and began rifling through her notes for the number. *What the hell did I do with it?* The traffic suddenly moved and Damiano with it. When she finally turned into her parking space, she saw Matte had just arrived. The teacher's number was forgotten.

As they rode the elevator, their heads dropped with the weight of unrelenting pressure and the oddity of too many good suspects. 'What about a profile?' Matte asked before they reached their floor.

'Good idea. I'll call Angela Marino later. Anything on the street searches?'

'Nothing yet.'

'Holmes is conscious and recognized her father. As soon as the throat tube is taken out, we'll take hospital shifts. She's our best hope. If this news leaks to the press, Holmes is extremely vulnerable. Let's go with what we know.'

Matte began: 'We have a cold-blooded, deliberate murderer – it's a fluke Holmes survived –a premeditator, a planner, an assailant who wears a disguise, someone with a sense of irony who chooses a manuscript as a weapon, an angry, revengeful perp who plans his/her getaway. The question is why?'

'That's good, Pierre.'

'Why? We know it's anger and revenge, but I feel the assailant had a backlog of these emotions. Holmes paid the price for past grievances. We have one angry bastard who meant to get even and took it out on her. That's my take. I'm not God. Who fits our profile?' Matte asked, deferring to Damiano.

'Galt, Beauchemin, Graham and Pauzé.'

'What about Angela Marino?'

'We can add to that list. Four is already too many!' The phone rang.

'Detective Damiano?'

'Yes.'

'Officer Picher. I have a kid who saw a man throwing dirt over his sneakers and stepping on them in the lane at the top of Beaubien. The kid thought it was *weird, man,* his words. Thought it was ketchup.'

'You have him with you?'

'Sure do.'

'Call his parents. We need one of them with him. Get the kid with a parent down to the division asap. Leave the rest of the questions to us. I don't want him spooked or so greedy for attention he'll exaggerate. How old is the kid?'

'Just a sec – he's twelve.'

'Good work! How come the kid was not in school?'

'Latchkey who played hooky.'

'The mother will be pissed. Just get them to us.'

'Soon as I pick them up.'

'Tape the area in the lane. I'll have Crime down there for samples. Blood is five times denser than water. It would take weeks for the rain and dirt to filter it out. Crime might find Holmes's blood. Call another officer –

I don't want the site unprotected.'

The phone was on speaker. 'What do you think, Pierre?'

'Good pickup. If Crime finds Holmes's blood, then the kid saw our assailant. Hope he saw more than the bloody shoes.'

Chapter Thirty-two

DAMIANO STILL HAD the call on speaker and punched in Tracey Doyle's mother, Angela Marino.

'Monette, Gravel, Pingitore & Marino.' The voice was all business, almost dour.

'Angela Marino.'

'Angela Marino is in a meeting. May I ask who's calling?'

'Detective Damiano of Major Crimes.'

'Oh. Well…'

'Well, I think you had better interrupt her meeting.'

There was a pause.

'Excuse me?'

'Please hold the line.'

'It's like getting through to the Pope.' Damiano flexed her fingers, frowning.

'How dare you ambush my daughter?' the strident voice jumped out at Damiano. 'I'll have you know I'm considering legal action.'

'I wish you good luck with that, Mrs. Marino. Actually, I'm calling you for an interview. We can…'

'What? This is outrageous! I'm very busy.'

'We can meet you at your office or down at Place Versailles.' While Marino was gathering more steam, Damiano continued. 'This is an attempted murder investigation, and we are interviewing anyone connected with Ms Holmes. I'm certain you are familiar with police protocol.'

'I never met the woman and I haven't time to waste. My daughter informed me you taped her and…'

Damiano cut Marino off. 'With her permission, also on tape. Now where would you like to meet? That's the only option I can offer you.'

'I work late.'

'As do I.'

'Nine o'clock at my office.'

'Good.' Damiano nodded in relief as she cut off. 'Made it to first base without injury.'

'Do we order in again?' Matte asked.

'No choice. Call Schwartz's. I feel like something heavy and greasy.'

'They don't deliver and you know it's cash only.'

'You're a detective in Major Crimes – you can pull some strings, like a COD for the cabbie and the smoked meat, fries and cokes.'

'That's a money bundle.'

'Not if we split it.'

'I'll do my best.'

'I hope the kid gets here soon. I'm going to take a quick shower and use my last clean shirt.'

'Do you want me to take that interview?'

'Do you have kids, Pierre?'

'We don't. You have to be strong as a couple before you think of children. We're not there.'

'I'd better take it – thanks to Luke – I know their lies and tricks.' Damiano rushed through her shower and got back into her clothes. Her mind raced. If Crime found Holmes's blood in the lane, then the kid saw the assailant. That one detail linked Holmes to the assailant, the man in the lane. Kids had great recall, but they had little interest in adults. She fought to resist assumptions. She couldn't rely on stupid. Stupid got her nowhere. Matte had locked Coupal's office and was gone when she got back. 'What the…?' Had he left to meet the kid? She hurried across the office, passing three badges working on files.

Matte was running up the stairs with a brown bag, and she smelled smoked meat. 'You did it!' She rarely saw Matte smile – he looked like a kid himself.

'A friend lives on rue St-Dominique, and I gave him tickets to a Habs game a week ago. My father still gives me tickets he knows I won't ever use. Anyway, Jean's quick behind the wheel and voilà!'

Damiano grabbed the bag and mumbled, 'I'm impressed. You're not a Habs fan though? They're going nowhere this year.'

'I'm not. That's why I handed off the tickets.'

When they reached the office and had locked the door, Damiano tore open the bag and smelled the familiar aroma that had seduced Montrealers for generations. They ate in silence like homeless men at a free Christmas dinner. The small office reeked of fries and Schwartz's smoked meat. 'I should have showered *after* this mess.' She saw that Matte looked no worse for guzzling the grease.

He caught her scrutiny. 'You could take a lesson.'

'Food's gotta be messy to really enjoy it.'

'Your looks carry you past the worst of it. Even with mustard on your bottom lip and meat caught between your front teeth, you still look good.'

Damiano blushed and swiped her lip.

Damiano reached for her purse, took out $30 and offered the money to Matte. 'My treat.'

'Thanks!'

'Sometimes I wonder how hard it is for you on the job.'

'No harder than it is for a woman.' Matte wanted to move on. 'Let's get this cleaned up before the kid gets here.' They waited thirty-one minutes. 'We can't miss the Marino meeting.'

Damiano frowned and checked her watch. Finally, the call came in. 'You downstairs?'

'Yes, Detective.'

'Wait there. We're coming down to meet you.'

Mathieu Roy didn't look twelve. Damiano learned from his mother the little bugger had just turned eleven. The detectives made the introductions and led Mme Roy and Mathieu up to the interview room. 'Thank you for coming.'

'Can you give me any help with this boy? Imagine ducking school at eleven? His father's not around to help.'

'Mme Roy, this is Major Crimes.'

'See, Mom, I told you. The cops need my help,' the boy boasted.

Mathieu's mother fidgeted and rubbed her eyes. 'I have enough with two jobs and trying to keep my boy in school. I do not want Mathieu to testify. I will not put us at risk. My boy's a handful, but he's mine and I love him. Our life is hard enough.'

The boy crouched in the embarrassment all kids feel about their parents at one time or another. He'd rather be there alone. Beneath large unblinking dark blue eyes, Mathieu had two big, perfect white front teeth, almost too large for his mouth. A thin scar ran across his bottom lip. He wore little boy clothes from Wal-Mart.

'May I ask Mathieu a few questions?'

'Yes, if he can help, but it'll go no further than this room.'

'Mathieu, just tell me very slowly what you saw in the lane that day.'

Mathieu was raring to go. 'It was a shitty day…'

'Mathieu, I've asked you not to swear!'

'Let's go from there, Mathieu.'

'Everybody was rushing 'cause it was cold and windy. I wasn't rushing 'cause I had nowhere to go.'

'You should have been in school!'

'Mom! Anyway, I see this guy at the top of the lane, he's kneeling on one knee. I thought he found something, but he was scooping up dirt and rubbing it on his sneakers. Then he rubbed the dirt in some more with his feet, like with one sneaker on top of the other. He was wearing shades and there was no sun. When he got up, he hurried like everyone else, and

I followed him. He went into the métro. Couldn't follow him there 'cause I had no money.'

'That's good detective work, Mathieu.'

The kid's face beamed.

'What did he look like?'

'He had on a wool hat, pulled down low. It almost touched the shades. That was weird, right. There was no sun. He had on a heavy, dark green jacket and the collar was pulled up. He had black pants and sneakers.'

'Did he see you?'

'Nah, I'm not stupid.'

'How old do you think he was?'

'With all that shit on…'

'Mathieu!'

'With all that stuff on – I don't know, like old.'

'Twenty?'

'Older, I think.'

'Like thirty?'

'That's old, right?'

'Was he tall?'

'Kinda, I don't know. I saw him mostly kneeling down.'

'When he passed people heading to the métro, was he taller?'

'I was looking at him, not other people.'

'Do you think you might be able to recognize him again?'

'Sure, from the side.'

'Anything about his face you remember?'

The kid thought.

'Don't make anything up. I need the truth. You're doing a great job.'

'Yeah, he had some snot dripping from his nose. I saw that! Is that good?'

Even Mathieu's mother smiled through her nervousness.

'Would it be alright if Mathieu came back here to look at some photos, Mme Roy?'

'Yes, as long as it's in this room and not in a courtroom.'

'Mathieu. You have the eye of a detective – that's the truth.'

He smiled over at his mother while rubbing both knees.

'To have my job, or Detective Matte's, you need an education. You can't skip school. We need smart people like you on the force.'

Mathieu listened to every word and nodded. 'You really think I could be a detective?'

'A very good one,' Damiano said. 'Here's my card and private number.'

Mathieu's eyes grew even bigger.

'If you think of anything else, call me, but don't show this card to anyone else. Can I trust you with that?'

'I swear. No one will see this card. I wanna be a detective. It's really cool.'

'How come you speak such good English?'

'My dad – he was Irish.' He took his mother's hand when they left.

'We need proper photos of Beauchemin, Galt and Pauzé in jackets and caps and shades. Set up a six pack photo spread. The mother won't consent to a lineup, and Pauzé can't stand. This isn't a door, but it is a crack.'

'We just need their photos. I can Photoshop the rest of it.'

'Really?'

'Really. Get photos from the SAAQ—the license bureau—because our 'spects don't have records. You have Graham's.'

'That'll save us both time.' Damiano began going through her purse and found the teacher's number. 'Pierre, excuse me for a minute. I have to make a private call.' It wasn't even a school night, but what could she do? 'Ms Barrett?'

'Yes, forgive the noise. I have a husband and three wild kids.' The voice was lively and friendly.

'I apologize for calling on a weekend, but I have no other option. I'm Luke Shea's mother, Detective Damiano. Luke really wanted me to call about his progress.' She felt as though she were back in Principal Clark's office. 'This is my only free minute.'

'I'm very impressed with his grades. He's a great kid who's very proud of you. He talks about you often. He calls you the lieutenant. I don't get that from my kids. He'd never tell you, of course.'

'Tell him I called. He's promised a 90% this term.'

'Sometimes, they grow up overnight. I'll be sure he knows you called.'

'Thanks!' For a few seconds, the tension of the case left Damiano, and she sat, enjoying the enveloping warmth a child could bring to a mother. It didn't last because she spotted Matte outside pointing to his watch.

Chapter Thirty-Three

DETECTIVE MATTE CAUTIONED Damiano in the car as they drove to one of the scenic streets in Montreal, McGill College Avenue, named for the university. The school's ancient Roddick Gates stood at the north end of the street, and Place Ville Marie Plaza at the south end. 'We have reins on this interview. She has contacts that can take our badges.'

'Are you that nervous?'

'I like my job.'

'At the outset, I said there was a professional smell to the assault.'

'The other 'spects are still looking good.' Matte turned north on McGill College Avenue and stopped beside the "Illuminated Crowd" sculpture – *La Foule Illuminée*, and looked at Maison Astral, the office building where Marino worked. 'You have to make the bucks to have your office here. High class stuff!'

'Stop being so impressed. If she *is* "connected," where do you think the money came from? Where the hell do we park? Know what? Pull a U-turn and park in front of the building. Leave the flashers and hazards on and leave our cards. Do we still have that "Urgence" card?'

'In the glove compartment.'

She found it and slapped it on the dash. 'Let's do this!' Damiano adjusted her jacket and shirt as they entered the impressive office tower at 1800 McGill College. They found Marino's law firm listed on the wall directory. When they saw the foyer door was open, they walked through and were met immediately by security. Damiano flashed her badge. 'We have an appointment with Angela Marino.'

'Suite 1400, 14th floor. Do you need assistance?'

'We'll manage.' When the elevator door closed, Damiano looked at Matte. 'I'd like to tear a strip off this woman. I haven't met her and already I can't stand her.'

"I don't want to lose my badge because of your temper!'

'Take it easy. I'm just blowing off steam.' When they left the elevators even the hallway was impressive and decorated in muted tones. When they reached the door of the law firm they found no buzzer or knocker, so Damiano reached for the doorknob, opened the door and walked in. The receptionist's elegant poplar desk was unoccupied. Damiano knew fine wood, something she'd learned from her father. For an uneasy moment, they stood staring down a short hall. *To hell with this!* She spoke loudly, 'Detectives Damiano and Matte!'

'Coming!'

They waited. Damiano began to fume. She knew Marino was playing them by stalling. Both detectives were taken aback when Marino appeared. She was tall – she was stunning! Both women took stock of one another and mentally took a step back.

'I haven't stopped all day. I gather it's been the same for you. Follow me.'

They did, and once they were inside the spacious office Marino pointed to two soft pale green leather chairs. She sat behind a massive oak desk, pushed her chair back and crossed her legs. 'So?'

'I won't bother asking where you were the morning of the attack, I…'

'I'd hope not, regardless of what my daughter might have said.'

'Why did you want your daughter to change agents when she already…'

'I want the big time for her. Holmes was just lucky like Tracey – no skill involved on either side.'

'I don't appreciate being interrupted. I am interested in knowing how you would have had the contract broken?'

Marino held out a long slender hand and appeared to study her nail polish. 'Not by the brutal beating of an adversary, I can assure you. I specialize in contract law. On that front, I have the skills to break any legal document. This assault has not pleased me at all. The fans won't let my daughter leave Holmes – the emails are multiplying by the hour. Tracey and Madison are joined at the hip now.'

'The assault was a botched murder attempt. Had that worked out, your daughter would have been free.'

'Are you implying my hand is behind this assault, Detective Damiano?'

'I stick to facts, Ms Marino. Had you started on the paperwork to break their contract?'

'My daughter argued with me and left. She'd need my help sooner or later. She always has in the past.'

'So you hadn't?'

'No, I hadn't.'

'You wanted your daughter with a big-time agent, but you never began the paperwork.'

'If you're insinuating that I…'

'Power people never dirty their hands – they hire out.'

Marino rose. 'The interview is over!' She walked to the door and opened it.

Damiano and Matte rose as well. 'That was just another fact you already know, Ms Marino.'

'Little badges, little games – all sub-par.'

'Thank you for your time, Ms Marino.'

Marino slammed the door behind them. Matte didn't say a word until they reached the elevator. 'That went well.'

Damiano laughed half-heartedly.

Angela Marino made two calls. The first was to Tracey. 'Whatever you want to do with your life when this affair is done will be your decision. I won't interfere. Now though, I want you home. We need to show a united front. I'm asking you, Tracey, as your mother.'

The second call was more important. Marino used a throwaway for that call. Better than most, she knew that trails, electronic or paper, all led back to the source.

Chapter Thirty-Four

As Damiano and Matte headed back to the office, Damiano felt her nerves tearing, one after another. She wasn't a good wife or mother. She felt both roles were subservient, and she wasn't going to use up her life waiting for Jeff to get home, to listen attentively to his day. It was nauseating to her that women slipped so easily into support roles. She had chosen to make things happen in her life and she was failing at that too. Four suspects! What was she missing? Something was off. It was there, but just beyond her grasp. Was the profile off? Had Matte made one of his rare mistakes? 'Pierre, step on it!'

'Take it easy. We'll be at the office in a few minutes. I know you figured you'd have this case wrapped up in a few days. But this is one tough bitch of a case, pardon my language. Accept it.'

'Don't you feel that there's something wrong? That we've missed something?'

'That's always a possibility, but I think our perp is in our circle. I'm waiting for the slipup. You have no patience.'

'I have no patience with failure.'

'We are nowhere near failure.' He jerked the car into the parking. Damiano grabbed the dash. 'Alright, you made your point. We have a chance. Patience, right?' She was out of the car and hurrying toward the cop entrance, but Matte caught up to her.

'Don't.'

'What?'

'Just don't.' Matte headed to the office.

Damiano made a beeline to her locker and drained the two miniature bottles of vodka she kept on reserve. Damn Matte. She had to come down. Mouthwash would be too obvious to Matte, so she grabbed a stale O'Henry and almost broke a tooth with the first chunk. The vodka fell like fire in her gut. She chewed hard and fast before she returned to the office.

Matte was studying their wall charts when she got there.

'The perp is somewhere in this widened group.'

'Mr. Detail!'

'Now that you've been to your locker, I take it you're all set now,' he said sarcastically.

'Don't take that tone with me. I was hungry. Is that a crime now?'

'Huh!' He turned back to the board. 'I've included Marino, Holmes and Aubin in the circle with the other four to see them all with fresh eyes.'

'Good. Let's not argue. I could easily rip into *you*, but I don't have the time to indulge in that kind of fun.'

'Forget what I said. Let's get to work. First though, get rid of that bar. What is it, a year old? The chocolate's gray. Here.' He pulled out a stick of Juicy Fruit gum.

'You are so predictable, Pierre.'

'Well, your mood swings quickly become tedious and familiar.'

'Well said, but enough!' Damiano scrutinized the board. 'There's something we've…'

'Detective, stop talking and start thinking…' It was rare that Damiano allowed Pierre the last word. It felt good.

Chapter Thirty-Five

DETECTIVE DAMIANO WAS busy with her suspect charts. She was assessing the anger level of her suspects when Chief Richard Donat charged into her office. He threw the door open so violently it smashed against the glass wall, almost shattering it. 'What the hell happened?'

Damiano thought Marino must have called him. 'Sir, we treated Angela Marino…'

'What? This!' He threw a copy of the *National Enquirer* on top of her pile of papers, and then tossed three more in the air. 'Open some windows! The room stinks of smoked meat!'

Damiano picked up the tabloid and read one of the front page headlines: *Celebrity Agent Madison Holmes conscious – expected to make full recovery!* On page two, the lead story went on to say her father was by her side. Damiano wanted to tear the rag apart. She walked stiffly and opened the only two windows. 'What the HELL!' Managing to swallow the bile in her throat, along with the gum, she tossed the rag against her board. 'I had this locked down, Boss. The doctors, nurses, Admin, orderlies, my men – I can't believe this!'

'Fucking believe it! Murderers or would-be murderers, like this prick, want to keep things simple. This cluster-fuck, 'cause that's what this is, has forced his hand and added another base to the field. The media will go at me because you haven't closed the book. Holmes is back in danger, and you are nowhere with your, your what?'

'Still four.' She didn't dare admit the entire list.

'Four 'spects. Holy Jesus! I could throw you to the wolves; you know that, don't you?'

Damiano was riding on four hours of interrupted sleep, still furious and shocked at the leak. 'Let me talk to the media.' Her voice was hard, controlled and challenging. 'I'll find the leak. I'll protect Holmes. I will close the file. You have my badge on that.' She spoke from a safe distance in case Donat could smell the vodka.

'And I *will* take it. From now on, you deal with the fucking heat of this file.'

Detective Matte waited for a pause in the tirade before he entered the office. He had the photos.

The boss grabbed them. 'What the hell are these?'

'Sir, Crime has a match for Holmes's blood found in the lane. We have an eleven-year-old eyewitness.'

The chief studied the photos. 'Why are we wasting time with these? These guys look the same to me in photos. This is a special file. I want a lineup. I want this kid to see these guys up front.'

Matte tried to explain about the boy's mother and Pauzé who was hospitalized.

'Damiano, use the charm and tiger skills I've heard about and get the kid to a lineup. Run Galt, Graham and Beauchemin in a lineup. We'll include some of our officers in it too. Aim for elimination. If that fails, use the Pauzé photo. What about alibis – have you broken any of them?'

Damiano had regained her composure. 'All three of them were alone with no corroborating witness.'

'Marino?'

'You've handcuffed me with her. Marino gave up nothing – we all know she could have had it done.'

'You believe she's that stupid – I never took her for stupid.' Donat's phone rang. 'What time? Take notes and numbers. Shoot them to Damiano.'

'You have a press conference in the interview room in 20 minutes.' He left and slammed the door.

Damiano bent down to pick up the magazines Donat had tossed.

Matte leaned down and stopped her. 'I got them, and I'm sorry.'

'Pierre, find the leak. If it was Beauchemin's wife, Louise Morin, I'm charging her with obstruction. Whoever leaked this will be charged. I need a few minutes to prepare for the media. I hate politics! Fielding questions and offering nothing up – what a waste. Holmes has to be moved immediately.'

'Catch your breath. I'll leave you alone to prepare and I'll get to work.'

She made a few notes before she ran to her locker to freshen up. The first thing she did was to grab her pumps. Her hands smelled of meat. In the bathroom, she splashed water on her face, washed her hands and re-applied her makeup. Lastly she brushed her teeth. Five minutes later, she went to meet the media.

As soon as they saw Damiano enter the interview room, the TV cameras began rolling. Members of the press pushed forward, shoving their microphones as close as they could get to her. Damiano smiled stiffly. A podium and microphone had been set up for her. Placing her hands on either side of the podium, she waited for the press to be seated, but they all chose to stand, edging one another for the top ring in front of Damiano. She wasted no time. 'Good evening! I'm Lieutenant-Detective Toni Damiano, lead on the Madison Holmes case. At present, the investigation is on-going. Ms Holmes is well protected and her health is improving,' Damiano paused, 'as the media has reported. We have made good progress with the case. I will keep you informed of any major development. I will take three questions.'

There was shoving and pushing and hands thrust in Damiano's direction. She chose a short attractive Asian woman who had caught her attention.

'Yes?'

'Detective Damiano, Mina Zin, *National Enquirer*. We broke the news of Ms Holmes's condition. We all know what 48 hours means in such an investigation.'

The snitch was after money. There might be an electronic trail. 'Ms Zin, your question?'

'Forty-eight hours have passed. Do you feel an arrest might have been lost?'

'Forty-eight hours makes for good TV. With a complex file like this one, we take the time we need for a solid investigation. Nothing has been lost.' Damiano looked past Zin, but didn't miss her scowl. 'Yes?' She chose a pie-faced male with a honker and a small mouth.

'Art Shooey, *The Globe & Mail*. Are you at present interrogating persons of interest?'

'Yes, we are.' Damiano looked away again to a pale thin-faced male who wore the smallest glasses she'd ever seen. 'Yes?'

'Maurice Côté, *La Presse*. Quand prévoyez-vous faire une arrestation?'

'Bientôt, Monsieur Côté. We do expect to make an arrest soon. You will be informed. Thank you for coming.'

'But…?'

'One more question, please!'

But Damiano left the room. There were tentative steps towards her, but most stopped. Mina Zin's didn't. Tapping Damiano on the shoulder, she forced her card into her hand and left. For the others, Damiano's height and presence alone intimidated most people, even the vultures, she discovered. She spied the boss at the end of the hall.

'Neatly diced and sliced, Damiano! Go get me the arrest.' His voice, as usual, vibrated with impatience.

Damiano was pumped. Good work and a little vodka took the edge off. Her phone rang as she hurried back to Matte. 'Hi Luke! I can't. . .'

'Yada, yada, Mom. Ms Barrett called me at home!'

'I called her.'

'Cool. Thanks.'

'Love ya, my boy.'

'Yada, yada.' Luke knew when to let go. He threw the phone across the bed. He was on a timer when they spoke and he hated that. He threw himself on the bed and bounced once.

Matte was on the phone when she walked into the office. 'How'd it go?'

'Better than I'd anticipated. The leak went to the *National Enquirer*. I want that paid snitch.'

'We're set for the lineup. Tomorrow at 3:00 pm. Then, I may have overstepped, but I called Mathieu's mother and talked her into bringing him to Crémazie. I worked her.'

She punched his right shoulder. 'Way to go, Pierre.'

'Figured you want to make the call to Galt, Graham and Beauchemin yourself. Pauzé is out of surgery. I can bring the hat and jacket to the hospital if we need them after the lineup.'

'We are in sync – only took nine years!' Damiano found Galt's number and made the call. 'Detective Galt, Damiano.'

'What now?'

'I request that you present yourself at Crémazie tomorrow at 2:30 pm. Detective Matte and I will meet you.'

'Why?'

'Just be there, Detective. Don't make this more unpleasant than it already is.'

'With my rep?'

'If you feel you need a rep, by all means, avail yourself of one.'

'Fine.' Galt slammed down the phone.

Damiano called Beauchemin. His wife answered. 'Detective Damiano. I must speak with Monsieur Beauchemin.'

'Just a minute,' her voice was weary and strained.

Damiano waited for a full minute.

'Claude Beauchemin.'

'Detective Damiano, Monsieur Beauchemin. I request that you present yourself at the Crémazie Division at 2:30 pm tomorrow. Detective Matte and I will meet you at the front entrance.'

Beauchemin's mouth went dry. His armpits flooded with a sudden sweat. 'Is this an arrest?' he croaked.

Damiano sensed his panic.

'I'll have a lawyer with me.' He recovered quickly and shot back.

'As you wish.' Damiano hung up. Matte was energized, she could see that. 'Imagine if…!'

Graham was an easy call. He'd be there. He'd given his word.

'Be back here tomorrow at seven. I want the snitch!' She had the card of the reporter who broke the story. Damiano would go after her.

'No problem, and I do too.' he agreed. He had all the details down pat. Matte knew that Damiano was different. She held all the strings – she had vision.

Chapter Thirty-six

THE MINUTE DAMIANO was inside her door, she began to peel off her clothes. She laid them on the bed in Luke's bedroom and went through the pockets before hanging them up. She found Zin's card and snapped it between her fingers. It had Mina Zin's private cell number. Damiano wanted the snitch. She had to think before she made the call.

Padding down the hall, she stepped into a hot shower, allowing the spray to loosen her lower back. A shower washed the day off and gave her time to reassess things with a clear mind. Zin? She thought of a counter-offer to grab their informant. When the tips of her fingers began to pucker, she towelled off and blow-dried her hair. Zin? For all she knew, the reporter might have left the city.

Wine, she needed a good glass of wine and she half cursed the cigarettes she'd given up eight years ago. She uncorked the white Alsace Pinot that she'd been saving, and stood while drinking the first glass. She took the second to her small desk in Luke's bedroom, took a sip and dialed the number.

'Mina Zin, *National Enquirer*, leave a hot tip and I'll get back to you.'

Shit! 'Ms Zin, Lieutenant-Detective Toni Damiano. We met at the media meeting earlier today.' The only thing hot about her message was implication. A charley horse in Damiano's left calf struck like a bolt of lightning. She got to her feet, trying not to scream, while bending down and rubbing her calf with both hands. When that didn't help much, she stood on that foot and spread her feet. She hopped around and went back to rubbing. The spasm began to ease. *I really need this!*

Her phone rang and she hobbled over to it. 'Yes?'

'Mina Zin. You called. You know, Detective, I can't...'

'Reveal your source, I know. What if I made you a counter-offer? You live for the media, but in a sense we both work with scum, cowards and perps. I can't offer you an exclusive on the arrest, but I will offer you a co-exclusive with the Montreal media.'

'I'm listening.'

'This case will sell more than one issue. And you'll have the co-exclusive report.'

'I can't give up the name.'

'How much was the payout?'

'We never disclose the payout, if any.'

'If you want information from me – I need an approximate. Less than $50,000?'

'Yes. That's all I can say. I want to keep my job.'

'Was it hospital staff – just a yes or no?'

'A first on the package, right? No payout to you?'

'Yes, and of course not.'

'Not hospital staff.'

'All inclusive – physicians, nurses, orderlies and Admin?'

'I've spoken English all my life, Detective.'

'No offence intended. I want to be clear.'

'Got it.'

Damiano hesitated. 'My guys?'

Zin was silent.

'Compromising a victim, obstructing an investigation and throwing away a decent career for less than fifty grand!' Damiano breathed heavily. She felt personally betrayed and saddened. 'How was the payout made?'

'Electronically – leaves a trail. You're dealing with an amateur. You shouldn't be so surprised, Detective. I'm not anymore. You rake up the scum. Mine stay just under the waterline while they destroy best friends, or family members. Words are weapons.'

'What does it do to you?'

'I'm a cynic and still single – but I'm good at what I do. And you?'

'I'm pretty raw.'

'I saw that first-hand, Detective.'

'I believe in justice.'

'And you think you arrive at that?'

'No, but I bring the scum to the surface.'

'Good to hear there's still some faith out there. Some scum carry badges. It's not a first.'

'It is for me.'

'We have a deal, then.'

'You have my word. I have the tape of this conversation too,' Damiano said.

'Ah. You don't take chances.'

'Not in my business.'

'I'll be in touch.'

'I know you will,' Damiano replied.

Damiano threw herself on Luke's bed and closed her eyes. *Dammit to hell! It couldn't have been Galt. It's not Matte – it can't be Pierre.* She raised her leg and rubbed her calf – it was as sore as her heart. *No, it wasn't Matte.* She had the portable with her and she called him.

'What's up?'

'The snitch is one of ours.'

Matte took a moment. 'That's a blow.'

Damiano gave him what she had. 'I think we're looking at the hospital surveillance.'

'I'll alert Crime and they'll begin mopping their phones.'

'A police suspect and cop snitch – good PR. The chief will be pissed.'

'Not our problem, Toni.'

'Toni?' she laughed. 'Dropped my title, did you, Pierre?'

'Gotcha! Get some real sleep. I'll see you tomorrow.'

Damiano was wound up like the neck of a wire hanger. She knew what relief would level her out. Jeff? He'd be over in a flash. Getting rid of him after the nasty would be complicated, and she'd be tight with guilt pushing him out the door. Tomorrow was another tense day, so Jeff couldn't stay. Solo acts were so much simpler. They were fast, and there were no post-coital arguments. The scented lavender candle came out first, the Bose Wave system second, Shirley Horne third, singing 'Don't Forget Me,' and finally, Damiano having little work to get sounds as low as Shirley's, even after Horne had done her thing. Damiano finally fell asleep admiring her one contemporary graphic. At least it had straight lines.

Chapter Thirty-seven

THE NIGHT CLAUDE BEAUCHEMIN received the call to present himself at the Crémazie Division, he began to drink heavily. Talk between Louise and Claude had turned sour since she had called his writing an obsession. He started a new book, non-fiction, and began purposely working nights to avoid her. Louise relented and looked in on him around midnight. 'Claude, you don't want a migraine tomorrow. Why don't you go to bed? If you want me to go with you, I will.'

'No thank you. You might break into one of your sermons.'

Claude Beauchemin and his wife Louise slept in separate rooms that Saturday night. Sunday morning, Louise made poached eggs on brown toast with Canadian bacon and cottage cheese. Claude would need something substantial to fortify himself. The coffee was brewed. She poured herself a cup and waited. With no Sunday *Gazette*, she picked up Saturday's *Globe & Mail* and tried to read. What was he doing? It was well after nine. Should she go up and check on him? She paused and stared into the den, what she could see of it. *What had happened to them? Where was the anger in Claude coming from – where would it end. Surely, he hadn't...*

Louise went to the front door and opened it. A dry blast of wind caught her robe and turned her stiff with cold. Shivering, she closed it. At least there was no rain or freezing rain. As she turned, she caught sight of Claude. She hadn't heard him and he was on the bottom stair. 'You should eat breakfast, Claude.'

Claude swayed before he fell face down on the carpet.

Louise ran to him. He was semi-conscious and struggling to breathe. 'Oh, my God! Claude! Claude!' She scrambled to a phone and called 9-1-1. Her words were a garbled scream.

The responder spoke slowly and with authority. 'Slowly repeat what you said.'

Louise rubbed her mouth and tried again. 'My husband is having a heart attack.' Her voice had risen to a scream with the last two words.

'I have your address. Urgence Santé will be there shortly. Is your husband breathing?'

'I don't know, I don't know!'

'Keep the phone in your hand and go to him and see if he is.'

Louise put the receiver down and rolled Claude onto his back. She put a shaky hand under his nose. 'Yes, yes, he is.'

'Good. Help is on the way.'

Louise stayed on her knees, rocking back and forth. Six minutes later, Claude was hoisted onto a gurney, wheeled from the house and rushed to the Montreal General. Louise went with him. The paramedics worked on Claude, bagged him, took his vitals, and then sat back. Louise sat as quiet as a stone until she remembered she hadn't taken the police card. Detective Damiano would have to be called. Louise didn't want police cars at her front door. *How can I even be thinking of that now?*

When they reached the hospital's emergency department, Claude didn't have to endure the long Quebec wait that might turn into a day. Cardiac arrests received immediate attention. Louise sat anxiously in the waiting room. She didn't have to wait long.

'Ms Morin?'

'Yes.'

'The prelims show no sign of cardiac arrest.'

'Thank God! I'm so relieved. What happened?'

'In layman's terms, your husband suffered a panic attack. Has he been under stress?'

'A great deal of stress.'

'I've written a 'script for Valium – he might not need those. Tell him to take it easy. Actually, you can come and take him home.'

Louise walked to Claude tentatively. 'You're fine, Claude. No heart attack. Let's go home.'

Claude's face was chalky. 'Do you think I still have to show up at Crémazie? I thought I was going to die! That's what it felt like.'

'But you didn't. Let me see. Your face isn't bruised at all. You were lucky. Let's just go home. You can call Damiano from there. The appointment is later today. I'll make some food for you and then you go to bed. Do you want to fill the Valium prescription first?'

'That bitch won't let me out of this!' Claude was sitting on the side of his gurney. 'The fact is that I don't know if this is a formal interrogation or an arrest. I should have asked Paul yesterday. When we're back home, would you call Paul and ask him to find out why I've been summoned to Crémazie like a common criminal? Know what, Louise? I should have had a heart attack. No Valium! The last thing I need is to be stupid on tranquilizers.' Claude was back and sullen.

Louise stared at Claude. He was a stranger to her now, and she was growing frightened of him.

Six floors up, Madison Holmes had been moved to a private room. On the appointed floor, all the doors had been closed and the halls cleared when Holmes was wheeled into the new room. This practice was the hospital's procedure when there was a death on the floor. The measures ensured the dignity of the deceased and it saved patients from additional distress. Detective Damiano wanted only a select few to know the whereabouts of Holmes. She couldn't afford another leak. She had a bad feeling about the first leak.

Thomas Holmes hadn't left his daughter's side. There was space for a small cot and two officers carried it into the room. They wore white hospital coats to deflect attention. Thomas had pulled his chair closer to Madison and he fell asleep holding her hand. He woke with a start early Sunday, when he felt his hand in a vice-like grip and heard a guttural moan. Wiping the crusted sleep from his eyes, he got to his feet.

Madison was looking right into his eyes and moaning.

'Maddy, I'm here. You're safe now honey, I'm here.'

'Urts, URTS!'

Tears streamed freely down Thomas's cheeks. 'It's okay, Maddy, I can get something for the pain. You're back – you're talking. Do you know that, Maddy? You're talking!'

Madison's face was so sore she was aware she couldn't move her eyebrows, or tweak her nose. She could move her hands and her feet. It was her head – her head felt like broken glass. 'Daa, Daa…' She knew what she wanted to say but she was afraid to move her lips.

'You can say DAD. You can do that Madison.'

She gripped her father's hand tighter – she was alive. She felt tears in her right eye. Madison tried to raise her right arm.

'No, Maddy. You'll pull out the IV.' He took her free hand and lifted it gently to her face where it explored the damage. 'That's enough, Maddy. It'll take some time, but you'll be fine. Who am I, Maddy? Do you know who I am?'

Madison heard her father and she grew bolder. 'Daad – DaaD - Dad!'

Again, Madison said, 'Daad, Dad.'

'What's your name? Can you try that?'

'Maaa.., Maaaad,…Maadssonnn.'

'That's it! Madison! Thank you, Becky. You are your daughter's angel.' He held Madison's hand and wet it with tears. Thomas now knew that his daughter's brain was functioning. When he finally looked up, she had fallen asleep. He didn't want to share his daughter, but he wanted justice. He slipped his hand free. Madison didn't moan. He took out his cell phone in the bathroom.

Damiano caught the call on the first ring. 'Dr. Holmes?'

Damiano and Matte were back in the office Sunday morning. 'Yes, Detective Damiano. My daughter said her first word a few minutes ago. There appears to be no brain damage. She was able to answer simple questions. I didn't want to call you, but…'

'I understand. When…'

'As a physician and her father, I'm telling you that Madison needs time. Be patient – I want this bastard as much as you do. Once the first word is spoken and understood, some patients progress very rapidly. Madison is strong. I'd bet on very soon. Dr. Stephen Orr can get back to you on her progress and a time when you can safely question her. That's a promise. I'm not leaving my daughter's side and I won't permit you to rush her. I hope we understand one another.'

Damiano wasn't finished with Thomas Holmes, but this was not the time to pursue the battering of Pauzé. 'I'm happy for you.' Damiano felt the file closing and her heart pounded.

Chapter Thirty-eight

DAMIANO LOOKED OVER at Matte. 'We've come a long way on this file. You've done excellent work. Galt and Beauchemin will be well out of their comfort zone. If our young witness Mathieu has a good eye – we might close today! The snitch? Hours away from a grab. At the very worst, Holmes is recovering and answering questions. I am lit today! Pierre, you're too quiet.'

'I'm a slow burn. When we have this perp, you'll see me lit.'

'I can't stop the adrenalin when it explodes.'

'Let me call Mme Roy one last time. I have an officer picking her up.' He found her number and called. He spoke quietly, admiringly and gratefully while he shot Damiano a thumbs up. 'Let's go to Crémazie. We should check on the ID room, to be sure that everything is in place. Why did you choose Crémazie?'

'It's the only division that still has a makeshift ID Room for extreme scenarios. The Holmes assault is that for me. I want to use everything available to us. Crémazie was more convenient for the kid, worse for Galt, closer for Beauchemin and me. I didn't want to hear anyone was snarled in traffic, and I didn't want the headache of setting something up at Place Versailles. I want the lineup to go off as scheduled.'

'Makes sense.'

They weren't on the road two minutes before they were jammed by Sunday drivers and construction. 'Why the hell are they working on Sunday?' Damiano wanted to know.

'Deadline penalties, I guess.'

'I hate concrete and construction. I feel we're driving inside a cell.'

'We're not moving.'

'Funny! Pierre, use the flashers. Move some of these cars out of the way!'

He made a right on Crémazie Boulevard West and pulled into the underground parking. The North Division was located on the corner and that made quick turns dicey with traffic coming at you from all angles. When they were out of the car, Pierre brushed the shoulders of his suit. Damiano had worn a dark suit with a double-white cotton shirt and pumps. They walked up to the first floor, to the ID Room for the lineup they had raised. There were officers they needed to see and jackets, hats and sneakers they wanted to check. This was a high-purpose lineup. Both detectives went through the clothes and talked to the stand-ins, other cops. Matte made certain they had the sunglasses.

In case they needed them, Matte had brought a photo array that he showed to Damiano.

'Keep these safe in your folder. I hope today works for us. We have all the perps near Holmes's condo the day before, probably the day of because their alibis don't hold water for the day of the assault, but that's not enough to book any of them. Let's go talk with Mathieu. He should be in the interview room by now.' Damiano felt a hesitant twitch when she saw their young witness. His mother had washed the street off of him. The boy had morphed into a child with his hair combed straight back. Without his spikes, he was a little Samson after his haircut. Damiano was determined to get the punk back into Mathieu.

'Good afternoon, Mme Roy and Mathieu. Thank you both for coming. Mathieu, this will be very easy for a smart boy like you.'

Mathieu took a step closer to his mother. Damiano ignored that and went on. 'In a few minutes, I'll take you in with us. There is a window in the room that we stand behind. There will be six men brought into another room, and they will have numbers on them. All you have to do…'

Mathieu stepped away from his mother. 'I know. I surfed the web last night and I know all about lineups.'

The punk was back.

'Very good! I'll ask you a few questions…'

'Then you ask me to pick out the number. See, I know it all.'

'Detective Matte, I think we have a cop coming up the line.'

Mme Roy pulled her son back close. 'I've made it very clear that Mathieu will not testify in court. This is the end for us.'

'Thank you for this help, Mme Roy. Detective Matte will stay with you and take you in when I call him.' Damiano left and walked back to the front door to wait on Galt and Beauchemin. When she saw a couple of cameramen with their portables begin to set up, she fumed and called for help. Holmes's case was huge media-wise, but if Beauchemin and Galt were innocent and found themselves labelled as suspects in the broadsheets and media, her head would roll. The lawyer and the cop would sue the department. The boss would lose his brass for failure to supervise. In layman's language, he'd go down for mishandling a case. Damiano called for help and began to worry about another leak. The sad fact was that all departments sprang leaks.

Another detective appeared. 'Jean, big favor. It's not your job, but I need you to clear those cameramen. Inform them that it's against the law to take unauthorized photos of any judicial building. I have a lineup and I don't need lawsuits mixed in with it. I don't want Galt's career jeopardized.'

The detective agreed and went after the cameramen who backed off the property but stood their ground on the sidewalk.

'Shit!' Damiano tried Galt. 'Detective are you nearby?'

'As ordered.'

'Come around the back way as usual. I'll meet you at the ID Room. There are cameramen. Wanted to give you a heads-up.'

There was a pause. 'You're covering your ass, but thanks.'

She called Tom Graham and explained the back entrance. He told her he'd find it. The cabbie would know, he felt.

She called Beauchemin.

'What is it now, Detective? I'll be at the division in a minute.'

'Use the underground parking on the side of the building. I'll meet you at that entrance. There are cameramen out front.'

'Ah.'

Damiano heard the wind go out of Beauchemin. At least she had covered herself and her boss. She hurried down to meet Beauchemin and the lawyer he'd brought. It was cold down there and each time the garage door opened, a fresh blast of cold air zeroed in on her. She saw Beauchemin and directed him to park in a visitor's space. His lawyer must have instructed Beauchemin to say as little as possible because he got out of the car without a word. Beauchemin was wan and almost apathetic, as though she'd already arrested him.

'Follow me, please.' Damiano walked briskly up to the ID Room and handed Beauchemin over to a receiving officer who led him away. Damiano looked for Galt. When she saw a rep, she realized he must already be inside. She walked into the ID Room and the two men followed.

Nearby, Galt and Beauchemin were sharing the same thoughts. *She has an eyewitness! Surely it can't be Holmes…* Both men were sweating before they put on the woolen hats. Graham stood to the side with his own thoughts.

Damiano didn't speak to the lawyer or the rep before she went back to the interview room. 'Mathieu, are you ready to help me?'

'Yeah.' His mother took his hand.

There wasn't a whole lot in the kid's *yeah*. 'Mme Roy, please let go of Mathieu's hand when we enter the room. There will be two other men in the room with us.'

'Is there more than one witness?' Mathieu wanted to know.

'The men represent the suspects.'

'But they'll see me!' Mathieu suddenly let loose.

'You don't have to worry, Mathieu. One man is a lawyer and the other is a representative.'

'Yeah, but what if they tell the suspect what I look like?'

'They work for the law, Mathieu.'

'Oh.' But the boy wasn't convinced.

Damiano saw that. 'Once we get inside, let me ask the questions, Mathieu. Is that okay?'

'Yeah, yeah.'

'You have to really understand. I'll ask you a question and you answer, just the question, nothing extra. You are the important person, so what you say will be recorded with my questions. Got that? That's not hard. Just no extras.'

Mathieu reached for his mother's hand.

'Once we're in the room, you and I will stand together with the others behind.'

Damiano led Matte, Mathieu and his mother into the ID Room. The lawyer and the rep followed. Mathieu stared back at both men. Then every eye was glued to the side door.

Chapter Thirty-nine

THE DOOR OPENED. Six men in hats, sunglasses and jackets walked in single file and stopped. Mathieu saw a large measuring board behind the men. Damiano saw Galt was first and looked like he'd come for a fight. Was he trying to hide the demeanor he'd shown Mathieu the day of the assault? Galt knew he could change the odds. Beauchemin and Graham were at the end of the line. Beauchemin seemed blank. Graham stood indifferently. A clever guise or real, she didn't know.

The game was on. Damiano lived for this moment – for life, breathing and pounding in a minute that might explode – or deflate. This was the life she had chosen and she loved it. She looked down at Mathieu. She looked beyond him too. If she didn't close, she'd have the snitch most probably by the end of the day. She'd toss him to the news dogs and let them chew on him for a day or two while she waited for Holmes or for Crime.

'Mathieu, do you see anyone that you saw in that lane? Take your time, look at each man.'

The boy balled his fists. 'Could they kneel on one knee? That's how I saw the man.'

'Which side?'

He pointed to the wall opposite the door.

Damiano took a few steps forward to a phone attached to the wall. 'Ask the men to turn left, kneel on their right knee and look up at the window.'

Mathieu nodded to himself.

The men began to comply. Galt was the first to kneel and the rest followed like a folding accordion, all except Beauchemin. The man beside him began to blur, his heart jumped, he couldn't breathe. Beauchemin fell forward into the stand-in and then straight back onto the floor.

In the immediate silence, only two words were spoken.

'Oh fuck!' They pretty much summed up the situation.

'Mathieu!' Mme Roy pulled her son back and hid his head against her body, but Mathieu squeezed his head around and he saw the show before Damiano turned off the light in their room.

'Detective Matte, please take Mathieu and his mother to the interview room.' It wasn't easy to pull Mathieu from the live action, but his mother grabbed both arms.

Damiano did not want the kid to see Beauchemin or, frankly, the men without their hats. She rushed into the ID Room. 'Has 9-1-1 been called?'

'As soon as he went down,' the supervising officer replied.

Damiano knelt beside Beauchemin and peered closely into his face. He *was* breathing. 'Heart?'

'Dunno,' Galt smiled. 'Might be a panic attack. Saw one in this room six years ago – same MO.'

'Detective Galt, take a breather.' She caught herself before he could mock her with that comment. 'Don't go far – we might have the chance to repeat the lineup later today.'

'Wouldn't bet money on that.'

Graham handed Damiano the cap and jacket. 'Don't see this happening today. I can't get back for another lineup. My health takes precedence. You'll have to deal with my lawyer from now on.' He handed her his card and went looking for the exit.

The paramedics arrived in nine minutes and carted Beauchemin off, but not before Damiano caught one of them. 'Can you distinguish between a cardiac arrest and a panic attack?'

'Same symptoms really – hospital tests will tell the story.'

'Could he be faking this?'

The paramedic leaned over Beauchemin and pulled his eyelid back. 'Nope, he's out! He might have induced the attack, but tests will reveal that. I can't tell you any more.'

'Take my card – tell the ER physician I want to know asap. We're in the middle of an investigation.'

'Do my best, Detective.' He gave her a wide smile and a once over.

When they left, she headed to the interview room, trying to formulate a question for Mathieu. The rep and the lawyer caught up with her. The lawyer spoke up. 'I, we, want to be present if you pursue any formal questioning of your witness.'

'That won't be the case. The boy is as rocked as we were with what just occurred.'

'The kid was enjoying every minute. His mother had to yank him away. What room were you in?'

'Give me your cards and I will call you when or if we can reconvene today. If not today, I will keep you both informed. Take a break because you are not coming into the interview room with me.'

They walked off in a huff.

At the door, she thought of the photo array in Matte's folder and she wondered if Mathieu had already recognized one of the six men. If she worked behind the lines, the court would toss the ID the kid might have made. She walked into the room and spoke before Mathieu could say a word. 'This is a very serious procedure, Mathieu. I'm not going to ask you any questions without the lawyer and the representative present. Please, don't say anything for now. What happened to one of our suspects is awful, but I hope it's not serious. I was proud of you, Mathieu, except for the bad word. You handled yourself like a pro.'

Mathieu smiled like a winner.

'We do have a photo spread. We call it a six pack. We also have one more suspect, but I'll save that until we can repeat the lineup.'

Mathieu waved his arm impatiently.

'You can't tell me a number.'

'What if I know who it wasn't?'

Dammit. I'll chance it.

Matte cautioned her with a nod.

'Will you come back for another lineup?'

'I promised we'd help out this once – we will,' Mme Roy said reluctantly.

'Mathieu, it's best to wait.'

'Ah!' His mother pushed him ahead of her. 'I wish he felt this way about school.' Mathieu broke free and ran back to Damiano. He jumped at her ear. 'It was not #2, #3 or #4. A secret doesn't count as talking.' Mathieu ran out.

'Well?'

'He knows who it wasn't.'

'The kid just added more work for the next lineup. Now we have to change the stand-ins.'

She had turned her phone back on and it was humming.

Chapter Forty

MARIE DUMONT of Crime was finally calling.

'It's about time. I was beginning to wonder if you'd gotten stuck in poutine.'

'Very droll! I have some interesting info. We've found fragments of the weapon in the blood collected at the scene. There was so much blood that we first thought we were looking at clots. The pieces must have torn on the broken glass. You were right about the box. It's a Canada Post box, the kind authors frequently purchase at a postal station to send manuscripts. We dried out the most legible bits and realized we had a bar code. I called Canada Post. They can't track the destination of the package without the tracking number.'

'So you have zilch.'

'Patience, Toni. We're pulling up other bits of paper – we have five of the tracking numbers. If we can pull up the rest, you'll know where your perp was sending the boxed manuscript at least.'

'How many numbers are there?'

'Sixteen – we need all of them.'

'Why would a meticulous planner batter Holmes with a box that had a tracking number? Makes no sense to me.'

'Canada Post helped with that too. Nearly 40% of buyers attach the sticker to the wrong side of the box. Your perp is one of those. We have no address pulled up so far. Maybe he didn't see his mistake or saw it and felt a blank sticker wasn't trouble.'

'What are your odds of clearing all 16 numbers?'

'We'll do our best – it's a slow process.'

'His first mistake!' Damiano was shocked. 'But if we don't have the sender's name?'

'Then the tracking number might not amount to much. We don't want to waste our time with this.'

'Still such a stupid mistake. Thanks, Marie.' Her phone had been on speaker so Matte could hear and she wouldn't have to repeat the information.

Matte wasn't surprised. 'Tells me our perp is cheap – too cheap to buy a new box.'

'I saw boxes in Beauchemin's office. The warrant's still valid. Send Crime to see if there are boxes that have stickers on the wrong side.'

'How do they get back into the house? His wife must have been called to the hospital. Beauchemin might have suffered a cardiac arrest.'

'That's the last thing I need to hear. Pass her number to Crime – they can arrange a time.'

'What about Galt?'

'Can you handle that, Pierre? I want to see Thomas Holmes.'

'About?'

'Pauzé's attack.'

'Still?'

'Galt would have busted his nuts to close the file, but he hasn't. Holmes looks good for that battering, to me anyway. I want to see our victim – I hate waiting.' Another call came in from Crime.

'Toni, this just came in. We have your snitch. The idiot used his own cell phone. Guess he thought the *National Enquirer* would never reveal his name.'

'Let's leave it at *he never thought*. Who is it?'

'Officer Troy Turner.'

Damiano didn't respond.

'You there?'

'He is, or was, the best surveillance I have. He works the ICU door, takes notes, texts his fellow officers – kid had promise. Dammit! What an idiot! I hate waste.'

'What are you going to do?'

'I'll haul him in, charge him with obstruction, speak to the boss who'll take his badge and feed him to the media. His leak might have led to another attack on Holmes. Dammit to hell! Better go – have to report to the boss.'

'You didn't do this, Toni.'

'I liked the kid.'

'He's young – he'll move on.'

Damiano called the boss on his command line en route to Place Versailles. 'I have to see you. This is important. I'll be at your office in minutes.'

He growled. 'Bad fucking news! I can smell it.'

She took rue Saint-Hubert to Sherbrooke and exceeded all speed limits. When she arrived, she ran to a washroom and freshened up. She didn't want the boss to think she was caving under the stress. She placed her head under the tap and sucked in some water, wiped her mouth and walked into Chief Donat's office. The door was open.

This case was hers – she'd have to fight to keep it. First, the bad news – then a rundown of the file.

He gave her a hurried wave. 'Go! You're already wasting time.'

'Officer Troy Turner, head of the hospital surveillance team, is the snitch who called the *National Enquirer*. Crime informed me half an hour ago. I'll drive to the hospital and bring him back here. Boss, better than most, you know the force is *sous le gun* where transparency is concerned. Due to the recent uniform shootings, the in-house suicide, and the bad press, we should not hide the snitch.'

'Have you lost it?'

'I have not. The media can hurt us. They have more power. They mutate like a virus.'

Donat bristled but kept listening.

'I bring Turner to you. The file is progressing as you will…'

'You mean with suspects dropping in lineups?'

'Let me finish.'

Donat did a double take. He hid a thin smile. He'd chosen well for the file.

'We fire his ass, charge him with obstruction and have him return the snitch pay. Then you call a press conference. I'll be with you, but it will look better if you conduct, and I add only a few comments. The media will fight over Turner's bones for a day or two, praise you, and give me the breather I need to close the file. Please send a replacement for Turner.'

'Do you sleep?'

'Not well.'

'Good. This file has a bad smell. Four 'spects who all look good. That number has to be cut. You hear me, Damiano?'

'To the file: Crime is pulling up tracking numbers from the box, i.e. the weapon, used to assault Holmes. We need 16 – Marie has five. If we get those, we'll know where the box was headed. Crime is back in Beauchemin's house looking for other boxes. Turns out the label was attached to the wrong side. That's the first mistake we've found. You'd agree that this is a smart assault. Matte is at Galt's. Then I'll direct him to Pauzé's.'

'We have an eyewitness, a kid who saw the perp and he will be back for a second lineup.

'Madison Holmes is answering simple questions. I'm driving back to the hospital to see where we are there.

'Can't crack Marino – I have no tools for that one. You have to help me there.' Damiano stood and waited for another barrage.

Donat looked Damiano squarely in the eyes. 'You have a good head for this work.'

She had the strongest urge to jump once and yell *yeah. I do*! She held his eyes. 'I know.'

Donat laughed a phlegmy laugh and coughed. 'Go down and get that shithead. I'll be waiting. Don't give him a heads-up. I like surprises. I'll call the press conference.'

Damiano's high didn't last. Thomas Holmes hung over her. Turner saddened her. The traffic didn't pick at her nerves because Holmes and Turner had got to them first. Once she was inside the Montreal General, she took the stairs – didn't want to wait for the crowded elevator. Turner was at his post. His replacement would be there soon. She approached Turner. 'Officer, please ask Thomas Holmes to come out here for a few minutes. I'll watch the door.'

'Sure, Detective.' He disappeared.

Damiano flinched when she considered what she was about to do. The secret would be as safe as any secret shared between two people who had a great deal to lose by disclosure. She was no better than Turner if she went through with her plan.

Holmes wasn't pleased to be away from his daughter. 'I promised I'd call you.'

'Thank you, Officer Turner. Dr. Holmes, I need a few minutes of your time. Please follow me.' Damiano began to walk toward a small office. Holmes followed reluctantly. Once they were inside, she closed the door. The room was sterile and claustrophobic. 'Please sit down.'

'Why am I here, Detective?'

'How's Madison?'

He softened. 'Much better. She's saying a few words. That's why I shouldn't be here. I need to be with Madison to protect her and guide her.'

Holmes's face was drawn. She saw hope in his eyes, but dark circles under them. He was leaning over like an old man. *Could he have done Pauzé?* 'I have to ask you something. Your answer is very important, but it won't matter if it's a lie. I have to know about Pauzé.

'It's blocking me from the man who assaulted your daughter. If you attacked Pauzé, then the road opens for me. I know that your daughter is all you have left in this world. I know you have regrets. The offer I'm about to make will risk my badge. If you admit to the assault, I won't charge you. It will stay between you and me because Madison will need you. I hope you understand the sacrifice I'm making to find the man who tried to kill her. Did you assault Pauzé?'

'Police lie to get confessions.'

'I'm not lying.'

'Are you taping this?'

'No.'

'Is this offer for Madison or for the case you want to close? Is my daughter real to you, Detective, or just a piece of a top profile case?'

'I have a son.'

'So who knows what you might do if someone tried to kill him. That's our bond?'

'The law matters to me, Dr. Holmes – my son matters more. Did you assault Pauzé?'

Holmes studied Damiano. He cupped a fist and put it under his chin and closed his eyes. Damiano kept the afterimage of his face in her head and left the room.

Chapter Forty-one

SECONDS LATER, she was back, to try again. 'Dr. Holmes, some rapists, batterers, pedophiles, muggers and the odd murderer walk our streets because we can't touch them. Not enough evidence. Most had violent pasts, some history for their acts. The suspects in this file disgust me. Greedy, ungrateful, vengeful sociopaths, macho shits who refused to accept a "no." This vicious crime somehow boosted their self-esteem. Men with decent lives stepped across the line and proved more violent than most perps I've come across. Yes, this is a good file, but I want this perp. I want him to face a slow guilty plea in court and be exposed for the monster he is. Will you answer my question? I'm on your side.'

Holmes sat up and Damiano saw a momentary flicker, a nudge. But Holmes leaned back and changed his mind. He smiled and saw for the first time an extraordinarily good-looking woman. Damiano tried her best, he saw, to conceal a softness in herself. He felt a stir and he swallowed because his mouth had gone dry.

'Well?'

'If I confessed, you'd keep your word, but the lapse would eventually destroy you. Experience has taught me that lesson.' He rose and walked to the door. 'Solve the case the proper way. Madison might be ready to answer your questions in a few days, perhaps two. I won't have her rushed. Madison has to be ready. My daughter is a remarkable woman.' Holmes turned back to Damiano. 'Detective, she needs me.'

'Your answer saves us both.' Damiano was back in the gray of her file. She watched Holmes go and she felt better that he hadn't taken her up on her offer. She hated cheaters. Holmes had understood that. At the door, she saw Officer Turner speaking to his replacement. As she approached she saw that he wasn't pleased.

'Detective, why am I...'

'I'm having a meeting with the chief – we want to go over what we have. Take your notes with you. You are in charge here and you'll sit in with us.'

She knew that hesitant excitement, like a kid who's asked to look for a puppy in the back of a dark van.

'Okay, ah... I have all my notes with me. Do I ride with you?'

'You're sharing the patrol car, right? Leave it for your partner and ride with me.' Damiano made quick work of getting back to her car. Turner had to keep up with her pace. 'You can ride up front.'

'I hate to leave my post. I guess you'll be going in to question Holmes pretty soon. She's a fighter.'

'And very lucky.'

'That too, I guess.'

'How long have you been on the force, Officer?'

'Three years! I can't wait to get in in the morning. The job feels right.' He was glowing.

'Know the feeling, the rush.' Damiano's phone hummed and she flipped it open. 'Yes? Is he still there? That's good. Stress-related? Uh humph. Thank you for calling, Doctor.' She hung up and dropped the phone. The kid wanted to ask about the call, but he kept his eyes forward. He did squirm – she saw it. She didn't talk the rest of the way.

At Place Versailles, she moved quickly to the elevator and they got off on the sixth floor. They were halfway down the hall when Officer Turner spoke up. 'Should I have written my notes up?'

She didn't bother turning when she said. 'No, it's all in your iPhone. No problem.' Donat's door was closed. Damiano had her hand on the doorknob and spoke to his secretary from there. 'Chief Donat is expecting me.'

'Just a second. I'll just check to make sure he's not on the phone.'

They waited quietly.

'You can go right in, Detective.'

The chief wore full uniform. He pointed to a chair for Damiano. He had purposely seen to it that the other two were removed, forcing Officer Turner to stand.

He stood rigidly a few feet to Damiano's left. His nerves began to crawl.

'Close the door, Officer!'

'Yes, Chief.'

Turner's palms were sweating.

'Officer Troy Turner, you are a disgrace to the force. Put your badge and gun on my desk.'

Turner wanted to ask how, but there was no point.

Donat waited for the gun and badge. He swept them up in his hand and shoved them into his right drawer. 'Before you leave today, leave anything that belongs to the department on your desk. Detective Damiano will officially charge you with obstruction. The money from the *National Enquirer* should be sent forthwith to this office. Why a young man who, according to Detective Damiano, had made a good start would put a victim in harm's way and forfeit a promising career is beyond me. Your job was to serve and protect. In a few minutes, Detective Damiano and I will hold a press conference and we will reveal your name. You should have thought of the dire consequences.'

'Chief…' Turner wept openly.

'Get out of my office. Detective Damiano, follow Turner. Make certain he leaves immediately. Meet me back in the interview room.'

'What about my iPhone?'

'Do you have notes on it?'

Turner nodded.

'Leave it – it will be mailed back to you. What about the throwaway?'

'I bought that myself, Chief.'

Donat put out his hand. Turner bent down, unbuckled the gun clipped to his ankle and handed it over. 'I don't want you eating your gun. Take the rest of the day to get your things in order before we serve the arrest warrant. You've done a real job on the Anglophone community, Turner!' Donat rose and turned his back on them.

Damiano and Turner left together. She walked behind him. He turned around only once. 'You could have given me…'

Damiano shook her head and didn't bother answering at first. She was just lucky that Thomas Holmes had left the battering of Pauzé in some question. Her offer had already destroyed some part of her. She had to say something to the kid. 'Troy!'

Turner stopped and turned back. His face was ashen.

'This is the end of your career – don't let it be the end of your life. No one is immune to stupidity. Good luck to you.'

He wiped tears away with the back of his hand. 'I really loved…' And he walked away, sliding into shock.

Damiano could feel his shame because she felt her own.

Chapter Forty-two

DAMIANO WAS RESTLESS. Matte was still at Galt's house or at Pauzé's apartment. She called Chief Donat to see how much time she had before the press conference. She sounded like herself, as though she were still the same person. Holmes might harbor the idea that she was playing him, but she knew the truth and she colored, thinking about it.

'Don't give away anything. I'll be brief. We don't want to be left sucking air. Gotta talk careful on this one – gotta be word-specific to the power they wield. I'll meet you in the small interview room first.'

'We're doing what needs to be done,' Damiano reminded Donat.

'Politics – that's all it is.'

Damiano looked out the window and saw the media circus, TV trucks: CTV, TVA, Global, CBC and Radio Canada, one from ABC and another from CNN that had succeeded in blocking an exit from the mall. She checked herself out and hurried down. In the hall, they saw the mob and the tangle of cameras. They elbowed their way to the podium. When Chief Donat began, she saw his hand pulling at the side of his pants. She had never seen the boss intimidated.

'… the safety of Ms Holmes is uppermost, second only to the integrity and transparency of this investigation and to the SPVM, Service de Police de la Ville de Montréal, in general. Officer Troy Turner has been dismissed from the force and will face charges… Lieutenant-Detective Damiano, lead investigator, will fill you in on the Holmes file.' He stepped aside and neatly avoided hands that sprung at him like arrows.

A familiar feminine voice shouted. 'Has there been an arrest on the Holmes case?'

'When?' another reported shouted.

'Ladies and gentlemen, I expect to make an arrest in the next few days,' Damiano tried to assure them.

'Can't you be more precise?' the reporter from CTV asked sharply.

'Rest assured, you will be informed of the exact time and day of the arrest.' Damiano almost missed seeing Turner because he was in civvies at the back of the mob, and standing behind the cameras, but she saw him before he dissolved like a ghost. He'd waited, she guessed, to see if he'd be named, Damiano wanted to apologize for not warning Turner about the meeting with the chief. She needed to remind him that he could start over – tell him she had guessed *why* he had leaked the information. *Something* to hold him together. Instead, she followed Donat out, and the urge passed. Like Turner, she loved her job, and she had the second chance the kid would never have.

Minutes later, as the media stood around grumbling that the press conference had been a waste of time, there was the terrible sound of crashing cars on Sherbrooke Street. The media ran with their cameras towards the noise as cars continued to collide. The horrific accident had occurred across from Place Versailles. Donat and Damiano heard the crunch of metal, the squeal of brakes and the smashing windshield glass. Like everyone else, they ran outside, into a swarm of people and into what looked like a high-action movie crash. Cops were everywhere. 'What happened?'

Black smoke, combined with motor oil, rose around the carnage. 'What happened?'

Injured drivers were pinioned inside their wrecks, dazed drivers stumbled around. Police and passers-by rushed to help the injured. It wasn't long before the wail of ambulances was the dominating noise in the cacophonous wreckage. The trucks were forced to jump the sidewalks to get to the injured. Time seemed suspended and there was a deadly quiet inside the noise.

Chief Donat stayed back, but Damiano ran on headlong into the chaos, trying to locate the source. She passed a victim lying on the street with paramedics performing CPR. One stopped, and the other did too. 'Un arrêt cardiaque!' There was no mistaking what he'd said. She passed a victim covered in a white plastic sheet, stained with blood. Damiano knelt and lifted the sheet. The victim was a woman. Then she heard a man screaming in shock, walking back and forth, screaming and unattended. She grabbed him.

'It wasn't my fault! There was nothing I could do! The kid saw me – I saw him. He walked right in front of my car and looked at me when I struck him! What could I have done?'

'Nothing. Sit down and try to calm down. It wasn't your fault.'

'It wasn't – I'm swearing it wasn't!' He kept repeating the same words.

Damiano saw the next victim, saw his bloodied hand first. It was sticking out from the plastic sheeting. She knelt and stopped breathing before she lifted the sheet. *We're doing what needs to be done, Chief.* One of his legs was caught underneath his torso. His arms didn't look as though they were attached. He was covered in blood as though he'd been splashed with it. She reached for his face that was turned awkwardly to the left side and wiped some blood off the eyes and cheek. She had to be sure. Then she covered him gently. Distraught and haggard, she walked back to Donat.

'The little shit!' Behind his words, she saw he was shaken. 'I'll be eating dog shit on this one. What a little fool. He was a kid! Jesus, Mary and

Joseph! He was just a kid. The media will make this a big fucking deal!'

'Stop swearing – show some respect!' Her words had just come out of her. 'Turner was twenty-four years old. We all screw up, don't we?'

Donat's face grew ugly, but he didn't retaliate. 'He could have been discreet, at least. Give me that.'

'You took his guns.'

'We did the right thing.'

'Turner didn't leave us any choice.'

'At least we agree on one thing, Damiano. Now, get back to the file.'

'First, I'd like to inform the family. He was under my supervision. What about the money?'

'I'll put someone else on that. In the meantime, the parents can use some of it for his funeral. The kid paid dearly for it. I need a collar. We can't afford to jerk the media around anymore. They'll turn on us and trash us. Do the job I gave you.' Chief Donat headed back inside Place Versailles. Damiano followed. She checked her phone. Matte had called twice. When she had emergency numbers for Turner, she closed the office door and called his father.

'John Turner.'

'Detective Toni Damiano…'

'I've heard the name. You're way up there on Troy's list. Kid loves his work, he… What's happened?'

Damiano revealed the details as best she could and broke the news of Turner's death. When she heard no response, she waited before asking, 'Sir, are you still there?'

'You sure, of everything?'

'I'm sorry, I am. I saw his body.'

'Humph.'

'Troy was a good officer. He worked hard and he had the smarts for the job. That's what I'll remember. Most of us foul up. If we're lucky, we stumble on. Regrettably, Troy wasn't lucky.'

'Ah.'

Turner's sigh struck Damiano with the finality of death. There was nowhere to go, no hope to offer. Over. Finished.

'The first day Troy learned to ride a two-wheeler, he tried to ride hands-free. I shouted at him to hold on, but he was beaming before he crashed into a parked car.' John Turner moaned.

Damiano shuddered and she grieved.

The moan became a sad whisper. 'I guess he never learned. This will kill his mother.'

Damiano said hesitantly, 'About the money from the *Enquirer*…'

'I'll find it and return the amount in full.'

'Chief Donat said you could use some of it for Troy's private funeral because he won't have…'

'I get the picture, Detective. What I don't get is why? Why? We're not ill – we don't need money. He was doing just fine. Why?' His voice was thin and near breaking.

'He was a kid – they take longer to grow up today.'

Turner regained some composure. '*I'll* bury my son with *my* savings. I could never touch the Judas money that brought about his death. It will be the last thing I can do for my son,' Turner said stiffly and punched off.

Damiano cried as a wave of sadness washed over her.

I can't wait to get in in the morning. The job feels right. Troy's words lingered.

Chapter Forty-Three

LATE SUNDAY NIGHT Damiano was back in her condo. She pushed through the door, slammed it, slumped down into her favorite chair and kicked her shoes across the room. Confused and scared and tired, she tried to understand what had happened. Turner's suicide had sucked the heart out of her. Eleven days ago Holmes had been savagely beaten and left for dead. Later, Pauzé had been assaulted, Beauchemin was having panic attacks in her lineup, and now Troy Turner had very publicly killed himself. Graham had refused another lineup because of his treatments. There were so many veins of suffering in this case. She'd offered a deal. Her, a deal! Dammit! Too tired to eat, no head for alcohol, she bent forward and ran her fingers across her scalp, massaging her temples. The connection she'd felt with the file a few days ago and the quick solve she thought she'd have had gotten away from her. The file was growing like a web and she was caught in the middle of it. Damiano was seeing a version of herself she didn't recognize.

In the next few minutes, Matte and Marie Dumont from Crime both called. 'Pierre, I'm really jammed tonight. Can you wait till we meet at seven tomorrow?'

'Threads can wait. At Galt's, his kid got home from school, and I gave him a lecture on hacking. Turns out Galt asked him to hack into Holmes's computer.'

'Ah damn, what a jerk! Means we have to grill him again. See you at seven, Pierre. Save the rest for tomorrow.'

Damiano took Marie off hold. 'Sorry, Marie. I'm scraping bottom. It's been raw, the whole day.'

'I know. I have information, lots of it.'

'Any part of that package that I can lay paper on and scare the shit out of one of our suspects? I want a warrant!'

'We need to meet. You need extra men, and the boss for the work I have in mind. The RCMP have to become involved. We'll need information from Canada Post. It's federal.'

'Chief Donat won't be happy. Frankly, neither am I. This is my case. I don't want the Feds interfering.'

'What about eight in your office tomorrow morning? I'll have all my notes ready – you have the boss there. You don't have a warrant yet, but this is a real crack that might require a warrant.'

'Tell me.'

'Get some sleep. You sound near collapse. All we need is another dead cop on this file – lead detective, dead from exhaustion!'

'Not funny,' but Damiano smiled ruefully.

'See you tomorrow fully armed.'

Damiano dragged herself off the chair and into the kitchen where she stood eating wilting Romaine lettuce and stale crackers. Standing was tough, so she padded back to the chair with a handful of crackers and leaves. She looked at the phone. It stared back at her. *Shit!* She finally picked it up, checked the time and called. Luke was a nighthawk like her, but she woke him.

'Whaaa?'

'Luke?'

'Yeah, Mom. Who else? I got school tomorrow.' He was surly.

'I love you.'

'Mostly when you're worried about a case.'

'That's mean.'

'That's true.'

'I'm sometimes sorry I'm me, for you.'

'Mommm, too late for deep. Whadayawant?'

'I have no food in the apartment. Would you and your father…'

'This is crazy – one person and you can't take care of yourself! Like what?'

'Like everything healthy.'

'Tomorrow afternoon?'

'Good enough. I hate needing you like this. I should be the one…'

'I'm toast, Mom.'

'I'm lucky to have a kid like you.'

'You're paying.'

'Of course. I just meant.'

'I never asked you to change – you're cool. I gotta sleep. Need my own time too, you know.' Luke punched off.

Damiano didn't believe much in grace, but there were times she felt it, times like that night. *You're cool.* She undressed and stumbled into bed. *Needs his own time – he's my son alright.* She fell asleep and didn't move till the alarm went off at six. Damiano roseenergized Monday morning. The bard had it right. Sleep was *great nature's second course.* Once she had the coffee going, she hurried into the shower. Dressed in no time, she drove back to work. Matte was waiting on her with a bagel and cream cheese. Men were feeding her. Men had good points.

He had notes neatly arranged on the table.

With her mouth full of bagel and cheese, she waved her 'go' sign.

'Galt had no extra boxes, but he wouldn't, he's a cop who'd know to get rid of them. His kid, I told you about. Galt did one hell of a cleanup where he writes. It was obvious and suspicious to me. Pauzé lives in a cesspool of paper. I found a grimy, shiny old sneaker under a mess. I assume Crime lit it up, but I bagged it anyway today.' He reached for his bag and held it up with two fingers. 'He probably has thirteen years of garbage on this shoe. Look closer and you'll see plain dirt. I wondered if…'

'I was thinking the same thing – maybe match it. He said Holmes blew up his life, blamed her for his fraud with the essays. We should go see this kid and grind *him*. He's out of danger. Can you set that up for later today, Pierre?'

'I notice I get stuck with the paperwork and appointments.' There was no anger in his tone, amusement perhaps.

'Doesn't pay to be a neat freak.'

'Crime says they did find four extra boxes at Beauchemin's, one labeled incorrectly.'

'It's hard to compute that these three jerks are still neck and neck. We can't roll on one and discover we've made a bad call. Can't happen.' Damiano checked the time. 'Clean this mess up. Chief Donat and Marie Dumont should be here in five minutes. This is what I know…'

'RCMP?'

'Here they come.' Damiano rose and opened the door. 'Chief, Marie. You both know Detective Matte. We've cleared the table for you.'

Chief Donat had added a melancholy mood to his already abrasive nature. 'Have you seen what the media is doing to us? They're questioning our training. It's our fault a stupid little prick got greedy. Blame the masses for the actions of a few. Now we're the mass. Damiano – keep up with the viral shit. I want you at my next press conference. The kid's funeral is tomorrow. Be there in full dress. We have to put some face on this affair. He *was* one of ours. What a little fool! Alright, Dumont, why am I here?'

The boss never flustered Marie and his outburst had given her a few minutes to arrange her notes. 'Damiano figured out that the weapon used was a Canada Post box often used by authors to send their manuscripts. The box is actually a little larger, 11¼" X 9" X 2½". In the attack, the assailant didn't see that fragments of the box were being ripped off by the broken glass. We extracted them from the blood gathered at the scene.'

Chief Donat jerked forward. 'Get to the point, Marie.'

'We assembled the bar code – meant nothing. Then we began to extract and bring up tracking numbers – we had 13 before I called Head Office of Canada Post. The rest of the label, the part that we salvaged was blank.'

'Another blank!'

'Chief, please.'

Donat leaned back in his chair as though he had gotten one over on Marie.

'I hoped the tracking number could locate the origin of sale. As the Chief aptly put it – another blank.'

Damiano was edgy. *Marie better be going somewhere with this.*

Marie continued unperturbed. 'We need the receipt. It has the postal outlet or office, the name of the postal worker, and the last four numbers of the credit card. If the assailant was smart enough to use cash, we might still connect him to the receipt. We have the exact price of the box, $3.79. According to Canada Post, the box is not a common purchase, except at Christmas. Chief, this is where you come into the picture. My team has located between three and four postal outlets or offices in a five-kilometer radius for each of the three suspects. However, Canada Post is federal and one of the most highly regulated agencies in Canada. We need at least two RCMP investigators to go to these outlets with our officers to get these receipts. Chief, you have good connections with the RCMP. You have to get the investigators.'

A knot appeared in the chief's neck. 'The last four numbers of a card – there are millions who'd have the same numbers. I know that much about credit cards. Cash – the cost? Sounds like blanks again.'

'Chief, can't you get the investigators?' Marie tested him.

Donat slammed his fist down. 'Of course, I can, but I'm not putting the file out there with BLANKS!'

'Let me explain. We have a timeline for the purchase dates. Holmes sent the rejection slips mid-October and was assaulted November 8th. Our time frame runs from October 17th to November 7th. Now, we have the range of dates, four digits of a credit card and the cash price. We feel that the box was a recent buy to avoid fingerprints of others he might have had at home.'

'A mountain of paper!' Chief Donat barked.

'The credit card companies said they'd short-list the receipts. If the assailant used a credit card without a chip, on the slim chance he was that stupid, we have his signature. If not, we've cut the paper mountain down to a size we can deal with.'

'Who'll do all the reading?' Donat was relentless, but they all saw that his interest had been piqued.

Damiano jumped in. 'Chief, we take uniforms off the street, guys who can read, and stuff them in plain clothes. We set up shop in the second conference room. If we can tie the purchase to one of our suspects, we have paper for a warrant. As it stands, we have motive and opportunity on all three.'

Chief Donat used every muscle to control himself. 'I've listened to this proposal. So far, Detective Damiano, I have not interfered with your investigation. Marie, I appreciate your efforts. However, this whole venture is a waste of time. Don't proceed with it. The results will be tenuous at best. The weapon is long gone. None of these findings will hold water in court. Move on. Have I made myself clear?'

Marie gathered her reports, and Damiano spoke. She saw the merits on both sides. There was no point arguing with the chief once he'd made up his mind. 'Understood, Chief. On another front, Galt just gave us another link.' She informed the chief about the hacking.

The chief's face contorted with anger. 'If Galt did this assault – we throw the book at him. For the time being, don't charge him with the hacking. We can't afford any more bad press before you make the collar.'

Damiano nodded.

'The lineup?'

'Chief, Beauchemin is back home, so we'll go with another tomorrow or Wednesday morning. The agent, Tom Graham, has refused to be present because he's beginning cancer treatments. Told me to deal with his lawyer.'

'Did Marie get anything on his prints?'

'No.'

'You have his photo.'

'Yes.

'Do you think he's a runner?'

'Unlikely. He has prostate cancer.'

'Well, you may have to consider a six pack. Keep Graham in focus. He has motive – future income and reputation. He admitted being in the city at the time of the assault. In your sights, Damiano.'

'Intend to, Chief.'

Donat jumped to his next point. 'Remember what I said – I want you at Turner's funeral in full dress.'

'Of course.'

'To close, you need a smoking gun, Damiano. What about Holmes?'

'I have to give her time – the six pack is ready.'

'Alright.'

Matte waited till the boss had left before he reached under the table and produced the shoe. 'Marie, I guess you used luminol on this for blood.'

'Where did you get that?'

'Under one hell of a mess at Pauzé's apartment. I see dirt. You might be able to match the dirt on the shoe to the lane when the kid saw our perp.'

'You know the location?'

'Yep.'

'Let's get samples right now. If there's something specific to the area that the shoe picked up, it's as good as blood!'

Chapter Forty-four

A FAMILIAR PANIC settled in Damiano's stomach as soon as she found herself alone. Too many unanswered questions in a file led to guesswork. Unproven theorizing wasn't just inappropriate, it was dangerous. Yet the urgency and the multiple leads had pushed Damiano off her usual course of action to the edge and she knew it. If the kid didn't recognize anyone, if Holmes couldn't remember... Turner's death hung on her shoulders, weighing her down. She grabbed the phone and punched in Beauchemin's number and was relieved he answered. She could hear the relief in his voice. The crisis was past. That meant he'd have to make himself available. 'Yes?'

'Detective Damiano.'

'Oh.'

'Glad the attack wasn't anything more serious.'

'What is it you want, Detective?'

'I need you in another lineup tomorrow afternoon. You should present yourself at one thirty, same place.'

'I'm not supposed to drive.'

'I understand – take a cab.'

'If I had been arrested and died, you could have laid the attack on me. Case solved. I know you, Detective. I knew you when you walked into my home.'

'Excuse me?'

'You heard me.'

'Mmmm. I *can* understand why Holmes rejected your manuscript. I don't want you dead. I have a selfish motive for wanting you to live. I want my perp in cuffs. I want cameras flashing in the face of the coward who tried to beat a woman to death and failed at that too. Do we understand one another a little better? Be there tomorrow.' She purposely hadn't used his name – he was a cipher to her anyway.

She called Mme Roy at her office and explained that she needed Mathieu at the division. 'I can't afford to take time off work.'

Damiano surmised it was a question of money. 'How about you give me the name of Mathieu's school and I'll send a patrol car to pick him up and take him back. I'll take good care of Mathieu here. You're not to worry. I promise you he won't be in harm's way.'

'My sister lives across the street from Mathieu's school. She's been laid off. Can she go with Mathieu in the patrol car?'

'That's even better.' Damiano could feel the young mother's relief. 'Give me the address and I'll set things up.'

'Mathieu will be thrilled for weeks. Remember, he's a young boy trying to impress you. He can exaggerate and he's not above stretching the truth.'

'I'll speak to him before the lineup. You're not to worry.'

'I'll call my sister.'

'Thank you.' Things had begun to move – her panic was lifting. Yet Angela Marino, Tracey Doyle's mother, had forced her way into the case. Damiano couldn't eliminate her. If Marino had set up the hit, that was the reason she couldn't nail one of the four men. That was the block. But a pro wouldn't have botched the job. Damiano was back to her main suspects. She reached for her bag, locked the office and headed down to the car. She stopped off at the mall and grabbed a *Gazette, La Presse* and *Le Journal de Montréal*.

Lighting in the garage was poor. When she spied a bench, she sat scanning the papers. Turner's photo was front page in all three papers, alongside unsettling photos of the accident and one of his body hastily covered with a blood-smeared white plastic sheet. Speed-reading, she learned Turner had been struck by three cars and he was blamed for the other two fatalities. The boss had been right. There was a front page article questioning the training of young officers who might be 'woefully' unprepared for the 'temptations' of the job. Turner might have thought exposure would force the assailant's hand. He might have believed *he'd* make the collar. Maybe it wasn't about the money at all. She took one last look at Turner and threw the papers in a recycling container.

On the drive to Hôtel Dieu Hospital, she did a quick review of what she had on Pauzé. He was Galt's case, so neither she nor Matte had grilled the post-grad as much as they could have. Then he'd been assaulted, and in a weird sense, he'd been spared the scrutiny the other two had faced. Her first stop was the nurses' station to learn about his condition. The nurse she spoke to was about her age. Damiano recognized the same authoritative edge on the tall woman who wore little makeup. Her hands were unnaturally red. 'Well, he's out of traction. We have him up. Right now, they should be wheeling him back from therapy. Despite his whining, he's doing well.'

'He's up to questioning?'

'I'll be glad of the relief. He's buzzing for a nurse every ten minutes. We need a break.' Damiano saw a wrinkle of humor play around her eyes.

'I can take care of that,' Damiano smiled back.

Damiano left and spotted the young uniform on security detail, holding up a wall, slouching, leaning on one foot, then the other, and texting. The kid had a thick neck and a square face, a poster boy. He didn't see her until she was beside him.

'Ah shit!' He slipped his phone into his pocket and straightened up. 'Detective, I just took a small break. Pauzé's not even here, so I thought…'

'You're on duty, Officer. You know what that entails.'

'I'm sorry. Have to take a leak – thought texting might distract me. I still have another hour.'

'Go and get right back. I want to talk to you.' Damiano didn't have the heart to beat up on another young officer. The kid was back in a minute.

'Any visitors?'

'His parents yesterday, and no one else I saw.'

'How much texting are you doing?'

'Just now, Detective.'

'Right.'

'Pauzé's really spooked. He's really fucked up.'

'Language, Officer.'

'You know what I mean. He jumps every time anyone goes into the room. I can hear his labored breathing. It's not normal. He's really jacked – I mean frightened. Detective Galt was here twice. One of his friends came, but I wasn't on then. Officer Michel said that Pauzé knew the guy. There was no problem. Pauzé never shuts up unless he's drugged.' The uniform looked quickly to his right. 'Here he comes.'

Damiano waited for Pauzé to be helped from an extra-large wheel chair and carefully lifted onto the bed. When the orderlies left, she went into the room with a different strategy. The kid was freshly shaved and sponge bathed, but no one ever looked clean in a hospital. His hair was matted in the back where he had been lying on it and his nails were dirty. 'This is quite an ordeal,' she said with concern. Her phone rang and she turned it off. Damiano kept her voice down. She could ill afford to have the name of a suspect leaked. The chief would be livid and yank her off the file. Two older patients in the room were sleeping. She closed Pauzé's curtain around them.

Pauzé squirmed uncertainly before he answered. 'I had to go under again to have bone chips removed from my right knee. They botched the first job.'

'At least I hear they have you up on your feet.'

'These casts are 22 pounds, each! I'm hobbling on crutches. My armpits are burning and my hands are aching. I'm not an athlete. I hurt all the time. I…'

'Detective Galt thinks you know the person who attacked you.'

Pauzé's face stiffened like a plaster cast.

'We can protect you.'

'Bullshit!'

'Jean, I'm being straight with you. You're facing gruelling rehab – I know because I've been through some. A few years ago, a suspect came at me with a hammer, broke my arm in four places. Coming back wasn't easy.' She waited for a reaction. 'And I wasn't a suspect in a violent attack.'

Pauzé covered his face with both hands. Damiano saw the deep cut on the side of his palm.

'Couldn't just break both legs, I had to fall on glass to top off the night.'

It occurred to Damiano that perhaps there were bits of glass remaining in the wound.

'Didn't feel it till yesterday,' he said, looking at the side of his palm. Docs didn't see it either. Cleaned it myself. What does it matter anyway? My life has tanked. My supervisor and parents know about the papers. I thought I'd buck today's trend of not doing better than our parents. The wasted generation, that's what we are, you know. Thought I'd be the exception. Holmes could have made that happen.'

'You could start over somewhere else.'

'Who in hell would give a rat's ass about the Roddick Gates at McGill if I left the city? Haven't written anything else, never had time.'

'Is there any way the hospital could take you to the division for a lineup?'

Pauzé stopped breathing.

'You might want a lawyer, but he or she can't help you. I already have you in a six pack photo spread. Lineups have been replaced by photos. However, this high profile case is an extreme scenario, so I'd like you in person. If you're wondering, I am questioning you. Do you want a lawyer?'

Pauzé took a shallow breath. 'I'm not going to trust what's left of my life to some shit from Legal Aid.'

'Alright.' Damiano wanted Marie to see Pauzé's hand and receive her professional opinion as to whether the wound might have come from the boxed manuscript. 'Holmes deserved what she got. I hope she never wakes up. You're as two-faced as she is, so get the hell out of my room!' He was building steam as he shouted.

'She's awake and talking, Jean.'

An elderly patient in the room pushed herself up to get a better look as Damiano left.

Pauzé glared and waited for her to get out of the room. Then he turned his fury on the older patient. 'What the fuck are you looking at? Vieille sacoche!'

Damiano was on the phone to Crime before she left the floor. She was a cop – she could break hospital rules. Marie was a quick study.

'I'm on my way. Door glass and bottle glass, I can do. Good thinking.'

Damiano liked to save her thinking for the car. The silence helped. Could a sliver of the door glass penetrate a glove and remain embedded in the wound and not be noticed until days later? Pauzé had kept the wound covered Did he not notice it because of the overwhelming pain in his legs, or had he reason to conceal it?

Chapter Forty-five

FEAR BEGAN AS A TICKLE in her throat, until she knew what it was. Had she and Pauzé been overheard? Had she just caused a leak? The boss would dump her ass on the street if that occurred. A deeper dread surfaced. All the tracks they were pursuing looked good. Yet there was that 'X' factor. The leads might just be smoke. In eleven days she hadn't been able to tighten the net on one individual. Was Holmes's case the one that got to her, the file she couldn't close? *Toughen up!* Another thought soothed her. Damiano wished Jeff were pouring her a vodka martini with two green olives. She could taste the vodka as it glided past her tongue.

'Enough!' Grabbing her phone, she tapped in Matte's number. 'Where are you?'

'I left the lab with Marie, taking notes. I'm heading to the office to set up for the lineup tomorrow afternoon. I'll notify Galt. And you?'

'You keep impressing me, Pierre.'

'I commune with details.'

'Give some serious thought to Angela Marino. We need to work her – *how* is the question. I'm driving to the General to see Holmes. We can't wait forever. I was calling to see if you wanted to come with me.'

'You kidding me? But you know I can't. Details, remember?'

'You're a solid partner, Pierre.'

'You're just running a little scared.'

'What?' Her anger flared.

'*Calme-toi!* It's that time in the life of a case. Details are jumbled pieces. One piece will shake loose.'

'Can't be too soon,' she interjected.

'I'll work something up with Marino. Exert more pressure with Holmes. We've been patient.'

'Pressure is my game.'

'So go to it.'

For once, the traffic was light and she reached Pine Avenue in good time. She made a quick stop at a water cooler and drank three cups. Turner's replacement was the first person she saw. He was young and alert and spotted her well before she was close.

'Good afternoon, Detective! All quiet here.'

Damiano nodded as she walked into the ICU without medical clearance. Holmes was busy rubbing lotion on his daughter's legs and feet and didn't see her approach.

Madison did. Propped up with pillows, she turned her head and shoulders about an inch. Her head felt like an NHL rink, wide, heavy, awkward. Her eye was still heavily bandaged, but the bandaging was removed every morning when her eye was flushed. That felt so good – cool and refreshing. During the night the eye crusted over and she didn't try opening it under the bandages, but she did right after the flushing. When her doctor held it open each morning, flashing his light across it, she followed the light. Her heart settled back into good rhythm – she'd see.

Events raced around her mind. Holmes was trying to place them in order. The events were there. She just had to work to synchronize them. She had begun. She remembered Tracey's call, remembered taping it, remembered her anger. The rejection letters and the names had come back into focus. Her appointment with Connor, the wine, the new sheets, they were all pieces of a puzzle she was trying to fit into place. Holmes looked down at her father and smiled. She'd never seen so much of him. His voice was quiet and soothing, but he kept her from the work of sorting that she needed to do. He didn't leave her side. She needed time to think. She recalled hearing the doorbell; she saw the UPS courier with what was probably a manuscript, but she couldn't see his face clearly. It was blurred like faces on TV when they wish to conceal identity. Strange, but Madison let that go. Had she solicited a new manuscript? That thought stalled her sorting. She couldn't recall requesting any new clients.

Madison abandoned the sorting and turned her attention to the woman standing at the foot of her bed. She'd seen her before. She wasn't a writer. She wasn't a doctor. Who was she?

'Detective, let's stand over here.'

Madison strained forward but she couldn't hear what they were saying.

Holmes took command. 'Madison is walking with help. She can't afford a fall. Her physician and I are extremely cautious. Hemorrhages and clots might still occur, especially if Madison feels undue pressure.'

Damiano employed her best diplomacy. 'May I introduce myself and ask questions around the attack, questions that won't cause the stress you've just mentioned? You can monitor them as I proceed. I am sure that Ms Holmes would like to know who I am.'

'I picked up on that. Proceed very slowly, Detective.'

Damiano stood at the bottom of the bed. 'Madison, I'm Detective Toni Damiano. Call me Toni. That's easier for you.'

'Police?' Madison got the word out.

'Well, we have to take good care of a celebrity.'

Madison gave Damiano a shut-up wave and smiled before she realized the smile hurt.

'Do you remember Martin Connor, the big author from the States?'

It didn't take long for Madison to respond. 'Yes.'

'Well, I have good news for you. Connor fell and is facing rotator cuff surgery on both shoulders. But he said that after you and he have convalesced he still wants to work with you.' Damiano had spoken very slowly and she waited to see if Madison had understood the lengthy comment.

Thomas Holmes walked to the side of Madison's bed. Damiano didn't move.

Madison's face softened. 'Good for me then.' She closed her eye, but Holmes and Damiano saw relief spread across her face. He smiled at Damiano. Holmes had a kind face which she hadn't seen before. They didn't at first see that Madison had pushed herself up with both hands pressed firmly on either side of her.

'Maddy, what's wrong, honey?'

'Toni, what happened to me?' Madison's voice was strained but demanding. 'Dad won't tell me.'

Holmes caught the sudden change in the heart monitor. 'Maddy, lean back, honey. I don't want you excited. Rest is the most important thing for you now. Detective Damiano can come back another time. Is that okay, Maddy?' He tried to help Madison to lie back down, but she resisted him. The monitor indicated that Madison's blood pressure was rising.

'Dad, stop.'

Holmes signalled to the ICU nurse. When she saw the monitor, she ordered Holmes and Damiano from the room.

Madison was still trying to lunge forward. 'I want to know what…'

Holmes lit into Damiano as soon as they were out of the room. 'I warned you!'

'Just stop! Control yourself. I didn't ask a single disturbing question. Can't you see that the pressure is in your daughter's head? *She* wants to know what happened. And, dammit, I need her help.'

'I don't want to take the risk of…'

'It's not what you want anymore. It's what your daughter needs that is uppermost. And I know she can help me find who put her here. The truth is her starting point for emotional recovery. Can't you see that? Have some faith in her. Look at how far she's come on her own. The demand came from her!'

'Just not today. Is that possible? I want to talk to her, to see if she understands the consequences. If she does recall the brutal attack, the fallout might be dire for her health.'

Dr. Stephen Orr hurried around the corner, past them, into the ICU. They waited anxiously until he came back out. 'Thomas, this was bound to happen. Your daughter is one tough cookie. Her heart rate is high but has levelled with some sedation. She asked *me* what happened to her. Detective, did you put the question to her?'

'I did not. Ms Holmes asked.'

'I told Detective Damiano that she can't pursue the questioning today.'

'Perhaps a day of rest is good, Thomas, but we have to get past this point. Madison's trying to recall events. That's normal for victims. She's already agitated, so I will be present and administer minor sedation. It's necessary and will calm her. I think Madison can get through the ordeal, Thomas.'

Damiano was firm. 'I'll be back here before nine tomorrow.'

'I'll arrange to be here,' Dr. Orr added.

Holmes's shoulders stiffened and he went back to his daughter. He ran his hand gently across her forehead. 'I love you, Maddy. You don't deserve any of this. Why don't we simply concentrate on getting you better?'

'Dad…'

'I know, Maddy. Detective Damiano will be back.'

'Good,' Madison whispered and grabbed her father's hand. Her mind was determined to sort, and Madison went with it. She remembered the manuscript. Did she take it? The wind – she remembered the wind. A sudden shudder shook her whole body.

'Maddy?'

Madison had released her father's hand during the sudden, brief seizure. When it passed, she lay rigid, staring at the ceiling. She knew she was close – she had to know. Her breathing calmed. She had no choice. She did not want to forget what was lodged in her head. Even if it took a psychological hammer, she wanted to chip away at the hidden face. The answer was breaking out of her like Michelangelo's marble sculpture *Awakening Prisoner*.

Chapter Forty-six

Driving back to the Crémazie Division, Damiano's spirits rose and fell when Marie Dumont from Crime called.

'I'm at the Hôtel Dieu. I had to discuss the situation before proceeding. Does Pauzé want a lawyer? You asked, of course.'

'Doesn't trust Legal Aid and has no money.'

'Well, I have to advise him that I'm collecting evidence when I clean and dress the wound. Why wasn't it ever attended to?'

' Pauzé said no one noticed it, not even him till yesterday. I think it's been three and a half days. Time has blurred on me. Did a makeshift job on it himself. Said he stopped caring because his life has tanked, his words. Marie, can't you expand the subpoena we already have to search his apartment?'

'His body is not the same as his habitat. He can refuse.'

'Ah damn! Where do we go?'

'I can't have him thinking I'm looking for evidence of *his* assault – won't stand up in court, Toni.'

'We lie to suspects all the time – it's legal.'

'We're talking about his body – very different. I have a plan, but it's a crapshoot in court.'

'Try me.'

'I'll take the bag with me not to break the chain of evidence. Then we have proof of the continuity of possession and integrity of this evidence.'

'You don't have to be specific with the event, right?'

'That's the crapshoot – evidence retrieved under false assumption. He's despondent and medicated. He might not enquire about the evidence. We take a chance he won't.'

'Are we good if he doesn't?' '

'For a better chance in court, he has to have given consent. We can't afford a whole lie. Any judge would toss the evidence.'

'Know what? Go with your plan. Pauzé might not know the law as well as you do. Without a lawyer, we grind him down before the file ever gets to court.'

'Remember one thing, Toni. This is your problem – you're the lead.'

'I did tell Pauzé he was a suspect in the Holmes case when I saw him. I even said he'd have to show up at the lineup tomorrow afternoon.'

'In his condition?'

'They have him walking with help.'

'You're tough.'

'Yep.'

'Your problem just got smaller. He knows he's a suspect in the Holmes case. He also is aware he's being called to a lineup. If Pauzé doesn't ask me which assault I'm referring to, the burden for specifics falls on him. We're looking better.'

Damiano told Marie about Holmes.

'You're going to close. I can feel it.'

'Till I do…'

'I'll do all I can. I'm even skipping my poutine today.'

'Devotion.'

'You said it.'

Damiano felt she was tapping on thin ice, waiting for the crack that would get her inside.

'Hôtel Dieu called about the lineup. They will do their best, but no promises.' Matte told her. Matte looked back at Damiano for some kind of recognition. He found exasperation. 'What's up with you? I'm the one who should be annoyed after having the postal work shut down. Details are my domain. Thought I could run with it and find something solid.'

'In the long run, Donat was right about that approach. We were reaching. Anyway, I'm hungry and I'm tired. There's something I can't – I don't know. We've both worked our asses off. We've rolled marbles in four directions, but we haven't had one closed circle. They're all *ifs*! You've heard of problem files, right? Marie is hunting for glass she might not find, Crime is analyzing dirt from the sneaker; we're planning a lineup with a kid whose mother reminds me he lies to impress people. Lastly, Holmes might not recognize the perp with the hat and shades, even though she saw him. The whole file will come down to her eyes – I just know it.'

'Try your hand at writing a book on depression. You're kicking the stuffing out of me. You have no patience, Toni. I look at one detail at a time – you take in the whole picture. The puzzle isn't completed. Go home, fill your face and get some sleep. I'll do the same.'

'Turner's funeral's tomorrow.'

'Yeah, tomorrow is the operative word. Go home!'

'My mood shifts are killing me.'

'You're an intelligent, complicated, foxy mood-freak. That's your woven basket.'

'See you back here early tomorrow before I drive over to the hospital. I'm the lead here.' She threw the words back half-heartedly because she was choking back a laugh.

Chapter Forty-seven

DRIVING TO HER CONDO on Hutchison in Outremont, food and sleep were Damiano's mantra. Had Luke come through with food? As she got out of the city car in her underground parking, every part of her body ached; even her baby toes had developed a separate pinching pain. Her condo was two doors from the elevator. She smelled turkey as soon as the elevator door opened. *Can't be!* Her door was ajar and she heard voices inside. The turkey *was* definitely in her condo. She had a good nose. The voices were familiar. She pushed the door open.

'Well, Mom, waddyathink?' Luke and Jeff stood together beaming. 'Dad taught me to do a bird and oven-baked potatoes. You got the works: peas, carrots and turnips, pickled beets – we bought those, and fresh cranberry sauce. Dad filled the fridge too. So? Ah Mom, don't start to cry!'

Damiano wiped her eyes. 'I could eat the whole bird.'

'No, you don't! I want a leg and Dad wants the neck and dark meat.'

Jeff gave Damiano an awkward hug and whispered. 'Get into the shower and we'll serve. We won't stay long.'

'This is all so…'

'Yeah,' Luke said, 'we know.'

Damiano stripped off her clothes and tossed them on a chair. In the shower, she rested both hands against the walls and stood under the hottest water she could bear. She threw her head back and the full force of the spray washed across her forehead, face and temples. When her body was warm, she grabbed an extra-large bath towel and disappeared under it. For the next few minutes, she curled under the towel and lay on the bed, secure and safe.

Jeff tiptoed into the room. 'Sleepyhead, don't fall asleep. Blow-dry that hair of yours and get out here.'

'I'm so tired…'

'As soon as you eat, I'll clean up and you can flop into bed. Deal?'

'Why are you being so good to me?' She said from under the towel.

'As a Brit would say, because I wanna shag you, Toni Damiano.'

'Alright, I'm getting up.'

The trio had polished off the pickled beets, turnips, carrots, small sweet peas and most of the turkey. If she was lucky, she might have a sandwich or two from what was left. Before Damiano fell asleep, she remembered Luke saying, 'Mom, slow down. You'll have indigestion.' But she was asleep long before the indigestion had a chance with her. Early the next morning she walked into a spotless kitchen and a short note. 'We're on your side.' She found a second note under the first. 'Better come home soon. We're getting used to the extra space. Luke.' She expected the guilt trip, and it came. Family issues could wait. Unlike Madison Holmes, Damiano had no desire to chip away at her flaws until she saw the truth. It wasn't going to be good for her.

Still the day began with renewed hope.

'Good luck with Holmes!' Matte said as she left the division. 'Remember – piece by piece, Toni.'

She used both flashers as she drove. The congestion and the newly announced road closures infuriated her as they did most city drivers, but she didn't swear. She stayed focused on her approach with Holmes. In full dress uniform as the boss had ordered for Turner's funeral, she relented and took a busy, stuffy crowded elevator and closed her eyes to the stares. Orr and Holmes were waiting for her. They seemed immediately impressed, but cautious.

'We'd better get you a white coat. The uniform might unsettle Madison, even with the mild sedative I've administered,' Doctor Orr said.

'I have a funeral to attend – I'm sorry about this.'

Holmes waited with Damiano. 'I know I can't avoid this interview. Madison wants it. She's recalling on her own. After you left, she suffered a minor seizure. It didn't last, but…'

'I'll do my very best. You have my word. Here's the white coat. I guess we're ready.'

Madison was sitting up, propped by pillows and hooked to monitors. She asked the first question. 'Tracey Doyle?'

That gave Damiano a good lead in. 'She's staying with you. She wants to. It was her mother who…'

'The dominatrix.' Madison had some trouble getting her mouth around the word without hurting her face, but she got it out. Smiles hurt, so she kept a straight face.

The others laughed quietly. 'Excellent choice of words. All Tracey's fans have texted, emailed and tweeted that she has to stand by you because you two are the best team!' Damiano said. 'All you have to do is get well and you'll have your life back.'

Madison relaxed.

Holmes looked at Orr, and one could detect they were impressed with Damiano's approach.

'If I ask you a question that upsets you, put one hand up, and I will pause.'

'I want to know what…'

'Do you remember Tracey Doyle calling you?'

'Yes, I taped it.'

'You did. Do you remember the next morning, Madison?'

'Yes, I had breakfast.'

'Then?'

'I worried about Tracey.'

'Okay, then?'

Madison took her time. *What then?* 'Dad called, I think.'

'Yes, that's right, Maddy, I did.' Holmes stepped closer to his daughter.

Damiano glared at Holmes, and he stepped back.

'After that, Madison, what do you remember?'

Madison steepled her fingers. 'Then, the doorbell, UPS.'

'And?'

'I assumed he had a manuscript.'

'Excellent, Madison. Would you like to take a break? Water perhaps.'

Madison looked at her father and she saw him wince. She brought a hand up to her mouth and chewed on her thumb. 'No.'

'Did the courier leave the manuscript?'

Madison thought about that. Her mouth tightened. 'No.'

'Did you open the door then?' Damiano kept her voice very casual.

But Madison felt the quiet all around her. Her breathing became heavy.

'Don't worry if you don't remember. It's just a question,' Damiano said reassuringly. 'We can take a break.'

'No!' Madison was gasping. 'No!'

Dr. Orr checked the monitor.

Madison began to rock. 'The wind, the wind.'

'Madison, just lie back. Detective Damiano can come back. You need to rest,' Dr. Orr said, signalling the end of the questioning.

Reluctantly, Damiano backed off.

Madison's body shook violently. Dr. Orr injected sedation into an IV line.

Madison shook with rage. 'I opened the doo…'

'Enough, Maddy.' Holmes laid both hands on Madison's shoulders and gently manoeuvered her back down on the bed. 'Don't cry, Maddy. You're safe. Don't cry. Just breathe slowly. You don't have to know, Maddy. It's not important. Your health is all that's important now.'

He's not helping. Damiano decided to wait outside, hoping there was a chance for the last few questions. She still had time before Turner's funeral.

Detective Matte had said, 'A piece will break loose.' Still she felt that edginess, the drive to break through the long list of suppositions. At least Damiano was current on all of them. Since her mother's death, she had hated the word closure – who ever got closure? Holmes was fighting for it. Damiano wished she could keep Thomas Holmes outside the room during the questioning. He was in her way.

Pauzè had been moved and Damiano had missed it. At Hôtel Dieu, an elderly patient had passed away. At his request, Pauzé was now across the room beside a window on the sixth floor. He examined the window and then he lay back.

Chapter Forty-eight

THE CHAIN DIDN'T BREAK. Madison's seizure was more serious than the first, another delay. Damiano walked out of the Montreal General Hospital into a wickedly cold day. Gusty winds assaulted her on all sides. The turkey sandwiches with cranberry neatly packed on the passenger seat beside her cap were her only solace. Luke's short note had rattled her. *We're getting used to the extra space.* She could not go limping back to Jeff and Luke without closing the case. She had her pride. Failure? Never happen!

Yet as she approached the West Island, she grew more somber. Damiano hung a left on Boulevard des Sources. Familiar with the West Island, she drove right along Donegani Street to Valois Bay. After another right, she drove past three stops and found Saint John Fisher Church on Summerhill Avenue. She was early and alone for the next few minutes. Two summers ago Jeff and Luke and she had ridden along the lakeshore to the iconic St-Joachim Church which had been the beacon to sailors years ago. After checking out Treks at Paul's Cycle and Sports, they had eaten at the corner restaurant, Le Gourmand. She was happy then. What had really changed?

The soul-searching ended abruptly when she saw two TV vans pull onto the church parking lot. To maintain their privacy, the Turners had purposely not published an obituary. Damiano whipped out her phone and punched Station 5 located on Saint John's Boulevard. 'I want these hyenas off church property asap!' Struggling with anger and sadness for Turner, she stayed in the car until a few patrol cars arrived.

The church was a large, plain, brown-brick rectangle, built up above street level. No shrubbery, or late fall flowers softened the building or offered inspiration. It was one of the dullest churches Damiano had ever seen in Montreal, a city of churches. Wide cement stairs led to the three dome-shaped wooden doors. Only the center door was open. Nothing about the exterior was comforting. She watched the TV crew arguing, then reluctantly backing off. A few people began to arrive, mostly walking. *Neighbors.* Cars began to turn onto the parking lot. Some of the drivers were Turner's age, but there weren't many of them. Damiano grabbed her cap, crossed the street, went into the church and chose a back pew. She counted twenty-one mourners. Their scant presence made the body of the church more sterile and severe. *You stupid jerk, Troy.*

An organ began to play and she turned to see the casket in the vestibule flanked by pall-bearers. Damiano turned back when she spotted the Turners. A priest with two servers walked down the center aisle with holy water. *You're a little late, Father.* When he reached the back, the casket was rolled just inside the church, and Troy's body and soul were welcomed home by the parish priest whose words suggested he knew Troy.

Damiano stood at full attention as the casket was wheeled slowly down the central aisle, followed by the family, to the front of the church. John Turner nodded his appreciation as he passed her. Damiano fought back tears and stood until the organ stopped and people sat. ... *This doesn't have to be the end of your life. Why didn't you listen to me?* Damiano didn't hear much else. All she saw was Troy with his notes, his high spirits, his youth, his innocence. One event had narrowed the direction of his life. Troy had taken a piece of hers as well and she profoundly felt the endemic cynicism that came with the job.

Damiano didn't hear the homily, but she listened when the priest began to speak of Troy and the family's loss.

'This is a loss that disrupts the natural rhythm of life. There is no tragedy worse than the loss of a child. Troy had no brothers or sisters, so John and Jennifer must travel life's journey alone now, without Troy. It took me some years to fully appreciate that work and titles, success and affluence pale beside the soul of life, the family – the pulse, the wings and the bond of love that survives death. On their road they will carry Troy in their hearts...'

Damiano closed her eyes and didn't see the soloist, but she heard his words echoing against the walls of the church. 'Be not afraid, I go before you...' Her tears came rushing. *Shit! I have no Kleenex.* She used her white gloves and waited for the casket to be taken out before she left. John Turner caught up with her. Damiano didn't miss the cameras aimed at them and turned her back.

'Thank you for coming, Detective. Here's the check. I didn't bother with an envelope. I wanted it out of the house. Troy sold his life for $15,000. I'd better get back to my wife.'

'Just a second, Mr. Turner. I don't think Troy was interested in the money. I think he felt by exposing Holmes, he'd force the hand of the assailant. He'd make the arrest and earn an upgrade.'

Turner smiled forlornly. 'Another one of Troy's "no hands" moves that crashed. My son always thought he could handle things on his own, that he knew best. Anyway, what does that matter now? Troy had a bunch of friends in the force, and not one of them showed up today, except you. I guess you had no choice.'

'I would have made it a point to come. The situation kept his friends away.'

Turner laid his hand on her shoulder for a second and walked away.

When Damiano looked up, she saw that the servers were closing the church door.

Chapter Forty-nine

DAMIANO APPROACHED one of the patrol cars and spoke to the officer. 'Don't allow any TV goons near the family. I'd like one car to follow them to Lakeview cemetery. Block the crew from entering.'

'I don't know, Detective. We were told to come here…'

'Call in!' Damiano grabbed the phone and quickly got into a heated discussion. 'Bottom line, Poste de Quartier 5 doesn't want bad press on the fallout if you do not protect the privacy the family has requested. The editor of the *West Island Gazette* will get her teeth into this human tragedy.'

'We know her. She'd make a good investigator – doesn't miss a good story.'

'Well?'

'Hand off to Officer Dubé.'

'Thanks.' Damiano got to her car and dropped down onto her seat. She waited until one of the surveillance officers spoke to the TV crew before she drove away undetected. Her immediate goal was a quiet street. She found King Street and parked. She tossed her cap on the back seat, and reached across for the sandwiches and ate both with a desperate hunger, filling the emptiness inside. She looked around like a shoplifter as she ate. The Kleenex box was in the glove compartment and she did her best to clean off the turkey remnants from her teeth before she drove back to Crémazie as fast as she could without mowing down pedestrians who made jaywalking part of their daily diet. She had brought a change of clothes with her.

The lineup had the feel of another crisis, but the division was quiet when she drove down to the parking garage. Word hadn't leaked about their suspects or lineup, so they weren't going to be blindsided by the papers. That was something. As she was reaching back for her cap, her car door was flung open.

Detective Galt grabbed her shoulder and hauled her out of the car.

Damiano pushed him off and steadied herself, but he got to his rant first.

'Some of the shields are beginning to think I'm good for this because you are fucking me up, Detective!' He tried to push her, but Damiano stepped out of the way. 'You went back into my house without the decency of letting me know. I am one of you! What do you have up your ass, speaking to my son? You could have given me a pass on the whole goddamn file. Why the fuck didn't you?'

'Right, your son the hacker!'

Galt's face whitened. 'You fu…'

'I don't have to pin anything on you. You're doing a good job of that yourself.' Damiano tried to walk off, but Galt stepped in her way again. 'Watch your back.'

'You're threatening a detective now? What? Like Holmes didn't watch hers when you went after her?'

Galt's fist came within a whisper of striking Damiano in the face. He brought his arm down. Another thought occurred to him. 'You taping this?' He gripped the top of her uniform and was about to rip it down the front. She smelled his hatred. 'Will I find a wire, Detective? Just so you know, we're outta camera range.'

Damiano let go with a vicious kick that stuck Galt's kneecap and he howled. 'Get yourself to the goddamn lineup!' Damiano forced herself to walk away without running. Every part of her body was shaking. *Watch my back, you fucker!* Once she was inside the division, she hurried to her locker, took her change of clothes and makeup and headed to the washroom. She hung her suit on the top of the toilet door and went back to the sink and splashed cold water up in her face. *Fucker!* She kept her head down and let the water drip from her face. The lineup was already a crisis, and it hadn't even begun.

Why hadn't she heard from Marie? How long did it take to analyze dirt? Or glass for that matter? When she had changed, she checked herself out. The garage fright didn't show on her face. Small mercy. At that point, she'd take what she could get. Matte was waiting for her. 'I've missed not having you with me.'

'Good. Haven't heard anything from Beauchemin, or Galt. Think I'll call the hospital. So far, we look good.'

'Mathieu?'

'Not yet.'

Damiano debated telling Matte about Galt and saw that she might need someone else knowing if Galt came after her.

'Arrest his ass!'

'No, not yet. That's exactly what he might want to get out of the lineup.'

'Well, right after. He told you to watch your back. He might have something else in mind. You can't ignore his threat.'

'We'll talk after the lineup. I want him for Holmes if he did her. Pierre, would you get down to the ID Room and see to the suspects? I want to talk to Mathieu before Beauchemin's lawyer is present. Give me a heads-up on any glitches.'

'Keep your eyes open for Galt.'

'Yeah, yeah.' Damiano took the stairs down to the main entrance on the first floor. The patrol officer who had picked up Mathieu and his aunt had stayed with them. 'Good afternoon! Officer, thank you, I can take things from here.'

'Mme Boucher,' Mathieu's aunt introduced herself.

'Detective Damiano. Thank you for coming.' The woman looked as nervous as her sister. Damiano took them to the interview room and soon discovered the reason for her nervousness.

'My nephew has something to tell you, Detective.'

Mathieu was dressed in his best white shirt and blue pullover, and he smelled cleaner than most little boys. He seemed somehow shorter. 'Yes, Mathieu. Remember what I said about honesty.'

The boy shook his head in shame. 'Yeah. It was just a trick, not really a lie.'

'What is it, Mathieu? We don't have a lot of time.'

'Remember I told you I knew all about lineups 'cause I'd surfed the net?'

'I do.'

The boy picked up speed. 'Well, I saw three. In each one they had the cops in the middle and the bad guys on the ends.'

'So when you said it wasn't two, three or four, you were just copying what you had seen? You didn't really know.'

Mathieu hung his head again.

Damn! Damiano sat on the nearest chair and pulled Mathieu in front of her. 'Were you telling the truth when you said you want to be a detective one day?'

Mathieu's face grew serious and a frown looked out of place on a child. 'Cross my heart!'

'You did see the man in the lane, right? Don't lie to me, Mathieu. I'll know if you are. Cops pick up on those things.'

'I don't lie when I cross my heart!'

'Good. When we go back into the ID Room, I want you to think back to that day in the lane. Get a picture in your mind of the man you saw and do your best to pick him out in the lineup.'

Mathieu had scrunched up his face in deep thought. 'Doing it.'

'If you do this job honestly and well, I'd be happy to write you a rec-ommendation when you want to join the force.'

He gave his aunt a great smile. 'See, I told you!'

'Remember, take your time. I can't give you any hints. If the lawyer asks you if I prepared you before the lineup, what will you say to him? Keep the answer short, Mathieu.'

'I gotta be honest and take my time.' He looked to Damiano for approval.

'Perfect!'

Mathieu grew an inch.

'I'll come and get you in a few minutes. Just picture that man in the lane.' Before she got out of the room her phone hummed. 'Yes, Pierre.'

'Beauchemin with his mouthpiece and Galt are here. Hôtel Dieu just called. Pauzé has a blood clot in his leg – he's not going anywhere. I suggest we go with the six pack, following the lineup. Beauchemin has dropped about seven pounds.'

'So he won't look the same.'

'That's right. We are ready to go. Bring Mathieu down. We'll go with what we have.'

Mathieu walked beside Damiano and she greeted the lawyer at the door.

'Did you instruct your witness, Detective?' The lawyer was a short, stubby little man, a good match for Beauchemin. A small man with a small man complex. 'May I ask him a question?'

'Go ahead.'

'What did Detective Damiano tell you to do when we get into the room?'

Mathieu didn't blink. 'Detective Damiano said I had to be honest and I had to take my time.'

'Did she give you any hints?'

'NO!' Mathieu shouted. 'She's a detective!'

Satisfied, he turned and together they walked into the room. Seconds later the side door opened and six men in caps, jackets and shades walked single file into the room. As instructed, they knelt on one knee and looked at the glass mirror. Galt was forced to kneel on his bruised knee.

'Can I go closer to the window to get a better look?'

'Yes,' Damiano said.

Mathieu walked up to the two-way mirror, put both hands on it and took his best studied scan. On his side the room was dark. Detective Damiano had told him that the suspects on the other side of the mirror couldn't see him, so he felt safe. On their side it was very bright. He could see them perfectly.

'No coaching,' Beauchemin's lawyer warned Damiano.

Chapter Fifty

THE COURIER KNEW, without question, that he could have taken a life and gone on with his own without any urge to confess. He might have been fearless with the power of a kill behind him. He might have gotten what he wanted. He had a goal.

But he had failed. His world was cracking and shifting underfoot. Exposure flickered around him. Damiano had eyes on him. She held him in contempt, and he strained every part of himself to ward her off and protect what he had left.

He hated waiting. He hated being afraid – he'd been afraid for too long.

Chapter Fifty-one

MATHIEU WAS TAKING much too long to decide if he recognized anyone in the six-man lineup. Damiano readied herself to deal with another blank. Mathieu turned back to Damiano. 'It's not fair. The guy who took the dive, number four, doesn't look the same. Number three has something wrong with his knee. How can I tell now? Everything's different! The guy in the lane looked okay, just scared.' Mathieu was too young for failure. The boy hung his head and walked over to Damiano. 'Guess I'd never make a good detective.'

Maître David in his lawyer suit looked pleased, but the feeling didn't last.

'Detective Matte, please shut down the lineup. We'll go with the usual six pack.'

'When?' the lawyer asked, invading their space.

'Step back, please.' Damiano pointed to a corner until the lawyer walked in that direction, but he refused to be sidelined. 'When?' he called again.

'As soon as the room is cleared.'

'When were these photos taken?' he shouted back.

'You are not entitled to that information. Your client is not under arrest.'

The short lawyer wouldn't call it a day. 'Were the photos Photoshopped? The men were asked to wear hats and sunglasses and the rest.'

'I'm not under any legal obligation to divulge that information. I repeat, your client is not yet under arrest. Excuse me. Mathieu, I need you for a few more minutes.'

'Okay!' Mathieu said with renewed enthusiasm.

'Detective Matte will bring you a group of photos. Excuse me, Maître David, today's session has ended.'

'I should be...'

'This meeting is a gathering of circumstantial information. You'll have to leave.'

'Advise me of the findings as they pertain to my client,' he said, clearly miffed.

'Rest assured you will be informed.'

Mathieu waited until Maître David had left. 'Is it the same guys again?' he asked without much hope.

'You did your best. I can't tell you about the photos, but we'll go to the interview room and you can see them there.'

'I was kinda looking at the shoes and the shades. They had black rims and the shades were real dark so I couldn't see his eyes.'

'And the shoes?'

'They were real old.'

'Because they were dirty?'

'I mean like years old.'

When they reached the interview room, she told Mathieu and his aunt to sit and she'd be right back. She looked down the corridor for Matte and couldn't see him. A quick call to Marie might help. 'How long can dirt take to analyze?'

'Hello, Toni. You need poutine to bring you down.'

'I need something I can use on that shoe. What happened with Pauzé's cut? What about the dirt?'

'You got nothing with the lineup right, Toni?'

'Nada. Zip.'

'Considering what the perp was wearing, there wasn't much of him to see. Sorry anyway.'

'You have to have something, Marie. Damn! Matte's almost here with the six pack. I'll have to call you back.'

'Great talking to you, Toni!' Dumont intended the sarcasm in her tone.

Damiano hung up and turned immediately to Matte. 'Sorry for the delay, Pierre.'

'No problem. First Galt and Beauchemin were relieved; then they were pissed. I have the photos,' Matte said.

'Good. Let's get inside. I have another idea.'

'Mathieu, I'm going to put a sheet of photos on the table. Try those. Take your time.'

Matte slid the sheet in front of Mathieu.

'Can I ask questions this time?'

'Yes, but I still can't coach you.'

Mathieu's aunt backed away while he studied the photos. The boy was near tears. He pointed at Pauzé. 'This could be the guy, but the dive-guy and the knee-guy could be too. It's not fair, they all look the same.'

'What about the other three men?'

'I dunno, maybe. I'm never going to be a detective.'

'Mathieu, I might not have done any better. This part was hard. I have another test. If I showed you old sneakers, do you think you might recognize the ones you saw that day?'

'You have to mix them up again?'

'Maybe four pairs.'

'Well, I saw them. I might do good.' The kid was straining to get something right.

'Well, I'll call you when we have them, and I'll send a patrol car for you again.'

'Maybe at my school, so all the kids can see.'

'You can't tell anyone you're helping the police. You don't want your friends to think you're in trouble.'

'No, no.'

'Okay then. Thanks for the good effort. You have to work at things to succeed and I do too.'

'You're going to get this guy, right?'

'I will.'

Matte smiled as they left. 'Shoes?'

'The kid said the perp's sneakers in the lane were really old.'

'Glad I found it then. I better go back for the partner.'

'I'm going to send Crime as well. We need that shoe. This might be the break. I'm revving up again. We are so close. I have to slow down, be more like you.'

'Wow!'

'Maybe. The sneaker has to be in his apartment. I can't have the kid looking at one damn shoe.' Damiano was on the phone again. 'Marie, will you send Crime to Pauzé's for the other sneaker?'

'Can't believe we missed it.'

'What's the news? I have time and my notepad.'

'We took various samples of dirt from different places in the lane. Unfortunately, there was nothing remarkable or distinguishable from the top of the lane where your witness saw the perp and the samples we picked up elsewhere.'

'Ah, damn.'

'I assisted in the clean-up of Pauzé's wound. Worked the book on this. Asked him casually if he wanted to keep the "souvenirs." I was about to gather up the cotton swabs and slivers, there were two, but he's not a PhD for nothing. He smelled a rat. He decided he wanted them, as a lesson he said.'

'That's something, Marie!'

'I had the same thought.'

'You have to locate that bloody sneaker.'

Chapter Fifty-two

ANGELA MARINO SAT behind her cherrywood desk with folders, explaining what she had found on her first reading. Her client listened anxiously, wringing his hands as she spoke. 'Unfortunately, clients never understand the depth of their case. A close study exposes the perimeter of the work involved. The good news is that I can work with this case with results that will put your mind at ease. I need additional hours of study and I'll have to hire two investigators. That amounts to an additional $25,000 for my work and $15,000 for the outsourcing.

'Before you give me your answer, let me just say, that going "cheap" won't move this case forward. In the end it will drain your resources. With me you get what you pay very well for, you prevail.'

'What about the $10,000 I have already given you?'

Marino didn't seem offended in the least. 'That money will be spent when we conclude this two-hour session.'

'Do you have a ballpark figure for the entire case?'

'With sessions, paperwork, court time, the inevitable delays of course, and the unexpected that never fails to rear its head, easily $200,000. You walk away with your company and a dismissal of the charges. That means no record.'

'You can say with certainty that you will achieve those results?'

'In my career, I have lost three cases, all due to clients who withheld information from me. I demand complete honesty. You will receive a statement following each session. The money is paid to me as the case progresses. Unlike many litigators, I don't provoke delays. My client list is healthy. I work for results.'

'I don't seem to have a choice.'

'It seems to me you have two that I have explained. You are in serious trouble. You want to walk away from this – come aboard. It's that simple.' A phone in one of the desk drawers rang.

The client saw Marino's face stiffen.

'I'm sorry, this is an emergency. You'll have to excuse me. If you wait in the outer office, I'll be right with you.' The phone kept ringing.

'I hope this doesn't happen in one of our sessions,' the client said pointedly. 'I'm in. You'll have a money order tomorrow.' He left, buoyed and shaken. *$200,000!*

Marino slid the drawer open and reached for the phone. 'Angela Marino.'

'I'd like to meet.'

'May I inquire as to why?' But she already knew.

'Roberto's in one hour.' It was a premier Italian restaurant on Boulevard St-Laurent.

'Yes.' She took the disposable phone with her when she left the office. Marino made a last call from the office phone. 'Tracey, I'm glad I caught you.'

'I'm usually home writing, Mom.'

'What exactly did you say to the police about me – the precise words if you can remember?'

'I'm sorry, Mom.'

'Sorry doesn't do me any good. You're a writer, try to remember.'

'I was so mad at you…'

'Tracey, please.'

'They asked me how you could get me out of the contract.'

'And?'

'I'm sorry.'

'Tracey!' Marino's voice rose.

'I said you had connections – you could do anything.'

'Ugh.'

'Mom, I also said you weren't stupid.'

'I have to go.' Marino hung up and steadied herself against her desk. Her nose began to run.

'Mom! MOM!'

Marino went to the bathroom. The lighting was recessed and soft. The faucets were brass, the counters granite, the floor tiles, large white squares that glistened. She felt she was applying makeup to a block of ice. Too jittery to drive, she called a limo service. *Keep everything brief and be confident.* When she arrived at Roberto's her palms were slippery with perspiration. She was quickly escorted to a table in a dark corner at the rear of the restaurant. The two men were already there. Three glasses of wine were poured and waiting.

The shorter man spoke first. 'I understand there was a recent interview.'

'Anyone with any connection was interviewed. All routine and I saw them only once.'

'Confidentiality is uppermost in everybody's mind.'

'You have the added wall of client confidentiality.'

'It's not the same world today. People are weak and self-centered.'

'My licence to practice is my livelihood and my bond.'

'That is very good. You know we require an impeccable record with employees of your stature.'

Marino crossed her legs under the table and braced herself. 'You have that with me.'

The man smiled at her and the man beside him. 'Enjoy the wine! Your daughter is well?'

'Home and working.'

'You must be proud.'

'I am.'

'I won't keep you.'

Marino bowed and left.

These clients feared the plea deal Marino might make for herself if she were arrested. The lawyer had the 'book' on them. The beautiful Angela had suddenly become a redoubtable adversary. The man spoke again. 'Still nothing with our search?'

His companion shook his head.

'I am not a patient man, but I dislike waste.'

Out on St-Laurent, Marino kept her composure until she was in the limo. Then she crossed both arms under her chin and dropped her head.

'Are you alright, Ma'am?' The driver was studying her in his mirror.

'Let me out just ahead on Prince Arthur Street.' She threw a bill over the seat and rushed from the car. The driver watched her for a few seconds before he drove off. Marino hurried past closed terraces, past St-Dominique, de Bullion, Hôtel de Ville, Laval and Henri-Julien, all small streets leading nowhere. When she reached rue Saint-Denis she was panting and caught the first cab she saw. Little did it matter that Marino had prepared for such a day, that she wouldn't go down alone. *Her* world had changed and she'd have to live within the culture of fear. She had become a liability.

Chapter Fifty-three

DAMIANO WAS ALONE in the office. Matte had returned to Pauzé's apartment where Crime would join him. The pile of evidence had come down to three vital pieces: Holmes's possible identification, the receipts and the shoes.

Chief Donat came barrelling into the office. He threw himself down in front of her. 'Where are we?'

Damiano spoke with brevity and optimism. 'There are other possible breaks. We might get lucky. I still have uniforms on the street with the photos Matte had printed from his phone.' Should she inform the boss about Galt? As if on cue, he jumped into the lead.

'What about Galt? The hacking is the latest on him? Nothing else?'

Damn him! 'Well, he attacked me in the parking garage...'

Donat laughed raucously when she told him how she had connected with Galt's knee. 'You should have aimed higher. What do you want to do with that?'

'Nothing for the time being. If he's good for the assault, I want him on that.'

'Agreed. This is day 12, you know.'

'Have you given any more thought to Marino, Boss?'

Donat leaned back against the chair. 'Do you know how long she'd still be breathing if we arrested her? Wouldn't need a conviction. She'd disappear like Paolo Renda, like Jimmy Hoffa.'

'What if she believed she'd get it done? She's arrogant. She might have made a mistake.'

'Arrogant, not stupid. If she did hire a pro, we'd find no connectors from the victim to the perp. Her clients would never have given permission for the assault. She works for them. It's not the other way around. She didn't hire in. If she got outside help, we're totally screwed. Crime can't do anything with zilch. Pros don't mess up. Holmes survived. Keep that in mind.'

'Are you alright?' Damiano asked. It alarmed Damiano to see Donat quiet, pensive. She missed the assurance of his bark.

'Turner. The kid just threw his life away. The young are so unpredictable. We did the right thing. I do not doubt our actions.' Though it appeared Donat was doing just that. 'What about the funeral?'

'Not one cop showed up, except for me.'

'I didn't want them there. That's why.'

'I handed the $15,000 check in to control.'

'His father didn't want to use any of it for the funeral?'

'Not a penny.'

'Too bad the kid didn't take after his father.' Donat saw that Turner had left his mark on Damiano. He saw it in her eyes. 'You share no blame in his death, Detective. You did good work here. No matter his motives, Turner put Holmes at great risk. Dammit! He exposed her. He also obstructed this investigation. He violated his office. What he did to himself was tragic and final. In the process, he destroyed his parents.'

'Understanding doesn't treat grief.'

'True, but we move on. Good luck with the file, Detective Damiano! Who's on the shoe you've told me about?'

'Matte and Crime.'

'Get down there and help them out. I'll keep an eye on things here.'

Her phone rang. 'Ah, Maître David?'

'You said you'd keep me informed,' he warned Damiano.

'You will be, Maître David, but the file is ongoing. Your client doesn't have direct access because he's hired you. I make the calls. Understood?'

'See that you do.'

Damiano was cautious walking down to her car, on the lookout for Galt. When she reached the garage, she hurried over to it. Once inside, she made certain the doors were locked before she called the Hôtel Dieu. The officer posted on the sixth floor of the hospital, at Pauzé's door, picked up as soon as he heard his phone. He did not take his eyes from his charge.

Pauzé didn't appear to hear the call. He was looking out the window beside his bed, staring at a future he might have lost. He saw a kid on a bike and looked down at his leg.

'I need you to pull a double,' Damiano said. 'There's no time and a half with the budget cuts, but there is time off.'

'No problem.'

'Can you see the trash can in Pauzé's room?'

He kept his response low. 'It's between both beds.'

'Pauzé used swabs to clean his wound. I want every piece of evidence I can lay my hands on. Do you see them?'

'They're on the tray beside the bed. I'll position myself so that I can see if he tosses them. I won't miss anything.'

'My gut tells me he will. He has no place to hide the swabs. If he does, go in and strike up some small talk. Make some joke about hospital work and take out the other basket and leave it in the hall. Then say you're bored and needed some action. You figure out a scenario. Don't touch the swabs with your fingers. Do you have a bag?'

'Lucky day! Two Ziplocs. I use them for my allergy meds. I'll put my pills into one bag and use the other.'

"Don't take your eyes off the swabs. Make certain Pauzé doesn't get on to you.'

'He won't!'

'Call immediately for backup and take the sealed bag to Crime. No one else touches that bag. Maintain the chain of custody, or the evidence is contaminated.'

A sudden case of nerves gripped the officer. 'I have to ask, Detective Damiano. I'll do my best, but what if he does catch on?

'Scoop the swabs out in the hall, so he doesn't see you. If he suspects, don't hand them back. Get to Crime. The prosecutor can argue the legalities. I'm counting on you, Officer.'

Pauzé was looking his way when he got off the phone. 'You as bored as I am? Damiano can be a real bitch. She's testing my job skills! No one will get by me. You're safe.'

'You should hear her interrogations.'

It was that simple to be buds.

Chapter Fifty-Four

Marino saw that her cabbie was Lebanese and she sat back, feeling a little less anxious. He wasn't one of theirs.

'Where to, Ma'am?'

Where to? She had no choice. Her office was out of the question. Its dark halls offered no protection. Calling the police was out of the question. 'Chesterfield Avenue in Westmount above Sherbrooke.' She had the day. Her clients wouldn't touch her because they'd suspect her meeting at the restaurant had been under surveillance. She felt like her last client who feared losing his business. She might lose her life.

During her career, Marino had moments of clarity about some of the clients she had taken on and a day such as this one. Yet this sudden fall from grace, the alacrity of it, struck her like a bullet, like a victim who didn't know he'd been shot until he fell to the pavement. One police interview, that was all it took. Perception was more important than guilt. Her clients were not men who took chances. They didn't operate in doubt. They looked for guilt and they rid themselves of its tracks.

When the cab pulled into her driveway, Marino looked around before she ran to the side door and locked it behind her. She reactivated her alarm and dropped onto a chair in the kitchen, trying to catch her breath. Seconds later, she shot back up. There was no time to waste. Her study was her first target. The wall behind her antique Chippendale desk was a wall-to-wall oak bookcase of leather-bound law books and first editions. Marino reached for her favorite first edition. She tapped the wall behind it, and an oak panel slid two feet to the left revealing her safe. Her fingers trembled and it took her three tries to open it. She stacked the $100,000 on her desk, pulled out a new licence plate, a set of keys to a blue BMW X3 and a .22, the 'family' gun. The shooter had to be very close to the victim to 'take him out.' She stored the SUV at Baltec, a luxury car dealership on rue Jean Talon. It was serviced and ready for an emergency pickup. Marino had made weekly calls to BMW to verify the service. That practice had begun three years ago when the settling of accounts against the principal Montreal crime family began.

Next, she showered. Who knew when she'd feel safe again in a shower? She chose only casual clothes, nothing that she had worn that might be recognized. She didn't take many clothes, except what she could fit into two overnight bags and one piece of luggage. Tracey walked in while she was packing. 'What's happening?'

The urge to rant and cast blame was habitual, but Marino fought both and kept packing.

'Mom? You look awful.'

'Tracey, I haven't always been fair to you.' Marino knew that she might never see her daughter again.

'Contrition doesn't become you Mom. Now, what's wrong?' Tracey got to her feet and went over to her mother. 'What's the matter?'

'Nothing I can talk about. You can't know anything. Don't say you saw me this afternoon. The last time you saw me was this morning. The police will believe you. The house is large and it's possible I could be home and you not know it. My car's still at the office.'

'For shit's sake, Mom, tell me what's going on?'

'Please, get out of my way! I have to hurry.'

'It's Holmes, right?'

'Tracey,' there was desperation in her mother's voice she had never heard before. 'Leave me alone.'

'Are you going to be arrested, is that it? Are you responsible for the attack?' There was venom in her words.

Marino whirled around. 'I'm trying to protect you and I'm trying to save my life! Get out of my room and leave me alone! I can't think with you around.'

Her mother's hands were unsteady, and Tracey was shocked, appalled. This woman who ran roughshod over anyone in her way was afraid? That thought came before her mother's fear spilled into her. She froze watching her mother's frantic movements. She wanted to step forward and help, but she didn't dare.

'Are you still here?'

'Mom, you can't just go like this! You're my mother, even if you never wanted me.' Tracey held back tears. 'Why couldn't you have left my life alone? Why…'

'You claim to be a writer. You should know un-ringing a bell only occurs in fiction.'

'This isn't my fault if you're hinting at that.'

'Have I accused you of anything?'

'Can I help?'

'Wait here.' Marino went to the window and took a careful peek out at the street. It was another gray, cold day. She saw three parked cars, but she couldn't see if anyone was in them. She half ran back to her room and rechecked what she intended to take with her: cash, casual clothes, licence, keys, minor cosmetics, three disposable phones, her wallet and the gun.

She'd take no ID, but the papers for the car and her licence. Anything more and she'd leave tracks. 'You can.'

Marino pulled on a suede jacket that matched the color of her brown slacks, reached for a scarf and began to carry two bags downstairs.

'I'll take the last one.'

When they were at the side door, Marino put her bags down. 'Tracey, I don't know when I'll see you again.'

'This isn't just a drama play, Mom, is it?' But Tracey knew it wasn't.

'For what it's worth, I'm sorry. I *am* proud of you.'

The feel of the apology was paper thin and didn't get through to Tracey. Too many rough years had eroded such a connection. Tracey offered up a lopsided half smile. 'What do you need me to do?'

'Let me borrow that trademark floppy hat you wear. We'll put the bags in your car. I'll drive and you hunker down. That way, you're safe. I have an SUV at the BMW dealership, then you can drive back home safely.'

Tracey hesitated. 'How safe am I if you're hurt? Whoever they are will find me in the car.'

'Forget it! You're right. Just lend me the bloody hat.'

'Can you at least tell me the truth?'

Ignoring her, Marino went looking for the hat.

'Damn it to hell! I'm coming.'

Marino backed out of her driveway without taking one last look at her home. She pulled the hat down over her ears as she drove to Autoroute Décarie, checking her side mirrors and the cars that passed on either side. Her breathing was shallow and loud. Her shoulders ached from the strain. The only sound in the car was breathing. Once, Marino caught a driver at a traffic light staring over at her. She stopped breathing ready to duck. The light changed and she drove across the overpass to the dealer. At the service door, she honked until the door began to open and she drove Tracey's Beemer inside.

Marino tore off the hat and got out of the car. A serviceman was about to ask her what she was doing driving her car inside the service center, but she cut him off. 'Get Jean-Pierre down here, please.' Jean-Pierre was the general manager, so the serviceman got on his phone and called for him. A few minutes later, Jean-Pierre led Marino and her daughter down to the basement storage that housed new vehicles and offered better security. Hers was near a door. After signing the papers, Jean-Pierre walked over to open the security door and tapped in a code.

'I have to go, Tracey. Thank you for coming this far with me. As much as anyone may enquire, you know nothing about this car or where I've gone. Your safety depends on that. Now go back home as if you were just out here for service.'

'Will you call me?'

'For your protection, I can't.'

'Mom, I have to report you missing. We live in the same house.'

'Give me a day. I need a day.'

Tracey grabbed her mother's arm and held it tightly for a few seconds.

'Now go, before you say something you don't mean.' Marino watched her daughter. Tracey looked back once. Marino drove north until she reached Autoroute 25 and turned east on Autoroute 440. Her destination was Rawdon, a municipality and tourist destination on the Ouareau River in southwestern Quebec, sixty kilometers from Montreal. She made it as far as Terrebonne 41 minutes later.

Chapter Fifty-five

CLAUDE BEAUCHEMIN was on the phone with his lawyer and didn't at first notice that his wife had gone into the study and picked up his new manuscript. She was sitting near the piano reading it.

'What do you mean you have nothing from Detective Damiano?'

'I have no legal right, as you very well know, to demand information from her. You haven't been arrested, Claude.'

'She still has me in her crosshairs.'

'You're not the only suspect.'

'Why didn't you have me cleared when the boy couldn't make an ID?'

'Because, I've told you already, he zeroed in on you and someone else. That kept you in the mix, maybe not front and center. Your appearance has changed. Otherwise, of course, I'd have had you dropped from the suspect list.'

'Did your gut tell you that Damiano is waiting for Holmes to make the principal ID?'

'She didn't reveal anything, but I feel she has other evidence. She wasn't relaying solely on the lineup.'

'You've nothing further on Holmes's condition?'

'That's tighter than Fort Knox.'

'What am I paying you for? I heard you worked detours.'

'Within the law. If you'd be happier with someone else, by all means take the file elsewhere.'

'Just a second. Louise, what the hell are you reading?'

'Claude, are you still with me?' his lawyer asked impatiently.

'I have to go.' Claude turned his attention to Louise.

'You're setting yourself up for a cardiac arrest,' Louise cautioned.

'They were panic attacks!'

'Yeah, the next one might not be.'

'I have to go, Maître David. Keep the file.'

'Your check?'

'I'll get to the damn thing today.' Beauchemin slammed down the receiver, strode over to Louise and snatched the manuscript from her. 'How dare you read this without my permission? The study is my private place.'

'Didn't I proof your first book, what, seven times? Doesn't that suggest we are a team? By the way, I'm already midway through it.'

Beauchemin took a step back and held the manuscript to his chest. His breathing grew erratic. 'You had no right.'

'What in God's name are you doing? Do you want to be arrested? Writing about the assault on Holmes? Have you lost your mind?'

'I want a bestseller and this is my ticket. Can't you see the demand out there?'

Louise had remained seated, but she rose then. 'Anything you've written can be used as evidence against you. When I read your description of the assault…'

'It's fiction, for God's sake.'

'The savagery of it…'

'Now who's losing it?'

'Claude, you're beyond listening to anyone. I can't go to work every day carrying the tension and the upheaval from home. My mother will welcome the extra help.'

'That's it, Louise. Just take off. Leave me. You think that's going to bother me?'

'Are you hearing me? I'm near collapse myself with worry and stress. I have to work. We need the money.'

'Rub that in too, Louise.'

'I'm going up to pack. There's food in the house.'

'Waitasecond!'

'I don't know you, Claude. Maybe I never did. I don't know if you assaulted Madison Holmes, or you're just wallowing in self-pity because she rejected your book. I told you once, I don't want to know.'

Beauchemin stormed back to the study and brought the manuscript with him. The room began to shift and grow fuzzy and he reached for the desk and held on. He grabbed his water bottle, put his head back and splashed water on his face. He began to gasp and fell to his knees. He couldn't call out. Covering his mouth and nose with his hand, he forced himself to breath more slowly. He held his hand there until the room righted itself and cleared. His face was clammy and he felt nauseous. He crawled from the room and managed to haul himself up to his chair. Then he held his mouth and nose a second time and waited.

When Louise finally came back down with a suitcase, he could tell she'd been crying. He canted forward. 'You can read the manuscript if you still want to.'

'Claude, I can't stay. You have to help yourself, and…'

'You have to work.'

'I have to sleep at night, Claude.'

'I need you.'

'You need more than me.'

'This is it then? Twenty years just blows up in my face?'

'For now.'

'Louise, I can't believe this.' His heart felt like Jell-O.

'I've coddled you and your hobbies, listened to your ideas, the tedious details of your day and cooked your favorite foods. When I couldn't sleep last night, I tried to think of something you've done for me over the years and I couldn't think of…'

'Blah-blah-blah.'

Louise left quietly.

Chapter Fifty-six

IT WAS NO EASY TASK for Damiano to find parking, even illegal parking, on Hutchison Street near Pauzé's apartment on Barcelona. She heard the familiar sounds of a search at Pauzé's door before she knocked. The impoverished conditions of the small apartment surprised her. The lopsided book stacks she expected, but the general mess, the hovel Pauzé lived in, saddened her. She understood why he had undertaken his paper scam. Pauzé was a post-grad who should have moved back home until he found work.

'We've moved everything in this studio but the Murphy bed, and we're about to do that now,' Matte told her.

Marie was busy on the floor taking samples. 'This guy has managed to spill food everywhere. It almost turns me off eating. He had hot water. That's the best I can say for this place.'

'Does he have a locker somewhere?' Damiano asked.

'I have the super's number. I'll call him.'

'Pierre, what's your gut on the second shoe?'

'Can't see us finding it in the locker – wouldn't make sense.'

'The super will be here in a few minutes. I have the warrant that covers it. Marie, what's your take on the shoe?'

'If the one we have at the lab is *the* shoe, I think he bundled up what he wore that day and the shoe fell out in this clutter. He must have been pretty sketchy at the time, and racing around, and he didn't hear it fall out. By the looks of things here, he didn't own much to bundle anything. We looked for garbage bags, but he used bags he got from stores, when he went for food.'

'We had the same thought,' Damiano said, agreeing with Marie.

The super knocked. Damiano opened the door. 'We're ready.'

'This is legal, right? Learn a lot from TV.'

Marie produced the warrant. The super led them to the basement, turned left along a narrow corridor with yellow, numbered, locked doors. The super read his list and opened door seven. 'Pauzé's is #7.' He unlocked the wooden barred door that anyone could access. The super caught Marie's disapproval.

'The students know enough not to keep anything of value down here. Don't have much to begin with anyway.'

They began to wade through another pile of books, notes and a suitcase that they searched. Damiano stood up. 'Did you find any other shoes in the apartment?'

'An old pair of Docs, black boots, not shoes.'

'Huh. Pauzé was living on nothing. What if he was wearing the sneakers the night he was attacked, that he never tossed them? Let's say he cleaned them because he needed them. They'd be stored in his hospital locker.'

'That means another warrant.'

'This file is weird enough. Let's skip the bureaucratic bullshit and take a quick look at the photo of the shoes. If they look good – we go for a warrant. Pauzé goes for therapy every day. The surveillance officer is making "good cop" with him for the glass slivers. He can tell me when the kid goes to therapy. That's when we strike.'

'Drama queen!' Marie laughed.

'The best,' Damiano said. 'I'll call our uniform now.'

'Yes, Detective.' The officer shot a bored look at Pauzé who smiled. 'Any luck?'

'Nope, nothing on this front.'

'When does he go to therapy?'

'Before dinner. They serve it here at 4:30 pm. I'll starve. Just kidding, Detective.'

'Crime and I will be there when Pauzé's out of the room. We'll be there in an hour.'

'How are your legs?' the officer asked Pauzé.

'Heavy as tree trunks and hot as fire.'

'Does therapy help?'

'I feel like shit after it. They're trying to ship me to a rehab center in three days. They're hellholes. You have a name?'

'Hate it. Maurice, you know…'

'After the Rocket. No shit!'

'Yeah. It's a freakin' old name that no one uses.'

'Makes it distinctive then.'

'Among cops?'

'Guess not.'

Maurice wanted the swabs to impress Damiano. 'If I were in your place, I wouldn't be keeping souvenirs. I'd wanna forget.'

I have a PhD for Christ sake. This pompous little shit thinks he's going to get the better of me! Grabbing the bar above his bed with one hand, Pauzé reached for the swabs with the other. He tossed them into the trash can with other debris from the old geezer in the bed beside him who slept all day. He threw his juice on top of the mess, spilling some of it on the floor and splashing the side curtain as well. 'Gone for good, like you suggested.'

Pauzé wanted to say, 'Thought you had me, right, Maurice?' The devastation on Maurice's face gave him what he wanted, confirmation of a trap. *Let them try to set me up!* When Detective Damiano and Crime's Marie Dumont reached Pauzé's floor, they stepped out in the corridor with Officer Gauthier. They had twenty minutes before Pauzé was back in his room. Damiano felt sucker punched when she heard how Pauzé had gotten the better of them.

Marie saw the flash of anger in Damiano's eyes and stepped up. 'Toni, Pauzé knew what I wanted when I cleaned the wound on his hand. He played us both. We still have the evidence I got from him. It may be a wash, but I still have it.'

'Doesn't matter how we lost more evidence. Fact is we did! If there were any slivers, they were in the swabs he had. He got to his wound first.'

'Hold on!' Marie said. 'Officer, take the trash to your vehicle.' She reached into her case. 'Here, seal the bag and drive it to Crime. I want it on my desk. I might still find the slivers. You have to realize that Pauzé may have gotten that cut during his own assault. None of it might matter.'

'Great, and what we have today is already contaminated, Marie. What…'

'Hold on. If that's not the case, I might be able to match one sliver with the glass in the door, you turn to Pauzé exclusively. I'll do my best with it. Pauzé might have already hidden the slivers and kept the swabs as decoys. I wouldn't put that past him.'

'Ah damn.'

'Your suspects aren't stupid. You know that.'

Officer Gauthier's cheeks were crimson. He took the plastic bag, poured the contents slowly into it and was about to leave.

'Just a second, Officer. Which locker is Pauzé's?'

'The first of the four, the one closest to the wall.'

Damiano had her hand on the handle when a nurse dispensing meds walked into the room. 'Excuse me, who are you?'

Damiano bit her lower lip and turned. 'Detective Damiano and Marie Dumont from Crime.'

'Have you been given permission to open the locker?'

'Jean Pauzé is a suspect in the assault on Madison Holmes. I want to take a photo of the shoes he wore the night of his attack.'

'I gather then you don't have permission. Do you have a warrant? My sister's a cop, so I know you need one.'

'I can easily obtain it.'

Marie got on the phone.

'Did you hear what I said? He's a suspect in…'

'I heard you, Detective. To you he's a suspect. To me he's a patient. Pauzé's not here, so please wait out in the hall. You're disturbing the other patients.'

Two other elderly patients were snoring with their mouths wide open. 'I can see that. I appreciate your cooperation.' Damiano walked out stiffly and saw that Marie didn't look hopeful with her call. *Ahhh, shit!*

Chapter Fifty-seven

'MARIE, DON'T YOU know a soft judge at this point in your career?' The question was mean.

Marie snapped her phone shut. She looked both ways along the corridor, making sure they were alone. She whispered so nurse Duty wouldn't hear her.

'You're a smart, pretty woman who gets the better of most cops because they'd all like to get into your pants. Par for the male course. I'm your equal. This is a tough file. I've worked overtime, skipped meals to get work done faster for you and accepted your foul moods. But, I won't tolerate you questioning my credentials. Understand that today and throughout this file. I will try another judge. I don't give up either. You should know that.'

Damiano tapped her head against the wall. 'I'm a rotten mother, worse wife, but I thought I was a good cop. I can't close my first lead! I'm strung out, gave up my Red Bulls, hungry and ready to put my fist through that locker. As lead, the pressure falls on me. I accept that. I'm navigating in a confused space because all the 'spects look good for the assault and they're doing their best to obstruct my investigation. I'm looking for a handle. Can't get my hands on it because they are all viable 'spects! Haven't broken a single alibi. The chief and I have almost eliminated Marino because Holmes wouldn't be alive if a pro had done the work. Yet, to be on the safe side, we can't just eliminate her. I always relied on my job. I knew my job. I'm not sure of anything right now.'

'I wish I had a small violin for your pity whine. Let's get out of here. You're about to stuff your face with poutine. When you finish the bowl, I may think of forgiveness if that whole speech was your idea of an apology.'

'It was. Right now though, I have to arrange for another cop to cover Pauzé.'

'You're not getting out of this. And, I don't want a running commentary on our arteries as we eat! You need to reboot.'

'Maybe I'll like it,' Damiano said without conviction.

'This case has taught you miracles don't happen. They need roll-up-your-sleeves work and head-banging. Call Matte and tell him you're meeting with me.'

'First, I want to speak to nurse Duty.' Damiano spotted her two rooms down. 'Pardon me again.'

'You have the warrant?'

'We will very soon. I do have to advise you not to mention this visit or its intent to Jean Pauzé. I know you work hard but I wouldn't want to charge you with obstructing an investigation.'

Nurse Duty was sincere in her reply. 'You have my word.' She was a full-breasted, commanding woman.

'Thank you.' Damiano caught sight of another officer coming down the hall. *They must have called up the officer at the hospital entrance.* Approaching him, she asked, 'You're replacing Officer Gauthier?'

'I am, Detective.'

'Keep an eye on the first locker near the far wall on your right. Don't make it obvious or touch it.'

'Understood.'

Marie took Damiano to The Main restaurant on St-Laurent and ordered cherry cokes and a heart-attack-in-a-bowl for both of them.

Damiano needed Marie and wanted her friendship. She made her calls while she sat and ate and listened to the history of poutine, stuffing her cheeks with cheddar curds and fries drenched in gravy.

'Poutine has a history. Fernand Lachance, who hailed fromWarwick, Quebec, came up with the best junk food sensation in the world in 1957. For the best poutine, the fries should be fresh and hand-cut. Lachance's cheddar curds are so good that they're sent all over the world, and the gravy, that's still best in Warwick. The Main does a pretty good job though.'

'Please don't tell me you've gone to Warwick?'

'I'm proud to say I have.' Marie was laughing and a little gravy dribbled out the side of her mouth. 'Lachance was a young man when he created poutine, and it didn't kill him. He was 86 when he died.'

'The curds squeak when I chew them.'

'Good sign!' Marie laughed again. 'That's what they're supposed to do.'

'Friends again?'

'You're a good sport, but you have to clean the bowl.'

Damiano hated to admit it, but she didn't have that hollow feeling. She felt better. Her phone hummed and she flipped the receiver open. 'Ms Doyle?'

Tracey felt the bile of betrayal, but her mother's secretary had called three times. How could she ignore that, reminders that her mother was in trouble. 'My mother is not at the office. She's not at home either.' Tracey didn't add anything.

'Have you called her?'

'She's not picking up.'

'Does she always pick up when you call?'

'No.'

'She might be meeting with a client.'

Tracey thought of her mother's plea. *Give me a day.*

'Ms Doyle?'

Her mother needed help. 'She would have taken her car, but it's still parked at her office.'

Damiano didn't finish the poutine. 'What else do you know?'

'The secretary saw her go out of the office – she never came back.'

'Is she seeing someone? Is that possible?'

'I don't know. I don't think so. No, no, she's not! Something's wrong!'

'Give me her secretary's number. Have you checked the house carefully, for a note or something like that?'

'YES! Something's happened! Here's the number, but I've already called her secretary.'

'Keep calling anyone you think of. I'll look into it.' Damiano closed her phone.

'What?' Marie asked.

'Angela Marino's a no-show on all fronts. With my luck, she's running, or cancelled.' Damiano was up in a flash, wiping her mouth. 'I have to go to the boss with this. I'm sorry, Marie. Could be a false alarm, but I can't take that chance. She has the means to disappear. Locating her won't be easy if she doesn't want to be found.'

'Go. I'll work another judge. This is progress.'

'What? Adding another suspect is progress? It's addition, Marie. I don't care what happens to that woman. She fits right in with this bunch. I've never met such despicable people as the suspects in this file.'

Marie snorted.

'Right, probably why I have the lead. I'll be in touch.'

Chapter Fifty-eight

DAMIANO WALKED PAST Chief Donat's secretary.

'Detective Damiano, you can't just …'

'The chief will want to see me.' She opened the door and barged in.

'Detective, you've closed the file!'

'Angela Marino's skipped or been… I don't know. We can't locate her.'

' *Sapristi!*' He slammed both fists on his desk. Papers flew off one side.

Better than motherfucker. Damiano knew he was cursing himself because she had wanted a go at Marino. He had kept her away. She waited quietly.

'Department leaks!' His face appeared white and twisted because he was tilting his head.

'The office has been locked every night, and Matte and I have been there late.'

'I'm not jumping on you! They have eyes in every goddamn division. It's been that way since I was a rookie.'

Well?

'Stay with your gut. I still don't see Marino for this. She didn't hire a pro from anywhere in Montreal. Like I said, they wouldn't sanction a hit for her. She's too much of a liability. She'd have to have gone out for one. Don't see that either. She's no "stoop." They heard of the interview and they don't take chances. Marino knows that. She's running for her life.'

'What do we do?'

'I can't have you wasting time on her. If she's not involved in the assault, Marino's only chance is you closing this file. If she's not already among their disappeared, and you make an arrest, she bides her time for a few days and reappears. She goes on breathing.'

'It's that simple.'

'Black and white for them. Get back on Holmes. Fill me in. I may give Marie a call.' Donat said.

'I wouldn't if I were you. We kind of had it out. She's working a new judge.'

'You need another warrant.'

'She'll get it.'

'These damn bureaucratic delays! Just close the file, Damiano! I'm beginning to have second…'

'Don't replace me. Bad press for both of us.'

'Day 12.'

'I can count.' Damiano left and joined Matte. 'How are we doing here?'

'Good to see you. Anything from your side?'

Damiano gave Matte the rundown.

'There is movement on your end.'

'On yours, Pierre?'

'Nothing. We keep plodding. Keep the faith. Have you contacted Holmes's physician?'

'I wanted to give Holmes a few recovery days, but I'll call right now.'

Matte stood close while she made her call. The receiver was on speaker.

'Dr. Stephen Orr, please. Detective Damiano.'

'Please hold.'

'I'm on hold!'

'Patience.'

'Detective Damiano, he's in surgery.'

'Is there any way you could find out when he gets out?'

'I can't give you a projected time because there can be complications.'

'Pierre, you heard?'

He nodded. 'Why not just go down there? I'd like to go with you. We can take one car.'

Damiano needed a positive force. 'Why not? Think Marino's swimming with the fishes?'

'Leaving her office and not coming back is ominous since her car's still there.'

'I've been on the job seventeen years. I've never shot or killed anyone. My interview might have done just that. If it somehow got back to the people she works for, we both know the danger for her. Damiano's dejection wasn't lost on Matte. 'A dirty cop set her up if that's what happened. You were doing your job.'

'Right, but only one of our 'spects is guilty. We forget the damage we do to the other four or five.' Damiano stared pensively down at the floor. She felt doors closing. She was scared. Her life was shaky. 'Are you happy, Pierre, I mean, is it easier on the other side?'

'Why are you asking me this now?'

'I'm losing my balance.'

'Could be withdrawal,' he said sincerely.

'Come on! It's this hellish case. I thought I'd have it closed by now, but it's getting away from me. The swings from the file are far worse than any drugs. I like pressure when I feel I can succeed. It propels me. I scatter when I feel I'm losing. So, are you good?'

'I'll get to myself in a sec. You're afraid of losing because you don't know what it's like. You're the star. Think I don't know why I've never had the lead? I'm the best detail cop there is, just not a lead. I'm an investigator – you're a street cop. We all have to grow up. We'll close.'

'Psych course today.' Damiano didn't have the emotional energy to analyze Pierre's situation, so she let it pass. She couldn't add another person to her 'sorry' list.

'You asked for it. About me, I'm okay, like the turtle. This case *is* tough, I admit. Thought we'd close sooner too, but we have to go with it. I like you, Damiano. Don't make me lose my impression of your intelligence. And I'm okay in my personal life – no better than most. Apart from non-acceptance of gays, we have the same human problems. The whole weight of the relationship falls on the couple because we're still not out there, no matter what the law says. We're isolated. I'm a cop – that's a hard life on any partner. Dylan's gained a few pounds since I caught this file. That's good.'

'How?'

'He's hanging in and not at the bars.'

'Got it. Yet you love the job and the long hours just like me.'

'Told you already, I love details and puzzles. All have tracks. I like finding them. Good mental exercise.'

'You are a tight-ass.'

'Works for me.'

'Almost funny. I wonder who'll catch Marino's file.'

'We're not cut off – we just don't have the time. Something will pop. Let's hit the road. I'll drive.'

'As it should be.'

It was after six. They drove to the Montreal General in silence. Matte sat beside Damiano like a well-rounded friend.

Chapter Fifty-nine

THE OCCUPANT OF A RENTED black Lincoln MKZ had a gun with a silencer, an add-on rarely used. The man was muscled, early 40s, no amateur. Calculating and patient, he was at the top of his game. He got on the phone. 'She just turned east on the 440. I'm four car lengths back.'

'Is she squirrley?

'She's changed lanes – tells me she is, but hasn't made our car, or she'd be gunning her own'

'The man was right. She's heading to her property in Rawdon. There's no rush. Let her get well past Terrebonne. You're looking for an isolated stretch of highway. Take her out quietly. Leave no witnesses. You know speed and you know cars, should be a walk-on for you.'

Marino was no fool. She had picked up the trailer car. The rushing fear she'd felt at her home was gone. Her thoughts were raw and clear. The information she had on them was safe and would be sent to trusted authorities in the event of her death. Matching the tailing car's patience, Marino saw that the information offered her no protection whatsoever. If her body was never found, she wouldn't be declared dead for seven years. The miscalculation disappointed her. Her life was in her hands. Her destination was another miscue. *How did he know about my country home? I've never even been there.* Then she knew. Though the home was not in her name, she paid the property taxes on it. That was how they had traced her. She could write her missing report. *Angela Marino, a prominent Montreal lawyer, has gone missing. Police have found no evidence of foul play. A search is underway.* No one would ever find her. Approaching Île St-Jean, the traffic stopped in a tight bottleneck. She checked her rear-view mirror. The Lincoln hadn't moved up.

The idea struck like a bullet. At the last second, she turned a sudden right at Île St-Jean. The SUV wobbled violently for a few seconds before righting itself. *It'd be funny if I killed myself!* She cut her speed immediately, a cement truck grinding its brakes behind her. She had a friend in Terrebonne on rue Archambault, but she hadn't seen her in three years. Should she gamble that she was still there? The woman was an avid reader, a stay-at-home, a computer whiz. Did she dare? Marino even remembered where Jocelyne hid the spare key in the 14-unit building. The rear parking area wasn't well concealed, but if you weren't looking for it… If she could get inside the locked building. If, if, if… Should she turn around and speed back into Montreal? Marino was calculating the pieces of her life as though she were playing chess, as though she were watching the game.

She drove to rue Archambault; the gray building was on her right. She gunned the SUV into another sharp turn to the parking behind the building. She could hear her breathing but she couldn't feel herself. Grabbing her purse and the gun she ran to the back door. It was locked. She pounded on the glass door. She kept on pounding. She knew the front of the building was locked. She couldn't take a chance at that door. She'd be visible, out in the open.

'Did you lose her?'

'She turned off.' He kept his voice to a low whisper.

'Where are you?'

'About to make the cut-off. Heavy traffic.'

'Where's the runner?'

'He was ahead of her. I've alerted him.'

'This is quiet work. Complete it.'

The man in the Lincoln knew the consequences if he failed. 'Will do.' One might have thought, hearing the brief conversation, that the man was going to pick up a liter of milk.

Fear came back to Marino through her knuckles as she pounded on the back door. Finally, an elderly man came to the door, but didn't open it. She explained in French that her friend in Unit 14 was in trouble. The man hesitated until he saw the tears. Marino looked back at her SUV. At least it was parked between two cars. There was some concealment. She raced up the stairs to the third floor. There was no elevator. She wouldn't have taken it anyway. She was breathing through her mouth when she reached Unit 14 and knocked. She knocked harder. *Oh my God, I'm trapped!* She lifted the rubber mat at the door, no key. *No! NO!* She reached up to the door ledge and ran her hand across it. *NO!* She was standing on a runner. She dropped to her knees and ran her hand under it. It hit a key. Saliva dripping from her mouth, she got to her feet. *It's got to work – it's got to work!* The key turned. Marino threw herself inside the apartment. Her nose was stung with the familiar acrid odor of kitty litter. A Siamese cat stretched its head around a corner. *Thank God! Jocelyne's still here.* She made a promise then and there to buy her two cases of Glendronach whisky.

Marino ran to the living room, a large, comfortable room that offered a view of rue Archambault from two sides. She stood behind the verticals, carefully lifting one to the side. Marino didn't move a muscle. She watched for 15 minutes. The Lincoln didn't pass, or it had already and she had missed it. A bolder Siamese rubbed its body against her leg, and Marino jumped back as though she had been struck. She hated cats. They crept up on you like the sneaks they were. Her insides felt liquid. She found the bathroom and the kitty litter beside it. After relieving herself, she washed up as best she could because her hands shook and she felt cold, very cold.

She hurried to the door, to be certain it was locked. The wall reminded her that she had no view of the back parking lot, no way to see if the SUV had been spotted. She listened at the door. She heard nothing. She had to check the SUV, had to know if they were coming into the building. She couldn't stand there like a cornered animal. She listened again. Then she opened the door. She held her gun in the side pocket of her jacket. The hall was empty. There were only three units on her floor and she ran to the back stairs. *Goddammit! There's no window here either. I'll have to go back down the stairs.* Her head exploded with fear when she heard knocking, not at the back door. *They're at the front door!*

Marino raced back to the apartment and locked the door. She stood, trying to think. She chose a chair at the far end of the living room. She sat down and waited with the gun, knowing she had trapped herself. There was no safe way she could get back to the SUV. She wiped her hands on her slacks, but the sweat reappeared, and she wiped them again until she could hold the gun. Then she was past the sudden terror stage. She was alert and quiet. Her stalker was a killer. One of the cats circled her arm chair. Marino calculated the distance from her chair to the turn into the living room. If she stayed there, her .22 was of no use to her. When she rose, her knee buckled and she spilled the contents of her purse. She stepped over the items on the floor and crept back to the small study and stood beside a wall of books, and the urn containing the ashes of Jocelyne's father.

The loud knocking downstairs had stopped. Whoever it was was most likely inside the building. It was very quiet. The killer knew how to pick locks and he could do it without noise. She fell to her knees and crept back for her disposable cell phone. When she found it, she crawled back to the study with the phone in one hand. The other she kept levelled with the .22. The door across the hall opened, Marino was certain she'd heard it. There was no other sound but the opening of the door.

Chapter Sixty

DAMIANO AND MATTE were walking toward the ICU when Damiano saw there was no security at the door. 'Pierre, something's happened!' She rushed up to the door. Damiano opened it quietly and walked inside. Holmes's bed was located at the far end of the room out of sight.

The ICU nurse tapped Damiano's shoulder. 'Detective!' The woman was doing her best to whisper. 'You are not permitted to barge into the ICU without permission.'

Damiano ignored the nurse when she saw that Holmes's bed was empty. Her stomach flipped. 'What's happened to Ms Holmes? Where is she? Has she died? Where is my surveillance? What happened here?'

The nurse stepped out of the room. Damiano and Matte followed.

' Nurse,' Damiano repeated, 'I need answers! Was it Madison Holmes? Has she died?' Damiano's voice rose. She didn't care about hospital rules. Her victim was her concern.

Matte had his badge out.

' No, but Ms Holmes did suffer a cerebral embolism.'

'A stroke?'

'Yes. She's been taken for a CT scan to determine whether the symptoms are caused by a clot or some other disorder, like inordinate stress.'

'Has she lost consciousness?'

'No, and that's a good sign. She is being administered medication that helps to prevent recurrence. From there Ms Holmes will be taken to therapy.'

'Was she able to speak?'

'She was suffering from dizziness and her voice was somewhat slurred. In my opinion, this attack is not severe. But, occasionally, a minor stroke may be followed by a much more severe attack. My team is on alert.'

Damiano hid her concern. 'And my cop?'

'He's down there with her.'

'And that is where?'

'Detective, this is not my place, but my job is Ms Holmes's recovery. Your questioning is gravely impeding her progress. Why not wait – give the woman a chance to heal properly. She is lucky to be alive. Don't victimize her a second time.'

'Don't tell me how to do my job! I want to speak to her father. Where are they?'

'You're a determined young woman. Fifth floor, D5.' She turned on her heel and went back to her patients.

'Let's go, Pierre.'

'She had a point, Toni.'

'Give me a break. I want to speak to her father. Holmes saw her assailant – she was ready to tell when she suffered the seizure.'

'Do you hear yourself?'

'I do, but she's probably told her father. I won't interfere with Holmes's recovery. Holmes knows. My bet is that Madison blurted it out. Let's hurry to D5 before they take her somewhere else. Our cop should have called.'

'Is your phone on?'

'Damn!' She turned her cell back on and dropped it back into her purse, without checking. She had what she needed to know. Her cop was standing a few feet from Thomas Holmes. He was leaning against a wall, bent over, running his hands through his hair. The cop left his post and came over to her.

'Detective, I called you.'

'I know. Don't leave Ms Holmes unprotected. Watch the door closely.'

'I will.'

Holmes hadn't bothered to look up.

'Dr. Holmes! I'm sorry for this turn of events.'

He looked up then, his eyes red and full of anger. 'I had Madison up walking and talking. And you had to come back with your questions. I want my daughter back. I don't want you anywhere near her. Do you hear me?'

'Doctor, you can't stop an…'

Madison's physician appeared. 'Thomas, it's not as bad as it might have been. Madison's talking pretty clearly. We got her here quickly, and the ASA should prevent recurrences. I want her in therapy today, to get her up and moving.'

'Stephen, I don't want Detective Damiano in this hospital near my daughter.'

Matte came to Damiano's defence. 'Doctor, we're doing our job, trying to apprehend the assailant who attacked your daughter.'

'I've stopped caring about that. Try to understand my position. I want Madison well, above all else. She's *my daughter*!'

'Now, Thomas, you know, we both know that Madison wants to talk. Detective Damiano wasn't pushing her.'

Damiano's brow furrowed and she turned to Holmes's physician. 'Do you think she saw the the man who attacked her?'

'Stephen, we're colleagues. I know what's best as well as you.'

'Thomas, as long as this attacker is out there, your daughter is not safe.

I think she may have seen something. She mentioned gloves before she convulsed. Madison wants to talk, Thomas. That's what she was trying to do. Can't you see that?'

Damiano was determined and she pushed in front of Holmes. 'When do you think it will be safe to show her the photos we have? She won't have to say anything.'

'I will call you, Detective, in a few days.'

Holmes got up and stomped off, but not before he shouted at them. 'Why can't you all just allow Madison to recover at her own pace? You're hounding my daughter!'

'Huh!' *Why is he stonewalling?* Damiano's cheeks began to flare.

'Toni, calm down. It's good news,' Matte tried to tell her.

'I'll have gray hair by the time I see Holmes.'

'Didn't you check your phone for messages?' he asked.

'Another scolding? I turned it off for a while when I came into the hospital.' Damiano took out her phone and swore. 'Marino texted me.'

'What?'

'Just a sec.' Damiano scrolled down to the message. *I need help. 150 rue Archambault, Unit 14, Terrebonne.* 'Damn it to hell. She called 40 minutes ago!'

'Shit!' Matte never swore.

Chapter Sixty-one

MADISON LAY ON THE GURNEY after the CT scan and she heard her father's voice because it was loud and angry. She carefully guided her hand to her head and touched the contours of the bandages. For the first time, she felt her forehead and her eyebrow and massaged them gently. The heavy bandaging had been removed. She'd thought of it as the Hunchback of Notre Dame perched on the side of her head. Her head felt lighter; she rolled her shoulders without pain. She raised her arm, she pinched her thumb and forefinger and she smiled. Most of the numbness had gone. Pins and needles were receding too.

Her mind had cleared. The confusion and fear that accompanied it had lifted like a rising fog. Timelines began to fall into sequence as memory stretched into cohesive images. She lifted one leg, then the other. She rolled on her good side, just enough to know she could. Throughout the ordeal her father's soft, comforting, vulnerable voice had spoken for her. Madison took a deep breath, exhaled slowly and took another. She wasn't afraid. She wasn't afraid of what she remembered. Madison had joined an elite group of people who are shot, maimed, or beaten and left for dead and dismissed. Against those odds, they survive. Only they understand the exhilaration of knowing that they had the strength within themselves to come back.

Madison remembered the man who had come to her door. She saw the shorts, the gloves that seemed odd, out of place with shorts, the sun glasses and woolen cap. She heard his muffled voice, but his face still hid from her. 'Daad! Daad!' She brought her hand to her lips. Her left upper lip felt frozen, lopsided.

'I'm here, Maddy. You're fine, honey.'

'I reemmmbber – most of it.'

'I know you do.' Holmes held Madison by the shoulders. 'Let the rest go. There are physical dangers to your health. Another stroke? We don't want that. What's important is your recovery. We matter – nobody else.'

'Bbut Daad!'

'Trust me, Madison, please.'

'I want to…'

'Maybe later, when you're completely well, maybe then.'

I have to know. Madison closed her eyes and shut her father out.

Chapter Sixty-two

WE LEARN FROM OUR GREATEST FAILURES. It seemed strange to the courier that an author of some stature would put his name to such tripe. Failure exposes the large, crooked nose that puts a face behind the bench. Failure crumbles the attempt and it cripples the man who dared to think he might right a wrong.

I am nothing now. He could feel the pinch of handcuffs. His mind scurried from such thoughts. If she couldn't remember, he might, he just might...

Chapter Sixty-Three

DAMIANO AND MATTE dashed down the five flights of stairs. 'Damn, damn, damn! Now I have to worry about damage control.'

'Is there a Caller ID?'

'Think Marino would do anything simply?' Damiano called the Terrebonne police, advising them to get patrol cars to 150 Archambault, Unit 14. 'Might be mob related.'

'Who's in the unit?' the officer wanted to know.

'One Angela Marino, Montreal lawyer with connections.'

'Armed?'

'Assume it.'

'Are you coming out here?'

'I have to break the news to Chief Donat. Get out there asap. Call me.'

'I'm going with three men.'

'Good.'

Matte sped through the city, fighting traffic. Damiano clung to the door support. There was no point calling Donat. She grinned a tight smile. 'Marino might just be "gone" by the time the cops get there.'

'Do you mean that?'

'Her death would be on her then. No dirt on us. Donat will find a way to blame me because my phone was off.'

'I'll go in with you – you had no choice. I had mine off too. You've been a constant in the ICU. You couldn't have your phone on.'

'You're not Donat.'

When Damiano and Matte barged into Chief Donat's office, he jumped up and kind of froze mid-jump. 'This is motherfucking bad! No gold stars, I can assure you both. The press? Expect complaints of incompetence and judgment and whatever slime they can throw at us.'

Damiano stood her ground. 'I'm going to close this file, Chief.'

'How many times have I heard that?'

'Just so you know. Just so you remember you ordered me to stay wide with Marino.' Her throwback calmed Donat only slightly.

'Get out to Terrebonne, Damiano! Matte, work at the office or the lab. Keep the work up to date. I'm surprised Marie has come up empty. Push her, Matte. She'll balk, but that might produce results. We need something soon. Now get to work, both of you!' Donat's order lacked his usual abruptness and betrayed his concern.

'Well, that went well, Pierre.'

'What did you expect? We don't feel any better than he does.'

'Marie hasn't gotten back to me about the warrant for the shoes. We'll keep the single shoe from Pauzé's apartment on the back burner until I have news of the warrant. No results from Crime, but that takes time. Marie reminds me this is not TV. I'll be in touch. I'll go down there too.' In the garage Damiano was about to get into her car when she noticed Galt. Her hand slid into her purse for her gun.

'Forget the drama, Damiano.' He pointed to her purse. He raised his hands mockingly. 'See, no weapons.'

'I haven't got time for this bullshit.' She opened her car door.

'How's an unsolved case in the biggest file of the year going to fit into your résumé?'

Damiano took off, narrowly missing Detective Galt who stood in her path laughing and saluting her. She was at the apartment building in half an hour, driving as recklessly as a felon chased by patrol cars. She counted three patrol cars out front. *Who did Marino know here?* The nondescript apartment was white brick, maybe 20 years old, standing beside other apartment buildings erected by the same builder. The one she wanted was 150 Archambault, brick as well, with driveways and one poorly kept patch of grass. Damiano introduced herself to the uniform at the door before she climbed the stairs to Unit 14. Another uniform stood by the open door. Damiano could hear voices inside. She walked in and introduced herself.

'Detective Marchand. This is the tenant, Jocelyne Fortin.'

'Bonjour, Madame.' Fortin was a large, sixty-ish woman, who carried her weight like a jolly Santa. Her short, thick hair was completely white; her glasses were Prada. Her eyes sparkled with intelligence. Apart from a bag of food, she'd bought several books. One wall in the living room was carefully appointed with shelves of music. Damiano had seen, upon entering, that the study was a pleasant clutter of books. She wondered if Fortin was a retired professor. 'Detective, what did you find when you got here?'

'Madame Fortin was at her door. I told her what I had learned and entered the apartment first. I found no one.'

'Madame Fortin, have you checked your apartment?'

'*Bien oui*, of course. I found nothing out of place, nothing taken.'

'No beverages from the fridge?'

'Mon Dieu!' She went to her fridge and checked. 'No, nothing.' Her English, though pleasantly accented, was good and only the 'th' betrayed her. 'Nothing' sounded like 'nutting,' heavy on the 't.'

'Do you have friends who know about the spare key?'

'Only Jeannine and she was with me today.' A thought struck Fortin. 'Une seconde!' She walked to the door of her apartment and out into the hallway. She knelt on one knee and ran her hand under the liner more than once. 'My spare key is not here.' Her brow furrowed.

Damiano led Fortin back into the apartment. Fortin announced she needed a scotch, poured herself a double and sat in a very comfortable-looking blue leather chair. She didn't look at the side table when she set her drink down. The chair and the scotch were old habits, long practiced.

'Madame Fortin, do you know Angela Marino?'

Fortin relaxed and took another swig of scotch. 'Bien oui, mais je ne l'ai pas vue depuis trois ans.'

'Did she know of your spare key? Was it under the runner three years ago?'

'Yes, at times, she would arrive before me. I invited her to use it and enter my apartment until I arrived home.'

'Has she been in contact with you recently?'

'No, three years, as I have said.'

'Detective, you checked the lock on the door?'

'No jimmying.'

'Would you dust for prints, to be certain Marino was here?'

Marchand got on the phone.

'Madame, if Angela Marino does call you, take my card and call me immediately.'

'Is Angela alright?'

'That's what we are trying to discover.'

'I must have her private number, would you like me to try that now?'

'Please.' Damiano wasn't hopeful, but the call was worth a try.

Fortin went to her computer and was back in minutes, calling and waiting. 'No answer.'

'Thank you for your help.' Detective Marchand walked out with Damiano. 'What do you think?'

'Difficult to say. She's an adult with freedom of choice.'

'Between colleagues, Detective.'

'She's "gone" or she's climbed into another hole.'

Chapter Sixty-Four

DAMIANO DIDN'T MAKE any calls on the drive back. Thoughts crept across her mind like a slow-moving glacier. She wasn't where she wanted to be with the case. She hadn't reached the point of eliminating possibilities. With no single break, she couldn't feel the end, couldn't smell the catch. She'd wait, but she wouldn't wait long. Damiano had a plan, a daring plan that could blow up in her face. For a solve, she'd risk her job. She didn't see any other choice. Right now Matte and she were sputtering along like amateurs. She had a copy of case notes and took them home with her. The chief could wait for her update.

As soon as she was home, she spread the notes across the dinner table. In the bedroom, she undressed and rushed through a shower. Padding into the kitchen, she desperately hoped there was some turkey left. She guzzled a large glass of orange juice and made herself a turkey sandwich with cranberry sauce. She used what Romaine lettuce remained for her salad, surprised anything edible was found in the fridge. She ate first, then washed her hands and went to work. She separated the notes into four piles.

There was no point wasting time on what she already knew. Galt, Beauchemin, Pauzé, Graham and Marino all had motive and opportunity. There was no sign of guilt or remorse in any of these suspects that might be useful to her in forcing a confession. Damiano wanted to answer two questions. Who had the stomach for murder, because that's what the assailant had wanted to execute. More important, who had lost most because of the rejection letter?

For her first question, she listed Graham, then Galt and Pauzé, with question marks beside Beauchemin and Marino. Beauchemin was a weasel who couldn't face a lineup without falling face-down in a panic attack. According to doctors, he wasn't faking. Did he have the stomach for murder? He was an angry, snivelling little man whose best attack on her had been to burn a note in an ashtray and fill his face with nuts. Murder? Did squirrels commit murder? Beauchemin was a squirrel to her.

Marino? She had the stomach to set up a hit. There was no rejection letter here. Would she risk her career and her life to control a daughter she didn't love? She had everything to lose *if* she was behind the assault. One protocol interview must have sent her running. Donat was probably right about Marino, but she wanted a final assurance. Damiano got up from her notes, searched for her phone, found the number she wanted and tapped it in.

Tracey Doyle picked up on the third ring.

'Tracey, this is Detective Damiano.'

'Have you found my mother?' Her voice was near panic.

'I need your help. Don't play stupid or angry with me. We're beyond that. Your mother called me this afternoon. She wanted help. All I got was her message. When we reached the address she had given me, she wasn't there.'

'Oh, no! Does that mean she's dead?'

'I need you to be calm with me right now. Cry all you want later.'

Tracey cried anyway and Damiano waited. 'You need to help me, Tracey. Help your mother, really.'

'My mother told me she did care about me, and I was rotten to her.' More tears.

Damn! 'I believe in her own way she did love you. No one starts out cutting people off because of work. It happens before you know it. Listen carefully. Do you think your mother was behind the assault?'

Tracey went on crying.

'If you want police protection for her, I need the truth.'

'I asked her,' Tracey whispered.

'What did she say? Was this today?'

'She asked me what exactly I had said to you. She was angry that I'd asked about the assault, like I was stupid. I was the reason she had to run. She told me to say nothing, to protect myself. She must have cared.' A new wave of sobs, much louder, broke out.

'Today, Tracey?'

'Yes.

Donat was right. Marino didn't set up the assault. Her clients are after her because they can't take a chance she did.

'Do you know where she was going?'

'No!'

'What kind of car? Your mom called me, Tracey.'

'A black BMW SUV. Do *I* need protection? Will they come for me? I don't know anything.'

Damn! I don't have time for Doyle. 'Pack some things. I'll send a car for you. Don't go out. Don't open the door for anyone. Make sure you see the officer's badge. He'll mention my name. Don't make any more calls. He should be there in an hour or so. Sit tight.'

'Is my mother dead?'

'I don't know. She has to make the next move.'

'You are going to try and help her, right?'

'That's my job.'

Damiano called in to the office and set things up for Doyle. Then she went back to work.

Tom Graham? Was he the dark horse? Rifling through her notes, she found his attorney's card and tried calling the private number. She got lucky. He was there, working after hours. She identified herself. 'Mr. Chapman, I was surprised that Tom Graham refused to attend our second lineup.' Damiano didn't waste time with niceties.

'Detective Damiano, you seem rushed, so I'll get to the point. Tom's treatments began earlier than expected because another patient was sent to palliative care. That's the reason he couldn't get back to Montreal. No evasion on his part.'

'He did inform you that he is a suspect in this file?' Damiano enquired.

'He knows he has motive. Tom's thoughts were very clear. He said, "I'd blow Martin's head off. I wouldn't waste what little time I have left to salvage by assaulting some nobody from Montreal. I'd want to implode with a splash, not further humiliate myself. I had my target right here at home." I believed him. If Tom assaulted this Holmes woman, and you made the arrest, he'd be the butt of New York jokes. He'd lose what he has left of his career. She was a nobody to Tom.'

'A little nobody who attracted Martin Connor, you must admit.'

'I do, but I also know that Tom didn't assault Connor, and I believe he would have been Tom's target. He's deathly frightened about his medical problems.'

Damiano recalled that Graham had told her Connor had dropped off his map, and she believed him. 'He's not going anywhere, I hope?'

'You have my word and his. Tom appreciated you coming here to see him. Detective, another point of interest. Tom is a realist. Angry, heated words that can't be called back passed between Connor and him the day their team split. Tom knew that having this Holmes derailed would not have Conner coming back to him. Both men burned that bridge the day of their confrontation. I know because I was there.'

'I will be in touch.' The suspect with the strongest motive didn't seem right. She looked over at the cabinet with the vodka. She needed a real belt, but not the down side that came with it. She took one good gulp, drained the rest and went back to work.

Galt? He had the stomach for murder; she had no doubt of that. What did he lose? A contract, maybe a fat contract, consulting work, more books, money and fame. Galt wanted all those things. How important was that to a cop who'd never make lieutenant and knew he was plateauing? How important was the 'promise' Holmes had apparently made to them, to Galt in particular? Galt caught Damiano's attention because he was angry and arrogant enough to think he could kill Holmes and walk away. He was in her sights because he had the know-how to get the job done, a perk of his badge. Would he have attacked her if he hadn't assaulted Holmes? Why implode his career if he hadn't? Had he attacked Pauzé to throw her off? Damiano didn't think so, but Galt stuck in her head.

Jean Pauzé had the stomach for murder because he was desperate. In his mind, where it counted for the file, he had lost his life. That was his thinking. The teaching career at McGill he'd banked on was lost when Holmes rejected his book. Without the backing of a large publishing house, he wouldn't be offered the position. He was broke, practically dirt poor. His fraud of writing students' papers had been exposed. The general whine of all three men was that Holmes 'had wasted two years of my life.' Those two years meant, to Pauzé, that his world had crashed. Galt's world darkened. Beauchemin's world shrunk. Graham, well, she didn't know.

The assault on Holmes was a horrendous show of dominance. The assailant was trying to regain what he felt Holmes had taken from him. Was it time, ego, or his spirit? It was one of those. It didn't much matter which one.

In Damiano's mind, Thomas Holmes had attacked Pauzé. Why? Had Madison told him she was afraid of the post-grad? Beauchemin's anger revealed itself in his voluminous emails. Perhaps, he was just a windy lout. Holmes was too smart to attack Galt where he had little chance of a take-down with that cop. She wished she knew the reason Holmes had gone after Pauzé. Was there a chance she was wrong about Thomas Holmes? What were his exact words when she had offered him the deal – confess and walk. *Solve the case the proper way.* His response was not a denial, not how she read it anyway.

She had to see the shoes in the locker. Her plan had to be perfect or else the case, not just her career, collapsed. A media storm would follow. A would-be murderer would walk. She'd never involve Matte. Damiano felt if she didn't take the risk, Donat would yank her from the file – a defeat she would not accept. She scanned all the notes and couldn't help seeing the parallels between the risk she was about to take and the risks Officer Turner and Pauzé, if she had it right, had taken to their peril.

A sudden knocking at her door startled her for a second. In the next, she was running for her gun. Galt? At her home? Damiano kept the gun at hip level and walked quietly to the side of the door. A second knock.

Marino? How did the intruder get past the front door? 'Yes?' she asked tentatively.

'It's Jeff.'

'Jesus!' She opened the door. 'You scared me Jeff.'

'Only Luke has a key. Figured I should knock.'

'It's late.'

'I know.'

The food and the turkey dinner sprang to mind and she softened her tone. 'Come on in. I'm eyeball busy, so I have to kick you out pretty soon.'

'You're always busy.'

'I know. Bad wife, bad job.' She led him into the living room and made a point of sitting beside him on the sofa. She owed Jeff that much, and more. 'Can I get you something? What's up?'

Jeff shook his head and pulled on his ear, a clear sign to her that something definitely was.

Damiano stiffened when she saw the strain on his face. Moving out temporarily had picked away at their marriage. Time away from him had sapped his patience. Would she ever be free of guilt? Damiano leaned forward, rubbing her temples, waiting for the onslaught.

'This housing arrangement was not what I had in mind for us, for our marriage, or for Luke. You have a great kid you never see and me, hanging on the sidelines of your life. I've been pretty patient.'

'You have been.'

'Well, Toni, do you see this as something permanent?'

'Do you have any idea of the stress in this file? It's 24-7.'

'Spare me the work shit for once. You're not the only person with stress. I'm asking you if you want to make this separation permanent.'

'What about my lonely nights when you were at medical school?'

'That's long over. At least, argue fairly. Answer the damn question.'

'I love you, I love Luke, I don't know. I'm a failure – I love my work and it eats up my life.'

'And you do your work best away from us? Are you using work to get away from us? Have you given that idea any thought – do you ever even question yourself on that?'

'Why are we doing this tonight?'

Jeff got to his feet and chose a chair across from Damiano. He studied his hands, avoiding direct eye contact.

'Ah.' The question involved a third party. 'You've started seeing someone.' Her words came easily, but Damiano felt suddenly cold and unsteady. She smiled crookedly because she couldn't believe what she was hearing.

'I haven't started, but I am interested in someone. It happened. I wasn't looking.'

'I have no time to hash this out with you. So it's a choice then. Move back or lose you.'

'That's what life comes down to, doesn't it. Make that choice when you finish with this case of yours. I'm giving you that time. Use it. You're a selfish woman, Toni Damiano.'

'At least we agree on that. And you're generous.' Damiano shivered. 'I mean it, Jeff. You are generous, and patient.' *Just what I need!* 'You're right. I do my job best alone. That's me, for shit's sake. I'm not the only person to feel that way. I can't stand this guilt trip you're loading onto me. I deserve a chance to prove what I can do! You had that chance and you're a doctor! What's so wrong with me wanting that too?'

'Miss out on what, for God's sake? You practically sleep at the division. I didn't have to leave you to earn my career!'

'A priority file like the one I have. At home, I'm doing laundry, cooking, all that shit and losing opportunities. I can't think there! Lastly, I have…'

'Abuse problems, right? I can smell the vodka and whatever else gets the buzz for you. It's helping you to be alone where you have complete freedom to abuse yourself? That's good for that goddamn priority file is it?'

'I'm quitting most of it.'

'You're telling me you're turning a blind eye to Luke and me so you won't miss out. That's rich, I have to admit. Can you even love anyone but yourself? Idiots like Luke and me run after you because even with all your shit, we love you. We want you with us. I'd hazard a guess you don't even know if you love us. Does anything ever shake you?'

'Tonight has.' She wanted desperately to say more. Instead, she watched her husband leave. Damiano had an urge to knock the table over, but she didn't. She stood rooted to the floor instead. For some time, her head was stuffed with cotton, until it was stuffed with rocks. Then the pain started.

Chapter Sixty-Five

DAMIANO THREW A JACKET on twice that night on a quest for Red Bulls. Twice she stood on the street in front of her building. *To hell with them!* She turned and stared up at her empty condo before she walked back inside. What had she missed in the notes? Why hadn't Marie gotten her a warrant? Why had Jeff given her an ultimatum at the low point of this file? He read the papers. After rereading the notes, she lay in bed wide-eyed. Around three, she turned on a pale blue lamp and looked over at her candle. Bad idea! Sex relaxed most people. Damiano wasn't much different, but some nights, orgasms revved her engine and she couldn't sleep, no matter how many times she relit the candle. Tonight would be that kind of night. It had been that kind of day. Before morning, she had done three loads of wash, opened mail and written out a few checks. Being awake all night wasn't a total loss. Bills didn't stop coming because of high profile cases.

The next morning she was in the office well before seven, going over the photos. Matte surprised her by arriving a few minutes later, haggard and appearing as low as she felt. 'What happened to you?'

'Let's just get to work.'

'Dylan went to the bars last night, right?'

'And I'll forgive him as I've done before, but something between us breaks, something we don't get back. Then there'll come a time when I won't, and I'm alone again.' Matte looked over at Damiano. 'You don't look any better.'

'Jeff sprang an ultimatum on me last night.'

'We make a great pair.'

'But we play for different teams.'

'There's that. Are the photos alright?'

'They're good. Nothing from Marie yet?' Damiano asked.

'No, but she's still at it though.'

'I'll give her a call.' It was before seven. She knew Marie was enjoying her hot coffee. Her day didn't officially start till seven.

'Don't you ever sleep? I'm on my third judge. I have them close, but they renege, afraid the warrant will be tossed on appeal.'

'What about the slivers? Usually you surprise me, friend.'

'Everything I have is nebulous in this bloody file. I'm still working with the trash. No slivers on the swabs. I found vomit, mucus, saliva, orange juice and leakages from surgical procedures. Pauzé shared the can with an elderly patient.'

'Another blank, as Donat would shout.'

'I'm not finished. I had the damn slivers, but they were miniscule. They might be mixed in with the vomit. I'm working on that now. The shoe was a carrier of 71 substances, and paint was one of them. No blood. First, I thought the paint was camouflage, but you can't paint over blood. If it's there, I can find it.'

'Damn! Something has to work!'

'Stop swearing. I will find a judge for the locker shoes.'

'Alright, alright.'

'If *you* find a link there for any of your 'spects, I can have a warrant issued.'

'We're trying.' Damiano told Matte about Tracey Doyle.

'Have you checked up on her?'

'She's not really on our file. I want to close. Donat was right. Marino's not good for the assault. You think we should add Doyle to our clinic, that we have time for that?' Damiano asked more harshly than she intended. The intimate moment they had shared had passed. The stress was back.

'We played her and used what she gave us on her mother.'

'That's what we do.'

'I haven't got my game on yet, I guess,' Matte said with some unease.

'For shit's sake, I'll call.' Damiano ripped her phone from her purse, took time to find the number and called. 'Detective Damiano.'

'Officer Mercier, Detective. My partner and I picked up Ms Doyle. We're here at a safe house with her now.'

'You weren't followed?'

'We went through the usual procedures and don't feel we were. Do you have any idea of the time frame?'

'A few days.'

'Would you like to speak to her, Detective?'

'Put her on.'

'Hello!'

'Tracey, Detective Damiano. I hope the officers have explained the protocol. You can't call anyone, not even a friend.'

'Alright. What if my mother calls?'

Damiano thought. 'This is difficult. Don't pick up. Inform an officer and he'll get in touch with me. We will take the phone and listen to the message away from the safe house.'

'What if my mother needs help immediately?'

'She has my number. I'm very serious about this. I hope you understand. If you violate anything I've told you, you're putting your life at risk, and you'll be out on your own. Please cooperate with us. If your mother calls me, I'll get the message through to you. Are we clear?'

'Yes. This is all my fault.'

'No, it's not. I have to go.'

Matte didn't say anything about Doyle when Damiano got off the phone so abruptly.

'I'm glad I called Doyle. We did play her. I want to head back to the lab.'

'Marie won't be glad to see us. I was just there.'

'I want to push her along.'

Matte sighed.

It didn't take long to be snarled in traffic. Montrealers learned daily about new revelations of wide-spread mismanagement and corruption in the construction industry that included roadwork. 'With all these corruption arrests, at least we know why workers keep repairing the same roads and getting nowhere. Do you think the provincial anti-corruption enquiry will bring about change?'

'Let's not really depress ourselves.'

'Where are we going, Detective?'

Damiano parked on University Street, got out and began walking. 'Pierre, I need a warrant to see the shoes in Pauzé's hospital locker. I want to shake Pauzé up, freak him out – get him talking. He's a talker by nature. If I had the sliver of glass, I'd put it under his fingernail. He'd spill something. Marie says we need something solid. She's on her third judge.'

'All the more reason not to bother her.'

'I'm the lead, Pierre. We have to force a break with one of these guys. I'm choosing Pauzé first.'

'Alright, but we're both off our form today.'

'Donat is about to yank us off the file if we don't get some action. I could mislead Marie just a smidgen to get the warrant. There's something I'm not seeing. I know it – I feel it. I have to press.'

'Are you crazy? We don't play our own, ever.'

'We have to take some risks. Sometimes, different tracks into a case, works for us. Not with this bugger. I'm willing to skirt the bounds. I'll come clean when I have the warrant. Beg Marie to forgive me yet again.'

'It's the judge *and* Marie, *and* evidence that will fall in court, not to mention the charges we'd face. What are you thinking? I won't lose my badge for you and I won't cover for you. Get rid of the vodka. You might see more clearly.'

Damiano stomped down the street ahead of Matte, her face dangerously red. To keep from squabbling, they walked in an edgy silence back to the car, huddling inside their coats against the wind. Damiano was so angry her whole body shook as she walked. She hated being wrong and loathed being called on it. She'd heard of alcoholic mind freezes. Now she knew what they were. Damiano felt a shame she'd never admit. Playing her colleagues? It had to be the vodka.

Chapter Sixty-six

Detective Stephen Galt was on the night shift. He'd showered and changed. He thought of calling his wife Maureen and asking her to come home. After all, her money had bought most of the house, but he hesitated. Had Corey told her that he hadn't actually hacked into anyone's computer? Galt knew he'd be facing a disciplinary committee when Damiano reported the hacking and perhaps lose his badge for the assault on her. Over the years he thought, he'd accepted that Maureen was the more successful. She never brought up the issue, but now he saw that her success was ever-present to him. The house, the vacations, even the cars, all were mostly on her dime. He'd never measured up to her. In the early years, he'd tried. He had.

When he thought of the job, he remembered all the effort, the god-damn exams he'd taken, the files he'd jumped on when no one else wanted them. And yet cops like Damiano had made lieutenant, another woman, among others who had passed him by. He was the loudmouth in the department. What had his father called him? *A bully with a badge.* Now he was a man without a wife and son. He'd cleaned his gun last night. It was sitting beside his badge on the table. He thought of Pauzé's file. He should have closed it. Simple things seemed to dribble away from him.

He thought of calling Maureen, just to hear her voice. He thought of Corey, doing the right thing like apologizing. There were so many things he'd have to fix. Second chances didn't come in your forties, if they ever came. He tried to feel something for Holmes, but he couldn't. His life had shown promise, payback with her, and it had crumbled with her. Damiano? He hated her most for her confidence. Would she have it without her rack and ass? He'd give her the face. Her face did good things for her.

He picked up his badge and gun, took a last glance at his home and left. He found a quiet place under a tree with a few stubborn leaves and parked. He pushed the car seat back, stretched his legs and took out his gun. He cased the area. He was alone. He checked a few CDs. He didn't want music. He readjusted the headrest and lowered the seat. He recalled a few victims he'd found dead of gunshot wounds in their cars. They had all pissed themselves. Suddenly, that mattered to him. Galt saw himself inside the car with pissed pants, and behind him, hair and bits of his brain sprayed on the back seat and roof of the car.

Still he reached for the blanket in the back seat and laid it over his knees. What if he peed right through it and he ended up looking like all the other poor, pathetic fuckers? Showering and wearing good clothes didn't change the fact that suicides looked like a pile of dirty clothes stained with blood and globs of brain when he found them. He wouldn't be any different. His father wouldn't be surprised. Maureen would, he knew that. He'd never understood why she loved him. Maureen and Corey were the only good things in his life. His gun hand shook as he raised it and that unnerved Galt.

'Fuck this! Damiano wants to take me down. Let her try!' After that burst of words, Galt threw his gun on the passenger seat and tore out from under the trees with tires screaming. He could still make his shift.

Chapter Sixty-Seven

THOMAS HOLMES was holding Madison's arm and walking with her. She was finally free of tubes but wore a protective helmet. Stroke patients can suffer sudden falls. Dr. Orr wasn't about to take any chances. Since no further leaks regarding Madison's recovery had surfaced, the media had turned their cameras and notes to the thousands of mostly university students protesting tuition hikes and Bill 78. Some of the protests had turned violent and attention was riveted on them. The uniforms were out on the streets of Montreal, trying to maintain control of a turbulent, escalating situation. Police actions were videotaped and critiqued in the press and the nightly news along with the usual uploads to YouTube.

At the Montreal General two officers were posted at each end of the corridor in the hospital where Holmes and his daughter were slowly walking.

'Daad!'

'Uh-huh.'

'I want to idnnndtify the man.'

'I know you do. How about giving me one or two days. Your speech is improving. I don't want you stressed right now. I'm a doctor. Seeing this man's photo will upset you. Look at you now, Maddy. You're walking. You may not even need my arm. I don't want the progress stopped. Detective Damiano has the photos, and she'll still have them tomorrow or the next day.'

Madison wanted to see the photos today. She wanted her life back. She wanted her assailant arrested. Most of all she wanted to go home and sleep in her own bed. Without commenting, she asked. 'Daad, let me wakk alon, pleeas.'

Thomas thought for a few seconds. He signalled to the closest officer and explained what he needed. The officer positioned himself on one side of Madison, her father on the other. He let go of her arm. Madison stood without moving, revelling in the moment she'd felt might never come. She moved her helmet to the back of her head because it was putting pressure on her head wound. Without any hesitation, she began to walk, faster than she had with her father.

'Slow down, Maddy.'

But she didn't. She wasn't afraid – she was walking! She was walking! Everything good that had come her way paled in comparison to the euphoria of this walk. Moving her legs, swinging both arms, throwing her shoulders back and smiling, nothing was better! Madison had an urge to run – to run as fast as she could, to feel her heart race.

Holmes caught her by the arm. 'I'm impressed, but we can't keep up with you. It`s my job to take care of you, to watch out for you. I made that sacred promise to your mother.'

Madison turned to her father. Her cheeks flushed, her eyes, the injured one too, sparkled as she shed tears of joy. She hugged her father and her body shook with relief. 'Daad, I nee the speec therapist, right?'

'You do, but Stephen Orr says you'll have your speech back quickly. I'll have someone in today.'

'I wannnt to walk.' And she did, ten more lengths. 'Daad, I'll wat for the photooos.'

'That's what I want to hear. I'll give Detective Damiano a call and tell her she can meet with you in two days, maybe even sooner, the way you're getting around. Let's get you back to bed now.'

'Noo. Wakk.'

'You're the boss.' Holmes's heart was as full as his daughter's. He felt faith and hope's slow return. Life began to make some sense. Those intangibles emanated from Madison. Back in the room, he helped Madison onto a chair. She wanted nothing to do with the bed. He opened his wallet and took out a photo of Becky and kissed it. 'I know it was you, Beck!' He handed it to Madison. She kissed her fingers and held them to the photo and then rested it on her heart.

'You'rr rigt, Daad. It wass Mom.'

When he left the hospital it was late, but not too late for a visit to the cemetery. It was cold and the ground was muddy and he had no flashlight. Holmes ran his hands across the letters on the monument and then kissed it. 'You're still with us, aren't you Beck. I know that now.' Holmes stayed until he was shivering before he got back into the car and drove to Montreal West to his home on Ballantyne where he still expected Becky to call out to him when he opened the front door. The house was quiet. Thomas poured himself a brandy and tilted it to the light from the lamp. He watched the light brown liquid as it slid across the glass, easily, like a ball bearing. He picked up the phone. He knew what he should be doing on all fronts, but he took a few slow sips of brandy, playing them at the back of his throat before he let them go.

He put the phone down. Damiano and her case could wait another day. Today belonged to Madison, to him and to Becky. Thomas fell into the first deep sleep he'd had since the day of Madison's attack.

Chapter Sixty-eight

CLAUDE BEAUCHEMIN hadn't showered, shaved or dressed since Louise left. Incidentals meant little to him. He was dead set on finishing his latest manuscript before Damiano made an arrest. He'd found three publishers he felt would take the book. The air in his study was heavy and thick. Beauchemin could smell himself when he moved his head or arm, and he'd turn away. Cigar smoke lent a gray shade to the room. He had survived largely on the Pinot Noir and the five-pound box of cashews Louise had bought from some bulk store.

Generally he and Louise wouldn't think of drinking homemade wine, but Louise had attended a book club in Beaconsfield on the West Island where the hostess served homemade Pinot Noir made with no sulfites, the culprit that caused headaches. Louise quite liked the wine. She and Claude had driven out to the wine store on Grande-Côte in Boisbriand that weekend and bought a case for their evening meals. Claude reached for the vendor's card and rather liked the name of the store, Les Plaisirs du Vin. Well, he thought, he was most definitely getting his pleasure from the wine, at a bottle and a half a day.

The cashews were another matter. He had gone through well over two pounds and the indigestion had risen higher than his breastbone, but he drank more wine and chewed a smaller handful of nuts. Claude was a decent cook. His French pea soup, his apple and orange pork chops, his braised beef dinners, and lamb were all hits at the dinner parties the couple used to have before he began to write. After Louise left, he had bitten into his book and had no time for cooking. He could shower and shave in minutes, so that could wait as well.

Beauchemin was well aware that pulp fiction was often whipped together to coincide with some horrendous crime. Those poorly written books were cheap plugs to cash in when interest was high and readers wanted blood and guts and didn't care about style. Beauchemin wasn't writing one of those books. He was working, rewriting, editing, choosing and producing a worthy manuscript. The added plus was that he'd have the book in the hands of a publisher 'before' the case broke. He was upbeat. He was writing up both sides, the *why* and *how* of the assault. Let the readers affix blame.

He decided he could improve on the assault and scrolled back to it. After a rereading, he saw places where he might make the event more vivid, because that's what the assault meant to him, an event. The fine line for an author of true crime was rendering a realistic portrayal without the intrusion of the author. He knew that the assault on Holmes was the lynchpin of his book. He didn't want the assault sliding off the axle of the work. Yet he could not control the anger that began to surge in his throat. He coated his additional information with a violence he didn't realize he was capable of expressing. The words punched themselves onto the screen in the semblance of another attack. When he stopped, Beauchemin was winded and sat back in the glow of satisfaction.

He drank more wine. When the pages blurred, he cleaned his glasses on his shirt. He squinted while reading what he had written in a burst of exuberance. He rose unsteadily, slapped his thighs and shouted, 'Atta boy!' He patted his chest. 'My book will drag publishers to me.' He stumbled back and nearly fell. Had he gone too far with the story? 'What have I done?' Spit flew from his mouth. For a few seconds, everything around him seemed confused. His objective had been clear when he first began to write this latest book. What had changed?

Don't shoot yourself in the ass. Was that what he had just done? He rubbed his hands on his dark pants and felt cold wetness before he saw it. Damn! When had he lost control? Humiliation seeped into his head. He couldn't leave what he had written. He reached for the chair, missed and fell heavily to the floor. In a drunken haze, Beauchemin crawled up on his hands and knees until he was back where he should be, at his desk. He highlighted his new work, and pressed delete. He knew then that the best place for him if he wanted to hang on was not in his book. He crawled up the stairs, stripped and stepped very carefully into the shower, held the walls and let the spray of hot water begin to clear his head. When he tried to step out of the shower, he stumbled again and fell, striking his head on the gray marble floor. He didn't feel the pain. He was content to lie on the cold floor, trying to determine what he'd do with his manuscript, now that the best part had been deleted.

The cashews had settled into a ball of fat that caused him more than a few loud burps. He turned on his back and massaged his belly. Louise would know how to handle the indigestion. She'd have him well in no time. He was about to call for her when he remembered. Beauchemin didn't feel well at all. His stomach began to heave and he tasted foul-smelling bile in his mouth. He scrambled to his knees and dropped his head into the toilet bowl just as a jet of vomit shot from his mouth and nose. He moaned and held his stomach and was sick once again, and then he fell against the wall. He used toilet paper to wipe his face. That's when he noticed the blood. He tried to get to his feet but the floor was slippery and wet. He grabbed

Kleenex and wiped the stinging sweat from his eyes. The tissues were red with blood that had seeped into his eyes.

Beauchemin knew enough not to stand, so he crawled to the bedroom. With his hands smeared with blood he grabbed at the phone on the night table. He worked his lips before he spoke. 'Louise Morin, please.' At least he hadn't made a fool of himself. He waited.

'Yes?'

'I've fallen.'

'Claude, are you drunk?'

'Yes.'

'Shall I call 9-1-1 for you?' Louise was distant and uninvolved.

'There's blood and I'm not dressed.'

Louise didn't say a word.

'I need your help.'

'Damn you, Claude.'

He sat back on the floor. She was coming. He lay against the bed and waited.

Chapter Sixty-Nine

STILL BRISTLING FROM Matte's second correction, playing her colleagues to close the case, Damiano jammed the car into a no-parking zone on a side street, threw her ID card on the dash and turned on the windshield flashers. Without a word she dragged her heels to the St-Viateur Bagel Shop, bought a dozen piping hot bagels, two kinds of cream cheese and cold drinks. Matte walked a few steps behind and waited for her outside the shop.

'Where do you intend on eating them?' Matte asked. There was no counter at the bakery. He dropped the issue and any further lecture. He wasn't up to a Damiano argument. She'd fight till she ground him down, even when she was wrong.

'I don't know about you, but I can multi-task.' With that out came a bagel and it took no time for Damiano to cut through it awkwardly with the plastic knife. She smeared the bagel generously with cream cheese and bit into it. Matte hesitated. 'You big priss – go for it!' And he did. The duo was back.

'Did you think of serviettes?'

Damiano reached into the bagel bag and pulled them out. 'You're dealing with a pro. I'll save the drink for the car. My multi-tasking skills have limits.'

They talked together for a few minutes, discussing details of the file and probabilities. Matte still believed they'd have their perp. Damiano took heart from him. Then they headed back to find their car. Although it was still cold, a good blue sky was threatening to appear, and their moods lifted. Matte hadn't pulled back into traffic before Damiano's phone hummed inside her purse. She grabbed it hopefully. 'Have you heard from my mother?'

Damiano lit into Doyle. 'What phone are you using? I was very clear about no calls!'

'It belongs to one of the surveillance men.'

'You haven't used yours then?' She hoped she hadn't miscalculated by trusting Doyle to follow her orders.

'No, I haven't. What about my mother?'

'I have no news, but I assume you understood your mother wouldn't be making calls.'

'I know what a clean phone is and she had phones in the SUV's glove compartment.'

'You told us it was a black BMW SUV. Do you know anything that might help us locate it?'

'I was with her when she picked it up at the dealer.'

'Damn it, Tracey, why didn't you help us out and tell us earlier?'

'She warned me not to talk to anyone, so that I'd know nothing. She swore me to secrecy because she wanted me safe. She was really worried about me.' Tracy seemed touched by her mother's caring.

And we've just wasted valuable time! 'What dealer?'

'Baltec on Jean Talon. She dealt with the manager. I should have said something sooner.'

Damiano resisted slamming into Doyle. It was her mother after all. 'Did you hear the manager's name by chance?'

'Jean-Pierre.' Tracey divulged another secret to prove to the police that her mother could protect herself. She wasn't without means. 'My mother has a gun. She has a licence for it too and she knows how to use it. I've told you everything now.'

Wonderful! 'We can get the plates from him. Thanks.'

'I'm always coming up short. I know that.'

I haven't the time for pity tears. 'You're not.'

'Where my mother is concerned, I am.'

'You're not alone. Sit tight and hope.' Damiano snapped her phone shut. 'I can get the plates for Marino's SUV.'

'Thought you had handed off?'

'I'll do this bit and hand off the information. Marino's still attached to us. She called me.'

'Besides, you want to know.' Matte knew he was taking a chance he'd just spoiled the reconciliation.

'Damn straight I want to know.'

He relaxed his hand on the wheel.

'I have an idea. Since we're not going to bother Marie, we can spare half an hour. Drive to Mount Royal Cemetery. Do you know where it is?'

'It's on rue de la Forêt, right?'

'Yes. I'm going to see if we can find the monument for Holmes's wife.'

'Why?'

'I still see him for Pauzé. We've never felt we had to pursue a hard-nosed investigation on him. I want to see that he's really coming to her grave to commune with the dead. If he's lying, and her ashes are at his home, well...'

'Fine. You never know.' It took time to leapfrog through traffic and more time to locate the man they wanted. The manager offered to go with them.

'Anyone can get lost here. Take your first left, follow it and, right there, a sharp right. Straight ahead. Slow down. The monument is on your right.' The manager got out of the car, but stayed on the path.

The white stone monument was tall and wide. "Holmes" was centered at the top. Thomas Holmes's name appeared first with the date of his birth, below, Rebecca Wilson Holmes with both dates. Below that, Madison Holmes with her date of birth. The epitaph at the bottom read: 'Safe with the hallowed walls of eternity.' The garden beneath the monument was well tended.

'Well, she's here.'

Ignoring Matte, Damiano turned to the manager. 'Is it common practice to have all the family names engraved?'

'I wouldn't say common, but some families have the work done. I've met Dr. Holmes because he's a frequent visitor. He added his daughter's name months ago. He wanted the same engraver, and the workers do move around when business is better elsewhere. Nothing unusual, Detective. Dr. Holmes is like family here. The routine ritual is family visiting for the first few months, then for birthdays and holidays. Then they drop off. We have our faithful like Dr. Holmes and a Montreal legend who lost his wife, a small but steady, faithful group. They find peace and quiet here. I understand that.'

'Just odd that someone so young has her name on a monument.' *Then she's attacked.*

The manager looked to his right. 'Detective, look at that monument, same thing. It's done.'

'Huh! Thanks.'

When they were alone in the car, Damiano asked Matte, 'What do you make of that, apart from the fact that he does commune with the dead?'

'We're not in the manufacturing business. Perhaps odd, but done.'

Damiano's phone rang. 'Luke?'

'I can't reach Dad. Some kids in my school want to join the protest.'

'You're not going to be one of them.'

'Why not?'

'Because you're fifteen and you should be in school. Besides, do you know anything about these tuition hikes?'

'Yeah, we don't want them.'

'Quebec university students have the lowest fees in North America. The hikes amount to less than a dollar a day. Does their protesting, possibly losing their school year, sound logical to you?'

'What can you do to me if I go?'

'Luke!'

'It doesn't matter what I think anyway.'

'What do you mean it doesn't matter? It damn well does matter!'

'You and Dad are busting up, right?'

Damiano motioned Matte away. 'What are you talking about?'

'Dad didn't think I was home. I heard him talking on the phone. I heard what he said. That's how I know.'

'So now you're going to march. What happens to the math mark? Luke, I'm asking you to stay in school. I'll pick you up in an hour and we can order pizza at my place.'

'What's the point?'

'Will you be there if I go?' *Thanks, Jeff!*

'I guess.'

'Good.' She turned to Matte. 'Finish up. Personal emergency.' She tapped in Jeff's number.

Chapter Seventy

A MAN SPOKE from his clean phone inside his car. 'We've located the SUV.'

'Go on…' The voice on the other end was calm.

'We searched most of the building where she parked.'

'Unnoticed, I trust?'

'Yes. We were on the third floor when police arrived.'

'And?'

'We left by the back door undetected.'

'Must I pump you?'

'We had a car at the front of the building. The cops left without her, but they left a patrol car out front. She could have gone into another apartment building. There are two of them.'

'Sit on the SUV. Are you certain you have the right plates?'

'We know we have the right SUV.'

'But not the plates?'

'We had eyes on her and the SUV, but there was heavy traffic. The uniform is beginning to make runs around the building.'

'Take shifts without being spotted. '

'How long do we stay?'

'Don't disappoint me.'

Angela Marino was not about to risk leaving the apartment building. When she left her friend's apartment, she spotted a door that led to the roof. Once she was behind the door, she saw that it couldn't be locked from the inside. Without options, she climbed the five stairs to the second door and crept onto the roof. Its parapet walls were less than two feet high, so she crawled to one side and tried to steady herself. The wind whipped around the corner and swirled across the tarred roof. Grateful that she had chosen warm clothing, she pulled her jacket over her head and lay close to the door with her gun cocked. She had heard the sirens, and she had fought with herself whether she ought to come out from hiding and seek protection.

Her profession had taught her to examine details and where they led. Don't ask a question unless you know the answer. Never offer up information unless you know where it might lead. The tenets came down to a simple lesson: never show your hand. If the men saw her with police, her life was over. Marino would have to turn on her clients to have a chance at witness protection. Most of these witnesses lived anonymous lives in constant fear each and every day. Her clients would eventually find her. Marino had no doubt of that.

The wind picked up, and her teeth chattered. Her hand felt stiff on the gun. If she spent the night on the roof, she could well freeze to death. Soundlessly, she opened the roof door just wide enough to allow her body past it. She closed the door quietly. She lay across the two top stairs, trying to stop herself from violently shaking. Her teeth still chattered. Her hands prickled from the cold. At least she was out of the wind.

Her original plan had been to hide out until an arrest was made and reappear at the office and get back to work as though nothing had happened. Her client would see she had nothing to do with the assault, and he had nothing to fear from her. The darkness of the stairwell blocked out everything around her. She moved her head, and her hair caught in a spider web. She batted wildly at it and nearly dropped the gun. Was there a surveillance camera where she huddled? When she slid away from the broken web, a stair creaked. Marino listened for any outside noise. She held the gun in both hands.

She decided to make two calls. For those, she had to crawl back onto the roof and risk opening the door again. Then she heard a door open close by and she froze. She heard *Merde!* Then the door closed. She recognized the voice of Jocelyne whose unit was 15 feet from her. Marino remembered she didn't have the time to replace the spare key. Had Jocelyne told the police that she knew her? Marino had to know. She'd have to risk a third call.

As quietly as she could, Marino crawled back onto the roof. She laid the phone beside her, took out the clean phone, found Jocelyne's number on the net and called. 'Jocelyne, this is Angela.'

'Qui?'

'Marino.'

'Ah bien, bonjour Angela. What is happening? The police arrived at my apartment and asked if I knew you. I said you were a friend. My extra key is missing too. I am anxious, I must tell you.'

'I have no time to explain, but I *was* in your apartment for an emergency. The spare key is on the desk in the study. I'll explain when I can. Sorry, Jocelyne.' Marino cut the line.

'Angela? *C'est fou!*' Jocelyne walked into her study and saw the key. '*C'est fou!*'

Marino made her second call. Damiano picked up. 'I can't talk – I'm still safe.'

'Do you need help?'

Marino hung up.

The third call was the most difficult. Her client always answered on the first ring. 'I had nothing to do with the assault. May I come home?'

The line was silent. 'I'm disappointed you felt you had to leave.'

'We both know how this game is played.'

Her client smiled. He'd always liked her nerve and her ass. She'd be difficult to replace, but she'd become a threat.

'You are a man of your word. I have always believed in that.'

The client thought about the fallout if Marino's end was a mess. Files would lead to arrests and he wasn't immune. Marino was a smart broad. 'Come home, Angela. You're family.'

'The hunters?'

'I'll whistle them back.'

Did she believe him? Her client might smile at her while giving a nod to one of his men. The money was in the SUV. How was she going to reach it without being taken? It took little time for her to decide. She'd stay put in the stairwell till morning. She'd make her decision then about a new exit plan. Now that residents were back in their apartments, the men, she felt, would stay on her SUV. The door five feet from her wasn't locked. She couldn't allow herself to nod off, not once. Sometime during the night, she fell asleep and woke with a jolt. The .22 had fallen from her hand. Her mouth tasted sour.

Chapter Seventy-One

DAMIANO WAS DRIVING to Loyola High School on Sherbrooke Street in Montreal West, a largely close-knit English-speaking community with a history dating back to 1879.

When Damiano received the call from Marino, her day had already turned bad, and Marino made it worse. *What does this woman expect me to do for her if she doesn't give me her location?* Damiano had a bad feeling about Marino's chances. Once you ran, you were on your own out there. When her phone rang again, she scooped it up, thinking it was Marino. 'Detective Damiano.'

'Mina Zin, *National Enquirer.* We still have our deal, Detective?'

Zin's words rankled Damiano, renewing her need to have this file done with. She could almost smell the moss growing on it. 'I don't forget and I don't break my word.'

'It's a bugger then?'

'I could think of a better word but I'm on the clock.'

'Don't give up. Hard cases make careers.'

'The opposite's also true.'

'Won't happen. I'll wait to hear from you.'

When Damiano shut her phone, Thomas Holmes came to mind. If she didn't hear from him today, she'd call Dr. Orr. He was Holmes's physician. It was time for Holmes to see the six pack photo spread. Holmes might well close the file on her own assault. It was time for the agent to come forward. The traffic stalled. Laughing high school students wearing their raspberry school blazers were out in the street, marching and protesting the proposed tuition hikes. *All they want is a day off classes.* Damiano turned on her flashers and parked, deciding to walk the rest of the way.

Realizing she had never picked Luke up from school, she had no familiar pickup point. *Damn!* Kids in uniforms tended to look the same to outsiders. Pushing her way along the sidewalk, she headed to the entrance of the school. *This is just great! Taking time off work and I probably won't find Luke.* Damiano walked faster, straining to find Luke among the boisterous laughers. Soon, she was surrounded by jackets. *This is ridiculous! What do I do now?* She had no intention of embarrassing Luke or herself for that matter by calling out for him. He'd never forgive her.

'Mom!'

'Didn't think I'd find you.'

'Didn't think you'd come.'

'Well, I did. Now let's get out of this mess. Take a good look at your friends and tell me they're out here in passionate protest.'

Luke took a quick scan and tried hard to hide his father's smile. 'If you worked a normal job, you wouldn't see behind things.'

'Then I wouldn't have a kid who made a 90 in math.'

'Droll.'

'That's all you have?'

'It's vocabulary, Mom. New vocabulary word today. See, I already got a use for it.'

'Have a use – not got a use.'

'School's out.'

They were both quiet once they were back in the car, thinking of the reason they were together. 'We'll talk at home.'

Luke inserted his ear buds, lay back and stayed in the car while she picked up the pizzas. Inside the condo, they made a beeline to the table ate from the boxes and drank cokes. Luke inhaled his pizza and drank his coke in two swigs. He wiped his mouth with the back if his hand. 'So, what about you and Dad?'

'Truth or aspartame?'

'You're leaving us, right? How much more is there to add?' His eyes were angry and accusatory.

'Luke, the first thing about truth – get the facts straight.'

'I could use another coke.'

Damiano pointed to the fridge and waited till Luke was back at the table. 'Your father wants me to go back home.'

'Yeah, right, like you're going to come!'

'You don't know that I won't, Luke. We all grow up, we all learn at different stages of our lives.'

'Stay on point, Mom. What do you plan on doing?'

'According to your father, I don't have to make that decision until this investigation is closed.'

'What about this other woman?'

'That's not up for discussion, Luke.'

'I thought we were talking truth.'

'Ask your father about that.'

'Do you love Dad?'

'Yes and I love you best.'

'Lame, Mom. Why can't you live with us then? Dad told me it's your big priority one or something, but you left before you got the case.'

'My job is tough for me, tougher for family. A file takes all your time.

It eats you up.'

'Other cops have families – they get along.'

'Maybe it's easier for a man. If your father were a surgeon, he'd be up at all hours. He'd be away a lot of the time, like I am now. Wives put up with that. Kids do too. For women, it's often different. There's more stress on us.'

'Why move out? I never got that.'

'Here, I don't have to apologize for late nights. I function better at work. I like my own space. I'm on the job 18-hour days, mostly longer.'

'So you just drop a husband and a kid, like we don't matter?' Luke played with his nails, pulling at skin. 'Ah shit, Mom. Don't cry! Why can't you just come home?'

'I'm up to my neck in the case, I'm having trouble sleeping and I want to walk around the condo with the lights on at three in the morning. I'd upset both you guys and you'd do the same to me. I need to be alone to think. '

Luke stomped into the living room. Damiano gave her son a minute and then went looking for him. She found him plugged in and sprawled on her white leather couch. Luke's eyes were closed and she saw his thick lashes, the natural bloom of youth in his cheeks, and his lips, red as roses. His mop of brown hair shone with health. His limbs were long and strong. This beautiful boy was hers. Warmth spread through her body. 'Forgive me?' she whispered, taking out one of his buds.

'I don't know. S'pose. What does it matter? You always do what you want.'

Damiano couldn't deny the truth, so she bent and kissed him on both cheeks. They were cool and firm.

He turned into the couch. 'Geez, Mom! I'm too old for that shit.' His eyes said he wasn't. 'What you do is cool.'

Damiano savored the moment, away from the pressure of her file and the judgment of her flaws.

'What happens if you don't solve the case?'

'File.'

'Alright, file.'

'Good files will fly to other desks. My competence will be judged. I won't land another priority file any time soon. I'll get the dumb files any detective could close. The Holmes assault is my chance.'

'I guess you've gotta do it then, Mom.'

'I know, Luke.'

Chapter Seventy-two

DAMIANO PROMISED HERSELF that she would not go off half-cocked at Marie who hadn't found solid evidence she could use. Instead, after Luke left, she shopped for groceries, made herself a bowl of vermicelli cooked in chicken broth topped with rosé sauce that she bought at Pizzaiolle across the street. She drank only two glasses of Chianti and soaked up the sauce with a baguette. Once she had cleaned up in the kitchen, she showered, did her hair, weighed herself and discovered she'd lost five pounds from stress.

She planned her next day after checking in with Matte. That night her sleep was fitful. Jeff had thrown a scare into her. As long as she was calling the shots, she knew where they were coming from. She'd lost control, and she might lose him. Jeff was right. She hadn't given their marriage any real thought. In one way or another, she realized, most people probably felt trapped, even when love was present. A cop's all-consuming life, hers in particular, was hell on a family. Good files, and she wanted good files, were all-consuming. She was a cop. Everything, stress included, circulated in her blood. It wasn't her title, or the commendations, it was the grind of the work that pumped her life and kept her alive in the moment. Jeff didn't understand that. He liked his work; he liked leaving it aside too. She thought of extreme sports – her job was extreme living. She was no stranger to hard decisions. She had another thought. A cop's life was a lonely place. With that, she fell asleep into busy dreams.

The next morning, she dressed well and still made it into the office seconds before Matte who appeared with two coffees.

'How will you deal with Marie?'

'With the truth. I won't play her.'

'I'm glad.'

She sat while she called Marie at Crime. 'Give me what you have.'

'No slivers of glass. That's after puke, saliva – you name it. He probably threw them on the floor. Are you going to call the kid in with the one shoe?'

'Don't see that standing up in court. Judges?'

'Sorry, still trying.'

'What's the hang-up?'

'Donat didn't help us when he called off the postal search. He was probably right. They all had access to the damn boxes. Slim lead, but the boss killed it. I'll still keep trying. What a bugger of a file!'

'I'm still working it. I'm calling Holmes's physician. Pierre has his six pack all ready. I will exert pressure – we've been patient. Holmes should be ready to make the ID. It's strange that after all our work the file may come down to her ID.'

'I'll cross my toes.'

'I have a good feeling about her. She's strong, determined and wants to do the ID. It's a question of getting permission from her physician. He's told me Holmes wants to move ahead. Her father's being stubborn, trying to delay. I understand his motives. He doesn't want another threat to her health, but there's something off kilter. I just can't nail it. It might just be me too. I'm reaching – I know it.' Damiano closed her phone. She looked over at Matte. 'Here goes. I want you with me at the hospital.'

Matte nodded, pleased. He packed his notes and photos.

Damiano placed her call. 'Dr. Stephen Orr, please. This is Detective Damiano calling. The call is important.'

'Hold on, please.'

'Yes?'

'Detective Damiano.'

'You're lucky you caught me. I have surgery in ten minutes.'

'Detective Matte and I will bring the photo spread to Madison Holmes. Doctor, we need the ID.'

'Have you run this by her father?'

'That's not necessary. I have been patient, but the ID has to happen today. It's your permission I need. You're Holmes's physician. I would prefer if you didn't alert her father.' Damiano kept their conversation on a personal level.

'You have my permission, Detective. I trust your skills. I'd like to be there. I'll be out of surgery in two hours. How about 11:00 this morning?'

Damiano pumped a fist. 'We'll be there.'

'I appreciate that. Thomas will too. I have to tell him. He's her father. I'll say you'd like him there for support.'

'As long as he doesn't interfere,' Damiano said firmly.

'I'll leave those guidelines to you, Detective.'

Damiano closed the phone, and both she and Matte sat quietly looking at the six pack. 'Pierre, it's two weeks today that Holmes was attacked.'

'There's harmony to this then. Toni, you have to be prepared for the best and the worst. Holmes saw her assailant's face for a second. Like our kid Mathieu said, these guys look alike with the hat and shades and collar. The photos will shoot the attack right back in her face – a lot of pressure and shock. We have to know that going in.'

Damiano took a deep breath and exhaled. She took the coffee and sipped it. 'All true, but I have a good feeling about the timing.'

'Do we advise Donat?'

'Hell no! If Holmes gets spooked, he'll yank us off the file today. We stay out of his way.' She looked at the photos. 'Do you have a gut feeling about who we take down? Theory, something?'

'Yes, but I won't be the one to jinx the morning. You?'

'I do, but you're right. We go with Holmes. She deserves first crack. It began with her – it should end with her.' Damiano looked over at Matte and knew what he was thinking. 'ID evidence from a victim who was badly concussed, etc., etc., might not stand up in court. If it's Galt or Beauchemin, they'll know who to hire to represent them. Tom Graham? Then we have extradition. Pauzé? At least he's confined. Holmes saw her assailant for at best, a second, like you said?'

'Actually, that was my next thought. I was thinking that if Holmes hesitates…'

'She doesn't know.'

'Exactly.'

'If she's quick and sure, it's anything but a trash can ID. It's a warrant.'

Chapter Seventy-three

The courier's thoughts drifted from safe, familiar objects around him to traps and cages. *Real fear begins when the red light above the exit door burns out.* Could he find another door? He was afraid of traps, always had been. He twitched thinking of traps, there were so many possible snares.

Chapter Seventy-four

THOMAS HOLMES WAS SHAVING. He had a narrow face that made the daily routine more difficult as ruts and lines dug in around his mouth. He was lifting his nose with his middle finger and using the other hand to shave under it when the phone rang. He wiped off the shaving cream around his mouth and ran to the phone, fearing the worst. Last night, he'd come to a decision. Madison's recovery was a miracle to him. The apprehension of her assailant meant a further threat to that recovery and testifying, he knew what followed, would force his daughter to relive the horror of the morning. He was not going to call Damiano. Madison's recovery had made possible a new life plan for both of them, one he saw clearly and understood. No one would violate it. He wouldn't permit it.

'Glad I caught you, Thomas. Detective Damiano will be in to see Madison at 11:00 this morning for the ID.'

'What?'

'I gave her permission, Thomas.'

'Why didn't you call me first? I don't want Damiano anywhere near Madison. I don't care about an arrest. I did when I was sure I'd lose Madison. I just want us to try to go on with our lives. I forbid it!'

'I'm due in surgery, Thomas. I can't obstruct a police investigation. Neither can you for that matter. Madison is an adult and she's chosen to make the identification. I'm discharging Madison on Monday. She'll continue with her therapy as an out-patient, of course, but on the whole, she's doing remarkably well. Think of the possibility of having her home with her assailant still out there. Have you thought of that, Thomas? Lastly, I have faith in Damiano. Madison wants some kind of closure.'

'I demand to be there!' Thomas fought to keep from shouting.

'Damiano suggested I ask you to be present for support. I'll be there as well.'

'That was decent of her. I just...'

'I understand, Thomas, but life goes on.'

'I'm about to head down now.'

'Good. See you soon.'

Madison picked up on the concern in her father's face as soon as he walked into her room, and it worked itself into her nervous system. 'Daad?'

'Have you been to therapy, Maddy?'

'For one hour.' Madison was sitting in the large chair beside her bed.

'Whaat's happening?'

'Detective Damiano has some photos for you to look at. I'm assuming they're of the authors whose work you rejected.'

'Baad move, I ges!'

'No, it wasn't. It's just that no one knows what's in the mind of another human being.'

Madison ran her fingers across her eyebrows, gently on her bad side. A sudden shiver caught her off guard and she jerked.

'Maddy?'

'It's okay.' But it wasn't. She was back at her front door. The wind was blowing inside her condo, and she was turning to close the door behind her... It didn't seem fair to her to have to be brave again. The aftermath of her assault loomed dark and frightening and unending. This morning... What if she couldn't recognize... Then there was court... What if her speech was still garbled... Madison moaned and fell back into the chair as though someone had struck her head. Her head hurt. Her body tensed, every muscle stiffened. The face was there, but still blurred.

Holmes watched his daughter with the desperation of a father who can't make things right. He saw his world collapsing for a third time. He sat hopelessly on the sidelines, waiting for Madison to come around. A helpless calm descended on Thomas. Madison seemed to move away from his care. Stephen Orr had been right. She couldn't go home with her assailant still free. Holmes convinced himself that Madison might even find her assailant in the photo spread. If not, he'd take care of her, always. 'Try to settle down, Maddy. You and I can go for a walk. The police won't be here for another two hours.' His words did get through Madison's momentary fright. In a few minutes, she got up from her chair. Together with the officer on duty, they walked the corridors of her floor. Together they waited for the photo spread. Holmes tried to figure out what was worse, the infernal waiting or Madison knowing.

Damiano and Matte were discussing strategy with their door closed when the boss barged in, as he generally did. 'Do you two have any idea what day this is? I know because I have the media to remind me on a daily basis. Are you listening?' He was working on a decent rant.

'I can count, Chief. Matte can too. He's the best with details.'

'Your tone is very close to insubordination, Damiano.'

Matte was prepared to watch the two of them go at each other. The file had come to a scratchy edge.

'In less than two hours now,' Damiano checked her watch, 'Matte and I will show Madison Holmes the six pack. We know from her physician that she wants to identify the assailant. We'd be there now, but we have to wait for Dr. Orr who's in surgery as we talk. I spoke with him this morning.'

Relief and rage didn't sit well on Donat's face. Why wasn't I informed?' The boss was back in full force.

'I wanted to hand you a copy of the arrest.'

'It's not what *you* want, Damiano, it's what *I* tell you to do. Understood, yet again?'

'Understood.'

'With all the goddamn traffic and construction, get going. I want you there, earlier than late.' Donat looked at his detectives and dropped his harsh tone. They were all edgy. 'I'll hold off on the media till I hear from you. Good luck!'

'Delay that, Chief. You don't want to rush to judgment. We're looking at a formal lineup and hard evidence. I will hand you a close. Then we go to the press.'

Donat left the office, but stopped abruptly at the door. He waved his arm, kept waving it until Damiano and Matte left the office. 'Get it done! Day 14!'

When they were in their city car, Damiano said, 'I wonder if his mother breastfed him.' She added a few seconds later, 'Let's close this file once and for all – no more grind and pull.'

Chapter Seventy-five

IT WAS ALSO DAY 14 for Angela Marino, Claude Beauchemin, Detective Galt, Tom Graham and Jean Pauzé.

Marino's shoulder, neck and hip ached from her night on the stairs. Her gun hand was stiff. She'd filled her night with worried thoughts. She couldn't afford to trust her client. The SUV was as dangerous as a bear trap. Her money was lost. The men might well have gotten into the SUV and taken it last night. Her friend Jocelyne had already left. Earlier, she'd heard her door open, close and lock. The spare key was not available to her, so a quick shower was out. All she'd have with the police was short-term protection. That door closed. Marino was on her own. That wasn't something new in her life. Marino was the epitome of a self-made woman.

She had never, as an adult, used a back door, and she wasn't about to do so now. Marino called a cab and waited on the stairs another five minutes. She stood inside the front door till she spotted the cab. Marino walked out, her head held high. She kept her hand holding the .22 inside her right pocket.

When Louise Morin walked into the house, she didn't immediately go to Claude. She opened as many windows as she could. The air was foul and it caught in the back of her throat. Claude hadn't moved. He was slumped against the side of the bed in a small pool of drying blood. His head was bloody. A trail of blood on the carpet led to the bathroom. She knew he was aware of her presence, but he hadn't looked up. Louise went for her first aid kit, wet a towel and came back to Claude.

'I won't win the Giller fiction prize for this effort will I Louise?,' Beauchemin said in an attempt to thaw the ice between them.

Louise ignored him and went to the window and opened the verticals, returned, knelt beside Claude and began to clean him up.

'I am sorry, Louise.'

'Don't move, Claude.' She went for another towel, wet it and got back to work. 'You're going to need sutures. I'll help you up and get you dressed.'

'Louise, say something to me.' Beauchemin, using the bed for leverage, managed to get to his feet and took the clothes Louise handed him. He dressed as best he could.

'Just a minute. Your head's bleeding again.' Louise lifted off the gauze bandage and changed it for another. 'Alright. I'll take you to the Queen

Elizabeth clinic.'

'Not the hospital?'

'I can't take you to the General, Claude.'

Once they were in Louise's car, Beauchemin tried small talk that stayed small. When that didn't work, he said, 'I think I'll try my hand at something else.'

'What did you do with your retelling of the assault?'

'I deleted it.'

Louise didn't ask any other question. Blood was seeping into the gauze when they reached the clinic. 'Claude, go straight to the desk. The wound is bleeding again.'

'You're not coming in with me?'

'No, I'm not.'

'Louise!'

'When you get back home, call a cleaning service or that blood will permanently stain every place you crawled.'

'You're walking out on me again? Louise, please. I don't know anything about the cleaning service.'

'It's time you did. I work all day.'

'I can change. Just give me some help now.'

'I read the chapter – you scare me. I can't come home now. You will have to learn to be patient. I wish I had known you better, Claude.'

'I know you could have done better without me. I've always known that. You are the "better" in my life.'

Louise turned away and walked back to her car.

Beauchemin's sloping shoulders fell further. Shock mingled with hurt until he felt a line of fear. He had no anger to flash.

Detective Galt called in sick on day 14, the first sick day he'd taken since Corey was born. He began down in the basement, clearing out all the junk he had accumulated over the years. Half an hour later, he couldn't believe the stuff he'd hoarded. At the Loblaws supermarket he picked up cartons for the work ahead of him. Filling one box after another he didn't bother checking the memorabilia he was chucking out. When he came to his high school trophies, he stopped and examined each of them. MVP on his high school football team, MVP twice on the hockey team where he played center, those were good times for Galt. Those times of fame and promise had faded with the passing years.

He started on another box and found Corey's old toys, games, clothes and two trophies. In time, he'd have a room full just like his father's, junk that would mean nothing unless he made something of his life. Galt began rummaging to find something of Maureen's past but came up empty. He went into the small storage room, still nothing, well, very little, a pair of old cross-country skis. He sat and ran his hand over the warped, faded wood. Galt had filled nine boxes with his junk. Maureen had kept one pair of skis. The answer didn't really surprise him. She didn't need the past to bolster her ego.

Galt knew he wasn't going to walk away. He'd do time. He'd lose his badge. If he was lucky, he'd be left with part of his pension. When he walked into his writing room, he was amazed at all the paper and folders and drafts he had written over the past five years. Five years, and he had nothing to show for his work. He'd ruined his life and his family for a book! Galt tore into the room and had cleaned out every vestige of writing in three hours. By the time he was through he was slippery with sweat.

After a long shower, he flopped into his favorite chair, flipped on the TSN sports channel and went seriously at a cold beer. Galt was ready. Nevertheless, when the phone rang, his body clenched. He got to his feet and reached for the receiver without checking the ID. 'Yes?'

'Are you free for a dinner date?'

'Maureen?' He was still tight.

'Your wife.'

'Yeah, I am. I'm not even wearing an ankle bracelet yet.'

'I won't have to order in then.'

'What's the …'

'Miss you.'

'Really?'

'Unfortunately.'

'Do you know how beautiful you are to me?'

'That's part of the reason I'm stuck with you. I also like a man who can lift heavy things.'

'Bring Corey. We should be together.'

'Good idea, Stephen.'

Tom Graham sat in a blue hospital gown on a bench, waiting to be called in for the laser therapy. His thigh and groin had already been marked with indelible ink. He held the side of the bench with both hands and looked at the two men beside him. No one spoke. He pushed all thoughts of Montreal and Martin Connor off his radar. He didn't care about either one of them. The air was cold and he shivered uneasily. Ten minutes passed, thirty minutes passed. He began to sweat. *Mara was right. I should have brought*

War and Peace. He did wonder when Detective Damiano would contact him again. He had no doubt he'd get a call.

Jean Pauzé reluctantly closed the window beside his bed. The old farts in his room had called for the nurse, complaining of cold. He had no intention of leaving it closed. The room stank! With his crutches, it was easier to walk than to get down into a chair. The casts were long and heavy. He worked his way awkwardly out to the corridor, ignored the cop who walked a few steps behind him, and hobbled on. Once he swiveled and caught the cop bouncing on his heels. He decided no rehab center, and no parents' home to deal with their shame and disappointment. He'd return to his apartment if Damiano got off his back. If things worked out – it was a big *if*. He'd never been lucky, but he knew it took months to evict a tenant. The apartment was his only hope even though McGill would want nothing to do with him. The hobbling stopped. His legs hurt – they still throbbed. He missed his good legs. Even if he managed to get back to the apartment, even if… He got stuck there.

He wanted a pain killer – he needed its numbness. He hobbled over to the bed and rang for the nurse. 'Copper, shut the door. I need rest and the corridor is noisy. I'm on the sixth floor, so no one will try climbing up here.' He missed his privacy. An orderly had to help him take a dump! But there was something Pauzé had to do with the door closed. When he had the pill, he didn't take it right away. He thought of the one positive in his life. Holmes had said he was a writer! A writer! Of course that was a long time ago. She hadn't meant it anyway – she'd dumped him.

Chapter Seventy-six

So MUCH DEPENDED on Holmes's ID that Damiano and Matte didn't speak on the drive to the General, nor did they notice the traffic snarls. The air inside their car crackled with anticipation. Damiano's phone rang and she fished it out of her purse. 'Dammit! It's Donat.' She stretched her neck. 'Yes, Chief?'

'You there?' He was back to barking.

'We're just getting out of the car, but I have to turn my phone off.'

'The goddamn TV vans are back. They smell a development.'

'Not from us.'

'Forget them. I'll get rid of them. Get on the phone to me as soon as you have it. Don't make me wait!'

Damiano closed her phone. "I can almost forgive the boss today. He fields the heavy blowback.' Damiano hurried up the parking ramp with Matte tagging along behind her.

'You okay?'

'I'm thinking.'

'Get out of your details – I need you alert.'

'My lower back is seizing up on me.'

'You're human like the rest of us, Pierre.'

They took the elevator and walked together to Holmes's private room. Damiano was taken aback when she found Holmes dressed and pacing the small area. She no longer looked like a patient or a victim. Holmes had tried to hide the part of her head that had been shaven for surgery by pulling longer hair across it. The agent had a presence and that boded well. Dr. Orr rushed into the room and positioned himself beside Thomas Holmes. The room was very quiet.

Holmes stepped in front of his daughter. He kissed her on both cheeks and laid his hand gently on her head injury. 'Remember that I love you, Maddy. You take the reins now.' Then he stepped to her right.

The moment felt awkward.

Damiano cleared her throat and took the lead. 'Good morning, everybody! I can't believe how good you look, Madison. I'm very glad for you. You've come a long way in a short period of time.' Damiano pointed to the table and two chairs. Matte and the others would have to stand. With the bed in place, there wasn't space in the room for more chairs. Damiano had called ahead and had purposely set up the room. This was her interview, not a conference. 'Would you sit in one of the chairs? – I'll take the other.

Detective Matte will stand beside me. Your father can stand behind you with Dr. Orr.'

Thomas didn't move.

The rest stepped into position. Matte took out the envelope with the six pack, but first he walked over and closed the door. The air stilled in the room. Nobody moved.

Before Matte handed the six pack to Damiano, Madison anxiously twisted her fingers. She waited and shifted on the chair.

'Madison, you are a very strong woman. I admire that. Just relax, take your time and have a good look. No one is putting any pressure on you.' *Yeah, right,* Damiano thought. Matte handed the six pack to Damiano. She turned it around and slid it across the table to Holmes, so that she was seeing it head-on. Damiano and Matte kept their eyes on Madison, on her every move.

Madison let out a groan as though she'd been struck. Both hands became clenched fists, and her eyes teared. She examined the photos. She ran her fingers across one of the caps, then the shorts. Then she scraped her nails across the photos. The woolen caps cleared the blur. Madison looked down at the faces again, and then she knew! She pounded the table with both fists. 'Why?' she wailed. 'WHY?' She was seeing a face that her consciousness had tried to hide. The courier was back at her door, and she saw his face. She knew that face. Damiano's heart raced. She felt resolution was moments away. She leaned forward. The recorder was on. She was buzzing with her first close. She wanted to shout, *Who, Madison? Who is it?*

Madison turned to her father. Her eyes were wild with horror. 'Why?' Shock and fear gripped her throat half choking her. She saw it now, clearly.

Holmes backed away.

'Why, Dad?' Madison rasped. 'WHY?' she screamed hollowly, weeping and recoiling as though she had been stabbed.

Matte waited for her next word. Damiano didn't. She grabbed the cuffs from her bag. In a flash she was behind Thomas Holmes, pushing him towards the wall. She heard that click when Holmes stepped back as Madison asked 'why' a second time. That missing something, that odd piece she couldn't lock in was their monster, and he was standing in the room with them! 'Thomas Holmes, you are under arrest for the assault on Madison Holmes.' She knew. Matte hadn't yet made the connection, but rushed to help restrain Holmes who began to struggle viciously against Damiano, trying to kick her.

'I have to explain,' Holmes shouted, his face red and the veins on his neck bulging. 'I love you, Maddy.' He looked down at the cuffs, confused.

'Maddy, you must listen to me. Please, honey.' He fought Damiano and Matte, but they restrained him. 'I must explain so you'll understand!'

Dr. Orr had both arms around Madison, against the threat that Holmes might break free. Madison had fallen against his body. She couldn't look at her father.

'Don't take me away. I have to explain. Then you'll all understand,' he shouted desperately.

Matte and Damiano held Holmes against the wall, but made no effort to remove him from the room. Damiano wanted a confession. She wouldn't get one if he regained his senses and lawyered up. Matte sensed what she was thinking and nodded. With a firm grip on Holmes, Matte reached over for the recorder and held it closer.

'Listen to me, Maddy, please. I beg of you. Nothing went right after your mother died. Patients, my whole practice. I lost my footing. I'm facing malpractice suits and I'm about to lose my medical insurance. I was lost, Maddy. I needed to be with Becky. I miss her. No, that's not it. I have to tell the truth now. I *wanted* to be with her...'

'Doctor, I must advise you of your rights. You have the right...' Damiano had no intention of losing her case to a technicality.

'I don't care about rights. I waive them. Do you hear me, I waive them! Maddy! Maddy, please look at me. Honey, I couldn't leave you behind, not when you were so afraid. There was precious little time for planning. Don't you see, I had no choice when I struck you. I needed a perfect blind. The police couldn't suspect me! I couldn't have that! They had to think it was one of your authors. You see, don't you, Maddy? I never meant to hurt you. I could never hurt my child. I wanted us to be a family again, the three of us together like we used to be.' Holmes's words did not erupt in a sputtering spasm. They were clear and all the more frightening. His face bleached into sudden despair. 'I never meant to be cruel. You know me Maddy – you know me.'

Matte grabbed and pushed Holmes towards the door.

'No!' he shouted from the door. 'I have to tell my daughter. You have to know Maddy. I was so wrong – you lived! You are my miracle. I realized the error of my plan every day I saw you fight. It wasn't time. I readjusted my thinking because I understood what Becky wanted. I couldn't break my promise. I've tried to take care of you. You know that Maddy. I know you do. Madison, please look at me! I never meant you harm. You're all that matters to me.'

Madison buried her head in Dr. Orr's white coat.

Matte pushed Holmes from the room and he waited for Damiano.

She went to Madison. She grabbed Madison's fists with both her hands. 'You're okay, Madison. You are more than okay.' Damiano felt a sudden rush of pride in Holmes. 'Remember today. I hope this is the bravest, saddest thing you ever have to do in your life. You pulled yourself through all this mess. You will recover from this horrendous discovery too. I have faith in you. It wasn't a miracle – your recovery was hard work and strength.'

Madison wept but she managed to stand without any help and hugged Damiano.

'Why? Why would Daad hhurt me? Why?'

'I can't answer that, Madison, but your father loves you. It all got twisted.'

'He broke my heart…' Her lament was rock hard and final.

Dr. Orr stepped in and took over. 'I'll give her something. We'll take good care of Madison, Detective.'

For everyone in the room each of the fourteen days had been brutal and tense and now horrifying.

Matte and Damiano were professional and quiet as they led Holmes to their car. He too was finally subdued and appeared lost, shrivelling like a sprayed weed. Matte got into the back of the car with him. It bothered him that he hadn't fingered Holmes as quickly as Damiano. She was always racing ahead. He sometimes felt she missed details. But she hadn't this time. He had. Damiano waited till the door closed and grabbed her phone.

Donat must have been standing by the phone he picked up so quickly.

'Chief, I have a close.'

She heard a sigh of relief but wasn't quite certain if it was hers or his. 'I just arrested Thomas Holmes for the assault on his daughter a few minutes ago. I'm standing outside the car. He's cuffed and Matte is with him as we speak.'

Chief Donat was immediately alert. Damiano knew because he hadn't said a word. He was listening.

'I'm fully confident that a Crown attorney will determine we had reasonable grounds to lay charges. We have a confession, duly witnessed. Holmes waived his rights. We don't need a warrant. Holmes goes straight to trial. This file is closed.' Damiano paused, waiting for a response.

For all his short man bark, Donat had earned his rank. He recognized perception in his best cops. 'How did you know?'

'I was missing something – couldn't catch it, but I felt it was there. Then it clicked when Ms Holmes reacted to the six pack, and her father backed away. Something in those photos stirred her memory. I felt it.'

'Did Matte catch it? Just a matter of interest. I like to know my cops.'

'You'll have to ask him.'

'I won't bother. Had you figured for an ace. I'm not often wrong. You did me proud. I need details.'

'In brief, I read Holmes his rights. He waived them, twice. He confessed to his daughter in front of her physician, Matte and me. The confession was recorded. He's suffering some kind of breakdown. I hope he doesn't work that to his advantage in the courts. He's a monster! Holmes's attack on his daughter was ruthless, planned and viciously executed. He intended to murder her. He admits as much on tape.'

'Your job is done. Let the courts deal with him now. Bring Holmes to intake and book him – I'll meet you there. I'll set up the press conference. I'm very pleased.'

Damiano's adrenalin surged – she had her close! Yet the file had taken such an ugly turn that she found herself dragging as she got back into the car. Before pulling away, she noticed in the rear-view mirror that Holmes was glaring at her. She glared right back at him. Her phone rang minutes later and she scooped it up off the seat. 'Marie?'

'Toni, I have a warrant for the shoes! I fought like a billy goat for this.'

'We've closed, Marie.'

'Am I missing something? What's happened?'

'Later alright?'

'No problem. Good work, Detective. Good work. To you both.'

Holmes was still glaring when Damiano looked back. She saw that Matte was keeping a close eye on him. When they turned into the rear of the Crémazie Division, Damiano was grateful Donat had gotten rid of the media swarm. The building was quiet. Matte helped Holmes from the car and they led him, past a double steel door into the intake room. They stopped by a row of gray lockers on their left. Damiano opened one of them and spotted Donat. He didn't approach. He allowed his detectives to finish their work.

Damiano removed the cuffs from Holmes who immediately rubbed his wrists. Matte instructed Holmes to remove his belt and shoe laces. Matte took the items, bagged them and deposited them in an empty locker. He wrote Holmes's name on a label and stuck it on the locker door. Both Donat and Matte missed Holmes's next move. As he handed Matte his belt, he quickly reached into his right pocket with the other hand, closed his fist on something and brought it to his mouth. Damiano sprang at Holmes, grabbed his fist and pounded it against the locker.

He screamed in pain.

'Oh no, you don't!' Two pills fell to the floor. Matte scooped them up. Donat came running.

Holmes snarled at Damiano. 'You ruined everything! Why couldn't you have let things be?'

Damiano was shaking. 'Suicide watch and jacket. Let's get this done.' She continued processing Holmes. He was her perp. This bastard wasn't going out the easy way, not on her watch. When her phone rang, she swore. She was in no mood to pick up, but saw it was the Hôtel Dieu. She stepped back and took the call. 'Detective Damiano.'

'Detective, a patient, Jean Pauzé, has barricaded himself in his room with two elderly patients and is demanding to speak to you, only you.'

'Is he threatening them?'

'Pauzé has yelled to the surveillance officer in the corridor that he will injure them if the officer or anyone else tries to get into the room. It's an urgent situation. He was scheduled to go to rehab today, but that was delayed because we discovered more infection in one of his legs. We assume he has a crutch blocking the door. I don't know if he has a weapon, perhaps a knife from the dinner cutlery. He called the nurses' station from his room. That's all I know.' The voice on the other end of the line was shaken.

Dammit to hell! 'I'm on my way.'

'Matte, finish up here, please. Send the pills to analysis and get up to the Hôtel Dieu as soon as you can. I'll need you.'

'What is it?' Donat demanded. 'You can't leave!'

'Pauzé has barricaded himself and two elderly patients in his hospital room. He's threatened them and won't speak to anyone but me. I have to go.'

'Isn't Galt on this?'

'Chief! What if these patients are injured?'

'Then get it done and get back here asap.'

'I will. Hold off on the press conference, you owe me that, you owe both of us.'

'You have my word. Stop wasting time and get out of here. Matte, I can finish up with Holmes. Go with her.' He signalled to the two officers who were close by to assist with the processing.

Matte sped after Damiano.

Chapter Seventy-Seven

Matte switched on the flashers. Damiano reached into the glove compartment for the cherry, turned it on and placed it on the roof of the car. She also called for more backup. She checked her pocket recorder to see if it was charged. She had another case on her mind. She opened her purse and checked her gun. 'Blow this light, Pierre! Goddamn traffic! It's a wonder any ambulance reaches anyone in need.' She was leaning forward. 'Use the sidewalk. There's no one on it.'

'I'm doing the best I can, Toni.'

'Saint-Urbain is a one-way. You remember that, right?'

'Yes, I do. You should have taken the wheel.' Matte was angry.

'I'm sorry. It's just…'

'We're almost there.' After driving up a side street, he turned on Saint-Urbain and into the main entrance. 'Go! I'll take care of parking. I'll be right up. Be careful.'

Damiano grabbed her purse and ran into the hospital, up the six flights of stairs and raced to Pauzé's ward. Outside the room, the officer stood quietly with hospital staff and security. Officer Gauthier spotted Damiano. 'He's in there with two other patients. He must have opened all the windows. You can feel the draft coming from under the door.'

'Get these people away from the door, Officer. We have backup coming.' Damiano moved closer to the door. 'Jean!' she shouted loudly. 'It's Detective Damiano.'

Pauzé didn't answer.

She called through the door a second time. 'You said you wanted to talk to me. Is that right?' Damiano could feel her nerves revving.

'Detective, leave your weapon and your bag outside. Don't try anything or someone will be hurt. Do you understand?'

'I'm ready. May I come in?'

'Come ahead.'

Pauzé was the first person she saw. He was halfway out the window, more than halfway. He was hanging on to the side of the window sills. Any sudden move on his part or hers and she was sure he would fall. 'Jean, lean a little more inside the window, please.' Troy Turner flashed in her head.

'I'm just fine as I am. I want these old farts out of the room. I want to talk to you.'

'What do you suggest?' She wanted to keep Pauzé feeling he was in charge.

'First, open your jacket and don't move.'

Damiano had her digital voice recorder in the top pocket of her jacket. 'Is it okay for me to put the jacket on that bed next to you?'

'Do it and step back.'

Damiano complied. 'What about those patients, Jean?'

'Get Gauthier in here, only him. He can carry them out. If he tries anything or doesn't move quickly, it's over.'

'Hold on, Jean.' Damiano walked back to the door and called Gauthier and told him what to do. 'Okay Jean?'

'Do it now,' Pauzé ordered.

Gauthier followed Damiano's orders and had the elderly patients out in minutes. Both older men crouched in fear against Gauthier's shoulder.

'Close the door. Use the crutch to lock it.'

'Where do you want me to stand?'

'Stand at the bottom of my bed. You take one step closer and I'll jump.'

'I promise I won't. You wanted to talk. I'll listen.'

'You asked me who attacked me. I can tell you now, didn't want to before.'

Damiano had Pauzé talking, rolling and she knew enough not to interrupt him. She hoped he might look away and she'd edge closer to him. Pauzé was such a pathetic sight to her that she didn't have to manufacture sympathy. It was there. She'd prompt him, guide him until she could grab the kid and pull him back inside. She leaned forward.

'He packed a mean wallop for an older guy.'

'How did he know about you, Jean?'

'I got through to Holmes one night on the phone.' He smiled ruefully. 'Guess I did that right – put a real scare into her. She must have told her father.'

'Why are you telling me this now?'

'Don't fucking move!' He pointed to his right leg. 'Grave infection! That's what they tell me now. There's a good chance I'll lose my leg below the knee. I'll lose my freakin' leg!' Tears welled in his eyes.

'I'm sorry, Jean. I'm truly sorry,' she whispered.

'He came here to the hospital once. Scared the shit out of me. Thought he might kill me for Christ's sake. I swore I'd never reveal his name. He looked like he believed me, but I never trusted he wouldn't be back. I know you have me for Holmes's assault. I'm a likely target, a fucked up nothing. The shoes are under my mattress.'

'I don't need them, Jean.'

'What do you mean you don't need them? Why are you using my first name? You're not my friend. You and Madison Holmes did a real job on me. I'm going to lose my leg and I didn't do fuck all! You hear me? I didn't do Holmes.'

'I know, Jean. We have a confession.'

'What?' Pauzé's voice was shrill.

'Thomas Holmes assaulted his daughter.' Damiano watched shock and dismay turn to anger that distorted his mouth. She felt she could smell the sweat on his body. The kid was so poor, so beaten down, so alone. He held the window frame, but she saw him slump.

'So, he clubbed me with a bat to set me up. I was collateral damage to him. I didn't matter worth shit to his daughter or to him. That's actually true. I don't matter anymore, to anyone.'

'No, it's not. Damn, you earned a PhD. You're a scholar. You're a kid who can start over. They have very strong antibiotics. You probably won't lose your leg.'

'I pulled out the IV. Can't think of one time in my life when I was lucky – why would any of that change now?'

'You have your whole life ahead of you. I am truly sorry for what's happened to you. Fight back! You do matter. You don't have to jump, Jean.'

Pauzé laughed and she inched closer. 'That's where you're wrong.'

Chapter Seventy-eight

Matte had parked and was hurrying into the hospital when he spotted a small circle of people pointing up at a hospital window and using iPhones like telescopes to videotape plaster legs hanging from the sixth floor window. One person glanced over at him. Matte could make out the faint wail of sirens in the distance. *She's alone in that room with Pauzé.* He ran the same path Damiano had taken to help her. When he reached the corridor, he was panting and bending over at the knees.

Officer Gauthier was adamant. 'The kid said he'd jump if anyone tried to get into that room.'

'Can you hear what they're saying?'

'I hear voices, but I can't make out much more than a word or two.'

'Backup?'

'Our guys are on the way and firefighters too. They have the best equipment for jumpers.'

Matte wanted to barge in, but held back. He called Donat instead.

'She's alone in the room?'

'The kid will jump if I try to get in there. There's a crowd in front of the hospital catching it all on their phones.'

'Vermin! Can you inch the door open?'

'I tried but he has a crutch blocking both doors.'

'What about another room?'

'Already tried that but the kid's on the lookout. I don't want to cause him to fall. Damiano has him talking.'

'I'm coming down. We can't have another suicide.'

Matte gave Donat their exact location.

Pauzé inched further out the window. There was something hesitant about his gesture, and Damiano picked up on that.

'Wait, Jean. Just, just please explain to me why? Don't give up hope for your leg. Your plan was just a book. Are you willing to throw your life away for a bunch of words? You're twenty-seven – you haven't even made a dent in life. I want to understand.' If she managed to get Pauzé talking, he might look away for a fraction of a second and she'd lunge forward and grab him and pull him to safety.

'You've been inside the armpit of a room I live in. I'm in debt up to my eyeballs, so are my parents because of me. I'm a one-man train wreck. That book was my future. A large house…'

'A publisher you mean?'

'One with clout would have secured the McGill post for me – one break was all I needed. Holmes promised me she'd find a home for my book. She promised! Then she stole two years of my life and dumped me.'

'Agents try, Jean, but sometimes they don't succeed.'

'If she had kept me on a little longer, Doyle's success would have helped me. I know it.' Pauzé's face had hardened. 'Now, I'm just a cheat. Soon I'll be less than nothing without a leg.' He was crying.

'Find some courage. You had it to go through all that study with so little. You know what struggle is far better than most. Try to believe in yourself.'

'That's just it. I did once. I thought I had a great book and a great agent. Both blew up in my face. Now my leg. Could you keep your badge without a leg? Could you? See that letter on my bed. The bastard rented my apartment. I've got nowhere to go.'

Pauzé was so close to dying horribly, like Turner, that she felt a sudden bursting pity for him. She also didn't want a black eye for losing the kid. 'I'll find you a place. Don't fucking give up! Jean!'

Pauzé ignored her and went on as she wanted him to do, 'If Holmes had just… maybe all this…'

Damiano lunged forward and grabbed hold of Pauzé's arm, but he caught sight of her movement and pushed himself from the window. It was a flash, but she saw it. Pauzé lost his grip on the left window sill. He hadn't meant to. He hadn't meant to! His eyes were desperate. He grabbed her arm with both hands and held on.

His body weight and the casts thwacked Damiano's body smack into the wall and knocked the wind out of her. She couldn't scream for help. Searing pain from both knees cut into her. Pauzé's weight was excruciating. Her eyes teared and her face bulged. Her elbow hung out the window and Pauzé held on. She was forced to use her right hand to steady herself against the inner wall or she'd be propelled out the window with Pauzé. She rasped, 'Try to grab the window sill, Jean.'

She held his hands for almost thirty seconds. Without warning, the humerus, the large bone above her elbow, cracked like a thick peppermint stick. A shard of white bone broke through the skin. Dark red blood gushed out. Damiano lost her grip and Pauzé fell.

He never screamed, he never made a sound, but he looked up at Damiano until he smashed feet first onto the hood and windshield of a blue car. Her eyes were locked on his. He was still looking up at Damiano when he died.

Chapter Seventy-nine

WHEN DAMIANO SAW her arm dangling and gushing blood, she lifted it to her chest to protect it but fell back on her knees inside the room, dazed and numb with shock. Gasping, she crawled to the bed and pulled herself up with her good arm. Wheezing and coughing, she fumbled with her jacket until she found the recorder. Appalled and frightened by the jutting bone, she stumbled to the door, managed to pull the crutch aside and fell again when stabbing pain shot up her arm into her shoulder. Somehow, she called for Matte.

He flew into the room and knelt with her. Doctors rushed in with him. One shouted for a gurney. Matte tried to cradle Damiano, but doctors pushed him aside. 'We have to get her into surgery.' One was already cutting the cashmere sweater soaked with blood, exposing the jutting bone. She was gently lifted onto the gurney, covered with a sheet and wheeled into the corridor, past a clutch of staff and patients.

'Pierre!'

Matte was running beside her. 'I'm right here. You'll be okay.'

'I couldn't pull him back… I couldn't pull him…' she rasped.

'I couldn't have either. You were great, Toni.'

Damiano ranted in a delirium of pain, but she was stubbornly resolute. Her face glistened with perspiration and she writhed on the gurney, cradling her arm. 'Get Zin on the phone, promise. Tell her we closed.' She handed off the bloodied recorder. 'Holmes is good for the attack on Pauzé.'

Matte had to lean in closely to hear what she was saying. 'Huh! Good job!'

Damiano stopped writhing and said again, 'Call Zin.'

'Yes, yes. I'll call your family. I won't leave the hospital.' He bagged the recorder and slipped it into his pocket. *She wants the lead to the end.* He went back to the empty ward room and began making calls, waiting on Donat. Mina Zin called him back before he got to his second call to announce she was flying down. She wanted an interview for the *National Enquirer*.

'I'm impressed. I won't write this up till I have the blood and guts that sell our rag.'

Matte went to the window and looked down at the body of Pauzé.

Crime techs had already arrived, examining, chalking and taking photos. TV vans and reporters swarmed like seagulls on a crust of bread. The crowd of gawkers grew. More police arrived and began closing off the scene with orange tape, setting up a perimeter. Matte saw one man offering his phone to a tech who watched the video and posted it on YouTube. A physician pronounced the time of death. Minutes later, the team lifted the body off the car into a black body bag and zipped it up. As Matte looked on, he saw that there was little left of Jean Pauzé, except the deep impression of his body and blood left on the blue car. The crowd was still growing. Lights flashed as a white van took the body to the city morgue on Parthenais Street. Some reporters ran after the van, cameras held high and flashing.

Matte knew Chief Donat had arrived because he was immediately swarmed by cameras and reporters. He stopped, said something, watched the video, took it and rushed past them. Matte was out in the hall when Donat arrived. Without a word, the chief pushed Matte back into the room. 'What the fuck happened? I've scheduled a news conference at Crémazie an hour from now. Now that I've seen the video, we'll do it here but outside on the grounds. I repeat, what the fuck happened? I will not make a fool of myself at the conference!'

'The kid, Jean Pauzé, never meant to harm the elderly patients. When Damiano opened the door, he was halfway out the window. Officer Gauthier was allowed in to clear out the patients, but only Damiano was allowed in the room with Pauzé. The kid was deadly serious about that. He threatened to jump right then if I came into the room. Damiano got the solve on his attack. Holmes again.'

'Huh! Never quits, that one.'

Matte felt second-grade, but he continued. 'We could hear them talking, but couldn't make out more than a few words. When he tried to throw himself from the window, Damiano grabbed him and tried to pull him back inside.'

'I know. I saw the video. Damiano held on to the kid for a good half minute. The casts must weigh damn near 25 pounds apiece. Get to the point, Matte. What happened to *her*?'

'Her arm snapped, literally. And the kid fell.'

'How is she?'

'She's in surgery.'

'I'll stay the night.'

'I will too, Chief.'

Donat nodded. 'Make the necessary calls for the conference. We have black ink on another file. Good work. I'll keep this press conference here brief till I have you both on the podium with me at the division. Damiano was the lead. Knowing her, she'll find a way to get there.'

'She could have gone out the window with him, Chief. She might have been down there with Pauzé.'

'Damiano has balls of steel, a damn good cop. I want you with me at the conference. It's a makeshift thing, but necessary and great PR.' He left Matte alone to make the calls.

Outside the TV vans had set up flood lights and the talking heads were angling closer to the microphones hastily set up. Wire lines snaked around the podium. More media arrived. They set up their recorders and pads; some still did the note thing. On-lookers crowded in behind them. Donat left to locate Damiano's surgeon he wanted at the conference. Matte tried to tidy himself up. He kept the digital recorder in his pocket. He hadn't mentioned it again to Donat.

'You in there, Matte? Let's go down.'

Donat, Matte and a surgeon went to meet with the media. Once they were outside, Matte figured there were about two hundred people at the conference. He stood beside the chief, the surgeon on the other side. Staff had made their way out to hear the news.

Donat was formal. 'Good evening ladies and gentlemen. In a day or two I will hold a formal press conference at Place Versailles. I will not be taking questions tonight. Lieutenant-Detective Toni Damiano,' Donat spelled out the name, 'T-o-n-i D-a-m-i-a-n-o, and her partner, here beside me, Detective Pierre Matte, P-i-e-r-r-e M-a-t-t-e, employing strong investigative skills, successfully closed the file on the assault of celebrity agent, Madison Holmes. One hour ago, Detective Damiano and Detective Matte arrested Thomas Holmes for the assault on his daughter. Detective Damiano was then called to the Hôtel Dieu to deal with Jean Pauzé, a twenty-seven-year-old McGill post-grad, who was threatening patients in his room. Then the young man attempted suicide.

'This file has been beset by tragic incidents that began with the horrific assault on Madison Holmes. Ms Holmes is still recovering from her injuries, but is expected to be released from hospital any day now.'

A spontaneous round of applause erupted.

'One of our officers, Troy Turner, succumbed to the pressure of this file and became its second victim. Earlier, Detective Damiano risked her life to save Jean Pauzé, a former suspect in this case, from falling to his death. In another sad turn of events, Detective Damiano was critically injured, and Jean Pauzé became a fatality. For those of you who shot videos of this tragic event, you all know with certainty that Detective Damiano is a hero.'

A louder round of applause.

Chief Donat put his hand over the microphone and said something to Detective Matte. Matte stepped forward. 'There will be copies of Chief Donat's statement available to social media within the hour.'

The surgeon was brief. Damiano was in surgery. He hoped for a full recovery with rehab, barring complications. The media had what they needed to hawk their wares and rushed back to work. Chief Donat and Matte spent the next seven hours with bad coffee. Soon they were joined by Damiano's husband and son. Matte checked his iPhone. The video had gone viral. The digital headlines followed: *Hero Cop Closes Holmes Assault Case, Father of Holmes Taken into Custody, Holmes to be Released, Detective Damiano in Critical Condition after Attempting to save the life of PhD Grad.* The headlines went viral as well. The story would be the lead on all the national news channels. The coffee got worse. After brief introductions, Donat, Matte, Jeff and Luke sat alone with their thoughts. No one slept. Luke paced the room until his father told him to sit down.

At Parthenais, late in the night, Jean Pauzé's father stood behind a meager green curtain in the basement of the morgue. He identified his son and left without a word. No press was around to intrude on his sorrow. His privacy wouldn't last.

At Crémazie, Thomas Holmes had demanded to consult with legal counsel. His arms remained pinioned in a suicide jacket.

Before dawn, a weary surgeon walked into the waiting room, pulling off his mask and cap. 'Detective Damiano is out of danger. The surgery went well. Although I encountered multiple fractures in her arm, I expect a full recovery with lengthy rehab. We have your detective in a private room. She's a stubborn woman who insists on seeing you. She's groggy but awake. Please keep the visits very short. She needs rest.' He gave them the room number on the fifth floor.

Jeff and Luke jumped up and went to Damiano. Jeff went in first and alone.

Damiano lay on the bed propped by pillows. A heavy, thick white plaster cast, bent at the elbow and fortified by an aluminum bar, was going to make manoeuvering awkward. Her hair was damp, and her eyes were closed. Jeff walked quietly to her side and kissed her forehead. 'Hey, you!'

Damiano opened her eyes and realized that Jeff was crying. 'Guess I can't do things the easy way, huh?'

'I could have lost you, Toni!' Jeff sat down beside the bed and took her hand and held it to his cheek.

'But you didn't.'

'Not this time. Why…?'

'Not now, please.'

Luke barged into the room. He ran to his mother and kissed both her cheeks, in an unexpected burst of emotion. 'Mom, you're a hero. This is so sweet!' He laughed, 'Ha! Guess you'll have to come back home now. You can't get along without us now.' He pointed to the cast. 'I know I'm right. This is so cool.'

The awkwardness lifted. The decision passed with no objections, at least not for the moment. Jeff and Luke left guarded but happy. Damiano could taste another turkey. It wasn't bad at all, for now. Jeff and Luke stepped out to allow Damiano's boss some time with her.

Chief Donat walked into the room. He hated hospitals, hated their smells. They always scared him. His face was taut with concern when he saw Damiano and didn't know what to say. He never did when one of his cops was hurt.

Damiano helped him out. *Men!* 'Got both solves, Chief. Heads won't roll today.'

Donat ran his thumb across his lower lip. 'Not bad for a time-restricted high profile! You look pretty good for someone who almost went out a sixth-floor window.'

'You're not going to pretend to worry about me now, Chief. That's not you.'

'I suffer lapses. I rode you hard, and you closed the file. I respect that, Damiano. There was pressure on me to gangbang this file, but I wanted a single pair of eyes working it. I got what I wanted and you inadvertently gave the force a gold star. It won't last, but it's good right now.'

'Matte was right there with me, Chief.'

'He wasn't halfway out the window. You're a good cop. I'm glad to have you on my team. And you'll be the first officer I've ever nominated for the Medal of Bravery. If the nomination is approved, you'll receive the award from the Governor General at Rideau Hall in Ottawa. Either way, I plan to rent a club here to celebrate this solve and your courage.'

'Come on, Chief.'

'Don't tell me you didn't think you might fall with Pauzé?'

Damiano grew serious.

'Just as I thought. Use that stubborn head of yours to get the hell back on the job. A bed is no place for a cop.' He did barge out.

Detective Matte walked in quietly and stood at the end of the bed. 'You look pretty good,' he said, relieved.

'You don't lie well. You have the recorder, right?'

'Yes and good for you. Two solves in a day!' Matte pointed to the arm. 'Does it hurt?'

'I'm high on Demerol – but it hurt before surgery. I know what it feels like to bite the bullet. Shit!'

'How close were you to falling?'

'If my arm hadn't broken, I probably would have. I was scared, Pierre.'

Pierre grabbed her feet. 'But you didn't. That's a good thing.'

'Couldn't have done any of it without you, Pierre. I'm serious. We're a team.'

Matte patted Damiano's foot and left. 'I'll hold on to the recorder. No more visitors – so let the Demerol do what it does best.'

'Good point.' Damiano stopped fighting the narcotic and she fell into a jerky sleep and nightmares of falling.

Epilogue

DAMIANO WAS GLAD when the morning nurse came into the room with meds. An aide followed and gave her a sponge bath, and breakfast arrived.

'Are you up for visitors?' the young assistant aide asked. 'You have a strict three-minute limit.'

'Sure.'

DETECTIVE GALT WAS visibly ill-at-ease when he came into the room. 'I won't stay. I'm not here to plead for anything. I treated you roughly, par for the course with me. Doesn't make it right. You did great work and I'm glad you're okay. I wanted you to know that I'll present myself to Donat and see where that goes. My ag on a police officer might land me time, but I'm prepared to deal with the aggravated assault. You deserved better from a fellow officer. Now, I've said more than I've spoken to any other cop. My last point, you sure as hell can handle yourself. The Alouettes could use your foot.' He walked to the side of the bed and offered his hand.

Damiano took it. 'I'll ask the chief to write you up. He might go for a month's suspension, but that's his call.'

'Appreciated. Get better.'

MINA ZIN WASTED no time getting to her rag. 'I have new respect for Canadians. In the States, we'd call you a cowboy cop and that's an American compliment – taking on the rough rides. This story will sell! Now spill the blood and guts… I may sound trash to you, but you'll be a household name when I write up the story. Writers will come looking for you to advise them on their books! A smart, foxy cop who gets her man and risks her life in the process. TV isn't nearly this good. This story had all the elements good people eat up – courage, strength, and resolution. That's one of the many malaises of this generation – nothing is ever resolved. So?'

'Mina, I don't think I want to go that route.'

'Why?'

'I like what I do – I don't want to spoil it with my 15 minutes.'

'Remarkable!'

'You have enough for a decent story.'

MADISON HOLMES WAS unexpected and welcome. Though her recovery was remarkable, Madison was visibly suffering the physical and emotional effects of her father's brutal attack. 'I haad to come, Detective. Dr. Orr sent an orderly with me in the limo. I'm sorry for your injury.' The orderly helped Madison into a chair and left them alone. 'I can go home without woooory and start again. Howw did you know?' Madison was still shaken.

'For some time, I had a gut feeling something was off, or so close by that I couldn't see. When you ran your nails across the six pack, I knew the suspect wasn't there. When you turned to your father and asked why that second time, I knew in that instant. I knew. Odd pieces fell into place. How did you know?'

'For a long time, my mind focused on the caps. When I saw the suspects' faces at the hospital – I saw my father's.' Holmes looked away for a few seconds before she was able to talk again. 'You saved my life.' Madison allowed the tears to fall. 'If I haad gone home with my father…' Madison covered her face with hands. 'I won't ever feel safe with him again. He tried to beat me to death. I don't think I can ever forgive him, or be near him.'

Damiano knew that some emotional scars never heal. She didn't mention Pauzé. She didn't think Holmes would, and she didn't. 'It's too soon for forgiveness. Think of healing. Be grateful to your friend Michelle. She saved your life.'

'Yes, yes, I am, and to you.'

'Be proud of your own courage, Madison. I'm happy and lucky to be alive myself.' Damiano managed a smile through the day-after pain that lanced through her shoulder and arm.

'Me too.' Madison smiled through the tears. 'I better go. Take care, Detective.'

When Damiano was alone, she reached for her phone to check for messages. There was one from Tom Graham. 'Good close – get healthy. Therapy is some ride. You have a great book there. If you are so inclined; you have an agent.' Damiano laughed. *Galt would suck his teeth out for this chance.*

CLAUDE BEAUCHEMIN DISCOVERED he worked well with structure. Not only did he find the cleaning company, he learned he had a real knack for actual cleaning. In a week, he had gone through the entire house. Cupboards were his favorite target, especially the ones under the kitchen sink. To complete the task, he wrote up little Post-it Notes where he felt improvements might help. He wrote many Notes. When he was finished, the entire house smelled 'lemony fresh.'

Louise did not call that week, but she did come by eight days later to pick up clothes. She found Claude polishing the keyboard of the grand piano. He hadn't known she'd be coming by, but he'd showered and neatly dressed. His face brightened when he saw her. She smelled the lemon. 'What have you done, Claude?'

'Just let me show you.' And he did. Who could walk away from a man who loved house cleaning!

FOR THREE WEEKS, the police could not trace the whereabouts of Angela Marino. BMW did tow their SUV from Terrebonne. The manager did find the $100,000, but he locked it away in the office safe. He had no doubt that someone would come for the money. He enjoyed living. The police continued their search and took the daily calls from Tracey Doyle. On Monday of the fourth week, Marino walked into her office on McGill College Avenue. Her secretary had stopped coming into work at the end of the second week. Marino opened the safe and took out a clean phone and made her call. Only two words were necessary, but they were clearly understood. 'Thank you.'

'A small misunderstanding. We have work for you.'

Marino called her daughter next and told her she'd be home that night.

DETECTIVE DAMIANO ATTACKED her physiotherapy with the same passion she took to her work. She was keenly aware that Troy Turner and Jean Pauzé had no chances left. She determined to make the most of hers. When she was well enough, Chief Donat pushed her into interviews for PR because the file had drawn international attention. This was a file with benefits, he kept reminding her. At home she and Jeff and Luke were managing re-entry better than any one of them might have thought. Damiano attended the obligatory counselling that police are subject to after such traumatic events. Yet there were nights when she woke suddenly, sat bolt upright, and grabbed Jeff's arm to keep from falling onto the blue car. Then she'd roll on her side, haunted by a recurring question. If she hadn't lunged for Pauzé, would he have fallen?

Damiano didn't give up her apartment for the time being. She was a stubborn, independent woman – she couldn't relinquish everything. Once her arm healed, the next high profile case was hers!

On a sunny day in October Detective Damiano, in full dress uniform, walked across the impressive pedimented formal façade of Rideau Hall at One Sussex Drive, past the flags, the coats of arms and the official portraits in the magnificent heritage building. The detective was officially welcomed and escorted into the Ballroom. Damiano sat with 34 other recipients. 'Lieutenant-Detective Antoinette Damiano!' Blood rose in Damiano's cheeks as she stood, bowed humbly and accepted the Medal of Bravery from the Governor General of Canada. A one-paragraph citation was read by a director from the Chancellery of Honors. When she was back home, Damiano put the medal in a drawer. She didn't want to display it. *Pauzé might not have fallen if I hadn't reached for him.* Most good cops are haunted by ghosts.

A week later, Chief Donat threw his own celebratory bash in a legion hall. Damiano was a cop after all, a certified member of the 'blue' race.

THOMAS HOLMES WAS transferred to the Pinel Institute, a psychiatric hospital, for psychological evaluation and treatment. He refused therapy and remained "disordered and despondent" in the opinion of mental health reviewers. In the months preceding his trial, he fell silent under a gloom that had settled over him. Holmes was not about to trust his thoughts to medical personnel whose utter disrespect and callous loathing he saw and felt on a daily basis. Only Becky understood his heart and intentions. *Tell your father I forgive him.* He finally understood Becky's words and nodded to himself, fortified. He was already past the wash of guilt. After all, guilt had almost destroyed him. Thomas had a new goal. He was waiting for Madison. He knew she would come. She had to understand he acted out of love. If need be, he'd seek therapy. Thomas was well aware that patients never told their therapists the entire truth. Then he'd apply for day leave. He had the time.

Acknowledgments

The research on *The Courier Wore Shorts* led me to familiar and valued sources and introduced me to new venues and interesting information. To all the professionals who have helped me with their promptness, generosity and expertise in their various fields, I offer my sincere gratitude.

The SPVM (Service de police de la Ville de Montréal) has been invaluable to me. Anna-Claude Poulin of Police Public Relations set up interviews and sent key links for additional information I might be able to use. Lieutenant-Detective Denis Jr. Bonneau has kept his promise of getting back to me in five minutes unless he is caught up in a file. I have my questions and notepad ready for the precise details he is able to offer. Denis always adds, 'If you want this really tight…' I always do, of course.

For Cross-Border Investigations, I greatly appreciate the expertise of Victor Carbonneau, an attorney-at-law. Victor also worked with the RCMP. He took my call on a Sunday! I made notes of the precise and detailed information he gave me. I am fortunate to have such a resource.

Canada Post, the most highly regulated corporation in Canada, was informative, helpful and careful. From Head Office, the information was concise, but no one would give me a name for acknowledgement. Its regulations are in fine form. I did learn a great deal about bar codes, tracking numbers and receipts. At postal outlets, I studied the information on the cash receipts we rarely examine. Penny Doward and Tanya (no last name) explained further where I needed to follow-up.

CIBC VISA was my next stop. What I discovered from Aaron at VISA was first I needed the location of the Canada Post purchase. Even without a signature, a cash receipt together with the purchase price will permit him to shortlist the receipt and, in many cases, locate the buyer. These were all good facts.

Mike Deliva of Summit Computers sent detailed information on trojan viruses and how a relative amateur might hack into another computer and download information before the trojan is discovered. He also explained ID spoofing and its potential. He trusted I was working in fiction because there were new laws on the books for this kind of 'invade and steal.' When he set up my new Dell, I showed him my books and he let me off the computer hook.

I am indebted to the Press Office at Rideau Hall. I needed to know where the medals were presented, the general time of year, and the length of time it takes for a nominee to learn he/she has been approved. Two days later, I had rounded up the information and enjoyed a few virtual visits to the renowned heritage building.

All procedural errors in *The Courier Wore Shorts* are mine and I take full responsibility for them.

I owe heartfelt thanks to the usual suspects:

Gina Pingitore has gone beyond the measure of a best friend. From my memoir, *Sheila's Take* to *The Promise*, all eight books, she has proofed and reproofed, worked every signing, attended every talk and been constant in her enthusiasm. A 'thank you' falls short, but it's heartfelt.

Cynthia Iorio is a wonderful friend who puts aside her busy life to form the best sales duo with Gina. Cynthia works with a zest and generous nature that brought her to Ottawa with us and to every signing in Montreal. I am the lucky benefactor of this strong woman.

Margaret Goldik, a treasured, kind friend continues to contribute mightily through the final editing. She knows everything about changes in the style guides. Margaret's overall grasp and insightful ideas oil the bolts of the manuscript and tighten the screws in the paragraphs. She also catches those last little typos that manage to creep into the final copy.

Denis Coupal, my good friend the eternal optimist. If someone is in need, Denis is there to help out, at signings too. Thank you, friend, for the help and good conversation.

Bob Dillon is a quiet friend with a big heart. Bob has printed up posters and hundreds of colored fliers for my launches and signings. Thank you for your help and sustaining kindness.

Irene Pingitore never misses a book in her exact counting at the signings or the last few typos in her proofing. To those tasks she always brings her good cheer.

Anne Marie Gitto and Jan Lauer have invited me to speak this year and past years and have done all the work around such an event. I am grateful to them both.

Louise Morin always puts her daily work aside when I call for help with my French spelling, gently informing me of current usage rather than the stiff French I was writing. She is a good friend who gives solid advice with technical help.

Rose Murphy, Lucie Day, Kathy Panet, Shirley Shum, Hille Vires and Maggie Baxter have generously helped out at various signings.

Mary Tellett, my little sister, works hard in Toronto and has on my behalf for every book.

Brenda O'Farrell is an intriguing, well-grounded woman, a new friend whose company I thoroughly enjoy. She surprises me with wonderful support that I gratefully receive.

It was my good fortune to have Simon Dardick as my publisher for *The Red Floor*. His diligence, professionalism, insightfulness, humor, gentle calm and reputation impress all his fortunate authors as they did me. And my good fortune continues.

Véhicule Press